Revelation 911

Sun of Apollo

Revelation 911

Sun of Apollo

A novel by
Darab Lawyer
and Clinton Libbey

AF

Library of Congress Control Number: 2011940824
Lawyer, Darab and Clinton Libbey.
   Sun of Apollo / revelation 911 series. (Fictional book series.)

ISBN: Softcover   978-0-9847168-0-7
            Ebook   978-0-9847168-1-4

1. New Age—Fiction. 2. Religious and biblical prophecy. 3. Legendary Grail myth.
4. 2012 Mayan prophecy. 5. Metaphysical philosophy. 6. Mythological folklore.
7. New World Order. 8. Apocalyptic fiction. 9. Astrology—Fiction. 10. Science fiction.
11. Fantasy. 12. Age of Aquarius.

This is a work of fiction. All of the characters, organizations, and events portrayed in
this novel are either products of the author's imagination or are used fictitiously.

Visit our Website at www.revelation911series.com

Cover design by Virath Phongsavan
Cover photo of Stonehenge by Laszlo Ilyes
Cover photo of pyramids by Ricardo Liberato
Coat of Arms of Charles, Prince of Wales © Sodacan, p. 256

Printed in the United States of America.

First Edition
09 08 07 06 05 04 03 02 01 00

To order additional copies of this book, contact:
AtlasBooks
1-800-266-5564

In loving memory of
Erich S. Lawyer

Acknowledgments

In the development of *Sun of Apollo*, the authors integrated existing theories regarding metaphysical philosophy, religious prophecy, and mythological folklore. As such, the authors would like to recognize Robert Bauval for his work on the Orion Correlation Theory, Michael Baigent, Richard Leigh, Henry Lincoln, and Laurence Gardner for their work on the Merovingian dynasty and the bloodlines of Christ, C.M. White for his work on the Legend of the Scarlet Hand, Angelfire.com for their interpretation of Prince Charles' crest, Anne Wright and Vivian E. Robson for their work on fixed stars and constellations in astrology, Jon Stevens for his work on astrological analysis of comets, Mary Lawyer and Anne Wright for their astrological interpretations, Porus Havewala for his work on the Saga of the Aryans, and John Major Jenkins for his work on Mayan cosmology and philosophy. Without their work, this project would not have been possible.

In the 1960s the Age of Aquarius had dawned;
in the year 2012, it has finally arrived.

PROLOGUE

Cairo, Egypt, February 16, 2012, 6:38 A.M.

A S THE LEMON-YELLOW sun rose above the horizon, its life-giving yet deadly electromagnetic radiation slowed as it passed through the earth's atmosphere. The light that took eight and one-half minutes to reach earth, transformed the star-filled desert night into day.

The sun's rays felt good. Too good, thought Amon Ramsey as he gazed out of the eastern window of his twelfth-floor office on the southeastern banks of the Nile River. He yawned as he watched the last of the stratus clouds vaporize. Even the twinkling stars that graced the heavens evaporated faster than droplets of rain hitting the hot desert sand.

For two long hours he stared, almost catatonically, out of the window as he thought about the daunting task that consumed his every waking moment.

What was he missing?

As the sun continued its ascent above the arid desert landscape, waves of solar radiation waded lethargically through the thick desert air.

Nothing moved.

Not even the still waters of the ancient Nile dared to exert any energy, nor were the protruding eyes and nostrils of the barrel-shaped hippos visible. The few remaining crocodiles, like those that had patrolled the primordial waters for the past two hundred million years, refused to sun themselves along the banks of the longest river in the world. Camouflaged and motionless, their glaring eyes and narrow snouts barely showed above the calm water's surface. They seemed to sense a power greater than that of the sun resonating around them.

Gazing up into the heavens, a twinkling light caught the president's eyes. *That's unusual,* he thought, as he stared at the rising star. He realized it was getting brighter, and brighter still, as if it was attempting to outshine the sun.

Then it dawned on him. He smiled. It wasn't a star at all. It was a planet. If Venus could masquerade as a star and hide among the other stars, then maybe the answer he was looking for was cleverly disguised and hiding as well.

He needed more time, he thought.

Still refusing to be overpowered by the sun, it was as though Venus, the ruler of the nighttime sky, wanted to rule the daytime as well. He laughed. Never underestimate the power of a woman, he thought, as the morning gave ready to birth what he believed would be the hottest day on record.

As the only feminine planet finally conceded defeat and slowly faded away, the glaring eyes of the man-eating crocodiles submerged into the murky depths below.

Ramsey's smile faded and he moved away from the window. Even the cool air that circulated through his office did little to comfort him. Wiping the sweat from his brow, he moved through the sunlight that shone into his office through three oversized oval glass windows. The breathtaking views of Egypt to the south, east and west, went unnoticed. When he reached the southern window, he glanced at the atomic grandfather clock that stood like a sentinel in the right-hand corner of his office.

Less than forty-eight hours left.

He turned and stared at a portrait of his late wife hanging on the wall between the barren wooden bookcases behind his hand carved oak desk. He sat down on the tan leather sofa that faced the southern window and picked up the King James Version of the Bible from a small pile of books on the floor. He shook his head from side to side and tossed it onto the pyramid-shaped black onyx table in front of him. Landing next to a book on the predictions of Nostradamus, the delicate pages of the Bible slowly folded back. He stared at the bold black letters that spelled out *REVELATIONS* and laughed.

Angels of the Apocalypse . . .

Seas turning red . . .

Locusts with the faces of man . . .

What would they dream up next?

Fighting to keep his eyes from closing, he looked at the oversized painting of The Mythical Flight of Icarus hanging to the right of the window. Early on in his career he had looked to the painting of Icarus soaring toward the sun for inspiration. It had represented to him mankind's desire to reach new heights. Now, it was synonymous with failure.

He leaned back into the soft leather sofa and wondered if he could mend his wings and find the answer to the third-generation secret he was sworn to protect.

CHAPTER 1

New York City, February 16, 2012, 9:30 A.M.

THE OPENING BELL sounded. Darius Prince hit the enter key and submitted the largest order of his career. "I'll call you back with a confirmation."

"Make it quick," the hedge fund manager said.

Darius slammed down the phone. "Yes," he said, pumping his fist into the air. "This account's gonna change my life."

Watching the trades roll across the screen, he saw a hundred thousand share block of Zonoma Tonnai trade at thirty-three. He jumped to his feet and pressed the F3 key to confirm the trade. Placing his large hands shoulder-width apart on the desk, he leaned forward. His dark brown eyes anxiously awaited the trade confirmation. He was completely unaware of anything else around him.

The screen flashed.

What the hell? He slowly straightened. He stood with one hand on his hip perfectly still and with his other hand he slowly scratched the top of his head.

An emerald-green pentagram appeared, slowly turning in the middle of the screen.

Randomly hitting the keys on the keyboard in the hope that he would somehow reactivate the trading screen, he watched the pentagram start to change colors.

It had to be a virus. Darius grabbed the phone and called the trading department. "Come on, pick up," he said, bouncing his right knee up and down.

Following the rhythmic drumbeat of colors move from green to blue to purple to red to yellow, over and over, he found it hard to look away.

"Trading," a female voice said.

Darius arched his eyebrows and widened his eyes as though he was trying to stretch himself awake and shake off the image on his screen.

"Trading," came the voice again.

He looked away from the screen. "This is Darius Prince, I—"

"Please hold."

The aluminum micro-blinds covering the plate glass windows behind him and to the left of his mahogany desk were drawn to prevent the rising midwinter sun from creating a glare on his trading screen. The decorations in the high corner office he shared with his partner, Norman, who was late again that morning, were dedicated to achieving their hardcore dreams of becoming not just rich, but liquid. The framed motivational pictures hanging on the cherrywood walls preached achievement and success with one goal in mind. Whether he was staring at a trophy picture of a Ferrari, a private jet, or a gorgeous young starlet, the message was the same—*the key to success was money.*

Darius looked at the pentagram and slowly twirled the plastic wand to open the blinds. Thin rays of sunlight burst into the room from the south. He gazed out through the partially opened blinds at the Hudson River and focused on the Statue of Liberty. He smiled. There weren't many better ways for a twenty-nine-year-old man to spend his day than on the thirtieth floor of a Manhattan skyscraper trading millions of dollars in the pursuit of the American Dream.

Darius glanced at his watch. What the hell was taking trading so long?

He started hitting the keyboard keys again, but this time harder. The pentagram disappeared and the words *Zoro, Join Us* appeared.

What next, he thought, shaking his head. His lips were so tightly compressed he wouldn't have been surprised if they disappeared completely into his face.

His other phone line rang. He looked at the caller ID and quickly loosened his collar and paisley yellow tie. This was his first trade with the hedge fund. If he told them that his system was down, there wouldn't be a second. These guys didn't tolerate mistakes.

After the third ring, he put trading on hold and dialed his sales assistant. The moment her voice mail picked up, he pounded his right fist down hard on the desk. "Damn!" he said and pressed the trading line again, praying that they'd be waiting to confirm his trade. When he heard the classical music still playing in the background, he had no other choice but to answer the call.

"Darius Pri—"

"Darius! What the hell's going on? The stock's up twelve cents. Do I own it?"

Darius paused. He had to give his client an answer. He stared back at his computer screen. It was still there: *Zoro, Join Us.* If he confirmed the trade and was wrong, he was responsible for the stock and could take a hit.

"Darius," the fund manager said again. "If you screwed up this trade, you can kiss the account good-bye."

He looked across the office at a picture of a private jet that his girlfriend, Paris, had given him. The inscription below read *Money Isn't Everything, It's The Only Thing.*

He took a deep breath and exhaled.

"Relax. Your hundred thousand share block of Zanoma Tonnai is confirmed at thirty-three."

"Great. I'll call you later."

He watched his screen as *Zoro, Join Us* slowly faded away. His system returned to normal. What was he worrying about anyway? The stock was only up twelve cents.

He reentered the stock symbol and leaned forward. "What the—" His eyes widened. Large blocks of stock were going off at thirty-six dollars a share.

The phone rang again.

Please let it be trading calling to confirm my trade. He picked up the phone.

"Darius, it's Mike," his manager said. "I just received a call from trading."

He could feel his gut wrench in the pit of his stomach.

"Goldman Sachs claims you verbally confirmed their client on a hundred thousand share purchase of Zanoma Tonnai at thirty-three. They already sold the stock at thirty-six and want delivery. Did you verbally confirm the trade?"

If Darius could have disappeared from the earth in that instant, he would have. Sweat trickled down his temple. His heart was pounding. He typed the access code, D-M-A-C, into the computer and hit the F3 key again.

"Darius, I need to know right now! It just went across the tape that Zanoma Tonnai is a takeover target."

CHAPTER 2

"WHAT ARE YOU doing here?"

Darius smiled. "I ask myself that same question every day."

Laura Luv glided across the parquet floor, her small breasts firmly pressed against her red spandex top. When she reached the edge of the dance floor, she acted as though she didn't notice him staring. He looked up, trying not to be so obvious, and tossed her a towel. Laura Luv oozed charm.

"Philosophizing again?" She wiped her face and looked up at him.

The blood receding from her high cheek bones left a healthy pink complexion behind. For a moment, he forgot about the hit he'd just taken. She paused as though waiting for him to kiss her hello. When he didn't, she hung the towel around her neck.

"I feel so invigorated after every class." She unclasped her long light brown hair and swung it free. "I wouldn't trade this feeling for all the money in the world."

"I would." Darius tilted his head back and gazed through a skylight above the middle of the dance floor. The waning crescent moon rested comfortably in the arms of the nighttime sky. He looked around the familiar studio, and smiled. Little had changed since he had told Laura that the martial arts studio he trained at was moving. With the money she had saved from winning various dance competitions throughout the years, she had jumped at the opportunity to start her own dance studio, and two weeks later had rented the fifteen hundred square-foot location.

Other than the sign on the front door that now read *Laura Luv Dance Studio* the changes were subtle, yet obvious, to him. The U-shaped reception desk in the front of the studio was larger and well stocked with a variety of T-shirts, health drinks and power bars. The walls surrounding the lightly stained oak dance floor were fully mirrored and mounted with wooden ballet barres, and the locker room doors were painted blue for men and yellow for women.

Through the windows of the six-story walkup overlooking Broadway, the bright theater lights shone against the back mirrored wall which glared the reflection of his chiseled face and her long legs and tight buttocks. Yes, indeed, Laura Luv oozed charm. Beneath her green toe shoes, a thin layer of worn polyurethane hardly glistened under the bright studio lights. What the studio lacked in modern day conveniences, she made up for in talent.

"I took a big hit today," he said, snapping himself out of his reverie.

She reached out and touched his arm. "It's not all about money."

He cringed and stepped back as her arm fell heavily to her side. "Tell that to my firm." He took off his blue pinstriped suit coat. "They'll probably fire me," he said, and draped the coat around the back of a chair.

"Maybe God is leading you in another direction." She pulled him playfully onto the dance floor. When they reached the middle, she raised his hands to dance but he lowered them and stepped back from her.

"I feel as though the Devil's been leading me," he said. He stood there, one hand on hip, the other pushing slowly over his forehead and through his hair. She was probably going to think he was nuts.

"The Devil?"

"A multi-colored pentagram infected my computer today." He drew his hand down from his head and pulled slowly on his chin.

"Hmm. I just read in *The New York Times* that every eight years Venus forms a pentagram around the sun. What colors was it?" She raised her arms above her head and clasped her hands together and stretched from side to side.

Darius focused his gaze on a small pair of white ballerina slippers hanging on a wooden ballet barre. He turned his gaze back to her. "Green, blue, purple, red and—"

"Yellow?" she said, suspending a stretch midway.

"How'd ya know?"

She smirked and continued her stretch. "Those are the five colors Aristotle used to show the correlation between the pentagram and the five elements."

Darius held his pull on his chin and studied her skeptically. "Since when did you start studying philosophy?"

Laura laughed as her arms descended into another stretch. He wondered if she was ever still.

"There are a lot of things you don't know about me."

She was flirting with him, he knew it. But he couldn't get his mind off that goddamn pentagram. Or the hit. "I thought there were only four elements."

"Common misconception. Most cultures believe in five."

"What do you think 'Zoro, Join Us' means?"

"Darius, are you listening to me?"

"It was part of the pentagram virus."

She raised an eyebrow as she dropped her hands on her hips.

"So . . . ?" He half expected her to drop into knee bends or start jogging in place, but she stood taking in and exhaling deep breaths. "What's the fifth element?"

"The invisible matter that ties the universe together and transports the soul. The Greeks referred to it as aether or spirit," she said and reached for her towel. "I could lend you a book on it."

"I'm gonna be thirty tomorrow. I have a lot of things to do before my soul gets transported anywhere."

"I'm going to be thirty in September, too," she said, "but you don't see me freaking out about it."

"I think it's time I settled down and got married." He turned and walked toward the reception desk. He could hardly hear her footsteps behind him.

"Darius," she said and grabbed him by the arm. "Don't make the second biggest mistake of your life."

He turned and faced her. "Why do you hate her so much, Laura?"

"I don't hate her, I feel sorry for little Miss Perfect."

"She only wants the best for me."

"Don't kid yourself." She dropped her hand from his arm. "Can't you see you're falling into the exact same trap with her as you did with your father?" She reached for his arm again. "Darius . . ."

He pushed her hand away. "You have no idea."

"For Christ's sake, Darius, I used to be your girlfriend."

He felt his heart beating faster. *What the hell was I thinking when I nicknamed her Laura Luv and what the hell was I thinking coming over here to see her now?* He walked over to the chair and picked up his suit coat.

"She'll use the money to control you. Once she has you trapped in her web, the black widow will abandon you—just like your father did."

Darius stopped and turned back around. She stood with her legs slightly apart and her arms crossed. "The truth hurts. Doesn't it?"

He shook his head from side to side. One moment she was flirting with him, the next she was ripping out his heart and holding it hostage in front of his face. She had said some pretty nasty things in the past but nothing as cruel and vindictive as this. "What the hell's gotten into you?"

"Darius, I'm just trying to help you." She gave him one of her old, familiar sympathetic smiles.

"You're just jealous she's rich."

"Fine, take the easy way out," she said, throwing the towel at him.

The towel hit his chest and he watched it fall to the floor. He looked up, and said, "Like you did with Yasmin?" He kicked the towel toward her. "I didn't throw in the towel on that one, you did."

CHAPTER 3

"I WISH I COULD have seen his face when his computer came back online."

Roxanne, the twenty-nine-year-old former Miss Iran and so-called queen of the Islamic world, leaned back and spoke loudly into the speaker phone. "His eyes must have *expehloded* out of his head when he realized that the stock was up three points," she said with a hiss. Her Persian-accented English was good, but not perfect like she wanted it to be. In the patriarchal world she so desperately wanted to change, English was the language spoken among the world's elite. She felt inadequate to the point of embarrassment that she still had trouble pronouncing the letters p, s, and z, unlike the crisp English that effortlessly rolled off the tongue of her beloved leader.

"Even better, wait 'til you see the look on his face when he finds out that he was used to shift the balance of power in our favor."

"That will be a day to remember."

"Yes, it will," Artemis said. "How is Project Lucy proceeding?"

"The thirteen satellites are already in position."

"Excellent," Artemis said. "As a precaution, I want you to seduce your husband's brother, Zadam, but under no circumstances are you to sleep with him—at least not yet. We will need him when the time comes to execute the final phase of our operation. He is the only other person who has access to Mohammed's military installation beneath his palace."

"Consider it done," Roxanne said with great drama. "This has the makings of a Greek tragedy,"

"Persian tragedy," Artemis corrected sternly.

"Where are we going to meet to discuss Operation Andromache?"

"London, England. I have the *purrfect* place picked out." She sounded like a lioness in heat. "Thirteen Half Moon Café."

"How fitting." Artemis's purring aroused the animalistic nature buried deep inside her and Roxanne felt as if she had to have her right then and there. Then she crossed her legs and smiled to herself. She would be reunited with her Amazonian queen soon enough.

CHAPTER 4

"**G**OOD EVENING," CAME the polite voice from the elevator intercom. "Please select a floor."

Darius paused. He looked around the elevator car's blue and yellow art deco interior and extended his right-hand as if reaching to press a button. Then he pulled it back.

Paris laughed. "Lobby," she said and waved the back of her hand in front of the LCD scanner built into the console.

The mirrored doors gently closed.

Darius grabbed her wrist and squeezed it tight. "Didn't I tell you to get that chip removed?"

"Miss Templar," came the soft flat voice from the elevator intercom again, "there is a package waiting for you at the reception desk."

"Stop trying to control me, Darius." Paris glared at her hand, then up at him and back at her hand again.

"I'm trying to help you. There's a difference."

Paris pulled her arm away. "I hate that you're so against new technology," she said. "Personally, I love the building's new security system—especially the chip app that alerts me to my packages. How did I *ever* live without it?"

"Listen, I never said I was against new technology—just the chip."

She touched him softly on the arm and smiled. "Can't you just give it a try?"

"Never!" There was no way that he'd ever take the chip. He'd be defying his Christian beliefs, for one thing, but also *The Network* would track his every move. But even though he was loath to admit it, the chip did have its benefits.

Every day more and more lives were being saved by EMS workers who praised the chip for its quick access to medical records. And being denied access to all of those new cyber-bars and cafés just because he wasn't chipped would become a thing of the past. And all those long lines, he thought, shaking his head. Those seemingly endless lines that he was made to wait in at the bank, the stores, the airports, would be eliminated. He felt almost forced to take the chip. This high-tech discrimination was being interwoven into every aspect of his life. He had to figure out a way to stop it. And soon.

"Anything else you want to rag on me about?" Paris took a step back and crossed her arms as if she were looking for a fight.

"Yeah, Paris. Even though we practically live together, this is where *I* reside. *You* still keep an apartment downtown just in case things don't work out between us. Remember?" A short bitter laugh escaped him.

"Don't take your frustrations from work out on me," she said. "You need to grow up." She pointed to the mirrored doors. "Look at you!"

She's right, he thought, staring at the evidence in his reflection. He barely recognized the man staring back at him. He was going to be thirty tomorrow and already had bags under his eyes like somebody who was approaching forty. The person staring back at him was supposed to be a man who had already staked his claim in life. But all he saw was the reflection of a boy who dressed well and, as of today, was right back to where he started when he got out of college—dead broke. He had to be hard on himself, he thought. Men didn't make mistakes like he did today.

Disgusted with the boy hiding beneath his tough exterior, he arched his broad shoulders back, adjusted his light brown tie, and looked at Paris in the mirror.

She was taller than most women. As tall as he in her three inch heels. He turned and faced her. "I took a big hit with that new hedge fund account while trading your father's company's stock today."

She moved toward him. Her beige low-cut evening dress draped around her slender body accentuated her natural curves. "You're lucky the takeover rumors were false."

He looked into her light green eyes. "I screwed up big time," he said. "I should've saved my money instead of investing all of it in those long-term private placements."

She wrapped her long arms under his olive-green suit coat and around his fit waist. She snuggled her head against his broad chest. "How much was the hit?" Her tone was coaxing.

He took a deep breath and exhaled. The scent of her pheromone perfume aroused him. "Three hundred grand."

She looked up at him and straightened his tie. "Don't worry darling, I'll help you."

"You will?"

"Of course." She chuckled. "I made a fortune day-trading Daddy's stock in *my* trust fund today. You know I would do anything for you." She squeezed him tight. "I love you sooo much."

"I love you, too," he said as the elevator approached the lobby.

She pushed herself away from him with a look of disgust. "What's wrong?" He could see she was angry.

"I hate when you say the word *too* after I say I love you. It just sounds like you feel obligated to say something in return."

The elevator doors opened. He reached for her hand but she pulled it away and headed off into the ornate marble lobby. A cacophony of horns and sirens from the busy streets of the Big Apple mixed like water and oil with the classical music playing inside the lobby.

"So," he called after her, "what do you want me to say?" For reasons he couldn't put into words he always succumbed to these childish tantrums of hers.

Paris abruptly spun around and walked back toward him. She smiled and said, "How about . . . I love you *more?*"

"I like it." He reached for her hand. "But instead of saying the whole phrase, now all we have to say is '*more.*' I love you is already implied."

Paris's eyes lit up. "Love it!" she said with a devilish grin. "Now, we have a new game to play."

They walked over and stopped in front of the statuary white marble fountain in the middle of the bright lobby. The lobby of the Avalon Towers looked like ancient Greek architecture had collided with Italian Renaissance art. Large marble columns towered high into the air supporting a domed ceiling that replicated the Sistine Chapel.

He looked up at Michelangelo's nine narrative scenes from the biblical story of Genesis, and focused on the fresco of the Creation of Adam. He marveled at the masterpiece of the physically complete Adam extending his hand out to meet the finger of God so he too could become spiritually complete. Darius then gave a longing glance at the fresco of Eve.

Could there ever be balance between the sexes?

"Anyhoo," Paris said, interrupting his thoughts, "how did the conference call with the board of directors of Daddy's company go today?"

He let go of her hand. "Brutal. I felt like I was on trial for murder. They grilled me on my knowledge of bonds to derivatives and asked questions that an MBA graduate would have had a hard time answering. All I know is that

I'm still in the game. Down to me and the top woman broker from Goldman Sachs."

Darius loosened his ponytail and ran his fingers through his shoulder-length brown hair. With his right index finger, he gently lifted her rounded chin up. Their eyes met.

"Listen. The odds are definitely in my favor but I don't have the account yet."

Paris smiled and moved her arms up around the back of his neck. He loved how her long blonde hair glistened in the light. "Don't worry, darling." She ran her fingers through his hair. "You'll get the pension account. I'll talk to Daddy."

"Am I ever going to meet your father?"

"Daddy's extremely busy. He's in Eurasia taking another one of his companies public."

Darius rolled his eyes. He was beginning to think that they would never meet.

"Once Daddy sways the board into giving you the account, Tsumitomo securities might even offer you a partnership. Next thing you know, you'll be a member of their elite roundtable."

Darius unwrapped her arms from around his neck and gently pushed her off him. "I don't want to talk about the account anymore. Where are we going for dinner?"

"But why? It's so exciting."

"Look, I don't want to jinx the deal. You know how superstitious I am." He pulled his lucky Kennedy half dollar out of his pants pocket. He had no doubt that he'd be jinxed if he didn't put a stop to any further talk about the deal right that instant.

"I'm sorry."

"No, you're not." He rubbed the coin between his thumb and index finger. He noticed her admiring the nude replica of the Apollo Belvedere statue standing in the center of the fountain.

What were the chances of him breaking out of his father's shadow and having someone erect a statue of him one day?

"So, where to for dinner?"

"We have reservations at Da'Vine Bar on the Upper West Side," she said, not looking at him.

He frowned. "You picked a cyber-bar?" he said and turned toward her.

"Relax. You don't have to get chipped."

"Since when?"

"Since I became friends with the doorman. He'll give you an ultraviolet hand stamp instead."

"But they only serve wine and beer."

"That's the reason we're going there. You've been drinking too much hard liquor lately."

Darius's jaw tightened. "Is that so? Well, you know what I think?"

"Don't turn this around on me. I'm just trying to help."

"You wanna help? Start by getting that chip removed." He tossed the sterling silver coin high into the air and caught it. "I don't have a drinking problem. I've just been under a lot of stress at work lately."

"I *never* said you had a problem," she said with a hint of annoyance. "It's just that you need to slow down. That's all."

His mother had warned him about dating a Scorpio. "Do you remember what my mother told us when we first started dating?"

She averted his eyes. "Hmm. Scorpios have a hidden set of rules that they *never* tell anybody about until somebody breaks one of them," she said with mocking drama.

"I'm not a mind reader, Paris. Sometimes I think navigating a minefield would be easier than trying to understand you. It's like a constant setup." And he was tired of the set ups, tired of the games, tired of trying to be a mind reader. "You remember what else she said?"

Paris shrugged her shoulders.

He looked directly into her eyes. "C'mon Paris. You remember."

"Okay. Okay. Just keep your voice down," she whispered, and nodded her head in the direction of a neighbor who was waiting for the elevator. "No matter how hard a Scorpio tries," she said in a bored sing-song manner, "they will *never* be able to control an Aquarian."

"Exaaactly," he said, stretching the word out. "The last thing I need is another overprotective mother. Stay in your own boat and stop trying to row mine."

"Anyhoo, darling, we have a ten o'clock reservation," she said and took him by the hand. "We mustn't be late."

Darius pulled his hand away. "Wait a minute. I have to combat the jinx you just put on me."

"You're kidding. Right?"

He turned around and tossed his 1963 Kennedy half dollar high into the air. He heard her take a deep breath as he watched the coin flip through the air and land in the fountain.

"That was the coin Sargent Shriver gave your father just before Kennedy was assassinated," she said and leaned over the edge of the fountain.

Darius closed his eyes and then opened them. "Murdered 'cause he found out that the Office of the President was being manipulated by a secret society that controlled the Federal Reserve and United States Government from behind the scenes."

She laughed. She always laughed at any of his theories that conflicted with the official state version of events.

"Should I summon the doorman to get it?"

Darius leaned over and looked at the coin shimmering in the water. He frowned. "Damn! It landed on tails. Novus Ordo Seclorum," he mumbled, as he stared at the Presidential seal shimmering under the water.

"What did you say?

He grabbed her by the arm. "New World Order. Don't even think about retrieving that coin," he said, pulling her away from the fountain. "That would be a double-jinx."

"But—"

"I should have gotten rid of that coin a long time ago."

"Your father loved that coin," she said, freeing her arm. "You should have made up with him when he gave it to you at your college graduation."

"Too late now."

Paris smiled. "Did your wish include me in it?"

"Paris, wishing for something personal would be selfish. It'd be considered a triple-jinx."

"So what did you wish for, Mr. Humanitarian?"

"World peace."

She laughed. "It'll *never* happen."

Darius shook his head and walked toward the lobby doors without her. Although he was loath to admit it, even to himself, deep down inside, he was beginning to think that maybe Laura was right about Paris.

▲ ▲ ▲

Darius stepped out onto 69th Street toward the corner of Third Avenue and glanced over his shoulder. Paris was still in the lobby doorway chatting with the doorman. He stopped walking and tilted his head back to look up at the stars. It was a clear night sky. A breeze whipped passed him ruffling his loose hanging hair.

He smiled as he studied the Orion constellation. He thought it looked unusually bright among the brilliance of the city lights. As though it were alive and on the lookout, showing off its shiny belt stars as it stood guard over the city.

He wondered if the stars were ever going to align and bring him the recognition and money he so desperately desired. So far, things couldn't have been worse. If it wasn't for the possibility of Paris's father's company opening up a three-billion-dollar pension account, he would have been fired already. The mere one hundred share account that he had opened last year was now on the verge of becoming one of the biggest accounts in his firm's history. Now that's irony, he thought. Losing three hundred grand trading the stock of the company he had a good chance of getting a dream account with. He had to laugh to himself. If he got the entire account, he could easily gross three hundred grand a *month*.

His Ivy League colleagues, who he knew looked down on him because he graduated from NYU business school and not Harvard or Yale, had laughed at him when he was selected to compete for the entire pension account. Who was laughing now, he thought. He had put together a portfolio of high tech stocks that for the most part turned out to be the biggest performers of 2011. The only thing standing in his way now was the global investment banking arm of Goldman Sachs that narrowly beat him on a percentage gain basis.

"You're supposed to say *more*," Paris said, jumping on his back.

Darius lurched forward and gasped as he felt her hands slip off of him.

CHAPTER 5

A VOICE SPOKE SOFTLY near the southern wall, "Look."
The fifty-year-old president of Egypt jumped up from the tan leather sofa and scanned his office for the perpetrator. "Who's there?" he said gruffly.

Was there somebody in the room with him? Impossible. There was only one way in and nobody had the access code. Not even his brother-in-law and trusted top aide, Raj.

"Show yourself."

There was no reply.

President Ramsey took off his white linen suit coat, laid it over the back of the sofa, and listened closely for the intruder to make another sound. He moved cautiously around the various piles of discarded books—some stacked six feet high. All he heard was the constant tick tock, tick tock, tick tock of his Khronos long-case grandfather clock.

A thunderous boom echoed from the Giza Plateau. *"Come!"* he heard the voice say. Ramsey froze. He knew *exactly* what that meant. Every muscle in his body felt as tightly wound as the coils in the clock. Tick tock, tick tock—

The Bible said men would hear that word—come—when Christ broke the first four seals of the apocalypse and wreaked havoc upon the earth.

Ramsey turned and rushed toward the southern wall. Gazing out of the twelfth-story window southwest across the peaceful blue waters of the Nile, all he saw were the three Pyramids of Giza shimmering in the sun.

A trumpet sounded far off in the distance. His ears perked up. He strained to hear a second call of the trumpet—a call that sounded like a call to battle.

What the hell was going on? These were turbulent and dangerous times and he did not want to indulge in such an idea.

Maybe this was a hoax conjured up by the Queen of the Eurasian Union to make him think that he was losing his mind. It was no secret she despised his defiant rebel attitude. More importantly, he was the only remaining president in the Eurasian Union who hadn't implemented her chip-based cashless society.

Suddenly, the building started to shake. He felt the floor shift violently beneath him. The force of the quake threw him toward the window. He turned his head and his right cheek slammed hard into the glass. Ramsey grimaced in pain as the shockwaves continued, but he slowly regained his footing and was able to steady himself by pressing his palms and body firmly against the window.

The Nile started to bubble and turned blood red. It was as if the blood of Hebrew slaves, spilled thousands of years ago in the desert, had finally made its way into the river.

The vision of St. John the Divine was unfolding right before his eyes. *Was he losing his mind?* He had always thought the book of Revelations was the biggest hoax ever created. An imaginative story written as prophecy of the future to scare the Christian people into submission.

His short quick breaths fogged the window as he pressed his crooked nose against the glass. Then the quaking stopped as suddenly as it had begun. As the sun faded to black and a shadow spread across the land, he braced for an aftershock.

Had time run out?

The thought of failure spread through his mind like an infectious disease. Like his Pharaoh ancestor at the time of Exodus, he now knew what it was like to be at the mercy of the Christian God's wrath. All he could do was helplessly stand by and watch the prophesized events unfold.

A sudden flash of light blinded him. Then he heard a deafening sonic boom that shook the walls around him. With his eyes tightly shut, he covered his ears and fell to his knees. He could hear the sound of marble tiles crashing down from the vaulted ceiling above him. He opened his eyes and looked over his shoulder at the stacks of books swaying like palm trees in a gusty breeze. How was that possible? Then, just as quickly as the convulsion of the earth— or whatever it had been—started, it stopped.

Ramsey staggered to his feet and looked out across the desert plateau. A blood-red moon eclipsed the sun and stars fell like meteorites from the sky.

Could there be more to the biblical prophecy than he had originally thought?

Without warning, a comet streaked through the sky and struck the pyramids with what seemed to be the force of an atomic blast. He felt the floor shift violently again. Off balance, he reached out toward the window for support. He steadied himself and gazed out upon the Giza Plateau. His eyes widened. A pyroclastic cloud, as dense and dark as lead, mushroomed and raced across the sky. It blocked out the blood-red moon as it swept through the land—destroying everything in its path.

His shirt stuck to him like a soaked rag, his hair plastered his throbbing head. Yet he felt chilled to the bone, as if he were standing inside a cold, damp tomb. He held his trembling hands out before him as if discovering them for the first time. Was he dreaming? Having visions? Had this to do with his not yet finding the Chosen One?

▼ ▲ ▼

A spotlight attached to a high steel pole lit up, blinding Darius. He froze like a deer staring into the headlights of an oncoming car. His heart raced. When his vision returned, he focused in on the familiar black dome surveillance camera below the spotlight and realized he was being watched.

Oh God.

Darius turned. Paris was face down on the sidewalk. He rushed toward her. He could already see the police taking him away in handcuffs. He knelt down and shook her lifeless body. "Paris," he whispered, "you okay? Get up, sweetie. The Network's watching." Traffic had slowed and pedestrians stopped to watch.

"Paris, stop kidding around. If you don't get up they're going to send an ambulance for you and a squad car for me." He shook her again, this time, a little more firmly. The crowd they had drawn seemed to grow by the second.

The bright spotlight cast tall shadows against the red brick wall behind them. He could hear the whispers of the bloodthirsty crowd. He was nauseous with—what—fear? He felt the heat from the gathering people . . . from the spotlight. He was sure heat was emanating from the security monitor as well. He felt physically scrutinized to a cellular level. Then, Paris stirred. And none too soon. She coughed and slowly drew herself up to her knees. Darius gently took her by the arm and helped her to her feet. She covered her eyes with her hand and tried to catch her breath.

"I'm okay," she said groggily. "I just had the wind knocked out of me. Are we in trouble?" She looked at the mob of people almost encircling them.

He'd heard stories about the new monitoring system that was being deployed throughout the city. He placed her arm around his shoulder and practically carried her toward the flat-panel display screen built into the pole.

Wave the back of your hand in front of the scanner." He had to place his left hand on his brow to shield his eyes from the spotlight.

"Why?"

"Just do it! If you don't, I could be going downtown in a few minutes."

When she didn't respond, Darius grabbed her hand and waved it in front of the scanner. Then he pulled his license from out of his wallet and scanned it as well. The thought of making the eleven o'clock news for domestic violence made his stomach turn.

After a long moment, he heard a deep male voice from a speaker atop the pole say, "Miss Templar, your vital signs seem to be normal. Do you require medical assistance?"

"I'm okay," she said softly. "Just a little shaken up."

"Would you like to press charges against Darius Prince?"

After what seemed like a long pause, she said, "No."

The spotlight turned off. The onlookers, disappointed, moved on and the traffic resumed.

Darius breathed a huge sigh of relief. He stuffed his wallet into his back pocket and grabbed Paris by the arm and led her down Third Avenue. "Thank God they didn't dispatch the paramedics and police to the scene." He made the sign of the cross on his chest and looked back at the camera. He shook his head. "You can barely move in this city without constantly being monitored! The next thing—"

"For God's sake, Darius, you think everything's a conspiracy. The technology is here to stay. And you know what—I really don't care what you think, I feel safer." She shrugged her shoulders and shook her head indifferently.

"Well I don't." He waved his hand in the air to hail a cab. "If you'd been seriously hurt my face would have been plastered all over the eleven o'clock news," he said, looking back at her. It wasn't even quite so much the incident that had him so worked up, it was Paris's attitude. Her indifference.

Paris rolled her eyes. "Relax."

"I can't," he said as a taxi pulled over. "Nothing happened, but they've got a record of the incident now." He held open the door for her. "If somebody got a hold of that recording, they could use it to slander me. Goddamn Patriot Act."

She shook her head and got into the taxi. "You're paranoid, Darius."

As the driver sped off toward the Upper West Side, Darius silently gazed out of the window. A student of architecture, he admired the different architectural designs of the old and new buildings. They clashed with one another, he thought, as he watched them disappear into the night sky. Both, though, were status symbols erected by financial magnates symbolizing the wealth and power associated with what he thought of as the greatest city in the world. The towering skyscrapers he grew up around were nestled neatly among the large city blocks as far as the eye could see. They blended beautifully against the backdrop of historical bridges and waterways, giving New York City the magnificent skyline the rest of the world envies. He wondered if the passersby would ever wake up to the rapidly changing world around them.

Good morning, Elijah! He wanted to shout the Hebrew saying from the cab window. Wake up and smell the coffee! He wanted to shout it to Paris as well but with a slightly diffe emphasis in meaning: "Aha, finally you awaken from your slumber!" But stealing a glance at her from the corner of his eye, he doubted that day would ever come.

Making their way through Times Square, Darius gazed up at the colossal video screens and billboards that illuminated the streets around him. For a brief moment, a red pentagram flashed on one of the screens overhead.

Not another pentagram virus!

Why had no one else in the company been affected by the virus that afternoon? Maybe there was more to it, he thought, as he tried to look through the city lights that filled the nighttime sky. Out of all of the stars in the heavens, he noticed that only Venus could be seen through the bright lights of Times Square. Then it hit him. If what Laura had told him was true, and Venus would soon form another Pentagram in the sky, maybe the cosmos were trying to tell him something.

He was suddenly aware of Paris's hand on his knee. She smiled and waved two airline tickets in front of his face. "Happy Birthday. I was going to surprise you at dinner, but I couldn't wait. Two tickets to London, England."

"Tomorrow's my birthday," he said and looked at the nosy taxi driver who was watching them in the rearview mirror. "Take Park Avenue."

He looked over at Paris and shook his head. "You just don't give up, do you? I've told you a thousand times, Paris, I'm not going to any of Eurasia's seven zones that require me to be chipped. I'm *not* getting chipped."

"Nothing I *ever* do is good enough for you." She stuffed the tickets back into her handbag. "So, out of all of Eurasia, we can only go to Egypt? That sucks. Well, I guess you'll *never* meet Daddy," she said and pulled a rectangular box out of her purse.

"Egypt's nothing more than a cleverly designed trap," he said, "purposely left open by the EU to gather intelligence on anyone—chipped or un-chipped—in the hopes that they'll find a way to put an end to the resistance." He motioned toward the box. "Is that my birthday gift?"

"It's the next generation chip with GPS."

Darius stared at her in disbelief. "You got me *a chip kit?*"

Paris laughed. "No, silly. Daddy sent it to me. He insists I have it in case I get kidnapped."

"Greaaat," he said, stretching out the word. "So now when we're together, I'll be tracked, too."

"How will you be tracked?" Her voice rose with annoyance. "Honestly, Darius, what are you gonna do when the American Union adopts it?" She opened the box and carefully removed the chip. She held it out between her thumb and index finger.

As he silently stared at the tiny translucent chip the size of a grain of rice, he thought about the American Union's new power structure. Divided into three zones—North America, South America, and Israel—he wondered if the ministers who governed these zones might soon force the president to abandon the peace process in favor of a global chip-based cashless society. It was no secret that the president's poll numbers had plummeted ever since Israel joined the American Union and now things couldn't have been worse. Tensions between the Jews and the Muslims were escalating and his opponents in the upcoming election had already endorsed the cashless society. The ministers, he thought, needed to inject life into his campaign—and fast— or they all faced defeat. He prayed the president would stick to his promise not to deploy the chip throughout the American Union and find some alternative means to win re-election. The thought faded when Paris nudged him with her elbow and held the chip up in front of his face.

"Where do you plan on going when everyone has to get one of these babies implanted? Mars?"

"If that happens, we'll all be under the rule of the New World Order."

She placed the chip back into the box and tossed it to him. "I still don't see why you're so against it."

"It's called freedom, Paris, freedom," he said, shaking the box in the air. "With the exception of Egypt, you have to get one of these damn things to go anywhere within the Eurasian Union. The whole thing freaks me out." He sat back exasperated and opened the box; a shiver ran down his spine. Everything needed to chip oneself was neatly packed away like a backpacker's first aid kit. The lithium-ion powered chip sat protected in a foam mount next to a syringe that was used to inject into one's hand. He shook his head. How could she be so willing to trade her total privacy for so-called security?

"I'm dying to try out the new technology."

"That's the kind of attitude that's going to get us in trouble." He looked out of the window at a surveillance camera mounted on a steel pole.

"You know, Darius, in the beginning of our relationship your ideas were fascinating, but lately they've become borderline delusional."

"Don't you get it? That's precisely what they want you to think! This is a long-term global plan that's being masterfully orchestrated in secrecy."

And so it went. Their entire ride to the club was a heated volley about the merits and consequences of a global and total chip-based world.

The taxi made a sharp turn and headed west on Twenty-Third Street.

Just drop it, Darius told himself. He needed Paris's help to cover the hit; he had to stay in her good graces. And this was a topic that totally pissed her off. But the truth was, he was angry with himself for giving in and allowing her to take him to a cyber-bar. He wasn't going to let it go.

"Can't you see what the EU's up to?" Since its inception in January, citizens who refuse to take the chip can no longer buy or sell. They're stripped of all their rights, kept like prisoners in their own homes, and treated like outcasts," he said, practically tearing his hair out. "Their assets are frozen and they're required to attend mandatory rehabilitation classes that are designed to brainwash them into believing that the chip is beneficial to society's survival— and it's not!"

"It is," she said sternly, "and that's what you fail to understand. Look, if they agree to take it, they become part of society again. It's that simple. If they refuse . . . they won't survive."

"They will survive—and that's what *you* fail to understand. God will take care of them."

"They don't need God to take care of them," she said with a laugh. "The free co-ops take care of them. They're clothed and fed until they wake up and agree to be chipped"

"Those so-called free co-ops are another trap!"

Paris sighed heavily. "You're paranoid."

"It's true. You think they're safe but they're not. Everybody's being watched. I've even heard rumors that the EU's gonna arrest anyone that's not chipped by the end of 2012."

She laughed. "A high tech holocaust. I guess it's all part of their master plan."

He didn't have to look at her to see her eyes roll. His eyes narrowed and his lips thinned. "As long as there's a black market that allows people to buy and sell with gold and silver, their master plan's in jeopardy—and they know it."

When the taxi pulled up in front of Da'Vine Bar, she swung open the door and grabbed him by the hand. "Anyhoo," she said, looking back at him mockingly, "maybe you'll meet some of those people responsible for your so-called New World Order inside the bar tonight."

He felt like telling Paris to piss off, but kept it to himself. He loosely held onto her hand as she pushed her way to the front of the crowded line that stretched down the block and around the corner. She acknowledged the stout doorman with an air kiss to both cheeks and held out her right-hand. He waved a wireless scan gun over it and then waited for Darius to do the same. Instead, Darius pulled out his license and held it up to the scanner. When the doorman finished downloading his information, he stamped the back of

Darius's right-hand. No sooner did he feel the cold invisible ink seep into his skin did the doorman unlatch the red velvet rope and let them pass. It felt good being treated like a VIP again.

Darius followed Paris into the bar and was staggered to see a female nurse plunge a syringe into the forehead of a young man confined to a wheelchair. The nurse smiled at Darius as she wiped away a trickle of blood that ran down his forehead. Darius looked at the long line of people waiting to be chipped and sighed deeply. There is a common emotion we all recognize—contempt—and that is what he felt witnessing this scene. It is also what he saw in the doorman's face when he produced his license instead of his hand for implant scanning.

▲ ▼ ▲

When the dust settled, President Ramsey noticed a crater the size of a small city where the mighty pyramids once stood.

A trumpet, louder than the first, blared across the scorched desert plateau. Startled, he took a step back. Which of the seven plagues would this apocalyptic angel release upon the earth?

He didn't have to wait long as the answer revealed itself.

From the fires that raged across the plateau, he watched a cloud of smoke slowly roll out of the fiery darkness. Out of the smoke came a massive swarm of locusts that filled the blood-red sky and raced toward him. The sound of their wings echoed through the darkness like teams of horses pulling chariots into battle.

The hairs on the back of his neck stiffened. He couldn't help but marvel at their numbers. He must warn his people.

"Computer, get me central command."

There was no reply.

"Computer! Get me central command now!"

Still there was no reply.

What should he do? He recalled from the Bible that the army of locusts would have supernatural powers but those powers would somehow be limited.

Limited to what? Or how?

Gazing into the fiery darkness, he watched the locusts swarm, and realized that they were not here to feast on the land. If the chip contained the number of the beast referenced in the Bible, he knew very well what they were coming for. Ear-piercing screams of men, women and children penetrated the palace walls. His heart fell. He felt sorry for his people who had willfully received the chip from another member country. But what really turned his stomach was the fact that most of those people never had a choice and had been forced to take it. He thanked Allah for giving him the strength to defy his superior's orders to integrate the chip-based cashless society in Egypt.

As the fires danced across the plateau, he saw the face of the enemy for the first time. The locusts were genetic mutations. On their tiny heads were crowns of gold and their faces were that of mankind. With his mouth agape, he quietly watched the supernatural creatures from behind the shatterproof window. Their armor-plated breast plates led the way under the blood-red moonlight.

They whizzed by in all directions; then suddenly, they came to a grinding halt. They fluttered weightlessly in front of him. "Unlike us, you have failed to find the Chosen One—kill yourself," the locusts chanted as they gnashed their razor-sharp teeth.

He pressed his palms against his ears to block out their shrill voices. His efforts proved futile as more and more joined in chorus, still gnashing their teeth and screeching and chanting, "You have failed, kill yourself. Do it now!"

Ramsey's hands trembled. Sweat trickled from beneath his white head cover and down his unshaven face. Maybe they were right. He had only to find the Chosen One and he had failed at even that. His ancestors, famous for building the Pyramids, what must they be thinking?

"Go away," he shouted, pressing his hands harder against his ears. He shook his head from side to side; their screaming accusations of failure taunted him.

Suddenly, there was a dead silence. He slowly removed his hands from his ears. He willed himself to open his eyes and then watched the swarm retreat into the shadowy darkness. The breath of relief that escaped his throat sounded more like a hoarse choking as he staggered back from the window. Had they given up?

Hardly. He reached about blindly to steady himself, and as he moved forward, the massive swarm reappeared and split into two. Then a bugle sounded—and the charge began.

Why were they attacking him? He didn't have a chip implant. Or did he? The first swarm with their armor-plated breastplates on full display, led the way. He raised his right-hand to his face and looked at his tiny scar. Had the doctors deceived him and implanted the chip when they surgically repaired his broken hand? "Computer! Close shields," he said, staring at what appeared to be millions of locusts descending upon the building.

Nothing happened.

"Computer, close shields!" he said again.

Still, nothing happened.

The demonic creatures repeatedly smashed into the window like bugs against the window of a speeding truck. The sight of their twisted little faces and lion-sized teeth sliding down the glass made him gag. As he watched their scorpion-like tails continue to sting the window, even after they were dead, a gruesome portrait of blood and guts streaked down the glass canvas spelling the word "SUICIDE."

President Ramsey stood firm. As long as he was still alive, he still had a chance to change the outcome.

Wave after wave of locusts continued to smash into the shatterproof window. Slowly, the glass began to crack.

"Computer! Close shields," he screamed.

Judging by the crack in the window, he knew it could not withstand another attack. His heart pounded as the next wave of killer locusts raced toward him, readying their pointed tails. The muscles in his face tightened.

"Allah, save me!"

There was a loud crash. Instinctively, he put his hands up to shield his face and head.

CHAPTER 6

"**S**URPRISE!" FLASHES WENT off and the guests roared, "Happy Birthday."

Darius looked around the lavish room at the thirty or so guests who were standing and singing *Happy Birthday*. What the hell were all of Paris's snobby friends doing here? He smiled half-heartedly as they finished the song. He could tell already that he was going to need more than just a few beers to lubricate his brain if he was going to make it through this night.

Paris gave him a big hug and kiss. "Happy Birthday, darling."

Looking around the room, he felt her wipe the lipstick from his cheek with her thumb.

"You don't know how hard it was keeping this a secret." She leaned back with a self-satisfied smile on her face. The sound of her breath came out as a soft whistle. "I thought for sure you were going to find out."

He continued to search the room for a friendly face. When he couldn't find one, he pulled her to the side away from the guests.

"You are surprised, aren't you?"

"Shocked is more like it. I don't see any of my friends among your loyal minions." He absently rubbed at the tightness growing inside his chest. He didn't like surprises. He'd had enough surprises today to last him a lifetime. One more and he'd have a bonfire raging in his chest.

"I invited a couple of your friends, but honestly, Darius, I want you to make some new friends." She waved to a guest and looked back to Darius. "I'll be right back," she said and tried to move past him.

Darius put out his arm to block her. "I don't like your phony narcissistic friends," he said. "They give me the creeps."

"Darius, grow up. You're just like them. You grew up on Park Avenue being called Master," she said as she straightened his tie, "just as they did."

Darius rubbed the back of his neck as he contemplated this unwelcome truth. He might have grown up in similar circumstances, but he was *not* one of them. "I just don't trust them," he said.

"Nobody said you had to trust them. Just get to know them."

He grabbed her by the arm. "I'm not interested in making any new friends."

Paris frowned. "You should be. They all have big trust funds. Even if you exclude my money," she drawled, stretching back from him with a smile, "there's still a few billion dollars walking around the room right now."

It was typical of Paris to find an advantage, especially when it came to money to suit her purposes. Darius had to admit there might be some advantage to this particular surprise. But he still had misgivings. He felt a tap on his shoulder and heard a familiar voice say, "Happy Birthday."

Darius hesitated for a moment, still caught up in Paris's seductive smile, then he let go of her arm. "Thank God." He turned and smiled at his partner, Norman. "You're a sight for sore eyes."

Norman shook his hand. "Hi, Paris." He moved Darius to the side and gave Paris a big kiss on the cheek.

That was more than just a friendly kiss hello, Darius thought. Norm stepped back, ran his fingers through his short dark brown hair, smiled, and flashed Paris his baby blue eyes.

"Norm, you look simply divine. I love your outfit. Prada? Gucci?" Paris said with an exaggerated New England accent and hauteur.

Norman struck a pose and shot Paris a sly grin. "Medici-Venus."

"Even better. You're the only one of Darius's friends who has any sense of style."

Norman grinned. "If it wasn't for you, Darius would still be wearing his concert T-shirts."

The two of them laughed as though Darius wasn't even there. Darius crossed his arms and shot Paris a condemning stare. "Love you too, babe," he said with a forced smile.

Paris turned to him with a devilish grin. She squeezed by, facing Darius. "*More*," she whispered, seductively, as she passed by him. "I'll be right back, I need to say hello to *our* friends who just arrived. Toodles."

Darius watched her walk away. Once she was out of hearing range, he turned toward Norman. "Are you," he paused, but not for very long, because the notion wasn't that ridiculous, "screwing her?"

"Jeez, Darius, where'd *that* come from? She's hot, but I'd never do that to you. You're like a brother to me."

Darius looked at Norman's right-hand. "Did you get chipped?"

"Was tempted, but decided against it."

He embraced Norman in a bear hug, and lifted him off his feet. "I'm so happy you're here."

"Darius," he groaned. "I can't breathe. Put me down."

Darius tightened his grip.

"C'mon," he gasped, "let me go. I promise . . . no more jokes."

Darius gave him one final squeeze and released him. "I'm glad we understand one another."

Norman let out a big whoosh of air. He took off his camel hair sport coat and tucked his black cashmere sweater back into his black slacks. "I heard about the hit." He reached into his sport coat and pulled out a sterling silver flask. Darius could see the letters D-M-A-C engraved on it. Norman grinned devilishly and handed it to him. "This'll help ease the pain," he muttered in the somber tone one reserves for grave affairs.

"Now we're talking." Darius's lips were compressed and barely moved as he spoke. He looked around the room, unscrewed the cap, and took a healthy swig. He placed the flask into the inside pocket of his suit coat, unbuttoned his collar and loosened his tie.

"Darius, if there's anything at all I can do to help, just let me know."

Norm looked a bit maudlin, but sincere. "Everything's under control." Darius's lips broke a smile; actually it felt more like a wide grin. He couldn't stay angry at his buddy, even if he had reason to.

"Cool." Norman looked around the room. "Who're all these people?" he whispered. "They all look like they subscribe to the Robb Report."

Darius laughed. "I'll fill you in later. Where's Mike?"

"He's on his way," Norm said and extended his hand. "Here's a little something extra to help celebrate your birthday."

When they clasped hands, Darius felt the familiar small, plastic vial slip into the palm of his hand. "Is that what I think it is?"

"Shh. Put it away."

The mere thought of the drug resurrected old feelings. His stomach churned. For a moment, he felt like he had to go to the bathroom.

"Wait 'til I tell you why I wasn't at work today," Norman said as Paris walked toward them with three of her girlfriends.

Darius shot him a wink, and said, "G-L-O." It was their code for "good looking out." He slid the vial of endorphinate powder into his pants pocket just before Paris reached them. Darius froze. He didn't dare say a word—just stared into her questioning eyes. After a long moment she reached up, buttoned his collar and fixed his tie.

"That's better," she said, smiling.

"Happy Birthday, Darius," Paris's three six-foot girlfriends—her last remaining single friends—spoke in unison. All three were dressed in designer white galabias that loosely covered their tall bodies from head to toe.

Darius moved Paris to the side and gave each of them a hug and kiss. "You look like the three graces," he said, standing back and smiling.

"Enough!" Paris took him by the hand. "I want you to mingle with all the guests."

"Gotta go," he said as she pulled him away. The three women were Paris's best friends, but still he had a hunch she felt threatened by them.

"See ya in a little while," Norm said. He tipped Darius a little salute and shook his head with a soft chuckle. Darius tried for a smile but didn't quite make it. It was more like a pained sneer. Or at least that's what it felt like. He would much rather just sit and shoot the breeze with his partner.

Stopping to shake hands with a few of the guests who lounged on antique sofas, Darius glanced at the paintings of Roman goddesses hanging on an exposed red brick wall. He noticed Paris glance over her shoulder and give her friends a victorious smile. He would never figure her out.

He pulled her close. "I feel like I'm running for office," he said. "Let's get a drink."

She laughed. "Maybe one day you will."

They walked toward the long mahogany bar that spanned the entire front wall. It was stocked with a wide range of beers on tap and an assortment of wines in racks along the wall—all available by the glass. He slowly led her through the maze of guests nodding and winking as though he were, well, like he said, running for some office.

Neatly tucked away between two identical buildings, Da'Vine Bar typified trendy. The converted three-story brownstone was one of New York City's hidden hot spots. Along with wine and beer they served a wide array of tapas and full course meals. It was especially popular late at night, always with a famous DJ spinning the latest tunes. He pulled out a barstool for each of them and glanced up at the TV above the bar.

"Good evening," the bartender said and placed two coasters down in front of them. "What can I get you?"

"I'll have a glass of chardonnay," Paris said.

"And you sir?"

"Shot of Patron Silver and a Sierra Nevada." When the bartender looked at him as if he were crazy, he felt Paris hit him on the shoulder. "Hey, what'd you do that for?"

She leaned toward him. "Don't be a wise guy," she whispered and smiled at the bartender. "He'll have a Sierra Nevada."

"I was just kidding, Paris."

"Whatever."

When the bartender returned with the drinks, he pulled a wireless scan gun out of a holster attached to his belt and held it out in front of them. Darius's eyes widened. He watched Paris place the back of her hand under the scanner. The moment it beeped, the bartender moved the gun over and motioned for him to do the same. Darius glanced at his right-hand and leaned toward him. "I'm not chipped."

"Did they give you a mark?"

"Mark?"

The bartender rolled his eyes. "Did they stamp the back of your right-hand?"

Darius nodded. "Yeah."

"Hold out your hand."

He watched the bartender make the necessary adjustments to the scan gun. When the bartender looked up and moved the scanner toward him, Darius slowly moved his hand under the ultraviolet light. Staring at the familiar pattern of lines emblazoned on his skin, his hand began to shake. Before the scanner could read it, he pulled his hand away and looked at Paris. She seemed to be holding back a laugh.

Darius looked back at the bartender. "Nothing for me," he said and pushed the beer toward him. When the bartender placed the scanner back into its holster and took away the beer, Darius turned back to Paris. "You just don't give up. Do you?"

"Keep your voice down."

"I had a feeling you'd pull a stunt like this." He reached into his suit coat and pulled out the shiny silver flask and unscrewed the cap.

"Put that away. Now!" She spoke in that huffy, authoritarian voice she used whenever they—or he should say, she—discussed shortcomings or failings.

"Like hell I will. Why didn't you tell me they were stamping a barcode on my hand?" He tilted the flask in a toast. "Checkmate."

"What's so bad about a barcode?"

He took a big swig and smacked his lips together.

"This is so humiliating," she said, looking around the room.

Darius took another swig and leveled a condemning stare. "Every barcode has the number 666 encoded in it."

"That's ridiculous," she said, hands on her hips. "Put the flask away before our friends start to talk."

"*Our* friends?" Darius paused and gazed around the room at all the unfamiliar faces. A look of disgust crossed his face. "These are *your* friends."

"They're nice people once you get to know them." She flipped her hair back over her right shoulder with her hand.

She was a spoiled rotten little Daddy's girl, who always had to get her way. And always had to be right. Sometimes he had a hard time understanding what he saw in her. He screwed the cap back on the flask and placed it back into his inside jacket pocket. "If I can't trust you, how can I trust your phony friends?"

Paris looked incredulous, and she was twirling her hair with her French tipped nails—a sure sign she was beginning to lose her patience. He enjoyed pushing her buttons, but realized that he had better cool it before she threatened not to pay for the hit. He reached out and began caressing her hand.

"If I fix it so you don't have to use the barcode, will you give my friends a chance?"

Darius thought for a moment. "Deal," he said with a sigh, "but don't expect miracles."

"I love you."

"*More*," he said with a forced smile.

"Love it!" She squealed and took a sip of her wine.

Darius's cell rang. He reached into his pants pocket, pulled out his Solofōn and stared at the caller ID. His heartbeat quickened. He paused, glanced at Paris, and then stared at the phone again.

"Who is it?" she asked, leaning over ever so slightly to get a look at the caller ID.

Darius moved the phone away from her and stood up from the bar. He pressed the answer button. "Hello."

"Happy Birthday." There was a slight pause when he didn't answer. "I'm halfway up the block in a taxi. I'm leaving for Chicago and I need to give you your birthday present."

"Hello? Hello? I'm having trouble hearing you," he said. He got up and moved further away from the bar. "Just give it to me when you get back," he whispered.

"Darius," Laura said, "it's a gift from your father. He asked me to give it to you on your thirtieth birthday."

He cupped his hand over the phone and looked at Paris. "It's GE-Joe."

"Figures. Calling to wish you a happy birthday?"

"He's threatening to transfer the account again. I just need five minutes with him," he said, looking around the room, "but I need to go outside. The reception in here is lousy. There must be copper shielding in the walls."

Paris frowned. "Fine, but don't make me come looking for you. You know how Joe has a knack for keeping you on the phone *forever.*"

"I'll be right back," he said and rushed out of the room.

She sighed, looked away, then looked back.

▲ ▲ ▲

"Happy Birthday D-MAC."

Darius kept his distance.

Laura Luv adjusted her tan galabia, which hid her muscular five-foot-seven-inch body. She crossed her arms.

"How did you know where to find me?"

"I ran into Norman at Sachs and he told me." She let her arms fall to her sides.

Darius nervously glanced over his shoulder. "What's in Chicago? New boyfriend?" He didn't know exactly why he was being so sarcastic. Why shouldn't she have a new boyfriend? After all, they were long over with and he had Paris.

"I've been invited to try out for the lead in a new musical called 'Aphrodite.' So," she said without a pause, "did little Miss Perfect's father give you the big account yet?"

He would have to ignore Laura's remark about Paris. "You said my father gave you something that he wanted me to have on my thirtieth birthday." He glanced over his shoulder again and looked at the long line of people crowding the entrance to the bar. When he didn't see Paris, he felt relief and then an unexpected surge of anger. He noticed a camera above the entrance scanning the restless crowd of people still waiting outside. He shifted his gaze back to Laura. "I must be crazy being out here with you." He turned and headed back to the bar.

"Your anger's consuming you. You need to forgive him just like I forgave you."

He stopped and turned. "It's not the same."

"You're right, it's not," she said, walking toward him. "You abandoned me for a night of pleasure with my college roommate."

Darius took a deep breath and exhaled. "Listen, Paris is paying for the hit and if she sees us together . . ."

Laura moved closer and playfully poked him in the stomach with her finger. "Hopefully she won't require your soul as collateral." She smiled and handed him a silver chain. "It's Byzantine."

He backed away from her a couple of steps. "The only way he knew how to show love—with money or gifts." His father's voice echoed in the back of his mind. Darius decided it was best to leave it in the past.

He placed the chain in his suit coat pocket. "I don't get it," he said, looking at her galabia. "Why is a Jewish woman wearing an Islamic male robe? Why does any woman, for that matter, wear it?"

"Maybe in ancient times only men wore them," she said adamantly, "but not in this day and age. "And, to me, the dress has nothing to do with religion. It's about feminine power. Women all over the world are now wearing them in support of the movement." Her expression was completely neutral as she spoke.

"Movement? Feminine power?" He gestured to her galabia.

"I'm serious. There's going to be a revolution."

Darius nodded and noticed three tall young women wearing black galabias and combat boots march by.

She's not kidding.

▼ ▲ ▼

What was taking him so long?

Paris finished her glass of wine and excused herself from a group of friends. She looked around at the other guests who were merrily drinking wine or beer and eating the assortment of tapas she had chosen.

She pulled out her Solofōn, and looked at the screen. She had a full signal. If she had a full signal, then so did he.

Bastard.

She was the one who had told him about the Solofōn stock opportunity to begin with. Once she found out that they could provide a worldwide service at a fraction of the cost, she knew Solofōn would dominate the global communications market. He had used her tip to resurrect his charred book of clients and built a thriving new business on it. But now he seemed to have forgotten that she, too, was familiar with the technology.

She walked over to the bar and ordered another glass of wine. The more she thought about it, the more her Scorpio instincts made her fear for the worst.

▲ ▼ ▲

Darius glanced at his watch. It was eleven-thirty. He looked into Laura's soft brown eyes. "Look, I've got to get back to the party," he said and opened the taxi door. "When you get back, give me a call and tell me how the audition went."

"Oh, I almost forgot—that message, 'Zoro, Join Us,' I think it might have something to do with your father being a Zoroastrian."

How could she possibly know that? *Nobody* knew that.

Zoroastrian. His mind flooded with images. The three-bedroom apartment on the corner of 67th and Park Avenue; the ritualistic milk-and-honey bath with flowers on his twelfth birthday. But the one thing that stood out the most was the day when his mother interpreted his astrological chart and told him he had extremely rare symbols that, if used correctly, could make him a very powerful man one day.

"How did you know he was a Zoroastrian?"

"I stayed in touch with your father up until his death last summer. He was one of the most enlightened men I've ever met," she said, stepping into the taxi. She closed the door and rolled down the window.

Darius leaned his head down. "She would have been eleven years old last week."

"Stop living in the past."

He watched the taxi speed off and then tilted his head back and stared at the waning crescent moon. Maybe there was more to his life than just trading stock.

He felt a tap on his shoulder. Startled, he turned.

"Copper shielding, my ass," Paris said with her hands on her hips. "Who was that woman?"

Darius paused. "What woman?"

Paris crossed her arms and tapped her foot. "Okay, let's start over." She gave him a Valley Girl sneer. "The blonde woman who just . . . got . . . into . . . the . . . taxi. Duh."

He could see she was about to pump up the attitude. He knew he'd come to regret taking Laura's call. And especially meeting with her outside, even if it was for only a few minutes.

"It was Laura, wasn't it?"

If he told her the truth, she would be hurt, and he didn't want that. She would also be mad as hell. He, quite literally, could not afford to give her a reason to back out of the deal she had made with him. There was only one other option. "Okay. I'll come clean."

"I knew it. You're still in love with her."

"Laura's the past." He couldn't believe how cool he sounded. "You're my future." He reached into his pocket. "It wasn't Laura. She was a runner."

"A runner?"

"Delivers drugs." He handed her the vial Norman had given him.

Her eyes opened wide. "You told me that you gave it up right after your father died."

"I did. But I felt like doing it tonight. You know, the big three-O and all."

"You know what this stuff does to your mind," she said, dumping the white powder in the gutter. "I want you to be around to celebrate your next birthday."

God that was close. "You worry too much." He knew he was home free now and gave her his hundred-watt smile.

"And for good reason. Endorphinate powder was developed as a mind control drug by the American Union . . . to better help control their soldiers—remember?"

"Yeah. I remember. Then, the government lied and said it didn't work and sold the formula to drug companies who found different uses for it."

"And now it's in everything from baby formula to ADHD drugs."

"I know—part of the master plan to control the masses," Darius shuddered, instantly hating himself, because he knew what was coming next. He had just stuck his foot straight into his mouth.

"If you believe that . . . you, Darius, we're talking about you—Mr. Paranoid, Mr. Conspiracy Theorist, Mr. Anti-Master Plan—then why would *you* do it?"

Darius shrugged his shoulders. He realized that he had just added fuel to the fire. He wasn't going to add any more. He stuffed his hands in his pants pockets and just stared.

"For Christ's sake, Darius, it's made from human endorphins. Promise me that you'll *never* snort that shit again," she said. "Promise me."

"I promise, and I'm sorry for lying to you." He moved to the side and put out his arm for her to take.

"Now that's more like it," she said and took him by the arm. "I love when you act like a gentleman."

"Wait 'til you see the look on Mike's face when I tell him that you're going to help me."

As they walked back into the bar, Darius thought that he would be willing to make some sacrifices in order to make their relationship work. Because he really did want it to work. Besides, she was right. What the hell was he doing willfully accepting—not mind-altering, but mind-control drugs?

CHAPTER 7

T HE SUDDEN SILENCE was as unnerving as the crash had been only moments earlier. Or *was it* only moments ago? Time seemed to have stopped. He felt almost calm as he stood listening to the vast quiet. Then slowly, he dared to loosen the grip of his hands and lower his arms from their protective shielding of his head. The window was intact and the locusts had vanished.

Ramsey reached out and touched the glass. Was he losing his mind? If it didn't break, then what was the noise he had heard? Looking down, he noticed the painting of Icarus lying face down in a pool of broken glass.

He glanced at the grandfather clock. Six-thirty? In the morning? Had he slept for an entire day? His body must have just shut down. After all, he had been up for more than two days straight. Ramsey shook his head as if to clear it and then focused his gaze back out the window. The stars glistened like diamonds in the twilight. He looked downward and out upon the Giza Plateau. The pyramids were still there but the fire, the smoke, the crimson moon—they were all gone. Had it all been a dream?

He reached down and picked up the Icarus painting. Turning over the gilded frame, he noticed that the metal wire on the back had snapped. That was odd. The wire was strong enough to hold three hundred times the painting's weight. He leaned it up against the wall and peered over his right shoulder. Not one book had fallen off the various stacks of books he had already searched through. How was that possible? He tilted his head back and scanned the white marble ceiling. No broken tiles. He looked at his large oak desk; it was just as it had been—a chaotic mess.

He shifted his gaze back to the painting of Icarus soaring toward the sun. The painting was beginning to haunt him. Standing there in his now dead-still office listening to the constant tick tock of the clock, Ramsey felt as if he were all alone in the world with nobody but Icarus and the fleeting darkness to comfort him.

He turned and slowly made his way across the room, and plopped down into his desk chair. He glanced at the silver shaker and half-full martini glass that sat in back of the dwindling pile of books on the right of his desk. A long rectangular wooden case sat in front of him. He reached out with both hands and pulled the case toward him. Forbidden to open it until he had found the Chosen One, he defied his father's orders and clicked open the three bronze latches.

He gazed upon the beautiful, but deadly, contents for the first time. Protected within a shiny silver sheath, his hands trembled as he carefully removed the curved sword from the cases silk lining. With both hands, he firmly held the sheath and tilted it toward him. His heart raced as he stared at the three interlaced triangles engraved into its center.

The Islamic nine-pointed star.

With his left hand wrapped tight around the sheath, he slowly ran his right index finger up the sword's black onyx handle. Inlaid with diamonds and rubies, a silver lion's head protruded from the butt end. He wrapped his right hand tight around its smooth handle and pulled the sword out of its sheath. The sight of the shiny steel slashing through the air filled his body with nervous tension. He marveled at its majestic beauty, its yielding motion.

He dropped the sheath into the case and moved the blade from side to side—inches from his face. The president stared morosely at his distorted reflection. The dark bags beneath his eyes and the wrinkles around them were proof of the toll the last fifteen years in search of the Chosen One had taken on him. He gazed across the room and stared at the southern window. He could almost hear the locusts again, smashing against the window, sliding down the glass, noisily spelling out the word *SUICIDE.*

Was that to be his destiny if the Chosen One fell into evil hands?

Ramsey looked over at the clock—a gift from the late Princess of Wales. The big hand moved onto the twelve and the little hand touched the seven. With each stroke of the clock's chime, he felt the pressure twist deeper and deeper into his gut.

Twenty-four hours. That was all he had left.

Now that Islam had surpassed Christianity as the largest religion in the world, the next part of the prophecy was about to come true. Could he find the Chosen One before the comet aligned with Stonehenge? He slid the sword back into its sheath and placed it gently, reverently, in the case. Other than the prophecy, it was the only evidence that validated the existence of a Chosen One.

When he heard the last chime echo throughout the room, he lit a jasmine-scented candle on his desk, and said, "Close shields." This time, as expected, the titanium alloy window shields closed in a quick spiral motion. He felt comfortable in the shadowy darkness as the sweet smell of jasmine filled the room. Flickers of red light danced around the inside of the case as if performing a ritualistic ceremony, illuminating the nine-pointed star.

He marveled at the ancient symbol; a symbol, he reminded himself, that was also sacred to the Freemasons. Did it have something to do with the Chosen One or did it merely show a connection between Islam and Freemasonry? He'd heard rumors that they were somehow connected, but there was no time to chase down another conspiracy theory.

Ramsey felt a sharp and sudden panic. With every breath, he could feel the brick walls of his office closing in around him. The office from which he labored to change the world was beginning to feel more like a tomb. And not just any tomb—his tomb. Would future generations think of him as a king and praise him, or would they blame him because he had failed to find the Chosen One? He looked at his desk and stared at the last of the books he had yet to search.

Only three left.

He exhaled deeply and pulled an eleven-by-fourteen-inch framed document out of the middle drawer. He looked at the brittle edges of the yellow papyrus protected beneath a thin layer of high-tempered glass and moved the prophecy toward him. He stared at the seal emblazoned on top. Every time he laid his eyes on the six-pointed star, he felt his blood pressure rise.

The State of Israel, Astrologers, and secret societies all used it, but what was the true meaning behind the controversial star? And, more to the point, what did it have to do with the Chosen One? There had to be an answer, or a clue, hidden somewhere within the faded ink.

He studied the Egyptian hieroglyphs for a few moments, and then read the opening of the prophecy aloud.

> *"In a time when Islam rules the world a fireball from space will align over the monoliths and pour its knowledge upon the land. A pure Aryan-Zoroastrian who has the power of the pyramids embedded in his soul will connect to the divine energy released by the heavenly bodies above. He will have the power to retrieve the Sword of Orion and crown a young prince, king. The Chosen One will hold the fate of good and evil in the palms of his hands."*

He had read the prophecy hundreds of times before. Why did he think it would look or say anything different now? He had scoured the planet for the man prophesized about, but had been unable to find him. There just weren't that many pure Aryan-Zoroastrian men to begin with, and he had checked each one of them twice. The majority had intermarried and their sons were now considered to be westernized half-breeds. Was it possible that he could have overlooked one?

If so, and he found him after he was gifted with what he believed to be supernatural power, would he be able to determine, beyond a reasonable doubt, whether the Chosen One was good or evil? Knowing him before the transformation took place might help aide him in his decision. For the Zoroastrian, it could mean the difference between life and death. He placed the framed document back in his desk and closed the drawer.

A hollow feeling filled the pit of his stomach. What if the prophecy was incomplete? Or, even worse, a false prophecy?

He couldn't bear the thought of his father and grandfather dying for no reason. The thought of their suicides being covered up and made to look like assassination attempts tormented him even further. Lies covered by more lies. Would it never end?

He thought about his late wife. She had once told him that since he was a Pisces, he could be so in tune with the world that he could easily mistake the world's psychic pain for his own.

Maybe she was right.

He leaned back in his creaky chair and thought about her and his son. A tear ran down his cheek. He had never gotten over the tragic day of their deaths. If he had only listened to his wife, they would still be alive today.

His wife had been Hindu and he studied Hinduism as a source of comfort while in mourning; it made him feel more connected to his beloved. The cosmos, according to Hinduism, as well as people's souls, experience an infinite number of deaths and rebirths. If Hinduism was part of the cosmic equation, which she firmly believed was the case, then there was a chance that he could be reunited with them in this life or possibly in another.

He wiped away his tears and hesitantly reached for the top right-hand drawer of his desk where he kept his late wife's pendulum—a metaphysical object she had always used to guide her.

He missed the fights over whether or not it had mystical powers. It was one thing to use it for, say, matters of one's private life, but not for making important political decisions. Especially since it was considered fortune telling which was strictly forbidden by his Islamic beliefs. If he had agreed to use it even once and the results were positive, she would have probably wanted to run the entire country with it. But, then again, the moonstone pendulum did indicate, according to his wife, that the man they were going to meet on that fateful day was not the Chosen One.

He thought back to the assassination attempt on his life twelve years ago. He could still hear their screams as he stood by helplessly and watched his family burn to death. The foul stench of burning rubber and charred flesh remained fresh in his mind. He clenched his jaw. They would still be alive if he hadn't insisted they go with him. He should have died that day, not them.

If the pendulum had the power of sight back then, it seemed reasonable enough that it still did today. And if it was able to guide his wife, perhaps it had the power to guide him as well.

He reached for the drawer but pulled his hand back when he noticed the time. "Set lights on high," he said. Squinting through the harsh fluorescent light, he made his way over to the clock.

He marveled at the exquisite craftsmanship, and noticed that it seemed to possess a certain human-like quality. Patterned with squares, circles, and triangles, he focused on the clock's square antique head which rested comfortably on the strong but narrow shoulders of its tall wooden body. He felt his heartbeat quicken. How could he have missed it, he thought, staring at the twelve-pointed star carved into the clock's face. He leaned forward to get a better look.

That looks like a—

There was a knock at the door. Startled, he turned and rushed back to his desk.

"President Ramsey, I know you gave explicit orders not to disturb you, but there has been a major change to your agenda," his aide called from outside his office door. "Would you kindly let me in?"

He glanced at the clock. It was seven-thirty. He stared at the heavy metal door that separated him from the rest of the world. "I'll be right out," he said. The clock and the three remaining books would have to wait.

▲ ▲ ▲

"Norman, I can't hear a word you're saying." Darius turned toward Paris and saw his manager, Mike, walk through the red velvet curtains covering the entranceway next to the DJ booth. "Paris, can you tell the DJ to turn it down a bit."

"For real? Our guests aren't going to like that. They practically worship the young Brit," she murmured dramatically, then bobbed her eyebrows.

"Just do it," he said. "Mike just arrived and I need to discuss the hit with him." He put his arm around her. "Don't get me wrong, the trance music is cool but, hey, *I am* the guest of honor."

"I'll see what I can do. Toodles."

He watched Paris walk through the crowd of guests hypnotically swaying to the music and found himself tapping his hand on the bar to the rhythmic beat. When he saw her on the tips of her toes talking into the ear of the skin-headed DJ, he leaned back against the bar.

The lights dimmed and the music softened. He breathed a sigh of relief and noticed Mike looking around the room for him. Darius waved his hand high in the air and motioned him over. He turned back to Norm. "So, what were you telling me about last night?"

"You're not going to believe what happened," he drawled. "I was having dinner with my cousin at the New Age eatery, Aquarius, in SOHO, and just as we were about to leave, these three tall, gorgeous, women grabbed us and insisted that we do shots of Hpnotiq with them."

Darius shook his head. "Hate it when that happens," he said with a short laugh. When Norm placed his empty glass on the bar, Darius glanced at his partner's wrist. "Let me guess," he said. "They got you drunk and stole your Rolex."

Norman turned toward him. He had a surprised look on his face. "How'd ya know?"

Darius grinned and took a sip of his beer. He pointed to the tan line on Norm's wrist.

"They got me real good." Norman shook his head and sat down at the bar. "Damn watch cost me thirty grand."

"You're lucky they didn't cut off your balls," he said as Mike approached them. Darius took a step forward, away from the bar. "I was starting to think you weren't coming."

He stretched his arms out to give his stocky manager a hug, but Mike simply extended his hand. Darius reached out to shake it but when he noticed a small bandage on the back of Mike's hand, he pulled his hand back. He felt a sinking feeling rush through his body—not unlike the feeling you have when you're descending from the highest point on a roller coaster. "You got chipped?"

"Happy Birthday. Sorry I'm late." Mike's tone was detached and almost businesslike.

"You got chipped?" he asked again.

"I had'ta for work. Didn't you get the memo?"

"Mem—"

"Darius," Norm said in a piping voice, "do you really think that the girls were considering cutting off my balls?"

Both men faced Norman and just stared. There was a long silence during which Darius was afraid he might do something stupid, like kick Norm's bar stool out from under him.

Memo? Darius started to panic. He couldn't seem to get any words out of his mouth. It was like being in a nightmare and you're about to be attacked or go over some edge and your speech and movement are totally paralyzed. "The firm wants—*everybody*—chipped?" he finally managed to squeak out.

"Not everyone," Mike said, "just upper level management—and brokers who owe the firm money."

Darius wiped the sweat from his brow. "That's bullshit. They can't force me to take the chip."

"Oh, yes they can!"

"No. They can't," he said adamantly. "I know my rights!" At just that moment, Mike and Norman burst into laughter. Darius shot his manager a wry look.

"Relax," Mike said, "I was just kidding."

"That wasn't funny."

"Maybe not, but the look on your face was priceless." Mike gave Darius a reassuring pat on the back. "Yo, Norm, get us a round'a beers."

"Right away, boss."

Darius grabbed Mike by the wrist and ripped off his bandage.

"Hey! What'd you do that for?"

Darius stared at the tiny scab on the back of his manager's right-hand. After several seconds, he looked up. "You did get chipped." Darius practically threw Mike's hand back at him. He shook his head and handed Mike the bandage. "The firm? Did they force you?"

"If you call being promoted to managing director and a hundred grand raise a use of force, then yeah. Look, now that I'm in charge of all the managers, brokers and wire transfers, I had to do it since I'm in control of the firm's money." He paused, glanced at his hand, and looked back to Darius. "Still, it was my choice."

Darius shook his head. "Bad move bro . . . that's the number of the beast!" He ran his hand over the top of his head as his boss reapplied the bandage to his hand.

"Darius, forget about the chip. Top brass wanna know how you intend on paying for the hit."

Try as he might, he couldn't forget about it. How could he—it was all around him. He looked at a guest who was holding the back of her hand under a bartender's scanner and shifted his gaze back to Mike. "Don't worry, they'll get their money."

Norman handed both Darius and Mike a dark frothy beer in an ice cold mug and then reached back and grabbed his beer off the bar. "Did you know Paris's Russian girlfriend has bigger hands than we do?" Norman said with a perplexed look on his face.

Darius cracked a thin smile and cleared his throat. "A toast." He raised his mug in the air. His smile turned into a smug grin. "To Paris," he said, "for lending me the money to pay off the hit. Cheers, guys." When they both responded with astonished looks rather than join his toast, he lowered his glass. "What? You don't believe me?"

"Hell, no," Norm said and looked at Mike.

"Neither do I. Seriously, how do you plan on paying for the hit?"

"Here she comes. Ask her yourself."

Darius and Mike shared a multi-million dollar client they had nicknamed GE-Joe. Both recruited by Tsumitomo Securities straight out of college, they grew up in the business together. Once Mike was promoted to branch manager, he relinquished the GE-Joe account to Darius with the understanding that Mike would receive fifteen percent of the profits at the end of every month. Over the years, the ups and downs they endured in the volatile stock market had strengthened their friendship. Together, they possessed major mojo. But there was a tension now Darius had never sensed before.

Darius sipped his beer in silence as they waited for Paris to join them. He had nothing to worry about, he told himself. Paris would back him up and that would be the end of it. She'd probably pull out her check book and pay for it right then and there. He watched Mike run his fingers through his slicked back hair and unbutton his blue double-breasted suit coat just as Paris hugged him from behind.

"Fashionably late I see."

Mike turned and grabbed her around the waist. "How's my little sista," he said and lifted her off the ground.

"Put me down," she shrieked. After a long moment, Mike planted her feet back on the floor and kissed her on the cheek. "It's a damn shame what happened to Darius. Honestly, I don't know how you stockbrokers do it."

"Darius tells me that you're going to pay for the hit."

"Well," she said, stretching out the word like hot taffy, "I told him I'd help him. I *never* said that I would pay for his stupid mistake."

CHAPTER 8

"**W**AS THAT PRESIDENT Ramsey?"

Raj's ears perked up at the tone of the question. Wearing a white robe and head cover wrapped with a black felt band, Raj looked up from his tablet computer and glanced over his shoulder to see who spoke as he prepared to brief the president. He watched an aide disappear into one of the many offices that lined the corridor and then noticed the president hurrying down the hall. Perhaps whomever it was that had asked the question was just as surprised to see him as he was, since the president had locked himself away in his office. Not even Raj had spoken with nor seen him in the last three days. When the president had finally emerged from seclusion, at his persistent pleading, he had walked right by Raj, who was on his computer with his back toward him. Rushing after him, Raj struggled to catch up with the president as he continued to check his tablet for any more surprises to the day's agenda.

As the hall began filling with government workers, the rising sun slowly made its way through the large oval windows and skylights accentuating the thirty-foot cathedral ceilings and finely polished white marble floors.

This was the first chance Raj had had to get a good look at the president. "Oof," he said, looking the president up and down. Ramsey's usual perfectly combed dark hair was matted and his white suit was heavily wrinkled and beginning to turn yellow. But what really shocked Raj was the three-day stubble wildly protruding through his wheatish complexion. It was well known that President Ramsey despised facial hair and considered an unkempt appearance to be a sign of weakness. So much so that Raj was reluctant to hire anyone if they had a beard or moustache, or even a goatee, because he was quite sure the president wouldn't trust him. He was also quite sure that if he were to hold up a mirror to Ramsey, he too would gasp.

He had watched the president gradually become more and more detached over the last year and significantly more so over the last three months. It was obvious to him that the president needed to confide in someone and Raj thought, being not only his loyal aide but also the president's brother-in-law, it was obvious that that someone should be him. To make matters worse there was the mounting pressure that Eurasian Union officials were placing on him to find out what was wrong with the president. His constant defiance of their initiatives resulted in him being viewed as a rebel by many top officials, and Raj was running out of excuses as to why he couldn't be reached over the last few days. If things didn't return to normal soon, it was just a matter of time before they would both be removed from power.

Raj reminded himself that he must reduce his weight. He wasn't getting any younger and knew that being overweight combined with the stress of his job would be the death of him. He would start his diet today, he thought, and took President Ramsey by the arm. "Mr. President, I need to have a word with you," he said, and led him into an alcove that provided them some privacy. Raj placed his left hand under his rounded chin and studiously looked his brother-in-law up and down. When Raj looked back up, he saw that a deep crevice had formed between the president's eyebrows.

"What's on your mind, Raj?"

"Mr. President, I'm tired of watching you suffer. Would you kindly tell me what it is that is troubling you?"

His question elicited a gaze out of the alcove window, high above the hot city streets.

He hadn't really expected a reply, but Ramsey did seem to notice him for the first time. Now that he had gained his attention, how could he get the president to confide in him?

Then it dawned on him. It was a long-shot but maybe, just maybe, it would work. He looked at his tablet computer, took a deep breath, and moved next to the president. Ignoring the president's pungent body odor, he said, "Actually, my sister always used to say that your soul keeps coming back until you get it right and—"

"The reason most people fail is because they don't trust," the president said, finishing the statement. He took a deep breath, glanced at Raj and then turned and gazed back out of the window offering no further comment. President Ramsey had soulful black eyes that seemed to carry the sorrows of the world when he was serious like this.

Raj reached out to touch him on the back of the arm, then thought the better of it, and withdrew his hand. "She would have been very proud that you entrusted me to be your top aide."

Ramsey turned and faced him. "Unfortunately, there are some things I must do by myself."

Raj smiled half-heartedly. It was such a final-sounding statement. His response had been abrupt, resolute, but Raj didn't take offense. If he didn't find out something soon, he would be fired and they would start the proceedings to impeach Ramsey. The vultures would pick at the president until there was nothing left but bones. Raj looked up at him. "There is a lot going on in the world that needs your attention."

President Ramsey nodded in agreement. "Let's go to the lounge and have a nice cup of tea. You can tell me everything on the way."

"Listen to me," Raj said. He was going to have to stand his ground. There was simply nothing else to do. "You are in dire need of a bar of soap, shave, and a change of clothes. The less people see you like this the better," he said. "Trust me, the last thing you need is people spreading—"

"Am I that bad?" President Ramsey made a face of displeasure.

"I'm sorry but, yes."

He didn't look quite convinced, but seemed to take his word for it. "Give me your head cover."

Reluctantly, Raj removed it and handed it to the president who fit it snugly around his head.

"Better?"

"It's a start," Raj said, rubbing his cleanly shaven head. Then Ramsey did an abrupt about-face and started back down the hall, which was now teeming with government workers. Once again, Raj caught up to the president and then looked down at his tablet computer. The sleek device was protected with the latest encryption software to prevent cyber-terrorists from hacking into the Eurasian Union's billion-dollar petaflops computer network. The highly intelligent system, code named Patriarch, made it virtually impossible for anyone to bypass its firewall.

Checking the agenda, he noticed another high-profile name that had been added. The president was scheduled to meet with the prominent peace activist, Princess Zara of England, first thing that morning.

Raj admired the thirty-year-old princess and thirteenth heir apparent to the British throne. More importantly, he respected her. For the last several years she had been tirelessly working with the United Nations to achieve peace between Muslims, Jews, and Christians. The idea of the president meeting her in his current condition was unthinkable. To make matters even worse, he had a video conference scheduled with her grandmother, Queen Elizabeth, immediately afterward.

President Ramsey slowed his pace and then came to an abrupt stop. "So, what's on my agenda?" he said, turning to Raj.

"Actually, it's not a matter of what, but who. There has just been another change to your schedule. At nine you're scheduled to meet with Princess Zara, who has just made a stop in Cairo on her way back from—"

"Good, I have a few things I need to speak to her about." He motioned to Raj for them to get going and they continued down the corridor at a steady clip.

"I don't think you understand, Mr. President. This meeting is multifaceted and extremely critical." Raj tried to slow his breathing before he continued. He silently swore to himself that this time he would stick to his diet. "If you handle the issues correctly, which I will go over with you, you could lock up the majority of the women's vote in the upcoming election."

"Right now, I have the women's vote."

"I beg your pardon, sir, but after the riot that occurred yesterday, that could all be in jeop—"

"Riot?" Ramsey said, slowing down their pace again.

He didn't want to make the president more anxious than he already was. "Yesterday, a meeting took place in Babylon between women's rights activists and three religious leaders representing Islam, Judaism and Christianity," he said. "The women verbally attacked the religious leaders and questioned the patriarchal interpretations of their holy texts. When the activists accused them of using religion to legitimize their patriarchal agenda, the men walked out on the talks. Later, the three leaders were found dead—hanging by their necks from the rafters over the altar in the church they'd met in."

"Did anyone claim responsibility?"

"Not yet, but three women were seen leaving the church just before the bodies were discovered. Two of them were wearing black veiled hijabs which are associated with the extreme left-wing feminist group, and the other assassin was wearing a veiled black galabia that is now associated with the . . ."

"Peaceful women's rights movement," Ramsey said.

"It's hard to tell these days. Everybody's wearing them."

"That leaves almost every woman in the world a suspect."

Raj shook his head. "What bothers me most is that the hijab and galabia were once worn to show respect to God. And now—" He shook his head again and tittered.

"My guess . . . the Ghostriders are behind the attacks."

Raj glanced over his shoulder. The mere thought of the elusive left-wing feminist group made his stomach turn. They didn't just promote female superiority, they preached hatred for men. He placed his hand on the president's back as he steered him along. "Maybe. It's possible, I suppose. I must admit the thought did cross my mind."

"The problem is that we know virtually nothing about them."

Raj grunted as he directed the president to turn left. "It's imperative we find out who their leader is. Mr. President, if there is anyone who has the necessary resources to help you—it's the princess. By the look of things," he said, trying to pick up their pace, "it appears as though you now have two ghosts to chase."

The president took a deep breath and exhaled. He came to a sudden halt, and the two men stared briefly at each other. "Yes, but I don't know if I will ever find him," he said and then turned and started walking again.

Raj touched him on the arm as they quickly resumed their pace. "So you *are* looking for somebody."

"Hmm, clever," he said with a quick glance at Raj. "Maybe you can help me."

"Arey!" he said. This was wonderful news. His brother-in-law hadn't asked for his help in any personal matter since his wife and son had died.

"When we're done with our tea I want you to come back to my office and take a look at something."

"It would be my pleasure," Raj said. He was grateful that he was being taken into his brother-in-law's confidence and that they would be a team again. Right now, though, he needed to advise Ramsey on the issues currently facing him.

"The more I think about the princess's new taskforce on the benefits of life in a matriarchal society, the more I think it's the break we've been looking for," Raj said. "If you get involved, Mr. President, you can secure a stronger women's vote in next year's election."

"There's no time for that, Raj."

"Let me put it to you this way. If you don't help her, you'll lose the election. And, your successor will implement the cashless society."

"Don't worry, I won't let that happen," he said, patting Raj on the back.

Ramsey, always as steady as a ship at anchor, was finally regaining his composure and equilibrium, Raj thought. In other words, his old self. "Now, at noon you have a call with Queen Elizabeth."

"All she wants is to know when I plan on implementing the cashless society in Egypt," the president said with a dismissive wave of his hand.

"Of course she does. But with the recent attacks, I think she wants to entice you to help her niece find the culprits. Rumor has it that she's receiving death threats and fears for the lives of her family."

"They are always receiving death threats."

"True. But this time," he said, "I have a funny feeling that the group responsible for the attacks has threatened to kill her and her family."

As they continued toward the lounge that was now in sight, Raj caught the eye of a young Egyptian woman walking toward him. She was dressed in a black cotton galabia that covered her entire body from head to toe. Entranced by her heart shaped face and olive-gold complexion, he fell a step behind the president. In the flash of a second, their eyes connected deeply. He stopped abruptly as she passed and he turned to look at her. At the same moment she, too, turned and flashed him a smile that paralyzed him.

When he snapped out of his trance, he saw that President Ramsey was almost at the lounge, in front of which stood three oversized solid gold statues of the Egyptian god Amon-Ra and the goddesses Mut and Maat. If the president reached them and noticed that he was not at his side, he would be offended. Now that Ramsey was taking him into his confidence, it was a risk he could ill afford to take.

CHAPTER 9

D ARIUS FELT A sharp tightening in his chest. He could feel his
eyes ablaze. His face felt like it was on fire and he was sure it was
beet red. He put his arm around Paris's shoulder and looked at Mike. "Paris is
such a kidder," he laughed. "Ya know she gets that from me. Honey, please tell
Mike that you're going to lend me the money."

"I *never* said that," she replied. "I said that I'd help you. There's a big
difference. Do you honestly think that Daddy would ever allow me to give
three hundred grand to somebody I wasn't married to?"

A nasty combination of nausea and hunger washed around in his belly. He
hadn't eaten a thing all day. His voice sounded thin and hollow to himself. "I
think I'm going to be sick," Darius said and sat down on a barstool. He felt as
though he had been punched below the belt and then kicked in the head. He
looked at Paris. "So, what did you mean when you said you were going to help
me?"

"I'm going to move in and pay the bills until you get back on your feet.
When Daddy sways the board to give your firm the pension account, you'll be
able to pay it off in no time." Her tone was chillingly matter-of-fact.

Darius flashed a look to Norm.

"Don't look at me. All my money's tied up in real estate."

Darius rolled his eyes and looked at Paris. He could tell by the smirk on
her face that she was holding something back. "Is there something you're not
telling me?"

After a brief moment of silence she nodded in agreement. "Actually, Daddy
called while you were outside. He told me that he talked the board into giving

you the account," she said, clapping her hands together and smiling. "Now, it's just a matter of paperwork."

"That's great news," Mike said and took a sip of his beer. "The top brass will be pleased."

Darius grabbed her arm and pulled her close. "Why didn't you tell me outside?"

"I was mad at you."

"And what if your father doesn't come through or the account gets delayed?"

She laughed and pulled her arm free. "Like I said, I'll move in and take care of you until the account transfers or you find another job." She gave them all a smug smile and took off in the direction of her friends dancing over by the DJ.

Darius stared at her in disbelief as she walked away. She looked supremely satisfied with herself. He wouldn't be at all surprised if this was all part of her master plan to make him dependent on her so he would have no other choice but to marry her. Even if it was, he might still need her help just in case the account transfer was somehow delayed or failed to ever materialize. He thought it best not to confront her and kept his thoughts to himself.

"Now I see where you get your negotiating skills from," Mike said with a laugh. "Paris is one shrewd woman."

He was sometimes loath to admit it, but Paris was a good deal maker. "She's a Scorpio. Sneakiest sign of the Zodiac. Hard time trusting people, too."

"C'mon," Norm said, "you don't trust either. It took us years to become partners. You thought I was gonna steal all your accounts."

"My mom says I have Scorpio rising. I think that has something to do with it."

"Anyway," Mike said, "Paris is the best thing that ever happened to you. She's an angel."

"So what does that make me? The Devil?"

They all laughed.

"You were a goddamn wild man before you met her," Mike said.

Norman grinned. "Darius, Prince of Darkness. It's got a nice ring to it," he said. He finished his beer and placed it on the bar. "Hey, do you know anything about Taurens?"

"My father was a Tauren. They're ruled by the second house of money. Need I say more," Darius said as he listened to the DJ crank up the music.

"If you're not going to mingle with all these potential million dollar clients," Norm said arching his shoulders back, "I will."

"Do whatever you want with the guests, but stay away from Paris," he said, as Norman strutted over to the dance floor and began dancing with her friends.

"Women always fall in love with bad guys," Mike said.

Darius flashed him a devilish grin. "Yeah, well, you know, they don't even need us to procreate anymore."

"By the way, Genetically Perfect Baby is going public next week. Is Paris's father allocating you any stock?"

"I don't know if I want any."

"Are you crazy? Stock's gonna be up huge. Did you see their commercial?"

"No, but I heard it really bashes men."

"Does it ever! Starts off with a hot blonde flying down the road in a Red Ferrari Spider. Then it cuts to this guy who's crossing the street in a red, Jersey Devils baseball cap."

Darius moved to the side to let Norman squeeze past him. "Norm, grab me another brew," he said and handed him his empty pint glass.

"Sure." Norman wiped the sweat off his forehead with his sleeve and turned toward the bar.

"Poor Normy, not even one full dance and he's panting like a dog in heat." Darius nudged Mike with his elbow. "So what happens next?"

"It cuts back to the blonde in the Ferrari. When she sees the man, she shifts into high gear and floors it. Just as she's about to hit the guy, he looks up. His eyes open wide and . . . they cut. Next thing you see is the guy's Devils cap lying on the ground. Then the camera zooms in on the license plate that reads *Genetically Perfect Baby* and a seductive woman's voice says, 'Genetically Perfect Baby, who needs men anyway?'"

Darius grabbed the pint of beer from Norm and took a sizeable gulp. Why would Paris's father approve of such a commercial?

"That commercial gives me the creeps," Norm said. "I'm tellin' you, they're out to get us."

"I believe it," Darius said.

"C'mon guys," Mike said, "it's only a commercial."

"That's what they want you to think," Darius said and turned to Norm. "Dude, once I get the pension account, I'm gonna have to perform."

"I gotta hit the head," Mike said.

Darius pointed out to Mike where the bathroom was. Once Mike was out of hearing range, he said, "We need a new stock to pitch."

Norman glanced over both shoulders and leaned toward him. "I know a stock that's gonna put Solofŏn to shame," he whispered.

Darius put his arm around Norm's shoulder. "I'm all ears."

"You never heard this from me but I know somebody on the inside who assures me that over the next year Congress is going to pass a bill to make the American Union cashless."

Darius scoffed. "President Walker'll veto it."

An astrologer by trade, his mother had once told him that the President of the American Union was a Leo who had Aquarius rising and a moon in Gemini. Unlike a person's sun sign and rising sign, which provide insight into one's internal and external self, he remembered that a person's moon sign could tell you a lot about their emotional instincts and habits. He too had a Gemini moon, which he knew resulted in a person having a short attention span. Knowing this, he had always tried to prove his mother wrong by purposely trying to maintain his focus much longer than usual—in the president's case, he prayed that he too would intentionally stay focused.

"Trust me, Herbert Hussein Walker is a politician. He'll do whatever it takes to win re-election. That includes selling his soul—as you like to put it. Anyway, the majority of the voting public is in favor of a cashless society. And," he said, heaving his shoulders and arching his brows, "Walker's opponents have already endorsed it. President'll have no choice but to follow suit."

Darius sat down on his barstool. "I hope you're wrong." Suddenly, he felt exhausted. He didn't even have the energy to get worked up about Norman's news.

"Cheer up," Norm said and patted him on the back. "We're gonna make a fortune trading this one. If my source is correct, they're not gonna use the same chip as the Eurasian Union. They're goin' with another outfit that's invented a superior chip."

"What's the name of the stock?"

"Nero Technologies. Their chip technology makes it virtually impossible to steal someone's identity. That's the biggest problem plaguing the EU's chip."

"What's the symbol?" Darius said hesitantly as he watched Mike walk toward them.

"M-A-R-K. It's trading at six dollars a share. Once they pass the bill and Walker signs it into law, the stock's gonna shoot past Pluto."

"I don't know, man. The company stands for everything I'm against." He realized how foolish that sounded as soon as the words left his mouth.

"Then don't buy the stock. But remember one thing, Darius. Morals don't make men rich and, right now, you're three hundred grand in the hole."

Darius ignored him and pointed to the TV above the bar. "Isn't she beautiful?" He stared at the stock chart of the 800-pound corporate gorilla that had made them wealthy and their clients rich. He raised his glass in the air just as Mike rejoined them.

"To Solofōn," he said and recited the company's slogan. "Get in touch with your spiritual side." He smiled and turned to clink glasses with Norm and Mike. Darius licked the froth from his lips and looked back up at the TV. When the commercial ended, a live shot of Stonehenge appeared on the news. "The comet, Goliath, is scheduled to go over Stonehenge tomorrow night," he said and felt a kiss on his cheek. He glanced at Paris who slid onto the stool next to him.

"I think it's so classic it's going to happen on your birthday," she said. "I can't wait."

"Big deal," Norm said. "If it doesn't' make me money I couldn't care less."

Darius laughed and looked at Norm. "Spoken like a true Tauren," he said. He turned back to the TV. "Look at all of those freaks."

"There must be a hundred thousand people there," Paris said.

Darius nodded. "Central Park'll be crawling with 'em tomorrow, too."

"That gives Daddy's little girl an idea," she said. She smiled that kind of smile that told him she was up to something.

Darius watched her stand up and move behind him. He felt her start to massage his broad shoulders. He relaxed and tilted his head back. She leaned in, brushed her mouth against his ear, and said, "Let's dress up as hippies and go to the park after work to help ground and channel the energy that the comet is supposed to release when it aligns with Stonehenge."

"What? You hate the park and detest hippies!"

She leaned her face over his shoulder and flashed him a devilish grin. "I've had a sudden change of heart," she said. "Trust me, it'll be a night you'll *never* forget."

▲ ▼ ▲

Dashing through a minefield of staff who Raj was sure sought his highly coveted position, he finally caught up with the president. He hoped to God he wasn't offended by his temporary absence.

"I was beginning to wonder what happened to you," Ramsey said.

"Please forgive me." Raj glanced up at the goddess, Maat, as if she were responsible. She bore an uncanny resemblance to the woman he had just passed in the hallway.

He turned to find Ramsey smiling and staring at the cover of a magazine.

Ramsey looked over at Raj and raised a copy of *New Age Magazine* up in front of his face.

The cover showed a comet, streaking through a star-filled night, high above Stonehenge. He read the bold yellow subtitle aloud.

"When I don't know, I look to the stars."

Ramsey's smile widened.

Slowly, Raj tilted his head back and gazed through a circular skylight high above their heads. He didn't see any stars as he stared into the powder blue sky.

When his eyes returned to their surroundings, he noticed Ramsey thumbing through the magazine.

"Do you know this magazine?" the president asked.

"I read it from time to time. It's a metaphysics magazine . . . good for keeping abreast of the New Age Movement."

"I wasn't aware that there was such a movement. What is their cause?"

"Actually, it's not a cause, it's about change. New Agers believe that the Age of Aquarius is about the evolution of the soul. Apparently, humanity will soon ascend to a higher level of spiritual consciousness," he remarked. "In fact, sunrise tomorrow is believed to mark the beginning of this New Age." He motioned to the magazine. "Where did you find it?"

"Under the statue of Maat."

"Perhaps the goddess of universal order and balance is trying to tell us something," he chuckled and knotted the rope around his waist.

"There are no coincidences, Raj. Everything happens for a reason."

"So . . . what is it that you want me to look at?"

"The clock that the Princess of Wales gave me."

Raj frowned. "You want me to help you fix a clock?"

"No. There's a message hidden within the clock face that I need you to help me decode. Come by my office after work."

Raj half wondered if somehow in the vast reservoir of his intuition President Ramsey had always been searching for someone, someone of vital importance.

CHAPTER 10

"**I** UNDERSTAND YOUR HIGHNESS. I will follow up and get back to you shortly." Mohammed, the forty-year-old religious leader of the world's three billion Muslims and one of the queen's seven presidents, disconnected the call. He gazed absently out of the study window of his palace that was due south of the towering Alborz mountain range in Northern Tehran. He was a small man, but he was also the most powerful president in the Eurasian Union. Staring out at the magnificent snow-capped peaks, he thought about the queen's ultimatum.

Mohammed took a deep breath and exhaled. "Life has become full of threats," he said aloud in a philosophical manner. He liked the sound of his Persian-accented English. He pulled the belt tight around his traditional white robe and slowly turned. He looked at his younger brother who was dressed in desert-issue fatigues. Zadam's six-foot-three-inch frame settled comfortably into the chair behind Mohammed's expansive desk. He leaned back and clasped his large hands behind his head. Zadam had a way of taking possession of any place he occupied. He was street-smart; Mohammed had to give him credit for that. He was also a charismatic underachiever with a playboy attitude who thought everybody owed him a living—especially Mohammed. Against his better judgment, Mohammed had leveraged his power to further Zadam's military career by helping him obtain the highest ranking post of Field Marshal. Ever since they were youngsters, Zadam had always defended him and in so doing had earned Mohammed's trust.

"What does our beloved queen demand of us now," Zadam said. His tone was heavy. He grabbed a handful of shelled pistachio nuts from a bowl on the desk and tossed them one by one into his mouth.

Mohammed glanced at the tiny scar on the back of his right-hand and slowly moved toward him. "She wants me to put pressure on our dear friend, President Ramsey, to implement the cashless society in Egypt. She feels he's delayed long enough."

Zadam snorted. "More meaningless threats. She *should'av* gotten rid of him a long time ago."

"This time I believe she is serious. He's been a major thorn in her side. If he doesn't agree to implement the technology soon, you're going to be commissioned to remove him from power."

It seemed to Mohammed that Zadam was naïve. He didn't understand the New World Order power structure that now ruled the world. He would figure it out, he hoped, and hopefully in time to protect both of them from its influence.

Zadam grabbed another handful of nuts. "Brother, as usual you are looking at things in the wrong light," he said and leaned back again. "The depression in England has caused a separation of the classes. She is the one who is on the verge of being removed from power. It started with the death of Diana and will end with the death of her son, Prince Charles, and her two grandsons—Princes William and Harry." He smiled with a sense of satisfaction. "She will live only to see them die."

Mohammed stopped in front of his desk and leveled a condemning stare. "For now, you will do everything in your power to protect the British Royal Family." Mohammed knew that a breakdown in England would lead to chaos worldwide and many battles for power, including his.

"On the contrary, my brother, I will be late for work that day."

"You have much to learn," Mohammed said.

Zadam rose from the seat. His many meaningless medals jingled as he made his way out from behind the desk. Standing toe to toe, Mohammed tilted his bald head back and watched Zadam rub his neatly trimmed goatee.

"When are you going to wake up and realize that she is just using us to control the Muslim people?"

"Nonsense," Mohammed said. Zadam did an abrupt about-face and moved back behind the desk. He sat down and nonchalantly kicked his steel-tip boots up onto the corner of it.

"The queen has done much for the Muslim community," Mohammed said, "unlike your dirty boots."

Zadam laughed. "It's all an illusion. If I were you, I would already be the ruler of the Eurasian Union."

"Is that so," he said with a short laugh.

"Yes, even your wife agrees."

"Enlighten me. What has she told you?"

"Aries people are natural born rulers."

"Roxanne spoke this blasphemy?" He would put an immediate stop to that, he thought. It would be an embarrassment to him, but more importantly the Islamic faith as a whole, if word got out that she held such beliefs given the position he held.

"Yes," Zadam said, nodding in agreement.

"She is young and foolish. Astrology is nothing more than fortune telling," he said, "and in clear opposition to the letter and spirit of all religions—especially Islam. You must seek Allah's forgiveness and renew your faith."

His brother slowly removed his feet off the desk and stood up. "I assure you, brother, it will never happen again."

"Good." He would later demand the same from his wife. "Now, about your delusions of grandeur. Let's say you were the supreme leader of the Muslim world who was just pronounced King of the Eurasian Union. Tell me. What would be the first three things you would do?"

"That's simple," he said. "First, remove the Israeli Prime Minister Chaim Soloman from power. Then, the British Royal Family. And, finally," he said, flashing him the back of his hand, "rid the world of this godforsaken chip."

Mohammed rubbed the back of his hand. "That is why it is Allah's will that you are not in a position to rule."

▲ ▲ ▲

Roxanne removed the listening device from her ear and quietly slipped into her study. "Lock door," she said. When the mechanism clicked shut, she scanned the room and manually deployed an additional dead bolt.

She closed her eyes and tried to invoke her telepathic powers. For some reason, she was having a hard time doing so. Nothing seemed to work. Once again she placed her fingers on her temples and focused her energy. "Damn it," she said and took out her Solofōn and punched in the number. Pacing back and forth, her emerald green eyes were on the lookout for anything unexpected.

A female voice answered the phone. "Roxanne, I thought I made it absolutely clear that we are no longer to communicate by phone."

Roxanne could feel Artemis buzzing with anxiety. Lately, it seemed as though every little thing irked her. If she could have reached into the phone and shook her, she would have. At the beginning of their relationship, Roxanne discovered that Artemis was often hot one minute, lukewarm the next, and then cold, but never ice cold. This time she had a feeling it had nothing to do with her love for her even though Artemis had just ordered her to have an affair with her husband's brother. No, this was different. One moment she was critical and condescending, the next full of love and admiration. But what concerned her most was that her highs and lows were becoming more frequent and extreme. There was no more middle ground anymore—just red hot or now, ice cold. She had taken a turn for the worse, Roxanne thought. Before she confronted her, though, she would need more insight as to what was wrong. It was best to try and calm her even though she wanted to give her a tongue lashing.

"I am having *difficulteez* with our established mode of communication," Roxanne said.

"Yes, I know," Artemis said. "There's an unusual amount of electromagnetic energy in the atmosphere. And as the comet nears we may lose all telepathic powers. So, my dear, for now, we must be very careful when communicating by other means."

Roxanne swallowed hard and took a deep breath. Artemis knew that the comet was at fault but still she berated her. If the comet had the power to disrupt their communications, then maybe, just maybe, it was affecting her as well. Anything's possible when you're dealing with the supernatural.

"Roxanne! Are you there?"

"Sorry, my Queen. I was just think—"

"I do the thinking around here. Not you." Her tone was condescending, as if she were a mother scolding her unwanted stepchild. "Now, what is it that you want to tell me?" she said in a sing-song manner.

Roxanne shook her head. Hopefully this behavior was temporary and Artemis would return to her old self once the comet Goliath passed earth. "Queen Elizabeth just ordered my husband to force President Ramsey to implement the cashless society."

"And if he refuses, as he always does?"

"This time, Zadam is to remove him from power."

"This is of no consequence," Queen Artemis said with a laugh. "There'll be no need for cash or a cashless society once Lucy ascends into heaven with her army of angels and reclaims her rightful throne. Once Operation Andromache is complete and the balance has shifted—for the last time—she will return the earth in all its purity to the worshippers of the divine goddess, Artemis, as payment for their help. And you, my dear Roxanne, will be well rewarded for supplying the necessary component that put Operation Andromache in motion."

Finally, a little recognition. Unfortunately, it came at the expense of another mood swing. "Thank you, my Queen."

"Remember, it's imperative that our little Zoroastrian friend does not find what we have worked so hard to keep from him all these years."

"Don't worry, my Queen, when the time comes for the balance to shift, his soul will be as dark and empty as a black hole."

"A-WOMAN to that," Artemis said. "How is he doing?"

"He has," she hissed, "few friends left."

Artemis laughed. "And no money."

Roxanne smiled. "Funny enough, he actually hopes to run Zonoma Tonnai's pension account."

"I guess we are going to have to have a talk with their board of directors."

"I heard they're one tough bunch."

"Enough with the jokes," Artemis said. "Does Mohammed suspect that you are having an affair with his brother?"

Each of Artemis's mood swings was met with a sharp pain in Roxanne's heart. She took a deep breath. "No, he's too busy conducting his crusade for Islam to even notice. He's a typical Gemini," she said, "always thinking about new ways to get people to convert."

"When is Mohammed going to deliver the queen's ultimatum to Ramsey?"

"Seeing that they're such good friends, my husband will stall for as long he can."

"Good," she said with a sly grin. "Then I still have time to have a little fun with the defiant president before he is removed from power."

When they ended the call, Roxanne realized that she had her work cut out for her. Besides implementing the next phase of their operation, and maintaining order throughout the Amazonian kingdom, she would now have to keep a watchful eye on her beloved leader. She would do anything to protect her, anything, but nothing—not even an Amazon queen—was going to stand in the way of Operation Andromache.

CHAPTER 11

T HE FLAT SCREEN television mounted on the wall in front of Darius's desk switched from the financial news to a live feed of his Mayan sales assistant, Ixchel. He looked up from behind his desk and smiled as she moved her long jet black hair off her face and brightened the room with a smile that seemed to stretch across the screen.

"*Felíz Cumpleaños,*" she said as he heard the office door open.

Darius looked up. Norman strolled into the room impeccably dressed in a three-piece grey flannel suit carrying his Louis Vuitton brief case. Darius focused his gaze back to his assistant. He frowned. "Don't remind me. I'm getting old."

Norman laughed. "You can say that again. Happy Birthday, D-MAC."

Darius ignored him. "*Manda todos las llamadas a Norman porque tengo mucho trabajo, pero quiero hablar con GE-Joe,*" he said as Norman sat down at his desk.

"No problema guapito," she said. "Hola, Norman."

"Good morning, sunshine."

Darius winked at her. She smiled and winked back.

He saw Norman catch her wink. He smiled and looked up at the screen but Ixchel's image had been replaced with the Financial News Network.

"What's so funny," Norm asked.

Darius grinned. "I told her to transfer all the calls to you except GE-Joe."

"What's so important that you need me to field all the calls today?"

"Remember when the virus infected my computer? And there was that message, *Zoro, Join Us?* No one else in the company seems to have been infected by it. Norman, I think it was specifically aimed at me. It might have something to do with my father's ancient religion."

"What's that?"

"Zoroastrianism."

"Zoro what?"

"I'll tell you about it once I know more," he said as the phone on his partner's desk began to ring. Darius leaned forward and googled the word Zoroastrianism into his computer as he listened to Norman speak with a client. A plethora of information regarding the religion appeared on the screen.

It's going to be a long day, he thought, rolling up the sleeves of his white dress shirt before searching through the first of many documents.

▼ ▲ ▼

"Find the connection, Zoro?"

Darius swiveled his chair to the right and looked Norman dead in the eye. "For your information, Darius was the name of a Zoroastrian king whose empire was defeated by none other than Alexander the Great."

"I always wondered where your name came from."

"Me, too," he said. "When I asked my father about my name, he never answered me. It was like . . . I didn't exist." Darius stared at the circular clock above the door with the inscription *Money Never Sleeps* in bold black letters that stretched fully around its face. He thought back to that painful day at the family dinner table when he was six years old. The smell of freshly baked breadsticks lingered in the apartment. Quietly sitting in front of his plate he had placed his napkin neatly on his lap and looked at his father, who was seated at the head of the table.

"Daddy, can you please pass me a breadstick?"

His father had, for whatever reasons, started a family late in life and was by then an elderly man. What had his young wife, from England, Darius's mother, seen in such a cold and distant man? His father ignored him as he continued to fawn over his baby brother, sitting in a highchair opposite Darius. He watched his mother fill his plate with spaghetti and meatballs as he repeated the request a little louder. When his father ignored him again his mother looked up from the other end of the table, and said, "Your son would like you to pass him a breadstick." His father reached out over the breadsticks, but instead pulled his brother's highchair toward him.

"There are two other people in this family you son of a bitch," his mother had said, slamming her hand down hard on the wooden table. As he continued to coo and tickle the baby, his father absently reached out with one arm and pushed the basket toward her but just out of the reach of her outstretched arm. His mother stood up and grabbed the basket. She offered the breadsticks to him but Darius jumped up from the table and ran to his room.

A few minutes later, his mother knocked on the door. "Darius," she said, "please open the door."

He had his face planted in his goose down pillow soaked with tears. "Go away," he said. "I don't need you. I don't need anyone." His mother knocked on the door again, jiggled the door handle, and called to him over and over.

"Darius! Darius! Are you listening to me?"

Norman was sitting with his hands on his hips and his brows furrowed. With his arms stretched behind him, Darius shook his head as if to shake off that day and his father; that day when he vowed to never let anyone get close to him again. His brother had suffered as well when his father abandoned him three years later for a puppy he had rescued from an animal shelter. His father did try to make amends when the boys were older, but, up until the day he died, Darius never forgave him. He looked at Norm. "Did you say something?"

"Zoroastrianism. Sounds like something out of a sci-fi flick."

Darius swiveled his chair back in front of the desk. "You're not too far off. It was named after a prophet, Zarathustra, who foretold of a final battle in the future where good would finally conquer evil. It's believed to be the first monotheistic religion."

"I thought Judaism was."

"Judaism's an offshoot of Zoroastrianism. So are Christianity and Islam." Darius glanced at the ticker on the bottom of his computer screen. "Now, to find the connection between Zoroastrianism and the pentagram," he said as he watched a large block of Zanoma Tonnai stock scroll across the screen. He slammed his right-hand down hard on the desk.

"Damn. Zanoma Tonnai is trading at thirty-three. If the firm could have waited just one more day to cover the trade, I wouldn't owe them a goddamned penny," he said, adding pentagram to his search.

Darius read through numerous theological and philosophical entries, one by one, searching for anything that could point him in the right direction. He finally looked over at Norman who, trying to finish his sales pitch, seemed to be at a rare loss for words. "Hang up on this guy already," Darius said, and added Aristotle to his search. "I might have found the connection."

There were twelve matches; he clicked on the third link. A few minutes later he looked up stunned. *That's it.* When he heard Norman hang up the phone, he said, "Yo, Norm, listen to this. Zoroastrians worship the god Ahura Mazda and his holy elements of earth, air, water, fire and the stars. The connection is the stars," he said, smiling. "Aristotle believed that the stars and the heavens were made out of a vaporous gas he called aether, and he used the pentagram to show all five elements together."

Norman shook his head. He looked hard at Darius, the way someone does when they're deciding something important. "Earth to star-man, come in star-man. We need to find a new stock to pitch. Everyone's heard the Solofŏn story."

"What about grand trines," Darius said. He googled grand trine into the search engine and slammed his finger down on the return key. He knew he was on to something and felt a tingle rush through his body as he waited for the results.

"What's the symbol," Norm asked.

"It's not a stock," he said, clicking on the astrological glossary and scrolling to the letter G. "Grand trines are rare planetary alignments," he read aloud, "that occur in some astrological charts where three planets form an equilateral triangle. If the volatile energy associated with this configuration is not focused correctly, the power it releases can be difficult to control."

"Darius, we need to focus our energy on making money."

"Check this out, Norm," he said, clicking on another article. "The Star of David is really two interlaced grand trines that map the major stars of the Milky Way. It appeared in King David's birth chart but didn't become the symbol of modern day Israel until 1948." He shot Norman a sly grin. "Most people don't even have one grand trine in their chart. I have three." He leaned back and let this information sink in.

"What do you think about opening accounts on that chip company I told you about . . . Nero Technologies."

Darius leaned forward and gave him a longing glance. "I'm trying to tell you that I think I have a higher purpose." He knew how stupid this must have sounded to Norm, how egomaniacal. But who knew, anything was possible, right? Lot's of people feel they have a higher purpose. It was what drove great leaders, presidents, kings, prophets and the like. Not that he was putting himself in this category, but the idea of having a higher purpose gave him a little mental bounce.

"Unless this map in your astrological chart has a million dollar treasure attached to it, and your higher purpose is to find it and give me half, I'm not interested, Darius."

"The treasure, as you put it, are symbols added to your chart to show you've mastered something in a previous life," Darius said, ignoring Norman's rebuff. "I have three—that means I've mastered three things in three previous lives. According to this article," he said, pausing as he scrolled down his screen, "I've returned to win yet another grand trine so I can complete the next phase of my soul's evolution."

"I don't mean to interrupt your ego trip, but aren't you supposed to meet Paris in the park at four-thirty?"

Darius looked at his watch. "That's right," he said. "Gotta go."

Ixchel's face reappeared on the screen. This time she wasn't smiling. "Darius, Mike needs to see you in his office, pronto."

"Can't it wait 'til tomorrow?"

He watched Norman lean back in his chair and put his hands behind his head. "I love Ixchel," he heard him whisper.

"Negative, your job's on the line," she said and signed off.

Darius stood up. He turned and looked at Norman as he gathered up his wallet and Solofōn. "Do you have any idea what he wants?"

"No. But if by chance he fires you, can I have GE-Joe's account," he asked, still staring at the screen.

"Sure. And while you're at it," he said and headed for the door, "why not take my first born, too." He slammed the door behind him and rushed down the hallway. Ixchel was putting on her coat. "Are you going to the festival in the park?" he said when he reached her desk.

"No," she said. "What the hell did you do? Mike's been on the phone with attorneys all day long."

Darius began to sweat.

She touched the screen on her desk. "Mike, Darius is here."

"Send him in," his boss shouted.

Darius didn't like the sound of things. "I hope it's not about the pension account." He opened the door and quietly entered Mike's office. "What's up boss?"

"Sit down."

Darius walked up to his desk but remained standing. "Can we make this quick?" he said as he jiggled the change in his pants pocket. "I'm supposed to meet Paris in Central Park."

Mike removed his glasses and rubbed his eyes. "I have some bad news. The attorneys representing Zanoma Tonnai called today." Mike clenched his lips and rocked back and forth in his chair.

Darius froze. "Don't tell me they've changed their mind and are going with Goldman Sachs."

Mike burst into laughter. "On the contrary, you're getting the account but it's much bigger than we originally thought," he said and jumped up from his seat. "All they need to see are our insurance policies."

"You almost gave me a heart attack."

"What goes around comes around," Mike said with a grin. "I finally got you back for all those times you played around with my head."

"I just hope you didn't jinx the account," Darius said, shaking his head. "The deal's not done 'til the account's in our possession."

"You're right. Let me make it up to you," he said as he walked out from behind his desk. "Let's go to the Camelot Bar for a few cocktails."

"I already have plans with Paris."

"Wouldn't go anywhere outdoors tonight if I were you."

"Why, what's up?"

"A big storm's heading our way."

Darius gazed out of the window at the tumultuous sky. "The only way I'll be able to get out of going is if fire and brimstone start falling from the sky."

"That's about to happen. High winds, heavy thundershowers and severe lightning are forecast over the entire region," Mike said. "C'mon. One quick drink for your birthday. Paris won't mind if you're a few minutes late. Besides, it's probably gonna get cancelled anyway. Tell her to come join us."

As they walked out the door, Darius recalled the only advice his father had ever given him—be careful what you wish for. But it seemed an old man's useless warning.

CHAPTER 12

"THIS IS BETTER disguised than a pirated fifteenth-century Raphael that was painted over." Raj opened the glass door covering the clock face. He pulled on his chin and looked thoughtful, his expression a little pinched.

President Ramsey moved behind his eager aide who began inspecting it with an infrared magnifying glass. He looked over Raj's shoulder. Could this be the break he was looking for? "Princess Di went to such great lengths to hide the message from unwanted eyes," he said admiringly, "that it almost went unnoticed by the eyes it was intended for."

He moved forward, almost hunched over his brother-in-law's back. "What are the dots in the four corners?" the president asked. When Raj didn't respond, Ramsey reached over his right shoulder and repeatedly stabbed his finger at each of the four corners. "The dots," he said a little more loudly this time, "what are they?"

Raj moved the magnifying glass over the tiny black speck on the top right. "It appears to be the astrological symbol for the star sign, Leo."

"And on the left?"

He moved the lens over and studied it for a moment. "The symbol for Gemini."

The president inched back when he felt Raj nudge into him as he inspected the two other symbols.

"Whoever made this clock paid great attention to detail," Raj remarked. "The symbol in the lower left is a double-bladed axe, and the symbol on the right is a—"

The clock chimed. "What is it," Ramsey said.

"His brother-in-law laughed, somewhat falsely, the president thought.

After the sixth and final chime, Raj moved to the side, and said, "Take a look for yourself."

The president looked at his aide. He seemed to be slightly rattled. He took the magnifying glass from his hand, leaned forward, and placed the small lens over the dot in the lower right-hand corner. The tip of his crooked nose barely touched the clock face. "That's the exact same butterfly your sister wore around her neck," he said as he turned to his brother-in-law.

"Coincidence?" Raj said.

"There *are* no coincidences."

"So who is this person we need to find?"

Ramsey ignored his aide's question and continued searching the clock. He listened to the constant tick tock of the mechanical organs churning inside. It seemed as if it were busting at the seams to tell him its secret.

Could he decipher the cryptic puzzle before the comet aligned over Stonehenge?

In the center of the twelve-pointed star on the clock's face were three, very small, interlaced triangles that held the black hands in place. Gazing at the clock, he thought about the nine-pointed star on the lion sword's sheath. He froze. Was it possible she had information pertaining to the Chosen One?

Ramsey's father had told him that shortly after the prophecy was discovered, an archaeologist on the team was caught speaking Hebrew into a transmitter and was killed. Even though the blood-stained sand still remained as evidence in the secret chamber, it was unclear as to whether or not he was successful in informing his government. If he was, then it was possible that others could be searching for the Chosen One as well.

Ramsey clenched his lips and shook his head. "How could I have been so blind?"

Raj looked at him. "There's no way you could have known. She gave it to you on your birthday—six months before she died. We all thought it was just a diplomatic gift."

"What bothers me most is that I could never determine whether her death was an accident or an assassination. I did, however, learn a few things about those who might have been involved," President Ramsey said, and then looked directly into his aide's eyes. "It all starts with the place of Diana's death—the Pont d'Alma Tunnel in Paris. It was built on an ancient pagan sacrificial site that was sacred to the moon goddess, Artemis."

Raj nodded. "The Merovingian Dynasty of Frankish Royalty worshipped the goddess Artemis. Maybe they had something to do with this."

"Possible. But my search kept leading me to secret societies that have plans of total control and world domination through a New World Order—in particular the Illuminati." He sighed. "Diana must have found something out that jeopardized their plans. It may seem extreme," Ramsey said, crossing his arms over his chest as he leaned back to view the clock from a fresh angle. "But perhaps she was murdered as part of a Pagan ritual to usher in the beginning of their New World Order."

"Mr. President," Raj said excitedly, as if he had made an important discovery. "The symbols Gemini and Leo refer to people! She was trying to tell us that twin Leos are responsible for this New World Order."

"Hmm," Ramsey said. "Get me a list of twin Leos linked to the Merovingian Dynasty immediately." He noticed his brother-in-law glance at *New Age Magazine,* which was on the floor next to the clock.

"Earlier," Raj said, "you suggested I look to the stars. Maybe Diana knew about the person you are looking for and the answer is hidden amongst the stars of the Leo constellation." Raj looked back at the president. "What if I were to arrange a meeting with the top astronomers and we further explore this," he said, patting his belly.

"Sounds a bit farfetched."

"At this point it's our only option," Raj said. "It's going to take a while to assemble the men at this hour, so let's play it safe and reconvene in the main conference room at two-thirty this morning. We shall burn the midnight oil."

"For your sake, this better not be a waste of my time."

Raj turned and headed for the door. "If you change your mind, I can always cancel it." When he reached the door, he opened it and turned. "Started my diet today," he said, patting his belly again.

"I've heard that before," Ramsey said with a chuckle.

Raj smiled and walked out of the room.

"This time you better stick to it," he shouted as the door softly closed. Ramsey made his way to his desk and sat down. He stared at the lion sword's black onyx handle inlaid with diamonds and rubies and knocked back the last of his warm martini. He made a sour face and refilled the martini glass half way with what remained in the shaker. His religion forbade drinking alcohol; but with all the pressure he was under, he had decided to indulge anyway. Hopefully Raj had been so consumed with the clock that he had failed to notice the drink or, to make matters even worse, the sword that was resting on his desk.

He took a deep breath and placed the martini glass on the edge of his desk. With his eyes fixed on the glass, he rummaged through the drawer and pulled out a red velvet, double drawstring pouch.

He reached under his desk for his late wife's hangman stand. He stood up and carefully placed the metal stand in the middle of his desk. A tear ran down his cheek as he opened the drawstring of her pouch. The sight of her moonstone pendulum brought back painful memories as it fell harmlessly into the palm of his hand.

Connected to a nine-inch silver chain, he attached the lucid cone-shaped crystal to the s-hook at the top of the stand and pulled it toward him. "Will I find the Chosen One," he asked and released the pendulum, setting it in motion.

His bones creaked as he slowly settled into his chair and watched the pendulum turn around and around in a clockwise motion.

He looked around at the stacks of books he had scoured through and picked up one of the three books he had yet to search. Great . . . another voluminous book on quantum physics. He opened to the table of contents and slowly read down the list of chapter names. Each chapter seemed more confusing than the prior. This was a waste of time, he thought. Just as he was about to close the book, the title of Chapter Nine caught his eye.

The Black Hole.

He frowned and sat forward. For the last fifteen years of his life, he felt as though the answers he had been searching for had been sucked into a black hole and lost forever. Could the most powerful force in the universe, the black hole, hold the key to his salvation?

He stared at a diagram of a black hole positioned at the galactic center of the universe. The subtitle read *Time and Space at the Subatomic Level.* He heaved a heavy sigh, tossed the book onto the floor and pulled the open sword case toward him. He picked up the sheath and drew the sword. The blade glistened. After admiring it for a few moments, Ramsey placed both the sheath and the sword down on his desk and picked up the second to last book. He shook his head. "Why me?" He was doubtful the religious art book could provide him much insight but he flipped it open to a random page and propped it up inside the sword case.

He picked up the sword and rose to his feet. Slowly, he ran his right index finger down its razor-sharp edge. The pain felt good, he thought, as the blade sliced through his skin. Blood trickled down the blade. The page he'd randomly opened to was a full-page picture of a half naked man in a loin cloth. Ramsey, too, had sacrificed much over the years only to run into brick walls and false hopes when he thought he was getting close. He could see himself hanging next to the long-haired man in the picture. How could the condemned king have possibly bared the burden of all of mankind?

He held the sword horizontally at eye-level between his hands and shifted his gaze back to the pendulum. A tiny drop of blood fell from the blade and landed under the eye of Jesus Christ. He sat back down and watched the blood-red tear slowly run down Jesus's cheek. With his bloody finger, he traced the crucifix from top to bottom and then left to right. What was the prophet trying to tell him? He slid the sword back in its sheath, placed it on his lap, and then picked up the last remaining book.

Microcosmic Quantum Metaphysics

He cringed at the thought of suffering through yet another scientific treatise and read the first paragraph aloud.

> *Don't fear. The answer to life's most sought after secrets lie deep within your mind. Everything is cosmically connected.*

His wife used to tell him the same thing. Her memory caused his heart to pump faster and he could feel sweat running down his sides inside his shirt.

> *In addition to the elements of earth, air, fire and water there is a fifth essence called aether or aetheric matter. This vapor that appears with ghostly apparitions is the substance which houses the soul, thereby allowing its existence in the spiritual world. Think of yourself as a time traveler whose mind, body, and soul have always had the power to travel back and forth through time at speeds faster than the speed of light.*

Time travel? But how? He turned the page.

> *From the beginning of existence, the answers to all of life's questions were stored at the subatomic level buried deep within the abyss of your mind. Choose an animal to guide you on your journey and then focus your chi on an inanimate object.*

Was it really possible? And, more to the point, could it really be that simple? Ramsey scratched his head and looked at the swirling pendulum. There's only one way to find out, he thought. And right then, he was willing to try anything. He decided on a hawk as his guide, took a deep breath, and focused his energy on the black titanium shield covering the southern window. When nothing happened, he shifted his gaze back to the pendulum and watched it turn around and around and around in a clockwise motion.

Suddenly the lights went out. He felt the floor begin to shake. From the far end of his office he heard a deafening roar with the ferocity, he imagined, of a thousand lions thundering through the darkness. Ramsey dropped the book and covered his ears. Small rays of light penetrated the black titanium shield from behind. He watched in disbelief as it imploded and vaporized into atoms.

"What the—"

Encircled by a ring of white light, a tornado-shaped black hole emerged, slowly spinning where the window shield had once been. Then, as quickly as the deafening roar had started, it stopped. He dropped his hands to his sides and just as he did, he heard a crushing sub-bass sound vibrate through the room. He felt a steep drop in air pressure and heard a high pitched squawk. A hawk flew out of the black hole and circled the room three times before finally landing on the hangman stand in front of him.

Ramsey could feel the gravitational pull from the black hole begin to take a hold of him. His muscles tensed. With all of his might, he slowly inched his chair back against the wall. He found it hard to breathe. He felt as if his lungs were going to collapse. The hawk looked at him, squawked, and flew into the air.

One by one, the items flew off of his desk and disappeared into the vortex. As he watched the hawk fly back into the black hole, his chair slid forward. He let go and flew head first into the hot aetheric matter. His body felt as if it had been transformed into electrical energy and transmitted through the vacuum of space.

When his molecules realigned, Ramsey found himself floating inside a Merkaba. The three-dimensional Star of David seemed to shield him from the deadly radiation of the colorful subatomic universe that he now believed he had traveled to. Filled with red, white, and blue supergiant stars, he wondered if one of these stars just might be a stargate that led to the abyss?

If so, was this where he would find the answers that would finally lead him to the Chosen One?

Floating weightlessly in the middle of the vast universe, he frantically searched for the star that led to the abyss—the place where all of life's unanswered questions would finally be revealed. As he gazed out upon the billions of stars that graced the heavens, it became overwhelmingly apparent that it could take an eternity to find.

Suddenly, the hawk flew past him.

His guide! The Merkaba followed the hawk, bringing him face to face with a massive blue supergiant. Shielded from the intense light of the enigmatic star, he watched the three Pyramids of Giza emerge from its center.

So . . . the pyramids did have something to do with him finding the Chosen One.

The sound of the hawk's high-pitched scream snapped him out of his thoughts as it flew past him again and headed toward the star. The Merkaba took off after it and just as the hawk disappeared into the star, he heard a loud crash. He shuddered in fear. The star turned red and collapsed. There was a brilliant burst of light followed by a cataclysmic boom. The explosion reversed polarity and sent him hurling through space and back through the black hole.

CHAPTER 13

"MAYBE YOU LADS should call it a night," the bartender said with a deep Irish lilt. "You've put away quite a few pints."

Darius glanced at his watch as he listened to the rain begin to fall. "It's only 7:30," he slurred, "my birthday officially starts at 11:43 so keep 'em coming."

"Can't argue with the birthday boy," Mike said. "Give us anotha' round."

Darius took a deep breath and exhaled. The smell of stale beer lingered in the still air of the Irish pub. It had been their favorite hangout when they were rookies at the firm. The cheep beer and pool table fit perfectly within their cold-caller salaries.

"This place is exactly the way I remember it," Darius said, looking around the circular wooden bar in the middle of the room. The dark walls were still plastered with medieval coats of arms and flags from the United Kingdom. A neon-yellow Guinness harp hung in the center of each wall. The same old television, mounted above the old-fashioned cash register, flickered on and off whenever the lightning flashed through the small castle-like windows overlooking the city streets.

"What time did Paris say she'd be here?" Mike asked.

"She didn't. She's pissed off I told her the festival would be cancelled and it wasn't." He thought he heard female voices outside and glanced over his shoulder. The door flew open and a brilliant flash of lightning lit up the bar as three women slowly walked inside. A deafening crash of thunder rattled the wine glasses hanging upside down above the bar.

Now that's an entrance," Darius said. He watched a tall skinny blonde with a boyish haircut walk toward the bar. She wore an oversized black leather biker jacket and black leather pants and was accompanied by two brunettes dressed in short black tunics with black high heeled boots laced up to their knees. They were dripping wet. Darius imagined that they were no more attractive when they were dry. He turned his back to them and took a sip of his frothy Guinness.

Mike stood up and hitched up his pants with an exaggerated flair. "When Paris shows up, blame everything on me," he slurred. "I'm afraid of no woman."

Darius laughed as he watched his boss stagger backward away from the bar.

"In honor of these three broads, I'm gonna go to the men's room and rub one out," Mike said with a wink.

"Look out!" Darius said. Mike turned and bumped into one of the tall brunettes. She was absolutely oblivious of his presence and seemed to walk right through him, spilling his beer all over his crotch. Darius laughed and watched Mike's back hit hard against the bar. When he saw the two brunettes jeering at Mike, he stopped laughing and watched the blonde woman move into the shadows behind him.

Darius jumped off his barstool with his beer in hand and grabbed Mike by the arm with his free hand. "You're drunk," he said, pushing him in the direction of the men's room. "Go clean yourself up."

"That bitch did that on purpose."

"I'll handle this." Darius looked over at the two women and smiled. "Please accept my apologies," he said to them. "My friend has had a little bit too much to drink."

They both took a menacing step toward him. "Tell your comrade," one of the tall brunettes said in a hard-talking Eastern European accent, "that the next time he says something degrading about women, I'll break his jaw."

"C'mon, he was just having a little fun. Let me buy you a drink." When Darius glanced over his shoulder to see where the blonde was, the brunette to his right smacked the pint glass out of his hand up toward the ceiling. Simultaneously both brunettes jumped into the air and threw spinning back kicks at his head. He dropped, instinctively, into a full split and heard their boots whiz over his head. As he watched the two women kick each other and fall to the floor, he heard his beer glass shatter behind him. In one fluid motion, he jumped to his feet and went into a defensive stance with his knees bent and his hands raised.

Wow! *He had never moved that fast before.*

He maintained his stance as both women slowly got to their feet. Darius glanced at the bartender who stood motionless behind the bar. He seemed to be in shock.

"Nyet," the tall blonde shouted as she emerged from the shadows behind her comrades.

Her sharp voice and thick Russian accent echoed off the pub walls. Darius didn't flinch; he remained fixed in his stance. Holding a wooden case in her left arm, the blonde moved between the two women and stepped in front of him. She appeared to be missing her right breast. As her sharp blue eyes looked him up and down, he felt as if he were a stud that she was considering mating with.

"You move with the speed and grace of a gazelle," she said in a heavy Russian accent and extended her left hand. "My name is Bella."

"Darius Prince," he said, straightening himself up. He ignored her hand and brushed his shirt down. "And as much as I might like to become better acquainted, I have a girlfriend." He turned his back to her and sat back down on his barstool. It seemed like an eternity before he heard her walk away.

Darius took a deep breath and exhaled. That was close, too close, he thought, watching Bella move to the opposite side of the bar. She sat down facing him, while the two brunettes stood behind her.

Why the hell had they attacked him? He'd been completely respectful to them and always felt that as long as he treated women with dignity and respect, he wouldn't have a problem. This time, he was wrong.

CHAPTER 14

R AMSEY COULD HEAR what sounded like the atomic
grandfather clock echoing around him. He lifted his head from
his chest and opened his eyes. For a moment, he wasn't sure of where he was
or where he had been. Then slowly the hangman stand on his desk came into
focus. He was back in his office.

He *had* lost his mind.

Ramsey's hands trembled as he wiped the cold damp sweat from his face.
Zadam would come for him. Queen Elizabeth would see to that. Then they
would take him away to some obscure mental hospital, drug him, and leave
him to rot. He wouldn't give them the satisfaction. If only he could have found
the Chosen One in time, he thought, and reached for the sword on his lap.

Wait a minute.

Leaning to his right, he saw the broken martini glass on the floor beside
his desk. The sound of the glass crashing must have woken him from his
dream. He arched his brow and moved his chair forward, away from the wall,
and back up to his desk. He put the sword back in the case and looked at the
pendulum. It continued to turn but much slower now. He glanced at the
southern window. The titanium window shield was intact.

He no longer felt confident that he could tell the difference between
illusion and reality.

He shifted his gaze to the grandfather clock. What power did the Chosen
One's soul have over the pyramids? Just then Ramsey thought he saw the
minute hand move in reverse. He yawned and rubbed his eyes. The clock's
hands now showed the time as 2:01 a.m.

After a long moment, the minute hand moved again. Ramsey froze. The clock now showed the time as 2:00!

"I'll be damned," he said softly. It *was* moving in reverse. He pushed himself out of his chair and hurried over to the clock. Indeed he *was* seeing clearly; the long black minute hand was now pointing to the Roman numeral XII.

Could he still be dreaming? Impossible. He looked around the room for anything else out of the ordinary. Nothing. He walked back to his desk and sat down. Ah, but here, in fact, *was* something else: The moonstone had changed directions as well and was now spinning in a counterclockwise motion.

With renewed faith, he ripped the crystal from its chain. The clock stopped ticking. As Ramsey was fond of saying, and often reminded his aide, Raj, there are no coincidences—everything happens for a reason. There was no doubt in his mind that the counterclockwise motion of the grandfather clock and the pendulum were somehow connected. What had made them reverse polarity? Had he tapped into an unused part of his brain and transcended to the subatomic level? If so, why was he denied entry into the abyss?

He stared at a jagged piece of glass on the floor and smiled. "That's it," he said aloud. The book on metaphysics had instructed the reader not to fear. His fear, he reasoned, had triggered the explosion in his brain and was responsible for reversing the polarity! He had been living in a prison of fear long enough. It was time to turn his fear into faith.

"Thank you, my love." He placed the moonstone in his shirt pocket over his heart. For the briefest moment he felt as though their souls had crossed paths once again. He stared at the picture of Christ one more time before he closed the book and placed it into his desk drawer. He shut the sword case, jumped to his feet, and placed it back in the safe hidden behind the portrait of his late wife on the wall behind his desk.

"Open shields." The three window shields spiraled open simultaneously. Ramsey made his way over to the southern window and gazed out at the mysterious pyramids. Would the astronomers be able to unearth the secrets or mysteries that could finally help lead him to the Chosen One? Raj seemed to think so, but he wasn't so sure. It was a long shot but he hoped to God that they could.

"You have received an email," the Patriarch computer said, "with an encrypted video attached—entitled Chosen One."

He froze there at the window. Had he heard correctly? He turned slowly.

"Open file."

Ramsey stared at the holographic animation that appeared in the center of the room. A ghostlike woman warrior on horseback appeared, wielding a bow and shooting arrows into the heart of what appeared to be the Greek god, Apollo. The morbid image played over and over until the mighty Apollo fell to the ground. His body turned into ashes and spelled out the phrase, "*We have the Chosen One.*" He felt a sharp and sudden panic. His worst nightmare had been confirmed. He watched the warrior on horseback drag the message around and around the screen. After a few moments, the image turned into a skull and crossbones that faded away with a short haunting laugh.

How in the world did the Ghostriders know he was searching for the Chosen One? Did they know about the sword and the prophecy, too? Regardless, he now had no other choice. He would have to give Raj's meeting with the astronomers a chance.

▲ ▼ ▲

"Can anybody tell us what the comet Goliath is trying to warn us about," Raj said and tossed several copies of *New Age Magazine* onto the oval conference table. "Read the article on page thirty-three."

The aromatic smell of freshly roasted coffee filled the air. President Ramsey yawned, took off his white linen suit coat, and draped it around the back of his chair. He glanced at the two middle-aged advisors sitting midway down the table and then looked at the eldest advisor at the far end. He had a long grey beard and was dressed in a green satin robe embroidered with the sun and stars in yellow, and the moon in white.

The president sat down and continued studying the frail advisor. He looked familiar, but he couldn't put a name to his face. He leaned toward Raj who was seated to his right. "These are my top astronomers?"

Raj paused. "They're highly qualified to answer all of your questions," he said in a hushed tone.

"Did you find out anything about the twins," Ramsey said, scratching his cleanly shaven face.

"Very little, I'm afraid." Raj picked up a copy of *New Age Magazine*. "There's no record of any twin Leo's related to the Merovingian Dynasty."

"Maybe they're not on the record."

"I doubt twins from such a powerful family would not have birth records."

"Keep searching. If they do exist, it is imperative that we find them."

"That sword on your desk earlier," Raj said, hesitating as he slowly closed the magazine and set it back on the table, "does it have something to do with this person you are searching for?"

"My father left it to me," he said annoyed. "What did you tell Princess Zara and Queen Elizabeth?"

"That you caught the flu that's been going around."

"Did they believe you?"

Raj shrugged his shoulders. "We'll reschedule the meetings when you're feeling better. They both wish you a speedy recovery."

"Excellent." When the two advisors started talking to one another, Raj stood up and asked if anybody had any thoughts on the article.

The chief astronomer sitting across from Raj leaned back in his chair. "I can't speak for the gentleman dressed as a wizard, but my partner and I are men of science. New Age Magazine deals with metaphysical theories. There is no scientific proof whatsoever to back up their claim that a comet's path through the stars can foreshadow the future."

President Ramsey glanced at the other astronomer, who was nodding in agreement, and then looked back to Raj. "I agree, that would be fortune telling," he said, turning to the elderly advisor.

"You need to cut off that beard," Ramsey said as he studied the frail advisor. "Your good name please?"

"Aje," he said with a slight lisp.

"Aje the astrologer," the president said and turned to Raj. "What is he doing here? My wife secretly took astrology lessons from him after I forbade it."

The astrologer nodded. "Your Excellency has a good memory but, with all due respect, I happen to be a fully qualified astronomer as well as an astrologer." He placed his hand over his heart. "Your wife was an extraordinary woman," he said with faintly tinted speech. "She will always hold a special place in my heart."

Ramsey stood up from the table. "I consider your teachings blasphemy."

"Good heavens," the astrologer said and crossed his legs. "Your wife didn't think so."

"She wasn't a Muslim."

"Mr. President, do you believe that Allah created everything?"

"Yes, of course."

"Then Allah created astrology," he said. "Have no qualms about it. My theory will challenge your religious beliefs. It will analyze and incorporate all religions and mythologies associated with the constellations so that we may interpret the message the comet is telling us as it travels through the star systems."

"What religion are you?"

"I was raised a Muslim but wasn't accepted by my peers because I practice astrology—so I became spiritual. I do believe in a higher power but no longer harbor any guilt."

"This is a waste of my time," President Ramsey said in a harsh tone as if he were a judge throwing out a case. He glared at Raj and walked to the door. He could hear Raj jump up from his seat.

"Mr. President, perhaps we should hear him out."

Ramsey stood with his hand on the door. After several seconds he turned and stared at the astrologer. "You have thirty seconds."

The astrologer rose to his feet. "Mr. President, your ancient ancestors aligned the pyramids with the belt stars of Orion for a reason. They also believed that comets were actually messengers sent by God to warn us of things to come. If you leave now, you may never find whatever it is you are looking for."

Ramsey turned and opened the door. The only difference between Aje's theory and the prophecy found under the Sphinx was that one was written in hieroglyphs and the other in the stars. Whichever way he looked at it, he had already taken the first step by believing in the prophecy and was guilty of blasphemy. He closed the door and slowly walked back to the table. He looked at the other astronomers, who were both grinning. "Kindly remain available for further inquiry," he said with a dismissive wave of his hand. Their eyes opened wide as they looked to each other and back to him. He arched his eyebrows at the two astronomers as he sat down. It was clear they were being dismissed.

When they left the room, President Ramsey poured himself a cup of coffee. He took a large sip and glared at the astrologer. "This meeting is classified and must not go beyond these walls," he said as if their lives depended on it. "Do we understand one another?"

Aje the astrologer swallowed hard and nodded in agreement.

Ramsey placed his mug down and settled comfortably into his chair. "Kindly enlighten us with your theory."

The astrologer stood up, and in a high and rapidly changing pitch said, "It's believed that the path a comet takes through the heavens will foreshadow world events. If the comet travels within six degrees of a main *sthar* in a constellation, it can also provide us with clues as to the identities of certain people who will be involved."

Ramsey leaned toward Raj with his hand cupped over his mouth, and whispered, "Main what?"

"Star. He lisps when he is nervous. Just give him a chance."

"Hmm," Ramsey said and nodded. He leaned back over and turned his attention back to the astrologer. "How long will it take to analyze the path of the comet?"

"If you can provide me with access to the Patriarch network I can have the answers within seconds."

Ramsey leaned back in his chair and rested his elbows on the chair's arms and steepled his fingers. He looked at Aje through slightly squinted eyes. "Computer, provide temporary access to Aje and hold all communications during the analysis," he said, still studying the astrologer.

"Connected," the computer said in a soothing female voice.

"Computer, link to comet analysis program," the astrologer said. "Since two comets were sighted simultaneously, we must analyze the trajectories of both."

"Two comets?" Ramsey said with a shake of his head.

The astrologer nodded. "Computer, give me a visual of David and Goliath's trajectories through the constellations as seen from earth."

The three six-foot oval windows spiraled shut and the lights dimmed. A three-dimensional holographic image of the Milky Way appeared above the center of the table. Two comets appeared streaking through the night sky in a yin-yang formation against a background of twinkling stars.

"Very impressive," Ramsey said, marveling at the colorful display. But more than that, he had always associated the star system's power with that of God.

The astrologer picked up his tablet computer, cleared his throat, and said, "As the earth rotates around the sun, the entire circumference of the sky is divided into twelve sections of orbital view—known as the Zodiac." He aimed a red laser light pointer at a lion-shaped constellation. "David and Goliath first appeared on August 9, 2010, in the sign of Leo."

President Ramsey turned to Raj, who was nodding his head in approval, and shifted his gaze back to Aje. "What is the significance of them being discovered while in Leo?"

The astrologer shot a longing glance at his tablet, then aimed the laser pointer at a cluster of stars. "The lion," he said, "is depicted as the righteous ruler and king of the jungle, but it's also known to be a savage beast. When discovered, Goliath was in the Gemini constellation—which symbolizes the divine union of male and female. It's also associated with twins. Similar to Leo, Gemini also shows duality."

President Ramsey held up a hand to pause. "Can the computer tell us the sex of the twins?"

"It's too early to tell," he said confidently, as if he were a doctor informing his patient that further tests were needed to ensure a proper diagnosis. "Since David was first sighted in the constellation Ophiuchus, the stars are speaking of a struggle that has lasted forever. The constellation is always associated with Aesculapius in Greek mythology."

"Aesculapius," the president interrupted, "is the son of the god, Apollo, who was given the power to restore the dead to life."

"Very good," the astrologer said, "I'm impressed. "This implies that twins will play key roles in deciding the fate of good versus evil."

He averted the astrologer's eyes. By the way he was speaking, Ramsey would have sworn that the astrologer knew about the prophecy. It was highly unlikely, he thought, but it was possible—and that's what scared him. But what scared him most was that the Ghostriders knew he was searching for a Chosen One and may have already captured him.

CHAPTER 15

T HE LIGHTNING FLASHED through the small castle-like windows of the Camelot Bar. It was best not to tell Mike about the fight, Darius thought, even though he was busting at the seams to do so. If word leaked out that he was getting into fights, especially with women, he could kiss the pension account goodbye. And at this point in his life, he could ill afford to have that happen. In his mind, the fifty bucks with which he had bribed the bartender to keep quiet was already paying dividends. Some things were just better left unsaid. And this was one of them.

"Why's the bar so empty?" Mike said.

The bartender sighed. "Everybody's at some crazy New Age festival in the park."

Darius leaned forward. "I know. I was supposed to go there with my girlfriend but Mike talked me out of it."

"You're lucky you didn't, lad," the bartender said, "it got violent. 'Bout five hundred women in red satin capes were protesting the festival. They got into a brawl with a couple hundred bikers from the Hells Angels."

"No way," Darius said. "I hope Paris didn't decide to stop by the park on her way here." It was unlikely she would've gone without him. But still, he was worried and felt it necessary to send her a text message to see where she was.

"And get this," the bartender said, "the women killed one of the bikers. Kept stabbing and stabbing him in the face with a butcher's knife while the rest of the women beat the daylights out of the other Hells Angels."

"Yeah, right," Mike said.

"I'm dead serious. You lads are probably too young to remember but there was a similar incident during the late sixties, at the Altamont Music Festival in northern California. Mick Jagger, ya know, of the Rolling Stones, came on stage dressed in a red satin cape. Looked like Lucifer. When theys played their hit song, 'Sympathy for the Devil,' the Hells Angels provoked a fight with an eighteen-year-old black kid who pulled out a gun and was then stabbed to death." The bartender squinted his eyes and leaned closer to Darius and Mike. "I have a gut feeling," he said in a throaty whisper, "that the murder in Central Park tonight was more than just a murder."

Darius laughed and nudged Mike. "Don't ya miss Connor's conspiracy theories," he said with a lift of his head toward the bartender.

"Not really," Mike slurred out of the side of his mouth.

By the tone of his voice, Darius realized Mike was getting in one of his foul moods.

"So, Connor," Mike said to the bartender as he leaned back on his stool and opened his legs widely, "what's next? Women from Venus trying to take over the earth?"

"Don't be a wise guy," the bartender said, leaning back. "I think the biker was sacrificed as part of a satanic ritual," he said. "Like Princess Diana was." He leaned forward again. "Don't look," he said in almost a whisper, glancing at Darius, "but the blonde—Bella—hasn't taken her eyes off you all night long."

Mike grabbed Darius around the face, and said, "What do you expect when you're blessed with looks like this."

Darius glanced over at Bella, who, indeed, was staring at him, and pushed Mike's hands away from his face.

"Maybe she's looking for a boyfriend," Mike said.

"She's a dyke," the bartender offered.

"Definitely," Darius said, glancing back at Bella.

"You're both paranoid," Mike said. "Do you remember the one he told us the last time we were in here?"

Darius tensed. "Yeah. 'Bout Christ having kids with Mary Magdalene."

"That's the Merovingian bloodline," Mike slurred. "I'm talkin' about the descendants of Israel's King David who claim lineage through—"

"The Legend of the Scarlet Hand," the bartender said.

"That's the one."

Darius gave them both a quizzical look and tried to keep his head from weaving back and forth. "I don't recall that."

"'Cus you were too busy lolly gaggin' with some tart," the bartender said. "Bible claims the next Messiah will herald from the Royal Houses of Judah and David just as Christ did."

"I am aware of the Biblical Prophecy," Darius said annoyed. "Now, tell me more about your so-called Legend of the Scarlet Hand."

"Legend's true," he said and pointed to the wall to their left. "Proof is sewn into the Ulster Flag of Northern Ireland. Ever seen it?"

"Can't say that I have."

"That's 'cus it was abolished in nineteen seventy-two. Look at the flag directly under the Guinness harp."

Darius turned. "Yeah," he said and turned back to the bar. "I always thought that was a Jewish flag," he said as he turned on his barstool to have another look. "Why would the Irish have a flag with the Star of David on it?"

"So they'd never forget where they came from," the bartender said. Darius wanted another beer but the bartender ignored him and pointed to the flag again. "Look at the middle of the flag. See the scarlet hand inside the Star of David?"

Darius turned around again and studied the flag. He looked at the kingly crown sitting atop the Jewish Star and then focused his gaze on the scarlet hand. "What's your point?"

The bartender rose up his shoulders and pushed out his chest. "There was a breach when Israel's Royal House of Judah bore twin sons."

"Breach?"

"The hand of Zerah came out of the womb first," the bartender said and pushed his hand up high into the air. "And the midwife tied a scarlet thread round his wrist to mark that he was first-born." He pulled his hand down quickly. "But, the hand disappeared back inside the womb and his brother, Pharez, was born first. Thus Pharez received the right to rule—not Zerah."

Darius tugged on his chin as he kept an eye on Bella and her crew.

The bartender smiled. "The flag symbolizes the marriage of the Hebrew princess, Tea-Tephi, the last remaining heir of the David-Pharez-Judah line, to the High King of Ireland, a direct descendant of the Zerah-Judah line. Thus the breach was sealed and the kingly line of David transferred to the Royal House of Ireland."

"That's your proof?" Mike said and wiped the froth from his lips.

The bartender nodded. "Those symbols were placed on the flag so's the Irish would never forget that they were descendents of the lost tribes of Israel."

Darius nodded his head in agreement. "Irish, Scottish, and British-Israelism. I like it."

"God help us if the Irish are the Chosen Ones," Mike slurred.

Darius laughed as he watched Mike down the last of his beer.

The bartender turned to Darius. "What'r you laughin' about. You're part Scottish, right?"

"Yeah, so . . ."

The bartender leaned toward him. His face turned red with anger. "If you're Scottish," he said and slammed his hand down hard on the bar, "you're Irishhh! They're all related."

He always had a feeling he was part Irish—even though his mother denied it.

"Time to go," Mike said.

Darius heard his Solofōn chime with a text message. He picked it up off the bar and read it. He turned to Mike. "Rule number one. Never ever leave your wing man," Darius slurred. "Paris's gonna be here any minute."

"Oh, I almost forgot. The firm is going to take half of your paycheck until your debt is settled. So, on Monday, don't be surprised when you only see nine grand deposited into your account."

Darius took a deep breath and exhaled. "Great," he said, stretching out the word.

"I'd love to stay but I gotta get home to the old ball and chain," Mike whispered. He gave Darius a reassuring pat on the back. "Don't worry, we'll get through this." He slammed a crisp hundred down hard on the bar and turned. "Darius, I'll see you in the morning." He grabbed his coat and headed for the door.

The bartender leaned forward again, knowing, Darius was sure, that he had a captive audience now that Mike had left. Who else was he going to talk to until Paris showed up?

"Throne of David is no longer in Ireland," the bartender said with pursed lips and a slow, knowing, close-to-the-chin bobbing nod. Up and down the head bobbed. Up and down.

"Let me guess," Darius giggled. "The Irish lost it." When he saw the bartender's face turn red again, Darius raised his hands in front of him. "Relax. Now that I'm Irish I figured I could at least joke about it."

"Silly sod, throne of David wasn't lost; 'twas merely transferred to Scotland and then to England when Queen Elizabeth the First died without no heir apparent."

"Yeah? Who became the next king of England?"

"In 1603 King James VI of Scotland was crowned King James I of England."

"And he rewrote the bible," Darius said.

"Now you're gettin' it, lad. I'll let you in on another little secret."

Darius leaned forward. What did it hurt humoring this old Irish guy?

"Reason Queen Elizabeth of the Royal House of Windsor hasn't abdicated her throne to Prince Charles yet, is 'cus she's forbidden to. There was one very important bloodline he's missing."

"Which one is that?"

"Merovingian line of Frankish kings who claim to be direct descendants of Christ our Lord and Mary Magdalene. That's why Princess Diana from the House of Stuart-Spencer was chosen."

"The Princess of Wales was a Merovingian?"

"Not *just* a Merovingian, lad. But a Merovingian virgin! Prince William and his younger brother Harry . . . the first royals ever that can claim to be descendents of all the kings and queens of Europe and Israel."

Darius's body tensed; his eyes narrowed. He leaned forward on the bar. "The Merovingians are full of shit," he said, "Christ never had kids."

"Relax, lad."

"And Mick Jagger's not the Devil." Darius leaned back and chugged his beer.

"I was at Altamont. You've no idea what went on. Darius, my boy, believe me when I tell you that these women just reenacted the exact same murder I witnessed forty-two years ago. You should have seen the size of them."

Darius belched and handed him the glass. "Descendants of King David, too?"

"I'm warnin' ya, lad. One more wise crack like that and you're outta here."

"Okay! Okay! Any idea who the women were?"

"They claim to be members of the Amazon Nation. I know it sounds crazy but the Hells Angels swear that the Amazons provoked the fight."

"I find that hard to believe."

"News said it had something to do with upsettin' the balance that'll occur during the Age of Aquarius. Supposed to be balance'll be achieved between men and women. That's what the festivals all over the globe are celebrating."

"I think it's achievable," Darius said with a shrug as the bartender finished filling his pint glass.

"You'd have a better chance of finding a pot of gold at the end of the rainbow," he said, setting down the fresh frothy beer. "There'll never be balance."

"Why d'ya say that?"

"Too much hate in this world. Power struggle between men and women has been shifting back and forth since the beginning of time."

Darius heard a loud crash of thunder. He blew the froth off of his beer and took a big swig. "Put on the news, would ya?"

The bartender picked up the remote control and turned on the TV.

"Wow! Look at all those freaks," Darius said, staring at the live broadcast at Stonehenge. He realized how shallow the statement sounded the moment the words left his lips. No matter how ridiculous they looked chanting and praying and twirling around in circles, he had no right to call them freaks. If anybody was a freak, it was him, he thought. He was just like them . . . but would never admit it. He couldn't. He had a reputation to uphold. But thoughts didn't matter—it was how he felt that counted. Deep down inside he longed to be at Stonehenge to help ground and channel the energy the comet was believed to release. As he watched the crowds perform some ritualistic dance to usher in the New Age, he was sickened by the thought of not being allowed to go because he wasn't chipped. Suddenly, the screen flashed and turned to static.

"TV's 'bout had it," the bartender said, turning it on and off again.

"Come on!" Darius said, "the comet's gonna align over Stonehenge any minute now."

"I'm trying."

"Give me that."

The bartender handed him the remote control as he made his way over to the other side of the bar. Darius began pressing random buttons and the picture finally returned. He placed the remote down on the bar. "Thank God," he said, realizing there was still one minute left.

The bartender returned and placed two rocks glasses filled with scotch on the bar. "This round's on Bella," he said.

Darius smiled half-heartedly and raised the glass in Bella's direction. He looked at the bartender, and said, "Here's to the dawning of the Age of Aquarius."

"God help us," the bartender replied. They touched their glasses and sipped the scotch.

"Thirty seconds and counting," Darius slurred, staring at the comet's long tail as it streaked toward Stonehenge. "Would you look at that camera angle? It makes it look like the comet is only a few hundred feet above the earth."

Darius felt a hand on his shoulder.

"Hello, darling."

He looked over his shoulder and saw Paris glancing furtively at Bella. When she turned back toward him, she looked flustered. "You're just in time to see Goliath align with Stonehenge." He stood up and helped Paris off with her rain coat.

The bartender placed a shot glass in front of Paris. "Here's some sipping whiskey from the girls across the way."

Darius smiled. "I think she likes you." He watched Paris look across the bar, shoot Bella an awkward smile, and then turn her attention back to him. She didn't seem at all amused by his comment.

"I don't think so," she said and rolled her eyes.

Darius fixed his eyes back to the screen. Paris had sat down on one of the bar stools next to him but Darius couldn't sit. "I feel funny," he said and stood up. He took a deep breath and joined the countdown. "Three, two—" When he said one, the TV turned to static.

▼ ▼ ▼

Ramsey snapped himself out of his troublesome thoughts about the Chosen One and motioned for Aje to continue the analysis.

"David and Goliath," the astrologer said in a breathy tone, "are also known as eclipse comets since they were discovered during both a solar and lunar eclipse. The solar eclipse occurred over North America and the lunar eclipse over the Middle East.

Ramsey was taken back. "You said something about clues . . . to the identities of people . . ."

Aje held a hand up to pause. "I will get to that in a moment." The astrologer aimed the laser at the hologram. "Since David appears to be travelling directly through the star, Yed Posterior, which is known as the Star of Evil Influence," he said with a series of lisps, "there will be a highly intelligent person who has the power to start a great war."

"Who is this person?" Ramsey asked.

"Whoever has access to weapons of mass destruction," the astrologer replied.

Ramsey looked at Raj. "President Walker, Queen Elizabeth and—"

"Mohammed, and his brother, Zadam," Raj said.

The astrologer placed his tablet on the table and put his hands on his hips. "What bothers me is that the computer failed to show the true meaning of Gemini. The two stars are believed to represent the first man and woman on earth. This suggests that a man *and* a woman will have the power necessary to defeat good or evil."

A nauseating feeling overcame him. *Did he have to find a woman as well?*

The astrologer took a sip of coffee and held his mug thoughtfully as he glanced down at the conference table. "David then passed within six degrees of the star Altair—known as the rising one. It is part of the constellation Aquila, the eagle, and associated with the military and the old Roman Empire."

He set down his coffee mug, pausing, Ramsey thought, for effect. Then he shifted his fixed look to Raj, and slowly back to the president.

"Like the lion," he lisped, "the eagle has two sides. But, since David also traveled through the Star of Evil Influence, a new Roman Empire, much more powerful than the first, shall rise."

The conference room fell silent. No one moved. Ramsey could not even hear his own breathing.

There was a loud knock at the door.

CHAPTER 16

"**Y**OU SHOULD HAVE told me about the prophecy a long time ago," Raj said. "Why did you wait until the comet—" "I was sworn to secrecy."

"Did my sister know?"

"Yes," he said reluctantly. "But she didn't hear it from me. I was spending so much time searching for the Chosen One, she thought I was having an affair. One day she snuck into my office and found it."

"What about that sword on your desk?"

Ramsey exhaled deeply. "You weren't meant to see that."

"I didn't see the martini glass and shaker either," he said with a sly grin. "I take it the sword has something to do with the Chosen One."

"Clever, very clever," Ramsey remarked. "My grandfather found it next to the prophecy. It's the only weapon that can kill the Chosen One. Only I, my father, and my grandfather had knowledge of its existence. Regardless, the Ghostriders claim to already have him."

"Maybe they're bluffing," Raj said. "You said the prophecy only spoke of a male Chosen One."

Ramsey nodded.

"But the astrologer identified a female as well."

Ramsey rose from his chair. "If that is the case, she too has the power!"

Raj smiled with a sense of satisfaction. "So that means," he said, nodding and grinning, "the sword can be used on her, too."

"In theory, but that remains to be seen. Still, I like what I'm hearing."

"What I think Aje was trying to say is that they must combine their powers to be effective."

"So . . . even if they have *him*, we may still be able to find *her.*"

Raj watched Ramsey sit back down in his chair. They were off to an excellent start, he thought, as he stared at the president, who seemed to be rethinking the situation. He had opened his brother-in-law's eyes to the metaphysical world. But he knew not to get too comfortable. It could all change in an instant.

After a prolonged silence the president said, "Computer, provide a visual of the comet Goliath just before it aligned with Stonehenge."

Raj thought he detected a note of panic in the president's voice, which was uncharacteristic for his brother-in-law. Just then the comet Goliath, traveling through the night sky toward Stonehenge, appeared. As the alignment occurred, the astrologer walked back in. There was a brilliant flash of light and the hologram turned to static.

"Computer, is that all of the footage available," the president asked.

"Affirmative," the computer replied. "Global satellite communications were disrupted twelve minutes ago when the alignment occurred. Only historical data is available until the satellites are operational again."

The astrologer headed back to his seat.

"What happened?"

"The comet exploded," Raj said.

"Impossible—comets don't explode."

"This one did."

"Any meaning attached to a comet exploding?" the president asked.

The astrologer picked up the tablet computer. He looked at the president and then down at his device in silence. He held up his left hand without looking up.

Raj fidgeted in his seat as he listened to Ramsey drum his fingers on the table. Several moments had gone by and the drumming quickened to a pace that defied being ignored. Still there was silence. This was disastrous, Raj thought.

"Answer the damn question," the president said.

Raj had never heard such a gruff tone from his brother-in-law. He rolled his eyes up to Aje without raising his head.

The astrologer's bony hands were trembling. "Jus gi-gi-give me a little more time," he said, fumbling with his tablet.

This was worse than disastrous. Aje was stalling and stuttering and now as he spoke, his whole body was trembling so much that he looked like he was having a seizure. Raj's nerves were beginning to eat holes right through his stomach. The day's events kept going around and around in his head; he could barely think of a single coherent thought let alone figure out how to approach the problem of this nervous advisor. But if Aje didn't give the president an answer very soon, he knew Ramsey would get up and leave. He had to think of a way to calm the situation. And fast.

Finally Aje broke the silence. "I-I-I," he stuttered, "am unaware of any message associated with a comet exploding."

That's it? Raj was afraid to even look at the president.

Ramsey stood up from the table and threw his hands in the air. "I've had enough."

"Oof," Raj said. He jumped up from his seat and grabbed Ramsey by the arm. "Don't give up, Mr. President—not yet." He turned toward Aje. "With further analysis, do you think you can find an answer?"

The astrologer nodded. "Yes."

"Raj, let go of my arm."

Raj tightened his grip. He had nothing to lose. If Ramsey walked out of the meeting, he had a feeling he would never confide in him again. "Mr. President," Raj said, holding his thumb and index finger half an inch apart in front of his own face. "We are this close to finding out the identities of the Chosen One and his soulmate."

He could tell by the look on Ramsey's face that he wasn't so sure. The analysis was like an archaeological dig that had yet to yield a major discovery but still showed signs of promise.

"The analysis doesn't provide any tangible evidence," he said, "only speculation at best."

"Mr. President," the astrologer said.

Raj interrupted. "I disagree," he said, loosening his grip on the president's arm. "You know more about the Chosen One than you did before the analysis; not to mention the fact that the stars have identified his soulmate."

Raj looked deep into Ramsey's eyes. It was apparent his religious beliefs were standing in the way. "Come on, Mr. President," Raj said, lowering his voice. He held his chin tight against his neck and spoke out of the side of his mouth. "You were fine up until the comet exploded. Any further information the stars provide can only help us. Allah will understand."

There was a long pause before Ramsey shook himself out of his thoughts. "You have until the satellites come back online. Now," he said, looking down at Raj's hand on his arm, "can you kindly let go?"

Raj let go of the president's arm and they both sat back down.

Ramsey glanced at his watch. "Computer, please inform us as soon as the satellites are operational."

Aje looked down at his tablet, took a deep breath, and exhaled as Goliath appeared exiting the Unicorn constellation with a long dust tail that seemed to stretch between the stars. Raj looked on in amazement as the comet streaked through the stars in the hologram. He hoped to God that Aje would find something with which Ramsey could identify with before the satellites came back online.

▲ ▲ ▲

The astrologer aimed his laser pointer at what looked like a small planet. "Goliath appears as though it's traveling directly through the asteroid Ceres," he said with a series of lisps.

Raj began fidgeting again when he heard Aje lisp. If it got any worse he would have to repeat himself over and over and precious seconds or even minutes would be lost. Time he could ill afford to lose.

The president cut in. "Wasn't Ceres the first asteroid ever discovered?"

"That's correct," Aje said. "It's associated with the rise of a feminine consciousness—demanding social equality," he said with another series of lisps.

"I can't understand a word he's saying," Ramsey said with his arms held wide. He was looking back and forth between Aje and Raj.

Raj steepled his hands between closed eyes and leaned forward with his elbows on the table. He couldn't bear to watch, let alone listen. "Could you repeat that, please, slower this time," he said without looking up.

When Aje repeated his answer with almost total clarity, Raj removed his hands from his face. Dumbfounded, he listened to the words effortlessly roll off the tongue of the astrologer as he continued his explanation.

"Ceres is the great mother goddess who rules major life cycles," Aje said as if he were a teacher lecturing a class. Raj thought Aje was gaining confidence in himself, or at least control of his damn lisp. "The ancient Mayans believe that we are now at the end of a 26,000-year life cycle."

"Why was the asteroid named after a goddess?" Ramsey asked.

"To restore gender balance. Astrologers consider the moon a planet so they use ten planets in their analysis. Out of the ten, only the moon and Venus are feminine. To better balance the masculine energy, five asteroids, Ceres, Juno, Pallas, Vesta and Chiron were added. They represent the vital components of the emerging feminine consciousness."

Raj sat up in his chair. Once again, he could not believe how easily the words seemed to roll off the astrologer's tongue with a distinct, almost tranquil, calmness. Ramsey turned toward Raj with a bewildered look on his face. When Raj looked back to the astrologer, he stood almost catatonic staring straight ahead. He couldn't help but wonder if there just might be some kind of divine intervention taking place. Raj looked at Ramsey who seemed to be lost in thought and broke the silence that separated them. "This is consistent with the riots in Babylon," he said, leaning in toward the president.

Ramsey gave no indication that he'd even heard his aide. The president sat as frozen, as Aje stood, with his eyes fixed on the astrologer.

After a long moment, the astrologer rejoined the discussion. "Now, more than ever, women have established a powerful collective consciousness that is driving their participation in the economic, political and social development of society."

"Yes, they're learning to use the quantum field," Raj said thoughtfully, keeping a watchful eye on the president.

Ramsey snapped out of his reverie and looked at the astrologer. "So, if I'm hearing you correctly, this is really about achieving balance between the sexes."

"Precisely," Aje said.

Raj raised an eyebrow to the president and then shifted his gaze to the astrologer. "What role, if any, will Ceres play in achieving balance?"

The astrologer smiled. "When the balance comes into play, the goddess must return the genetic strain hidden within the Sirius star system in order for the next stage of the evolutionary cycle to take place."

"I'm aware of this myth," Ramsey said.

"And if she fails?" Raj knew he had interrupted the president. But this was not the time to worry about such strict formality.

The astrologer's smile faded. "The balance of power will shift and a matriarchal society ruled by nefarious leaders will reign supreme."

Ramsey interrupted. "Do you have any idea when this will occur?"

"I'm afraid not, but if I had to guess I would say at some point on December 21st, 2012. This date marks the end of the Mayan calendar."

Raj scoured Ramsey's face, looking for even the slightest sign of response. When he didn't see any, he cringed at the thought of the computer interrupting them before Aje finished the analysis.

Aje pointed his laser at the hologram. "Goliath then traveled extremely close to Canis Major's main star, Sirius. Sirius is better known as the Dog Star or Royal One. Zoroastrians—"

The computer interrupted. "Mr. President, the satellites are operational. Shall I terminate the comet analysis program?"

The president leaned forward, rested both hands shoulder-length apart in front of him on the table, as if he were about to push himself out of his chair. He held himself in this position, and without moving his head, his eyes scanned back and forth, then up and down. His eyes stopped and he pursed his lips. With lips tightly pursed, he leaned back in his chair.

Raj was sitting on the edge of his seat studying Ramsey's every move. He knew the mention of *Zoroastrian* was like music to the president's ears, but was it enough to convince him to stay?

"I'm sorry Raj," he finally said.

A hollow feeling filled the pit of his stomach. He felt as though he was going to be sick. Raj lowered his head.

Ramsey leaned toward him. "I'm sorry . . . sorry for ever doubting you."

"You are?" he said, lifting his head.

"More than you can imagine," he said. "Everything in the analysis is consistent with the prophecy. And . . . it has provided us with additional information that may prove useful."

Raj smiled with a sense of satisfaction. "There are no coincidences—everything happens for a reason." He glanced at Aje, who stood with his hands folded behind his back and his head tilted to one side. His lips were compressed into a thin line, but one couldn't mistake the relief in his eyes.

Ramsey gave him a reassuring nod and patted him on the back. "Computer, display imagery of Stonehenge," he said and exhaled deeply.

"Satellite signal is currently being streamed. Imagery will be displayed in three minutes."

Ramsey shifted his gaze to Aje. "Please continue."

Patiently waiting for the astrologer to stop fiddling with his tablet, he realized that Aje had most likely forgotten where he had left off. Raj cleared his throat to grab his attention. "You were discussing Sirius and the Zoroastrians, I believe."

Aje nodded with a grateful smile and pointed his laser at the hologram. "Zoroastrians refer to Sirius as the 'Spirit of Wisdom.' Next to the sun, Sirius is the brightest star in the heavens and a dual star. Goliath," he said, "reached its apex or highest point on February third 2010. The history and myth of Canis Major states that Orion had two dogs—Canis Major and Canis Minor."

"Ah . . . yes . . . the dog is greatly revered by Zoroastrians." Ramsey's voice trailed off as he leaned forward and rested his arms on the conference table. "Dogs guarded the Cinvat bridge," he said, steepling his hands and wrinkling his bushy brows, "which linked this world to the spiritual world."

"That's right, and since Goliath reached its apex close to Sirius in the sign of Aquarius, this speaks of a Zoroastrian born under the sign of Aquarius. This man will have tremendous power."

"He's out there somewhere," Ramsey said to Raj. "Hopefully the Amazons are bluffing, and we find him and his soulmate before they do."

Raj gave a firm nod to his brother-in-law before turning back to the hologram. It was good to see the president's self-assuredness and command restored.

Aje motioned to the hologram. "When you do find him, you must exercise caution," he lisped. "Unless this individual is able to control his super-ego, he has the potential to become a powerful dictator or deceiver."

Ramsey looked as if he was deep in thought. "Earlier," he said, raising and motioning with his right arm, "you mentioned . . . that . . . the ancients believed that comets . . . were messengers sent by God."

Raj could hear Ramsey working out his hypothesis in his brief pauses.

"Yes."

"Then . . . maybe Stonehenge . . . was set up to receive the comets message," Ramsey said.

The president leaned back in his chair and folded his right arm across his chest. He brought his left hand up and rested his elbow on his right-hand and rubbed his chin. Raj knew Ramsey was mulling over his hypothesis. But he also noted a hint of self-satisfaction in his pose.

The astrologer aimed the laser pointer at the hologram. "We shall know soon enough," he said. "Since Goliath traveled through the stars in Orion's belt—Alnatik, Alnilam, and Mintaka—my guess is there is a metaphysical connection between those stars and the three Pyramids of Giza. Some believe the pyramids were built in alignment with these three stars in the Age of Leo approximately twelve thousand five hundred years ago."

Raj thought the astrologer was rather dismissive of Ramsey's theory. Ramsey was the president after all. Aje was the expert here, true, but he and the president did know a thing or two.

"The Orion Theory?" Ramsey said with a dismissive wave of his hand. "That was discredited when carbon dating showed the pyramids to be forty-five hundred years old."

If Aje further argued the point, Raj knew Ramsey wouldn't back down. He shook his head for Aje to back off and redirected the discussion. "Was Goliath at its apex when it passed through Orion's belt?"

"Yes. And it came within six degrees of Bellatrix, the Amazon star." The astrologer paused and finished the rest of his coffee before continuing his thoughts. "Orion was a handsome hunter. Artemis, the Amazon goddess of the hunt, fell deeply in love with him."

Raj wondered what this had to do with finding whomever it was they were looking for.

"They hunted on horseback. Used spears, swords, and bows and arrows," Aje said. "But they did hold one weapon sacred above all."

Ramsey grinned. "The double-bladed axe."

"Exactly," the astrologer replied. "The labrys is the symbol of the female labia, situated at the entrance of the womb, and the butterfly, which is associated with transformation and rebirth. They are all sacred symbols of the Amazons."

Raj turned to the president, and said, "The late princess was trying to tell you that the twin Leos are Amazons." When the president didn't respond, he realized that something must be wrong. Wondering what Ramsey was thinking, he thought about the butterfly necklace his sister wore and everything became clear. His heart fell. He glanced at the astrologer and looked back to Ramsey. "You don't think my sister was an Amazon. Do you?"

Ramsey nodded and said in a somber tone, "As much as I'd like that not to be the case, she did wear their symbol."

The president was right, he thought. No matter how hard he tried, there was just no denying it. "Why haven't the Amazons appeared in any of our intelligence reports?"

"Because they're going under an alias," Ramsey said, tilting and rocking his chair back and forth. Ramsey had his left arm slung over the back of the chair. His eyes squinted and his right-hand tapped on the table as he continued to tilt forward and back in his chair. Raj had never seen his brother-in-law look so sure of himself. For the moment, it seemed as if the president had managed to block out the thought of his wife.

"So," Raj said, "the Amazons are the Ghostriders?"

"I'd bet my life on it."

CHAPTER 17

ZADAM RAISED THE envelope to his nose and took a deep breath. Her scent instantly aroused him. He pulled the moist paper out, his anticipation heightened with every breath he took.

> *My little lamb*
> *I call Mars.*
> *I will devour you*
> *As we play among the stars!*
> *Worthy is the lamb that was slain.*
> *Give me pleasure*
> *Or our souls will cry out in pain!*
> *Meet me in my chamber!*
> *Roars—*
> *The Lion*

He crumpled the paper and vowed that this would be his last time with her. Roxanne was his drug and he was addicted.

Zadam burst into the chamber and threw himself onto his brother's king-size, four-poster wrought iron bed. He grabbed his brother's beautiful wife and sat on top of her, pinning her thin wrists and naked body to the white silk bed sheets. He was captivated by her emerald green eyes.

"Who is this lamb you call Mars?"

"You, my lover," she said.

Her beauty was radiant and her seductive tone entranced him. Slowly, he loosened his grip on her and before he realized it, he was on his back and she was on top.

"You're an Aries," she hissed. "Aries, which some believe," she said in a somewhat softer voice, "to be symbolic of a lamb. And I, I am a Leo which is symbolic of a lion." She arched her back and rested her hands on her thighs and swung her hair back. "You're ruled by the planet Mars and *I'm* ruled by the sun. I thought that you would enjoy my little poem, but obviously you have other things on your mind that are more important than I am."

Zadam said nothing. He stared through her as if she were invisible. He was torn between the love for his brother and the lust he had for his brother's wife. He felt Roxanne loosen her grip.

"What is troubling you, my love?"

He moved her to his side and sat up on the bed. She moved around him and caressed his broad shoulders from behind. "We mustn't see each other anymore."

"It's not that easy," she said, digging her nails into his shoulders. "I've fallen in love with you. But now that you don't want me, I just might have to tell Mohammed the truth about us."

He laughed to himself. He'd had a feeling she'd pull a stunt like this. "It's not that I don't love you." He turned on her, swung his legs off the bed, and stood up.

She moved closer to the edge of the bed. "You musn't fear your brother. He is small and weak. You are big and strong, and would make a much better leader." She stood up and faced him.

"Tell me something I don't already know," he said and grabbed her by the shoulders. "I dream of being in his shoes."

"I think that can be arranged. Let's play," she said, drawing out the word play, "among the stars."

Her tone was light, teasing. And her manipulative and deceptive nature aroused him. But more importantly, it reinforced why he fell in love with her in the first place. Roxanne's stunning looks and streamlined physique were now just an added bonus to the complex mind that wielded it. She was his soulmate but he knew to be careful. Still, he decided to up the ante. He pulled her toward him but she resisted.

"Not that type of playing," she said. "I want to give you an astrological reading."

"Mohammed asked me if you are practicing astrology," he said, letting go of her. He threw back his shoulders and tucked in his shirt. For once in their relationship she was at a total loss for words. "I think he's jealous that we've been spending so much time together when he's away. He's looking for an excuse to keep us apart."

"I can assure you that he's bluffing. What did you tell him?"

"I denied it, of course."

"Good."

"But I don't think he's bluffing," he said, tightening his belt. "Somebody *must'av* said something to make him question me." He knew Mohammed would never tell Roxanne that he was the one who told him. Mohammed was much smarter than that. Astrology was taboo among all Muslims so Mohammed had nothing to gain and everything to lose by dragging him into it. It was bad enough Roxanne was practicing astrology, but if word leaked that Zadam had participated, the repercussions would be devastating. Their control over the Muslim people would diminish and they would no longer be of use to Queen Elizabeth. She would immediately have them removed from power.

"I will deny any wrongdoing," she said with indifference.

"That will just make matters worse. You must tell him the truth. It is the only way."

"I will do nothing of the sort," she said coldly.

"Think with your head not with your heart. This is bigger than you and I. If you don't admit your wrongdoing and assure him that this will never happen again, he will tighten his leash on you and we will never be together."

She paused. "I will do as you say this time, but I will not give up astrology."

"Fine," he said with a satisfied smile. "Now tell me more about myself." He pulled her to him and pressed her body against his.

She leaned back and smiled. "Well . . . your Leo moon tells me you're insecure about the fact that you're not the center of attention."

"I am not in the least bit insecure."

"It's not your fault," she said comfortingly. "You just happened to be born second."

"So what do you recommend?"

"Establish yourself as his equal."

"How's that going to get me my brother's crown?"

"Supreme Leader is not a crown," she said mockingly, "it's a title. And even though the public may think of me as a queen, in essence, I am not. Well, that is, not just yet," she said and chuckled softly. "You need to aim your sites higher—shoot for the stars."

"I don't wish to see my brother dead," he said, "if that is what you mean." Zadam let go of Roxanne and turned away from her. He began pacing back and forth.

"That'd be too easy. I have something better in mind." She reached out to him with one of her arms but he shrugged her off. "Your rising sign, Gemini, provides you the ability to be the greatest leader in history but first you need to be free of the ghosts that haunt you."

He stopped his pace and placed his hands on his hips to study her.

"You see, my lover," she said sweetly, "my moon is in Aquarius. And that gives me the power to rid you of your demons. When this is achieved you will soar to new heights and not only surpass, but shatter, your brother's legacy by becoming the first *King of the World.*"

"Kiss me!" he said.

She grabbed his thick wrists and pulled him onto the bed with her. She rolled on top of Zadam and sat up straddling him. "There's one more thing."

He smiled. With Roxanne there was always one more thing.

"Aries," she hissed, "remember, are ruled by the planet Mars; Leos by the sun. The sun, of course, is about the self." She paused, he knew, to let her last sentence sink in. "And Mars. Mars," she said, lustily stretching out the word, "is about aggressive energy." Her voice was now deep and throaty. She grinned and pressed her lips up against his ear and tightened her grip with her thighs. "That makes us highly compatible and a formidable team."

"I must have you," he said.

But she was in the position to resist him and he knew she was further leveraging her power over him. "You have very high nervous tension, my love, so it is important you redirect this built up energy in a positive way." She leaned down and touched her hot breath and wet lips to his ear. "I know of no other way than you having your way with me." She tightened her grip on his wrists. "But . . . if you are to become the most powerful man on the planet," she said, "you must never question my authority and must always do as I say. Are you with me?"

Zadam looked at her with swelling admiration. "I'll be with you 'til the end of time," he said and reclaimed the top position.

CHAPTER 18

"**G**OOD GOD," PRESIDENT Ramsey said, staring at the megalithic ruin. The ancient stone circle that lay dormant on the Salisbury Plain for the last four thousand years had finally awoken. He had expected something, but never dreamed of anything quite like this. He looked at Raj and the astrologer; both had their eyes glued to the three-dimensional image of Stonehenge, which was now covered from top to bottom with a powerful energy field. Green and white light flickered as the subatomic particles circulated through the giant sandstones.

Suddenly, the transmission ended.

"Computer," Ramsey said as he rose from his chair. "What happened to the transmission?" He paced back and forth as he waited for the computer's response.

"There is a security jam," the computer replied.

President Ramsey walked away from the table, hands clasped behind his back and looked at the floor. Not only had he failed to find the Chosen One before the alignment ocurred, but he now had to deal with yet another pressing issue. The Amazons knew about the prophecy. He closed his eyes and shook his head. Why had his wife betrayed him? Being a world leader he had felt the stabbing pain of betrayal before, but he never thought it would come from her.

"Perhaps you weren't meant to find the Zoroastrian and he was meant to find you," Raj said, "and Stonehenge is some type of gateway."

Ramsey's eyes opened wide. *What had he done?* He had just told Raj everything. If his wife could betray him then so could . . .

He felt a hand on his shoulder.

"I know what you must be feeling," Raj said, standing behind him, his hand still resting on his shoulder. "I'm as surprised as you to learn that my sister was an Amazon."

"The one person I trusted most in life . . ." Ramsey said, turning back toward the conference table.

"Oof. I hope you're not thinking I knew of her involvement with the Amazons."

Ramsey took a deep breath and exhaled. "I don't know what to believe anymore."

"If I had known, they would have gotten rid of me too."

True, Ramsey thought. He knew when Raj was lying. His voice inflections fluctuated from high to low. But there was no fluctuation as he spoke now. He could sense his brother-in-law looking at him, but he couldn't bring himself to return his look. "Raj, I believe you," he said, "but what can you possibly say in her defense?" Ramsey stopped. He glanced at Aje who was quietly sitting at the far end of the table and shifted his gaze, through the corner of his eye, to his brother-in-law. Raj moved in front of him and grabbed a hold of his arms just below the shoulder. He felt Raj give a tight, quick, almost pleading squeeze.

"Can't you see what's happening? You're letting your emotions get the better of you. You once told me not to place blame until I knew all the facts."

When Raj let go, Ramsey exhaled and looked into his teary eyes. "We already know all the facts."

"Actually, you don't," Raj replied. "She called me the morning of the assassination attempt and insisted we meet. She seemed agitated and nervous but I thought nothing of it because we had been fighting all week long." He sighed heavily, with what sounded like a lifetime of regret. "She'd said some pretty harsh things and I assumed she just wanted to make amends. We set up a time and place to meet but she never showed because you forced her to go with you."

"Enough!" Ramsey shouted. He closed his eyes and pulled his hands behind his back, as if these gestures could hold things in check.

"I think she was trying to figure out how to get away from the Amazons," Raj said. "That's why she wanted to meet with me in person and wouldn't talk on the phone. She was probably being watched. My dear brother-in-law, Mr. President—she obviously was in way over her head. Now I know why. She was trying to protect you."

Ramsey froze. *Protect him from what? The Amazons?* If that were the case he'd already be dead. As his mind traveled back to the hours leading up to the incident, he heard her voice as clear as day. "I remember her saying that the Zoroastrian I was going to meet was not the Chosen One I had been searching for. She begged me not to take her but I thought it was because she didn't believe in me anymore." He could hear the astrologer, over at the far end of the table, shift in his seat. He took a deep breath and exhaled. "I was so caught up with proving her wrong that I forced her to go with me." He gave a demoralizing look at the floor.

"The assassination attempt was never about you." Raj sighed softly, bringing his hands to his lips. "It was her they were after. But when you got into her limo instead of yours everyone assumed the attack was aimed at you. She was trying to protect you from—"

"Herself," Ramsey said, letting out a long whoosh of air. He felt the veins in his neck bulge. He looked up toward the ceiling. "How could I have been so selfish? So foolish?"

"We're both to blame. Nonetheless, we need to put this behind us and move forward. Now that it's clear the Amazons know about the prophecy, it's quite possible they only know half the story. There's a good chance they have no idea about the female Chosen One."

Ramsey heard the astrologer clear his throat. He looked over at him as he shifted in his chair once more. "We need to find out as much as we can about these Amazons," he said and with a renewed strength motioned Raj back to the table with him. "Aje, what are the Amazons up to?"

"Computer, give me a visual of the alignment of David, the star Aldebaran and Goliath," the astrologer said confidently.

Ramsey stared at the hologram of a bright star in the middle of the converging comets.

"Oh, my dear." The astrologer shook his head as he stood up from his seat. "I was afraid of this," he said. "This alignment is so powerful it could actually refer to the Devil himself." He aimed the laser pointer at the hologram and traced the comet's trajectory. "Since Goliath passed close to the star Bellatrix on March 21st, in the sign of Aries, and David had just passed through Algol, this implies a couple of things. The sign Aries and the star Bellatrix refers to the Amazons."

"March 21st, was my sister's birthdate," Raj said, smiling.

Silence filled the room. All eyes focused on Raj whose smile turned awkward with the prolonged silence and faded away.

Ramsey sighed deeply but kept his thoughts to himself.

Finally, the astrologer broke the silence that separated them. "The star, Algol," he lisped, "is the most evil star in the heavens. It connects the Amazons to the Evil One." Aje paused and took a sip of water. He took a deep breath and in a sharp distinct tone said, "In an effort to secure their place in the future, an alliance will be formed with a very small nation. This nation will follow the Evil One with blind faith in order to advance itself."

"Of course," Ramsey said. "In Amazon mythology two queens ruled their society. One was in charge of defense and the other domestic affairs." He paused and looked at Raj and quickly back to the astrologer. "Could these two queens be the twins the stars tell about?"

"It's possible." He wrinkled his forehead and squinted as he took another sip of water.

Ramsey leaned on the table toward Raj. "You need to concentrate on finding the twins. We find them, I have a good feeling we will find my wife and son's killer as well as the Chosen One."

Raj gave him an approving nod. "I will savor the sweet taste of revenge when I look her killer in the eye and justice is served."

"Next," the astrologer interrupted, "Goliath traveled through the three stars in the belt of Orion, which the Magi refer to as the *Three Kings*, and came within six degrees of the star Bellatrix—the Amazon Star. This tells us of three individuals. One will emerge as a king who will be the leader of a superpower. The other two individuals will be a man and a woman, who together will have the power to destroy good or evil. The man will house the souls of himself and two others."

"Is that possible?" the president asked.

The astrologer shrugged his shoulders as if to say it was possible but that he really didn't know. "Computer, display David's path through the Lacerta constellation." Aje pointed the red laser at the bright stars of the Lizard Constellation. "While David didn't pass within six degrees of any main star, it reached its apex in the sign of Aries. This indicates that an individual will attempt to deceive the people during the height of his or her power. The Greek god, Ares, is the mythological father of the Amazons, but in this case the computer is associating Ares with the fifth tarot card, the pope."

Could the pope be the leader of this new Roman Empire the stars spoke about? And what role did the Amazons play in the scheme of things? Ramsey thought about the email of Apollo being killed. If Artemis and Apollo were twins then . . . he sprang to his feet.

"The Amazons are going to try and upset the balance."

CHAPTER 19

"**W**HAT DO WE have here?"

Dressed in a yellow rain coat, the doorman held the taxi door open with one hand and an umbrella with the other.

"Thank God it's you, Benny. Could you give me a hand getting Darius up to the apartment?" She pushed Darius's limp body toward the muscular doorman. "He had a bit too much to drink for his birthday."

When Paris was sure that Benny had hold of Darius, she waved the back of her hand against a scanner to pay and climbed out of the cab. The rain pelted down hard as she watched Benny lift Darius up over his shoulder and carry him into the lobby. A couple walked in right behind them and looked on as Benny dumped Darius in a wheelchair. It was okay for her to gossip about other people but when it came to her and Darius, she didn't want anybody knowing their business. She sighed as Benny wheeled him to the elevator.

"He's a pathetic excuse of a boyfriend," she said, listening to Darius talk in his sleep.

"What's he saying?"

Paris took off her coat and draped it over his head. "Sounds like a foreign language."

Benny chuckled. "Shh! It's not healthy to wake somebody out of a dream."

Paris shot him a wry look and looked around to see if anybody else was watching. When the elevator doors opened, a few people got off the elevator and looked curiously at Darius as they passed. Paris practically shoved them into the elevator and scanned her hand. "Sixty-ninth floor," she said, frowning. "This is so embarrassing."

Benny chuckled softly. "All I know is he's gonna have one hell of a hangover in the morning."

When the elevator doors closed, Paris breathed a huge sigh of relief. She looked into the mirrored doors and tried to fix her hair. "Nothing's going right today," she said, looking at Benny in the mirror. "We need to get him into the apartment before anybody else sees him."

"Relax, there's a bigger topic on everyone's mind. The comet, Goliath, exploded high over Stonehenge tonight."

"The comet exploded?" The moment the elevator doors opened, she stepped off the elevator and ushered Benny down the hallway.

"Yeah, it knocked out satellite communications worldwide."

"How does a comet explode?"

"Who knows. Government probably thought it was too close to earth so they nuked it."

Paris stopped in front of their apartment door. "Open says-a-me," she said. The door opened and she led Benny into the bright twenty-five-hundred-square-foot duplex. "Put him in the master bedroom," she said, looking through her pocketbook for a tip.

"Seems like the storms are getting more and more violent nowadays, Miss Templar." He picked Darius up in a fireman's carry and followed Paris up the stairs and into the bedroom. He laid Darius fully clothed on the right side of the four-poster bed and Paris accompanied him back downstairs. When they reached the front door she handed him a hundred dollar bill. "If anybody asks, you have no idea who the man in the wheelchair was."

The doorman winked. "I assure you, Miss Templar, your secret's safe with me," he said and made an about turn.

Paris closed the door and walked into the living room. She curled up in a ball on the black leather sofa next to the window. Drenched in moonlight, she rocked back and forth and wondered how much longer she could put up with this.

CHAPTER 20

"**I** 'M SLEEPING." SHE pulled the comforter up to her chin. Darius shook her again but this time a little harder. "Did you have any weird dreams last night?"

"No." Paris yawned and turned away from him. "Go back to sleep."

Darius sat up in bed with his hands balled into tight fists. He stared at the three nude goddesses hanging in a twisted gold rope frame on the wall in front him and wondered if he might still be dreaming.

He swung his legs over the edge of the bed and stretched his arms behind his back as the morning sunlight shone through the half-moon window behind him. His head cast a shadow over the three models sitting and kneeling on the floor in the painting. Their arms were folded across their chests and their elbows rested comfortably on a white ottoman nestled beneath a large painted canvas of the goddesses Hera, Aphrodite, and Athena. The models' gazes focused not on the goddesses above them but on a smaller painting, or perhaps it was a mirror, on the wall in front of them. For a brief moment, Darius couldn't help but feel that the goddesses were judging him. The famous watercolor painting, by Sir Russell Flint, was the only thing his father had left him besides the brown leather attaché case he kept hidden under his bed.

As the sun's rays moved down the painting, the light reflected into his bloodshot eyes. His head throbbed. For a moment, the three goddesses appeared as though they were dancing around his head in a circle, smiling and laughing. He closed his eyes and shook his head to clear it. When he opened them, they were back in their original positions, kneeling against the bed with their elbows comfortably resting on the ottoman and their arms crossed over their chests.

He was probably just suffering from a major hangover, he thought, and massaged his temples. He laid back down, closed his eyes, and tried to remember his dream.

He could still feel the hot desert sun beating down on him as he tirelessly searched the stones at the base of one of the Great Pyramids of Giza. Sweat dripped down his sun burned face and into the cracks of his parched lips. He noticed a crusted layer of sand about the size of a dinner plate in the center of one of the stones. He picked up a jagged rock and chipped away at it. Hidden beneath, he discovered what appeared to be two very worn handprints.

Before he could take a breath, his hands had jerked forward and stuck to the stone. There had been a brilliant flash of light. Suddenly he was no longer at the pyramids, but standing under the star-filled sky in the middle of the stone circle at Stonehenge. When he looked up at the stars he saw a comet streak overhead and found himself showered in pure white light.

Darius jumped out of bed and walked over to the full-length mirror.

What's happening to me?

He looked hung over, sure, but other than that, he felt great. Opening and closing his fists he felt an energy surge through his body that made his hands swell and his mind race. Maybe he just needed a good workout. That was it— he'd go to the gym and take a kickboxing class.

▼ ▲ ▼

Darius warmed up on the treadmill at a pace far above his normal level as he watched the morning news. He read the scrolling headline, "BBC News Special Report: Comet Goliath Explodes. Up Next." Shocked, he missed a step and almost fell before shutting down the machine.

"I'll be damned," he said and looked around the gym. The few others who were working out were wearing headphones and didn't seem to be paying any attention to the newscast. He stepped off the treadmill and wiped his face with a towel. As he waited for the story, he wondered if he had actually witnessed the comet explode or dreamt it.

Typically he forgot his dreams shortly after he woke, but for some reason, this one maintained its clarity. In his dream, the comet never exploded. Why was he so sure it did?

After a lengthy block of commercials, the news returned. British Intelligence acknowledged that the comet *had* exploded, but also issued a statement that a terror attack had occurred in the area and, due to security issues, no one would be allowed within thirty miles of Stonehenge.

That's a likely story, he thought. What were they trying to hide? Wandering aimlessly about the gym, he tried to collect his thoughts. Suddenly, he stopped and stared through the thick glass wall of the gym's group exercise room. A feeling of uneasiness swept through him as he watched a group of women equipped with headgear and kickboxing gloves sparring on a springy hardwood floor. What if they knew he had a higher purpose? When he moved forward to get a better look, one of the women who was bleeding from the mouth motioned with her glove for him to step into the room. Instantly, everything became clear and everybody seemed suspect. Overwhelmed by the realization that they were on to him, he decided to leave the gym immediately.

When he reached his building on 61st and Third Avenue, the sun quickly disappeared behind a thick blanket of clouds. Darius glanced over his shoulder one last time to see if he was being followed. When he didn't see anyone, he hurried into the building and up into his apartment. He double-locked the door and jogged up the stairs to his bedroom. Paris, wrapped in a fluffy green towel, was combing the nots out of her long blonde hair in front of his full-length mirror.

He walked up behind her and looked at her reflection. "Paris, we need to talk."

Startled, she turned. "I hate it when you sneak up on me."

He leaned over to give her a kiss, but she turned away and walked into the master bathroom. Darius followed her to the doorway and watched her blow-dry her hair.

"We need to talk."

Paris turned the blow dryer on high. "I can't hear you."

Darius moved toward her and ripped the cord out of the socket.

She turned and faced him. "You embarrassed me last night."

She pushed him aside and stormed out of the bathroom. Her hair was still wet and her eyes were cold and distant. Darius followed her into the bedroom.

"Hurry up and get dressed," he said and began changing his clothes.

"You owe me an apology."

Darius pulled his black V-neck sweater over his head, and put his right index finger over his lips. "Shh," he said.

"What's wrong?"

"Shh," he said again, tucking his undershirt into his blue jeans.

"Do you think somebody is listening to us?" she said with a touch of annoyance.

He made an exasperated sound and opened his hands like she'd said something totally asinine. He grabbed his wallet off the dresser. "I'll tell you on the way to work."

"Work? Today's Saturday."

Darius winked and pulled her close. "We need to get out of here, now."

"Are we being bugged?" she whispered.

He watched her reluctantly wiggle into a pair of tight blue jeans. She pulled on her white turtleneck and slipped on her black leather boots.

When she stopped in front of the mirror, he grabbed her by the hand and pulled her to the stairs.

"Darius, I can't go out looking like this."

"You look fine. We need to get out of here—now." When they reached the landing, he grabbed their lightweight trench coats off the banister and dragged her out of the apartment and down the hall to the elevator.

"Where are we going?" she moaned.

Darius looked at her for a quick moment but didn't say anything. He helped her put on her yellow coat and took a sharp look around to see if anyone was following them. He caught the look of panic on Paris's face.

"Darius what's wrong? You need to tell me what's going on," she said as the elevator doors opened.

"I'll tell you when we get outside," he said and pushed her into the elevator.

▲ ▼ ▲

Against her will, and a strong wind that moved the clouds across the sky, Darius dragged Paris up the block. Leading her through a sea of people crowding the sidewalk, he glanced over his shoulder every so often to see if they were being followed.

"Darius, you're scaring me."

He stopped and eyed her yellow trench. "You stick out like a sore thumb."

"What are you talking about," she said, trying to catch her breath. "Listen, I'm not going anywhere until you tell me what's going on."

He looked up at the familiar high steel pole and stared at the surveillance camera attached to it. "Get over here," he said and pulled her into an alleyway. "I'll explain when we're safely in the park. Right now you need to ditch the coat."

"Ditch my coat?"

"Turn around," he said. He spun her around and forcefully pulled her coat down her back and arms.

"Stop it," she shouted and started to turn around.

In one hard yank and tug he had the coat off her. He tossed it in the dumpster behind her and then pulled her out of the alley.

"That was a three thousand dollar coat," she screamed.

Darius didn't respond but, instead, pulled her in the direction of the Plaza Hotel. When they reached the corner of 59th and Fifth Avenue, he led a stumbling Paris through the oncoming traffic like a star running back navigating his way through an opponent's defensive line. The sound of tires screeching and horns blaring echoed off the buildings adjacent to the park. He could feel her try to pull her arm free with every move they made. Once they were safely across, he hurried them around the long line of horse-drawn carriages that lined Central Park South. He glanced over his shoulder at Paris. She was white as a ghost and gasped when she nearly stepped into a large pile of steaming horse manure.

Panting and out of breath, she stopped dead in her tracks. "I think I'm going to barf."

Darius frantically looked around them for a secluded area, void of any cameras. He noticed a busted surveillance camera dangling from a pole near some trees. When he felt Paris try to pull her hand free, he tightened his grip and pulled her into the wooded area.

"We'll be safe here," he said and let go of her hand.

"Safe from what?" She looked almost afraid of him as she pushed her hair out of her face.

"From them!"

"From who?" She wiped hard at her nose. "Darius! What *the hell* is going on?"

"I'm not sure. All I know is that they need to talk to me."

"*They!*" she said, jamming her hands on her hips and tilting her head to the side. "Need to talk to you." She was nodding her head up and down. "About what?"

"About what I know."

"About what you know?" Her lips were pursed and she was still nodding. "What do you know, Darius?"

He thought she sounded sarcastic. "Everything."

Her brows were wrinkled and her nose scrunched up as she shook her head back and forth. "Are you high?"

He turned out his hands. "Why would you say that?"

"You're not making any sense. For Christ's sake, Darius, you almost killed us crossing the street back there!"

"Keep your voice down," he said in a loud whisper. "I had to make sure we lost them."

She brought her hands up to her face and rested her thumbs on her cheeks, and her fingers on her forehead. "What . . . the hell . . . is going . . . on?"

He looked around to see if anyone was watching them. When he was sure they were alone, he hunched up his shoulders, shoved his hands into his pants pockets, and looked deep into her eyes. "I had the craziest dream last night about the three Pyramids of Giza and Stonehenge."

"This is all about some dream you had?" She had moved her hands to the sides of her head.

"Yeah," he said. She was shaking her head back and forth, "but it wasn't like any other dream I've ever had."

Paris dropped her hands to her sides and moved toward him. "How was it different?"

"It's hard to explain," he said. "It just felt so real. Then I heard about the comet, Goliath, and what happened at Stonehenge and—*I did* see the comet explode in the bar last night. I know it sounds strange but I feel as if I have to go to the pyramids."

"Darius! I want you to listen to me very carefully." She pressed her fingertips against her forehead as she studied the ground. "It was just a dream. You are not going to the pyramids."

Darius began pacing back and forth in front of her. Then he moved forward and placed his hands on top of her shoulders.

"Paris, I was really there. You have to believe me!"

"Darius, listen to me," she said, resting her hands on his cheeks. "It was all a delusional dream."

Maybe they were using her to get to him. He moved his hands up around her face and squeezed it. "Is that what they told you to tell me?"

"Let go," she cried. "You're hurting me!"

"What else did they tell you?" He squeezed her face a bit harder.

"Darius, please stop hurting me!"

"Only if you tell me the truth."

"Okay, I am working with them, but they only want to help you." She tried to pull his hands away from her face.

"I knew it. Why do they want to help me?"

"They didn't say. All they asked me to do is take you to the Madison Café for lunch. There, they will contact you."

Darius released his grip and lovingly put his arm around her shoulder. "I'm sorry," he said, "it's my fault you're involved in this. Anyway, what am I supposed to do when we get there?"

"You are to order a bottle of Santa Margherita Pinot Grigio and the most expensive dish on the menu. After you pay the bill and the waiter says the code words 'THANK YOU,' we may leave."

Darius thought for a moment. "These are the Rebels, Resistance, right?"

"Yes. They only want to help you."

Darius smiled and grabbed her hand. "C'mon we mustn't keep our guests waiting," he said, and pulled her in the direction of the restaurant.

"What do they look like anyway?"

"They *never* show themselves."

"Did they tell you the location of the Rebel base?"

"No," she whispered.

He glanced over his shoulder to see if he could spot anyone following them. When he didn't see anyone suspicious, he looked back at her. "How do they contact you?"

"They text message me. And you?"

Darius grinned. "They use mental telepathy and talk to me in my dreams. I'm far more advanced than most people."

They exited the park on 66th and Fifth Avenue and he hurried them down the block to Madison. When they reached the café, Darius glanced over his shoulder one last time and then pulled her inside.

▲ ▲ ▲

The trendy bistro, frequented by celebrities and models, had been one of Darius's favorite hangouts before he got involved with Paris. He would often sit at a table outside when the weather was nice and people watch. But today was a gloomy day and there were no tables outside.

"Good afternoon, Miss Templar," the maître d' said in a strong Italian accent.

"Alberto? You work here now?"

"Sí," the man said, stepping out from behind the maître d' stand. He gave Paris a big hug and kissed her on both cheeks.

"So good to see you. Table for two?" He looked at Darius with arched brows.

"Oh, excuse me," Paris said. "Alberto, this is my boyfriend, Darius."

Alberto stuck out his hand. "Nice to meet you, Mr. Darius."

"Prince," Darius said. When the maître d' nodded in agreement, Darius shook his hand and held it. He looked at the full-length mahogany bar to his right and scanned the dining room in front of him. "Are they here yet?"

Paris's eyes widened.

"Are you expecting more people?" Alberto asked.

Paris laughed. "Excuse me. I have to go freshen up."

When Paris was out of sight, he let go of Alberto's hand and put his arm around the man's shoulder and grinned. "I am expecting a lot of people. I'll need a table for about twenty."

Alberto snapped his fingers and three waiters appeared. "Push the tables in the middle of the dining room together and set them for a party of twenty," he said and clapped his hands twice.

Darius noticed a young couple walk in and sit down at the bar. "On second thought," he said, "there might be more than twenty. You better make it for more like—"

"Thirty?"

Darius smiled. "You read my mind."

"Let's just say it's a gift. There will be no problem accommodating thirty people."

"Can you put a bottle of Santa Margherita Pinot Grigio at the head of the table?"

"Right away."

Darius watched the maître d' disappear into the kitchen. He looked around the dining room at the few tables occupied by young couples and wondered which of the patrons, if any, were there to spy on him. How could he distinguish between the patrons, the Evil Ones, and the Rebels he was there to rendezvous with?

He shifted his attention to the flat screen mounted above the bar and everything became clear. They were a lot smarter than he originally thought. They were monitoring him through the eye-shaped logo on the bottom right of the television.

The maître d' returned. "Right this way, Mr. Darius." He led Darius to the monstrosity of a table and pulled a chair out for him. "A table fit for a king."

"Prince," Darius replied with a hint of annoyance as Paris walked toward them.

"Yes, sir," the maître d' said, seating Paris to his right.

When Alberto left the table, Darius lifted his glass of wine and turned to Paris. "Anyhoo," he said, mimicking Paris with a short sinister laugh, "now all I have to do is order the most expensive dish on the menu. I guess they want to see if I can follow orders. By the way, I already met one of them."

Paris looked around the room. "You did? Who?" She picked up her glass of wine and took an unusually large sip.

Darius waved his hand in the air for Alberto to come back to the table.

"Yes, Mr. Prince?"

Darius didn't say a word. He just sat there looking at the maître d'.

"Mr. Prince, what can I get you," he said, glancing sideways at Paris as he refreshed their glasses.

Darius noticed the little glance, but decided to let it slide. "Alberto, you know what I want. It's alright, she's one of us. She just hasn't learned how to use her ESP yet," he said, smiling. "Now, I'm going to think really hard about what I want to eat and I want you to tell me what it is."

Darius concentrated on the menu Paris was holding in front of her face and then focused his attention back to Alberto, who pressed his two index fingers against his temples.

"You want the . . . Kobe steak."

"See, Paris, he, too, has the power." Darius looked up at the maître d' and smiled. "Please provide us with two orders."

Alberto looked at him for a long moment, but he didn't actually return Darius's smile. "Excellent choice," he said and rushed off toward the bar.

"Darius, when I was in the bathroom they sent me another text message."

"They did?" He set his wine glass down on the table and leaned toward her.

"*They* won't be joining us. We're to move to a table for two immediately."

"Alberto," Darius said snapping his fingers, "get over here."

Alberto rushed over. "Yes, Mr. Prince."

"I apologize, but I was just informed that my party will not be joining us. Can you please move us to a table for two?"

Alberto's eyes opened wide.

"I'm so sorry Alberto," Paris said. "I promise I'll make it up to you."

"Right this way." He led them to a small table opposite the bar.

When Paris sat down facing him, he glanced at the couple seated at the bar and then looked at the flat screen above their heads. "I've got it all figured out," he whispered.

"That's nice, honey."

Darius saw her look about the area where they were seated. She seemed a bit edgy, maybe even a little paranoid, he thought. For the next hour, he barely said a word and didn't even touch his steak. He had first to arrange the glasses and silverware in symmetrical patterns around his plate. But he couldn't get the arrangement right. What were they up to, he wondered and winked at the television.

"Did you just wink at the television?"

Darius winked at Paris and then winked at the TV again. "They're observing us through the 'ALL SEEING EYE' on the TV." When Paris turned to look, he reached across the table and lightly touched her hand.

Paris focused her attention back to Darius and shook her head. "You think the CBS logo is a camera?"

"Shh!" he said, watching Paris wave her hand in the air for Alberto. He didn't want them to know that he knew how they were monitoring them.

The maître d' returned to their table. "Mr. Prince, you haven't touched your meal. Can I get you something else?"

"No. I just lost my appetite."

"Would you like me to wrap it up for you?"

"Nah, give it to the poor," Darius said and completed a pyramid with his utensils.

"Can I get you something else? Cappuccino? Espresso?"

"No," Paris said. "That will be all." She handed Alberto one of her many credit cards. "I'm paying for this one in more ways than you can *ever* imagine."

When Alberto returned with the bill, Paris signed it and handed it back to him. Darius noticed a huge smile appear on his face.

"Grazie," the maître d' said.

Darius remained seated.

Paris laughed, "Alberto, what does grazie mean in English?"

"Thank you."

Darius jumped to his feet, and said, "Let's go." He grabbed her by the hand and wondered when the Rebels would try to contact him next.

CHAPTER 21

"PROPHECY IS FORTUNE telling." Mohammed stared at the life-size holographic image of President Ramsey standing in the middle of his office. The president was dressed in a white linen suit and head cover.

"Perhaps, but when the ink on the papyrus was carbon dated, the results showed that it was just over twelve thousand years old."

"Your faith is being tested," Mohammed said.

"I beg to differ. The only reason my family believed in it was because it clearly mentioned Islam."

Mohammed raised an eyebrow. "Why was I not told of this historical document sooner?"

"I had to be sure. Now that the first two parts of the prophecy have come true, I am positive the Zoroastrian exists."

Mohammed paused. "What other religions were mentioned?"

"None. A hexagram appears at the beginning of the prophecy, but there's no mention of Judaism anywhere."

"The hexagram's not a Jewish symbol." This document contained the proof he needed to finally end the controversy regarding the sons of Abraham, Ishmael and Isaac. Arab Muslims traced their lineage back to Abraham through Ishmael. If Allah revealed himself to the Pagans of that time period, then he had a very strong case that Islam predated Judaism. He could then argue that the father of Islam, Ishmael, clearly had the right to rule, not Isaac.

"Good work, Ramsey. This is the proof I need to show once and for all that Abraham's covenant with God was about Ishmael's descendants, not Isaac's. I need to see this document at once. Encrypt it and send it to me."

"If I do that, will you help me find the Zoroastrian?"

"I'll make a few calls. If he exists, I'll get you a name. From now on you are to refer to the prophecy as a historical document. Who else knows of it?"

"My brother-in-law, Raj, and the Ghostriders. I believe the Ghostriders are an alias for the Amazons."

"Amazons?"

"Yes. And it's quite possible they already have the Chosen One. I also believe that they are responsible for the deaths of the three religious leaders in Babylon."

Mohammed leveled a condemning stare. "When I find out the true identities of these Amazons, they will pay dearly for their crime. In the meantime, ensure Raj's silence," he said. "We don't want word of this getting out until the time is right."

"I understand," Ramsey said. "Are there any new developments at Stonehenge?"

"No. Our scientists still can't penetrate the magnetic field. I must go now," he said, "I have just been informed that President Walker will finally be coming to Iran. I'll be in touch." The hologram disappeared.

Zadam cracked his knuckles. "The Jews must pay for their insolence."

CHAPTER 22

"**A** NOTHER DREAM?"

Darius sat up and wiped the sweat from his forehead. He took a few deep breaths and glanced at the alarm clock on his night stand. It was 3:36 in the morning.

"What day is it?"

Paris yawned. "Monday."

Darius paused, rubbing his brows and staring at the three nude models and goddesses trapped in the painting in front of him. "My dream was more like a nightmare. The Devil appeared and turned into a baby—right before my eyes."

Paris moved behind him and started caressing his shoulders. "You need to see a shrink."

"Then, a group of heavily armed women picked up the baby and suckled it. It was like witnessing the birth of the Antichrist." He dropped his arm onto the bed and stared up at the ceiling. After an awkward moment or two of silence, he felt safe to tell her the rest of the dream. "When the women took the baby away," he said excitedly, "I saw myself on a white horse leading millions across the desert into battle."

Darius could hear Paris sigh.

"You should take the day off and see my psychic. She's excellent at interpreting dreams."

He got out of bed and looked at her. "Are you crazy? I can't afford to miss a day of work."

"She might be able to help you."

Darius felt the veins in his neck bulge. "What can she possibly tell me that I don't already know?"

"You'd be surprised. She's helped thousands of people."

"You don't listen, do you? For the last time, this has something to do with that damn comet," he said and lunged toward her.

She raised her hands in defense. "Don't touch me."

He grabbed her wrists and shook her. "This is real," he said sternly. "You have to believe me."

"Take your hands off of me," she shouted.

What had gotten in to him, he thought. He looked into her eyes as she tried to free herself. Suddenly, he realized he was hurting her and let her go. She smacked him hard across the face and scrambled out of bed and ran into the bathroom.

He tried to apologize but she slammed the door in his face. "I'm sorry sweetheart. Please come out."

"You need to get help."

Maybe this was a blessing in disguise. She'd be much safer if the Evil Ones thought he didn't care about her anymore. This way they wouldn't be able to use her against him. "Paris, I think we need some time apart," he said and turned away from the door. When he heard the door open, he turned and faced her.

"I can't do that," she said, "I love you. But you really do need to get some help."

"Oh, no, no, no, I don't need anyone," he said, his tone almost jovial, "especially you."

"If you're not gonna get help, I'm going to get it for you." She grabbed the comforter off the bed and draped it around her and walked to the door. "I'm sleeping on the sofa."

For the next three hours he stared at the goddesses in the painting and thought about the comet. When his eyes finally closed, he heard the front door slam.

One day she'll understand.

▼ ▲ ▼

Darius charged into his office overlooking the Hudson River. "Lock door," he said. He looked over at Norman sitting at his desk staring at his computer screen. He looked edgy, nervous.

"Solofōn halted trading in the pre-market and GE-Joe called three times looking for you," Norman said without looking up from his computer screen. "He wants to know if he should unload his shares or average down when it resumes trading."

"Don't frown, average down," Darius said and scooted through the gap that separated their two desks. Nestled in the corner of two plate glass windows with views to the south and west, he leaned over his chair and booted up his computer. He closed the aluminum micro-blinds and sat down.

Norman finished entering their buy and sell orders. "You better get your head out of your ass and call GE-Joe now!"

Darius ignored him and, instead, stared at the digital picture frame sitting on his desk. In the picture, GE-Joe stood with one arm around him and the other around Mike.

GE-Joe was what brokers termed a whale. His real name was Sy Kurtz but he preferred to be called Joe after the late great Yankee, Joe DiMaggio. The fifty-six-year-old Israeli-born New Yorker had opened up an account with Darius on a thousand shares of General Electric stock during his rookie year. When he asked Sy who referred him, he said he was an old friend of his father's. Since Darius was a rookie at the time, the branch manager made him share the account with Mike.

Born under the sun sign Libra, Joe was the type of guy who always picked up the check so he wouldn't feel obligated to anyone. When he wasn't actively trading his account, he was usually on a conference call with Darius torturing the investor relations people at the companies he was down on. Even if the stock was down less than one percent, the investor contact still got an earful from Joe on how to run the company.

"Norm, I need to talk to you," Darius said, looking under his desk.

"Bro, what are you doing? Why'd you close the shades?"

"I'm looking for bugs, and whatever you do, don't put on channel two," he whispered.

Norman stood up. He walked over to Darius. "Are we being investigated?"

Darius lifted up the Tiffany lamp on his desk and inspected the stained glass shade. "They're after me because I've got it all figured out."

"The SEC?"

"No," he said as he yanked open his desk drawers.

"Then what the hell are you talking about? Who the hell are *they* and *what* have you figured out?" Norm said, waving his hand around as he sat down on the corner of his desk.

"*They?* They're the people who control the world from behind the scenes. They're highly advanced and speak to me telepathically through my dreams." He rifled through his desk drawers a second and third time. When he didn't find any hidden microphones, he stopped and looked up at his partner.

"Norman! There's something going on at the pyramids and Stonehenge, and I'm the only one who knows about it. They . . . are trying to find out what I know so they can stop me from saving the world."

Norman jumped to his feet. He put his hand up in a defensive position. "Whoa, guy! You're freaking me out. What's wrong with you," he said and took a few steps back.

"What makes you think something's wrong with me?" he said, slapping his palms on the top of his desk and throwing his head back. "I feel great!"

Norman shook his head. He jiggled the change in his left pocket and ran his other hand through his hair several times. "I should've never given you that vial of endorphinate powder. You need'a go home and sleep it off," he said and picked up the baseball encyclopedia sitting on his desk. "Don't worry, I'll take good care of the accounts."

"You bought that book so you could steal GE-Joe from me."

"Bro—that shit's messing with your head."

"I'm not on drugs. It's that damn comet." Darius thought for a moment. His eyes widened. "Don't tell me they got to you, too. How much did they offer you," he sneered, "how much?"

"I think I should call Paris."

"Now I get it." Darius stood up from his desk so fast his chair tipped over. He put his hands on his hips and scrunched up his face. "Admit it. You've been screwing Paris behind my back. Well, we're not together anymore." He leaned forward over his desk. He pointed his right index finger at his partner and jabbed the air. "So, you can tell your people," jab, "they won't," jab, "be able," jab, "to use her against me," he said with one final jab. Norm had his hands up in front of his chest and he slowly backed up as Darius kicked his way out from behind his desk and stormed out of the office.

Was there no end to Norman's shame? At least Mike was still on his side. Or was he?

He needed to formulate a plan—and fast. He stopped and sat down at an empty cubicle in the cold-caller's section of the boardroom. For the rest of the day, he listened to the neophytes qualify presidents and CEOs of Fortune 500 companies; occasionally poking his head up to see if Mike or Ixchel were looking for him. Had they sold out as well?

Everyone at the firm now seemed suspect—especially the cold-callers who were right then staring at him. Every time he stood up, they would whisper to one another and then laugh. He couldn't trust anyone until he could figure out who the Rebels were. And that wasn't going to be easy, he thought, as he anxiously waited for Wall Street's closing bell to sound.

▲ ▼ ▲

When Darius arrived at his apartment he draped his suit coat over a dining room chair, loosened his collar and tie, and dove onto the comfy leather sofa that seemed to swallow him whole. He looked at the seventy-two-inch flat screen hanging on the wall in front of him.

"Computer, load *Braveheart*," he said and kicked off his wingtips. He pulled the white comforter Paris had left on the couch over him and watched the trailer for the classic film *Highlander*. When the swashbuckling highlander, Connor MacLeod, cut off the Russian highlander's head and said, "There can only be one," Darius's Solofōn rang. It was GE-Joe. He sent the call to voice mail and nodded off to sleep.

A smiling teenage girl with strawberry blonde hair appeared in his dream. Dressed in shorts and a t-shirt, her long curly hair glistened in the sunlight. She took him by the hand and led him through a white marble city with streets paved in gold.

Romanesque buildings lined the ancient city streets. He could actually feel the warmth of the sun on his face and, for a moment, he even felt a light pulse in her tender young hand. Suddenly a large marble column, thirty feet tall and six feet in diameter, fell toward them. He scooped up the girl and ran forward, narrowly avoiding disaster as he heard the column shatter on the street behind them.

When he put the girl down, she took him by the hand again and walked him down the street into a dense fog. Wandering through the cool mist, he felt the street turn to sand. The fog dissipated and he was astonished to find himself standing in front of the Great Pyramids of Giza shimmering under the hot desert sun. The young girl pointed to the smallest pyramid, and said, "Father, fulfill your destiny."

CHAPTER 23

T HE LIMO SPED off from the hotel on Half Moon Street in the heart of London. The once capital of the largest imperialistic empire in history regained its title when it was named the capital of the Eurasian Union.

As the paparazzi roared off in hot pursuit of Roxanne, armed with a wide range of telephoto lenses, a Catholic priest dressed in a red hooded cloak emerged from the hotel lobby. He was accompanied by an old bearded rabbi wearing a formal black robe and brimmed hat, and a young Islamic cleric dressed in a creamy white wool gown. Standing between them, the Catholic priest tilted his head back and looked up at the overcast sky.

"It always looks like rain in this country," he said and walked the spiritual leaders away from the remaining reporters. A young female reporter emerged from a van with her cameraman and headed toward them. The priest tried to cross the street but the dark-haired reporter shadowed him like she would follow him to the ends of the earth until he gave her a story. The priest did not want to make a scene. He raised his hand and motioned for his colleagues to stop. He took a deep breath and turned to the reporter with a forced smile. "Can I help you, Miss?"

"Yes, Father," she said in a heavy Manchester accent. "I missed my opportunity to interview the lovely Roxanne, and if I don't return with a story my superiors are going to have my head. Do you mind if I have a word with you?"

"Of course not." He smiled for the camera. "I am Father Simetra."

"Thank you, Father. You have no idea what it takes to get ahead in a man's world nowadays." She held the microphone up to his face. "Father Simetra, can you comment on the recent attacks on the religious leaders in Babylon?"

He handed his white leather Bible to the rabbi. "The tragedy has shown us the error of our ways," he said in a soft Italian accent. "Unless men wake up and recognize that religion was developed by men to control the masses, especially women, religion is destined for failure."

He glanced at the Islamic cleric to his right who nodded in agreement and looked back into the camera. "The days of a male-dominated patriarchal society are quickly coming to an end. If we don't respond to the cries of our sisters all over the world, they will unite and the biggest intifada the world has ever seen will occur. The balance of power between men and women will shift and a matriarchal society will reign supreme."

"Are you saying that the incident in Babylon was just a warning shot?"

"On the contrary, the revolution is well underway. Unfortunately for you, it is not being televised."

He glanced at his watch. "Would you look at the time," he said, looking back to the reporter. "We must be on our way."

"But I still have a few more—"

The rabbi cupped his hand over the microphone. "We're finished here," he said in a deep Russian accent, his English slightly broken. He gently lowered his hand. "No more questions."

Father Simetra reclaimed his Bible and led the spiritual leaders down the street. After several blocks, he stopped in front of a British pub. Three tall women—a blonde, brunette and redhead—stood blocking the door. All three women wore mirrored sunglasses. Each sported a blue denim jacket and a tight black leather skirt. Soft black leather boots were laced up to their knees; the heels of the boots stood at least three inches high.

"This looks like a nice place to eat," the good Father said and walked up to the women.

"Pardon me, ladies," he said loudly, and tried to move past them.

The muscular short-haired blonde standing in the middle put out her arm to stop him. He stopped and looked into her reflective lenses.

"Beat it you wanker," she said in a heavy Scottish accent. "This meeting is for members only."

"Meeting?" He paused and stared at the women. "Members?"

"Get lost, old man. I won't tell you again." The blonde turned her head, nodded to the redhead, and then turned and gave a quick nod to the brunette on her right.

Father Simetra took a menacing step forward and got in her face. "Blow me, bitch," he said. When the other two women started laughing and heckling their comrade, she turned red with anger.

"Out of my way," he said, trying to push his way past. The blonde pulled out a silver nine-millimeter and aimed it at his cloaked head. He froze and the women surrounded him. Staring down the barrel of the loaded gun, he slowly raised his hands in the air and took a step back.

"My child, you would kill a man of God?"

"I'd kill any man," she said. "Take off your hood."

He looked into her reflective lenses again to be sure there was no one behind him and dropped the Bible.

"How careless of me."

The blonde glanced at the Bible, and in that instant he triggered a mechanism that jettisoned guns down his sleeves and into his hands. Before she could focus her eyes back on him, he fired. He watched the blood trickle down her forehead as her now lifeless body fell to the ground. When the other two women reached for their weapons, he spread his arms and aimed the guns at both their heads.

"Sloppy, very sloppy," Father Simetra said as the Rabbi dragged the dead body into the pub. He nodded to the Islamic cleric who ripped off his mask.

The two women jumped to attention.

Father Simetra handed Roxanne his guns and reached under his neck. He ripped off his mask and tossed it to the ground by their feet.

"All hail, Queen Artemis," Roxanne hissed.

The two women dropped to their knees. Artemis unclasped her long blonde hair and let it hang free. She looked down at her incompetent subjects shaking in fear. "I should kill you both. You put our entire operation in jeopardy." She kicked the Bible and stared at Roxanne, who was shaking her head in what seemed to be disgust.

Artemis thought for a moment. It was a good thing she decided to test them. If she was going to rule the world, she needed to be absolutely sure her Amazon warriors were properly trained and prepared for anything. Now, she would see to this herself.

"Roxanne. You were in charge of security; I'm holding you personally responsible for this breach."

Roxanne turned and faced her. "You didn't have to kill her. You're the only one who could have gotten past them, and you know it." She turned back toward the two women who were still on their knees. "Stand up."

Artemis stepped toward the women. "Meeting . . . for members only?" she said, looking them over. "You never ever reveal our business to anyone," she shouted. "Anyone! That's why your comrade is dead. Do we understand one another?"

They nodded and in unison said, "Yes, Your Highness."

"Now clean up this mess and kill anyone who tries to enter the pub."

Artemis led Roxanne through the traditional dining room lined with armed women wearing panther skin capes. When she reached the bathroom, Artemis moved toward a young dark-haired Amazon, dressed in a short leopard skin tunic, standing guard outside it. Artemis smiled openly at the girl and looked her up and down. She let her eyes linger on her where they wanted.

"What is your name?" Artemis said, admiring her streamlined physique.

"You're Highness," Roxanne hissed, "we need to talk."

Artemis ignored her and moved closer to the mocha-skinned beauty. Roxanne moved over and stood next to the girl facing Artemis. She continued to ignore her and, to add insult to injury, she touched the girl's lips with her finger.

"Tell me your name."

Roxanne interrupted. "*My Queen*, may I have a word with you in private."

"I have a better idea," Artemis said without looking at her. "Why don't you make sure the building is secure while this sexy fraulein helps me off with these hideous clothes?" She shot Roxanne a sly grin and licked her lips.

When Bellatrix emerged from the bathroom dressed in a leopard skin tunic and holding her rabbi costume, Artemis smacked the girl's tight ass. She looked at Roxanne as she pushed the young girl into the bathroom. "I will not tolerate any more mistakes." she said and slammed the door shut.

CHAPTER 24

D ARIUS SAT UP in bed. He noticed Paris's side of the bed hadn't been slept in. She must have stayed at her place, he thought, and stared at the three goddesses watching over him from behind their protective glass frame. He yawned, stretched his long arms behind his aching head, and thought about the young girl in his dream.

Father, fulfill your destiny? Was his aborted daughter reaching out to him from beyond the grave?

The nude backs of the three models facing him made him feel as though he was being ignored. Darius rolled over and reached under his bed. He pulled the brown leather attaché case out from under it and placed it in front of him. He sat up Indian style and wiped away a thin layer of dust that had accumulated on the case over the last six months. His hands trembled as he clicked open the case and laid his eyes on its contents for the first time. While thumbing through the news clippings and black and white photos of his father's prize-winning bodybuilding poses, he felt his heartbeat quicken.

The articles traced his father's amazing journey—from the jungles of India to the Himalayan mountaintops, from the Hippodrome in London to famous meetings in Hollywood, and back again to the jungle; but this time, the concrete jungle of New York City.

He picked up a news clipping and stared at the bold black headline dated May 1934.

British Apollo Lands In Hollywood.

They called his father a god? With hungry eyes, he read through the article. When he finished, he dropped it into the case and looked up.

Something wasn't right.

Why wasn't he ever told that his father had the exact same measurements as the Apollo Belvedere Statue? Was it a coincidence that a replica of the statue just so happened to be erected in the lobby of his building the same day he moved in?

Darius stared at the goddesses. If they referred to his father as a god, then what did that make him?

He smiled. Of course. *He was the Son of Apollo.*

A gusty breeze from the open window whipped through the room and interrupted his thoughts. He slammed the case shut and watched a stack of bank statements flutter off his dresser and fly around the room.

Was his father reaching out to him as well?

Watching the papers mysteriously twirl around and around his head, his eyelids grew heavy. He glanced at the alarm clock on his nightstand and saw that it was almost nine o'clock. Suddenly, the wind stopped and the papers fell around him. He reached out and picked up a statement that landed on the attaché case. The thick black letters at the top of the statement read JPMorgan Chase and Company. The alarm clock went off, startling him, and filled the room with music.

When he heard the ethereal psychedelic sound of the Rush song, *Tom Sawyer,* a warm feeling overcame him. He laid back down, closed his eyes, and listened to the opening verse. *A modern-day warrior . . . mean mean stride . . . today's Tom Sawyer . . . mean mean pride.* Glorious battle images flooded his mind.

Surrounded by clouds and a light mist that felt good upon his face, he saw himself standing on the lush green mountains of the Scottish Highlands wielding a sword high above his head. As the sun rose above a rocky peak, far off in the distance, he saw what appeared to be a large bird emerge from behind it and fly toward him. Tilting his head back, he stared at the ancient sword, forged when the world was young and the elements were pure. When the sun's rays struck its razor-sharp tip, a hot flash spread through his body like a wild fire through dry brush.

As he listened to the synchronicity of the mesmerizing medley of notes, he felt as if he were one with the universe.

The Angels are communicating with me through music.

As the angelic notes reigned down upon him, his mind raced and everything became clear. He wasn't a modern-day warrior. *He was a living god.*

Relishing the moment, he watched the bird start its descent. No sooner had it begun than he realized that it wasn't a bird at all but the archangel, Michael, coming down from heaven to greet him. A wave of euphoria overcame him at the thought of knowing that he would soon learn the secrets to the unsolved mysteries of creation. The moment he lowered his sword, Michael's angelic wings turned black and folded out. Darius's eyes widened and his body tensed as he watched the angel transform into a dragon and fly toward him. He stared into the reptilian beast's cold yellow eyes as black smoke spewed from its nostrils. Its scaly dark-green body and long tail cast a huge shadow over the mountainside. He reared his sword back and waited for the dragon to attack. Gnashing its razor-sharp teeth, it swooped down on him.

When he heard the loud car horn intro of the Van Halen song, *Runnin' With The Devil,* blast through the airwaves, he swung the sword with all his might. A cataclysmic explosion echoed throughout the mountaintops, followed by an intense fire with plumes of smoke that mushroomed high into the sky, as if a nuclear warhead had just been detonated.

The electrifying guitar chords ripped through his mind as he listened to the chorus sing, *Runnin' with the Devil.* His t-shirt was soaked with sweat, plastered to his chest. Then, it dawned on him. The Devil wanted *him* to run with him. He ripped the alarm clock out of the wall. The room fell silent.

"Christ is my King," he shouted and threw the clock at the painting, shattering the glass that imprisoned the goddesses. He gasped as it fell to the ground.

The goddesses were free.

He looked at the bank statement again and studied it for a moment. Were the goddesses telling him to check out JPMorgan Chase and Company? That had to be it, he thought. The brick-and-mortar bank controlled trillions of dollars worldwide. He felt no remorse for the people who controlled the bank's money from behind the scenes now that the goddesses were free. The money lenders were finally going to get what they deserved, with interest. His mind seemed to race faster than racecars on the final lap of the Daytona 500. He thought about the effect the first song had had on him, and realized that he had made a terrible mistake.

It was all an illusion.

The angels who played the first hypnotic song weren't good at all. They were evil. They must have manipulated his thinking with every musical note.

That's why he felt immortal.

When the Rebels realized what was going on, they snapped him out of his trance by using a song that referenced the Devil. Brilliant, he thought. They did this to show him that the Evil Ones would do anything, even masquerade as good, to try and turn him to their side.

If they hadn't come to his rescue, he might have disclosed everything. Now, more than ever, he had to remember to keep up his guard. They were capable of anything—he couldn't afford to make the same mistake twice. One thing was certain: both sides wanted him and could use different modes of communication to reach him. He thought back to the little girl in his dream and wondered what kind of father he would have been.

Would he have learned from his father's mistakes or would he have followed in his footsteps and inflicted the same cold and distant cruelty on his own child that his father had on him? His mind seemed to race even faster.

What if one of his ex-girlfriends had been pregnant when they broke up and had secretly had the child without telling him? Would the confused child one day show up on his doorstep and demand to know why he had abandoned her? What would he do? What would he say?

What if he had fathered a child during one of his drunken stupors that resulted in a one-night stand? If the child showed up at his doorstep, would he see a part of himself in the child's innocent face? If he did, would he be so overwhelmed with guilt that his first reaction would be to deny even the possibility and send the child away?

What if the girl in his dream *was* his daughter? What could he ever do or say to make it up to his child, who was a blameless victim of his lust? What if he did turn his child away and she grew up to be a beautiful young woman? Would she use his lust to inflict the same pain on him, perhaps by deceptively picking him up in a bar and then sleeping with him several times before telling him that she was his daughter? Could he even begin to imagine the pain she had endured all of those lost years?

Could the unborn child he sentenced to death eleven years ago ever forgive him? His excuse being that he was too young and the timing wasn't right. The truth was, even if she did forgive him, he could never forgive himself.

What's gotten in to me?

Why, for the first time in his life, was he so concerned with all this? Maybe God was getting even with him for his infidelities. Had he been so self-centered that he failed to care about anybody else but himself?

Maybe all he had to do was accept the fact that he was not guilty. After all, how could he be if Jesus had already died for his sins? Did the church forget about that minor detail purposely so they could scare the masses into submission? The thought of mankind killing the Son of God saddened him.

Could he ever find the courage to change?

Common wisdom held that one person couldn't make a difference, but he always felt the need to prove that theory wrong. He had to go about this alone; as if he were an Olympian training for the gold, and do what he thought was right for a change, even if the others didn't exactly understand what he was doing.

For the sake of the collective, he had to make a difference.

He got out of bed and walked over to his bedroom closet. He reached into his olive suit coat and removed the Byzantine chain his father had asked Laura to give to him. He stared at it a moment and then placed it around his neck. In a sudden feeling of rushed frenzy, he put on his white dress shirt and tie, selected a pair of blue suit pants, shoved his legs in, and then whipped the trousers up around his waist. He grabbed a pair of socks and a belt and put them on. He couldn't be sure what color the socks and belt were but he picked out a pair of brown wing-tipped dress shoes and put on his olive suit coat to finish off his ensemble. Perfect, he thought. He grabbed a handful of change and the bank statement off of the dresser, trotted downstairs and out the door.

CHAPTER 25

"**I** HOPE YOU'RE SATISFIED."

Artemis turned. Roxanne marched into the dining room wearing a short leopard skin tunic with one breast exposed. When she reached the round table in the center of the room, she placed her hands on her hips. Artemis despised her manipulative tactics but thought it funny her dear Roxanne expected an apology from her. Artemis looked around the heavily guarded room. "Satisfaction will get you killed."

Roxanne sat down across from her. "Your Highness," she purred. "I'm worried about you. I think the comet is having an effect on you too." She reached for her hand. "One minute you're full of love and the next, rage."

Artemis pulled her hand away before she could touch it. She scoffed. "You need to think more with your mind and less with your heart."

"I gave you my heart and soul. But not out of fear like the rest of your subjects," she hissed. "I did it out of respect. When I pledged my loyalty to you, it was undying, forever."

Bellatrix wheeled the dining cart over to their table and stood at attention in her leopard skin tunic. Artemis placed her napkin on her lap, over the bottom half of her two piece gold girdle, and looked at Roxanne. "That's the only reason you're not downstairs with the rest of the stiffs," she said and adjusted the sacred leather belt that hung diagonally across her chest.

The china and silverware rattled as Roxanne pushed her chair back and stood up. She placed her hands on the table and leaned forward. "If I recall," she said in a hushed tone, "I was the one who supplied you with the missing component necessary to form the Amazon alliance with Lucifer. Before that, only you were guaranteed a place in the new kingdom. Now, we all are."

Roxanne said this with a smile, but Artemis knew she meant it. Her comment was rife with insinuation and suggestiveness, but she purposely said it softly enough so no one else could hear.

"Perhaps the next time you feel the need to humiliate me before our subjects," Roxanne said louder so everyone could hear, "you will think twice."

"Sit down, Roxanne. And don't ever raise your voice to me in front of *my* subjects again," she said. "Is that clear?"

"Crystal," she said, shrugging her shoulders with indifference. She sat back down and pulled her chair back to the table.

"And how many times must I remind you that our divine leader's name is Lucy, not Lucifer."

Once again, Roxanne shrugged her shoulders with indifference.

When Bellatrix placed a domed silver serving tray in the middle of the table, Artemis smiled lovingly and motioned for Bellatrix to remove the lid. Artemis grinned with a sense of satisfaction as Roxanne gasped at the sight of the Spanish girl's head sitting in a thin pool of congealed blood. The moment Roxanne looked up, Artemis nodded and tilted her wine glass in a silent toast. She enjoyed watching Roxanne recoil when she cast her eyes back down at the platter.

"I get it," Roxanne said. "You're *jealous* that I'm spending so much time with Zadam?"

Artemis chuckled softly as Bellatrix removed the platter from the table. She winked at her loyal general who palmed a dagger and stood behind Roxanne with her back against the wall.

Roxanne leaned forward. "Do you think I enjoy constantly being groped by him? His mere touch repulses me."

"Just making sure you don't get any funny ideas."

"Like decapitating an innocent young Amazon?" Roxanne said, looking Artemis straight in the face. "I'm not the one you should be worried about. If I remember correctly, the goddess Artemis is the defender of young women. Not the murderer of them."

Artemis gazed around the room. Her guards were looking at one another with nervous stares. "Everyone but Roxanne and Bellatrix out of the room. Now!" When the guards were gone, Artemis sighed and looked at Roxanne.

"You're right," Artemis said. She smiled at her lover. It was a nice smile— for once unguarded. "I am changing, but for the better. The goddess's soul inside me has finally awakened."

"On the contrary, my Queen, I believe there are other divine forces at work that are affecting you. Maybe they don't want to see Lucy upset the balance. She paused. "What if Lucy hasn't told you everything?"

Artemis saw Bellatrix slowly move toward Roxanne with the dagger in her hand. She stared at her beloved, contemplating her fate, and kept her face neutral. "What are you trying to say?"

"Maybe you never received the other half of the goddess Artemis's soul when your twin sister died and it was gifted to somebody else. Think about it," she said, leaning back in her chair. "If the goddess's soul was alive in you, do you think that she would have allowed you to kill that young Amazon without a good reason?"

Artemis paused. "Nonsense," she shouted. "I can feel her power flowing through my veins. I killed that girl to show the goddess that *I'm* in control."

"You're not in control and that's what scares me. Maybe you received more than you bargained for when the comet exploded. There may be other goddesses inside of you that we are not aware of."

Artemis thought about this for a moment. She let the idea sink in and then nodded to Bellatrix to put the dagger away and start serving the food. Once she finished serving them, she made a plate for herself and sat down.

"As usual, you are the voice of reason," Artemis said, looking across at Roxanne. "But, the only way to find out for sure is to wake up Lucy—and I am forbidden to do that." She looked up and gave Roxanne a smile. Big mistake. It was a lousy, soulless smile, and she knew Roxanne didn't buy it for a second.

"It's possible that Lucy has no idea what's going on either. That's why you *must* wake her."

"Mind your tongue," Artemis said, smiling. They began their meal. "At this point there is not enough evidence to warrant waking her. Maybe the Zoroastrian can shed some light on the situation."

"Right now he is suffering from dementia as his mind tries to interpret the information bestowed upon him by the comet."

Artemis dipped a piece of broccoli into a bowl of blue cheese dressing and crunched off the head. "We must use his weakness to our advantage. Find out what he knows before he realizes what's really going on."

"I'm already on it."

"Excellent. Is Zadam still under your control?"

"Yes. He actually believes he would make a better leader than his brother," she said with a laugh. "Trust me when I say that nothing will stand in the way of Operation Andromache. Nothing!"

"When the time comes, I will supply you with the necessary information to implement the final phase of our operation. You will need to gain access to the war room beneath Mohammed's palace in order to arm the satellites surrounding Jupiter and send them crashing into the gaseous giant," she said, crunching into another broccoli head. She smiled lovingly at Roxanne. "Once the planet ignites it will herald the coming of Lucy, the supreme mother goddess." A bittersweet laugh escaped her. "That is when you are to launch the nuclear strike on our selected targets."

Roxanne raised her glass in the air. "When that day comes, Lucy will ascend into heaven and reclaim her rightful throne. And you, my Queen, will have total control over the planet and all the men on it."

CHAPTER 26

"**Y**OU CAN'T BE serious."

Mohammed tilted his head back and stared at the middle-aged president. The African-American leader stood a little over six feet tall and had a boyish face. His short black hair was now slightly graying, which made him look more distinguished than when he first took office. He wasn't your typical looking president but then again, Walker was anything but typical. A brilliant thinker who spoke with the conviction of an evangelical minister, he was relentless in his crusade for peace. Despite their different cultural and religious beliefs, Mohammed and the American Union president were the anchors of the peace process.

"Please have a seat," the supreme leader said, motioning to two oversized chairs. After they sat down, Mohammed picked up a box of cigars from the table between them. "Cigar?"

The president raised his hand up in front of him as if to say no.

Mohammed placed the box of cigars back down. "Mr. President, I will not sign the peace treaty with your State of Israel. Your Israeli prime minister does not want peace."

The president crossed his legs. "That's absurd."

"Your special interest lobbyists have rendered your country a superpower for sale and the Israelis were the highest bidders. Now, they control you."

"I disagree," the president said. "Less than fifteen percent of the American Union's population is Jewish. I really don't see how they control anything."

"Don't patronize me," Mohammed said. "Less than one percent of your population controls ninety-nine percent of its wealth. Wealth is power. Numbers and statistics can be manipulated. More Jews live in New York City, or what I call New Jerusalem, than live in the entire state of Israel."

Mohammed watched President Walker reposition himself in the chair as if his pants were hiking up on him too much. He glanced furtively around the room until he had no choice but to look back at Mohammed. He could tell the president was uncomfortable and he had every reason to be. He had to strike now.

"Mr. President, wake up! They are using you, just like you are using the peace process as a platform for re-election. We don't have a problem with the Jews. They have a problem with the Muslims. That's why they refused to become part of the Eurasian Union and joined forces with you. While you were asleep at the wheel, Israel pulled your country right out from under you."

The president balked. "Did you expect Israel to just hand over their military? No questions asked?"

"It was a test," Mohammed said, "and they failed. They never wanted peace."

"What's really behind your sudden change in thought?"

"Let's just say that I have proof that God's covenant with Abraham was about Ishmael and not Isaac."

"And am I to assume that you are going to attempt to suggest that God promised Jerusalem to the Muslims?"

"Yes."

"This is turning into a war of cultures. You must put your religious differences aside and work out a plan for peace."

"So must you," Mohammed said. "Your middle name, Hussein, is a Muslim name. And in Arabic culture, under Islamic law, if your father is a Muslim, then so are you." He grinned with a sense of satisfaction. "Once a Muslim, always a Muslim."

"My religion is not the topic here."

"Where do you think all of those small contributions that helped you get elected came from?"

"You think you can buy me?"

Mohammed frowned. "By no means. But, we can ensure your re-election. You sold your country to the Jews for pennies on the dollar, Mr. President; we want you to help us keep ours."

"So how can we put an end to this conflict?"

"There is one way," Mohammed said and rose from his chair. He turned and looked at the map of the world on the wall in front of them. "Tell Chaim Soloman to pull out of Jerusalem and you shall have your peace."

The president slapped his hand down hard on the table. "Impossible! And how can you possibly prove that God's covenant with Abraham was about Ishmael and not Isaac?"

"You shall know soon enough."

"I will do everything in my power to defend Israel."

"Mark my words," Mohammed said staunchly. "Soloman will do everything in his power to undermine your authority and turn your country against you. That's why we are going to help you win re-election. Once this is achieved, you will realize that your loyalties lie with the Muslim people."

The president paused. "Don't make me do something we are both going to regret."

"Is that a threat?"

"Just call it a warning."

The supreme leader scoffed. "Then this meeting is over." Mohammed walked over to his study window. After a long moment, he heard the president stand up and heave a heavy sigh.

"Realistically, what is it going to take for you to make peace with Israel?"

Mohammed looked out into the clear blue sky above the Alborz Mountain range and then turned to him. "An act of God."

CHAPTER 27

D ARIUS DIDN'T ARRIVE to work until lunchtime. He opened the door to his high-corner office and saw Norm standing behind his desk with his back toward him. He was on the phone, peering through the micro-blinds. He sounded like he was arguing with a client.

Darius hurried into the room. He was bursting at the seams to tell him about his rebellious walk to work. "I showed them," Darius said loudly. "They can't control me with money."

Norman spun around. "I gotta call you back," he said and slammed down the phone. "Darius, where the hell have you been? Everyone's looking for you."

Darius grinned. *Word of his power was spreading.*

Norman shook his head and chuckled softly. "Nice suit."

"It's my best one." He noticed his shirt was hanging out on one side so he tucked it back in and moved behind his desk. Darius leaned over his chair and stared at his trading screen. He tried to run his fingers through his hair but it was knotted and tangled. He could feel his face was covered with perspiration.

"You look terrible."

He turned and looked at Norman. "I feel great."

Norman paused and gave him a wry look. "The market's down six hundred and sixty-six points and Solofön halted trading. They're looking for a new CEO to run the company."

"That's the code the Evil Ones are using to show me they're responsible for this." He focused his gaze back to his trading screen and snickered. "This morning I sent fear into the hearts and minds of the bankers. They're panicking."

He closed the blinds and turned on the lights. "From now on, keep the shades closed."

"Evil Ones?"

"Yeah. They've been spying on us with satellites."

He heard his partner take a deep breath and hold it before finally releasing it. "Darius, there are no codes, no Evil Ones, and no one's spying on us. And you're definitely not responsible for the market crash. Or in shape to speak to clients."

Darius looked up from his trading screen and turned toward Norm. "That's exactly what they want you to think." He jumped out of his chair. "Why do you think all of our stocks are up while the market is tanking?"

"Bro, you need to see a shrink. Go home. I'll take care of your accounts."

Darius turned around and peeked through the blinds behind him. He stared at the crowded sidewalks below. He looked over at Norm, massaging his temples. "Soon after I started walking this morning . . . I looked over my shoulder . . . *hundreds* of people were following me." He smiled with a sense of satisfaction. "Norm, I did it. I single-handedly mobilized the masses."

Norman paused and frowned. "You walked to work?" he said sadly.

"I had to. Since I won't tell them everything I know, they wiped out my bank account. There's supposed to be nine grand in there. But I showed 'em," he laughed. "Now they're afraid of me. I wouldn't be at all surprised if they made me the new CEO of Solofōn."

His partner regarded him for a moment. "Really," he said, stretching out the word, "what do *they* want to know?"

Darius made a face as though Norm knew exactly what he was talking about. "Everything!" he shouted.

"This is all my fault," he said. "I should've never given you that vial of endorphinate powder. Bro, you're delusional. Go home."

"I'm not delusional." He turned and pointed down to the streetscape below. "Hey, you don't believe me? Take a look for yourself." He turned back. Was Norm looking away . . . in disgust? Darius marched over to the front of his partner's desk and placed his hands shoulder-width apart on it and leaned forward. "The bastards are terrified of my ability to mobilize the masses. They'll do anything to please me. Can't you see? That's the reason our stocks are up today."

Norm stood up. "Bro, you're really scaring me. You need help." He walked around his desk and headed for the door. He reached it in three long strides and flung it open so hard it nearly put a hole in the wall. "Stay here," he said, "I'll be right back."

Darius moved back behind his desk and sat down. If Norman was scared, he thought, then the Evil Ones must have gotten to him. Norm, too, used money to control people. He picked up the phone and called his bank. They'd probably put the money back into his account the second they heard of his power to mobilize the masses.

A synthesized female voice instructed him to enter his account number. Darius froze. "I am not a number, I am a free man," he shouted.

"I do not understand your request," the voice said. "Please restate your request."

For their sake, I hope they're still not messing around with my money, he thought, as his sales assistant's face appeared on the flat screen. He hung up the phone.

"Darius, Mike wants you in his office, pronto."

Darius stood up just as Norman walked back into the office. "Mike wants to see me," he said, moving toward the door. "Bet the big guys upstairs told him to make me a partner before I'm offered the CEO slot at Solofōn." He opened the door and looked back at his partner. "By the way, who do you think would win in a fight? Braveheart or Highlander?"

Norm dropped with a thud into his chair.

Darius slapped his right-hand hard against his chest. "I think Braveheart would kick the crap out of Highlander." He slapped his hand hard against his chest again. "He had heart—unlike some people around here," he said and slammed the door behind him.

Darius hurried down the magnificently designed Art Deco hallway that was inspired by the 1925 World's Fair in Paris. Ixchel wasn't sitting at her desk and he burst into Mike's office unannounced.

Mike looked up from behind his desk. Darius thought he looked startled to see him. "Paris, I'll call you back," Mike said and hung up. "Haven't you heard of knocking?"

Darius stood in front of his desk and looked around the office. The plate glass window behind Mike's desk didn't have shades. *They probably had them removed so they could watch me.* "You don't waste any time, do you?" he said, looking back to Mike. "Doesn't matter anyway. We just broke up so she's fair game. Go for it."

"You've got it all wrong. She's worried about you, as am I. Please, Darius, have a seat."

"The only person you need to worry about is Norman. He's after her too." Darius sat down in the chair that had witnessed its share of hiring and firing and began searching for a hidden camera.

"What are you looking for?"

Darius focused his attention back to Mike. "Nothing." He sat back and wondered how long Mike would keep up the charade before he informed him that he was being promoted. Everybody would want to see the surprised look on his face when he heard the good news, so he'd play it cool and go along with it.

"Nice suit."

"Norman liked it too."

Mike sighed and leaned forward. "I'm getting reports . . . that you're . . . acting bizarre. Saying some . . . well . . . some really strange things. Both in the office . . . and at home."

Darius stood up. "Lies, all lies. I feel great." He began pacing back and forth in front of Mike's desk. "I've been working fourteen-hour days and working out like an animal. Look at these guns," he said, flexing his right bicep as if he were competing in a bodybuilding contest.

"I know you've been under a lot of pressure to pay for the hit, Darius, but is there . . . anything else . . . bothering you?"

"Nope. Couldn't be better. I'm benching three hundred and fifteen pounds for twelve reps now."

Darius watched Mike lean back and run his fingers through his hair. "Norman said you walked to work today."

"I was gonna take a taxi. But they wiped out my account, so I decided to walk and I'm glad I did."

Mike leaned forward. "Was there a problem with the direct deposit?"

Darius paused. He remembered Mike saying that his money would be deposited on Monday—and now it was Tuesday, so it had to have been deposited and then taken out. "Nope."

Mike picked up the phone. "You want me to check?"

"No sense involving you in this," he said and watched Mike hang up the receiver. "They're holding onto my money 'til I tell them everything."

"*They?* Who the hell are you talking about, Darius?"

"The people who control the money and talk to me in my dreams—and through music. They know that I've got it all figured out and are trying to get me to tell them everything I know." Darius looked out of the tinted window to see if anybody was watching him from the adjacent building.

"What have you figured out? No, no," his boss said, raising his right-hand. "I've heard enough. Darius, we've been through a lot together and you're a close friend. But, I'm your manager and right now, I've gotta separate business from friendship."

Mike had dropped his hand onto the desk and Darius thought he looked a bit hesitant. Darius grabbed both chair arms and readjusted himself.

"Darius, I'm gonna have to—"

The phone rang. Mike glanced at the display. "It's the head boss in Japan."

He must be calling Mike to tell him to throw a party in honor of the promotion he was about to get. Thank God he had worn his best suit. Darius reached into his pants pocket and pulled out a handful of change. He separated the lint from the coins. Now how the hell did that get there, he thought, staring at his Kennedy half dollar. Had Paris retrieved it from the fountain—or was there divine intervention at work? The thought faded when he realized that he had just encountered the dreaded triple-jinx.

"I understand," Mike said and hung up the phone. His boss stretched his arms out onto his desk and clasped his hands together.

"Darius, I feel as if I know you better than anyone else at the firm. But . . ." He removed his glasses and rubbed his eyes with his thumb and index finger, sighing heavily. "I believe you're suffering from a condition known as Financial Insecurity Disorder. It—"

"You're joking, right?"

"No. It was caused by the monetary loss you incurred," he said. "I want you to take a leave of absence and get some help."

"Mike, listen, don't be afraid of them. I'll protect you."

Mike sat quietly with his hands clasped. "I'm sorry, Darius, my decision is final."

Darius stood up. He put his hands on Mike's desk and leaned toward him. "I should've known," he said, "you sold out just like Norman did."

"Darius, if you want your job back, you're gonna have to get some psychiatric help."

"Is that so? Well . . . ya know what I think?"

"What?"

"If you want your soul back, you're gonna have to get that chip removed."

"Darius, go home. That's an order."

"You'll be sorry," he shouted. He looked around the room and shook his fist at the window. "You'll all be sorry!" He walked to the door and pulled it open. "Wait 'til you see what I do next," he said and slammed the door behind him.

CHAPTER 28

NORMAN STARED AT the baseball almanac on his desk. Like a hunter stumbling upon a mythical Unicorn, this was his dream come true. Very few brokers ever came close to bagging a client of this size and now he was going to get his shot to trade him. He shifted his gaze back to Mike, whose face took up the entire television screen. Norman put on his game face and leaned forward in his chair.

"You can count on me to take good care of GE-Joe while Darius is getting treatment."

Mike shook his head. "That was one of the hardest things I've ever had to do."

"What about the pension account?"

"You just make sure GE-Joe's account stays here," he said and signed off.

Norman picked up the baseball almanac and stared at the cover. "GE-Joe, you're mine." He put the book down and placed the call.

"Hello." Joe sounded groggy, as if he had a terrible cold. When Joe cleared his throat, Norman moved the phone away from his head and felt as if he needed to clean his ear out.

"Hey, Joe, it's Norman St. John from Tsumitomo Securities. I wanted to let you know that Darius has taken a leave of absence. I'll be handling your account until he returns."

Joe coughed again. "Why the leave of absence?"

"Mental exhaustion."

"Are you serious? What happened?"

Norman paused and thought about what he should say. Joe was a client after all. But Joe was not the kind of man who appreciated being lied to. "I'm not sure. Some kind of mental break—acting paranoid, delusions of grandeur."

"Delusions?"

"He was babbling about the pyramids, Stonehenge and," Norman hesitated, "saving the world." There was silence on the other end of the line. "I think he just had a nervous breakdown—from a huge loss he took. It happens to most stockbrokers at least once in their career."

"I see," Joe said. "Tell Mike I'm transferring the account. You shall have the signed forms within the hour."

Norman's heart started to race. He had to save the account.

"Joe, do you know the saying it's not what you know, but who you know?"

"Norman, I am a very busy man. Please get to the point."

"Joe, whether you know it or not I'm the guy Darius gets all his stock picks from. I'm wired in from New York to Hong Kong." He could hear the client breathing into the phone. But that was all he could hear. Then, Norman sucked in a deep breath. "Joe, you love money just as much as I do. What's it gonna take for you to keep the account here?"

"Norman, I enjoy talking to you when Darius isn't around. You're the only one who knows more about baseball than I do. But I'm only interested in working with Darius. Where is he right now?"

"Mike sent him home." He paused. "Joe, I'll make you a deal. You keep the account here and I'll charge you six cents a share on block trading."

There was a prolonged silence.

"Three cents and you give me fifteen hundred shares of the Genetically Perfect Baby IPO Darius told me you're getting a piece of."

Norman cringed. He cursed Darius's name under his breath. "The best I can do is five cents a share and five hundred shares."

"Four cents and one thousand shares or I'm transferring the account."

Norman took a deep breath and exhaled. "Fine," he said, pursing his lips. "You just bought yourself one hell of a trader."

"Mazal. Now buy me sixty-thousand shares of GE and give me Darius's number."

▲ ▲ ▲

Sy Kurtz entered the access codes into his Solofōn and called the Israeli Prime Minister. He held the phone tight against his ear and anxiously waited for the call to connect.

Sy was a highly influential and politically connected man. For years, he had tirelessly worked with the prime minister to facilitate peace between the Jews and the Muslims. As with any politician, there were a few select people who helped them achieve their position and keep it. In this case, Chaim Soloman, known as the Lion of Israel and the Butcher of Lebanon, perceived by some as honorable and by others as insidiously dangerous, owed his success almost unilaterally to Sy Kurtz. Both men knew it and Sy never missed an opportunity to leverage that power.

"Shalom, Dr. Kurtz." The prime minister had a strong, deep voice.

"I think we've found our man."

"You sound terrible," the prime minister said.

"Did you hear me, Soloman?" Sy coughed. "I think we've found our man."

"I'm listening."

"I believe it's someone we've already checked out."

The fifty-three-year-old prime minister sighed. He had a strong connection to the land and a deep sense of responsibility for ensuring the long-term security of Israel. A Pisces with Aries rising, he was obsessed with survival, and it was well known that he was not a team player.

"What makes you think that he's the Chosen One?"

"He's having delusions consistent with the prophecy."

"Mental hospitals all over the world have suddenly become jam packed with people suffering from the same delusions. We don't have the manpower to chase down every lead, especially a second time."

"Mr. Prime Minister. He fits the profile—although he's not a pure Aryan or a Zoroastrian."

"Send me his name and I'll put him back on the list of potential candidates. That's the best I can do. By the way, I'm attending a meeting at the UN tomorrow. Let's have lunch at Carnegie Deli afterward. Say, one-thirty?"

"Perfect." Sy Kurtz disconnected the call and stared at the picture on his desk of himself with the prime minister, President Walker, Princess Zara, the Dalai Lama, and Mohammed. He sighed. They had been so close to peace that day. Why had Soloman gone back on his word with the Eurasian Union just weeks after coming into office? By joining the American Union and maintaining power over the Israeli military, he had single-handedly destroyed any chance for peace between Israel and its Arab neighbors. Now, the Muslims didn't trust him—and for good reason. He had lied to Sy and everyone else to get into office and, shortly thereafter, went back on his promise to join the Eurasian Union and make peace with the Arabs.

Sy had to do something to clean up the mess the prime minister had created—but what? Maybe he could resurrect the peace process by going public with the prophecy. It was a long shot but he didn't see that he had any other choice.

CHAPTER 29

D ARIUS STORMED OUT of Mike's office and passed Ixchel who was talking on the phone.

"Darius," she called in a hushed tone, "wait."

He ignored her and hurried down the hall toward the elevators. From the nervous look on her face, he had a· gut feeling that she was part of the conspiracy as well. After all, she had access to everybody's accounts, including the big bosses upstairs.

It was getting to the point where he couldn't trust anyone. As he waited for the elevator, all he could think about was starting a revolution.

Darius looked up at a camera mounted on the wall and shook his fist.

"My money better be back in my account when I get to the bank or there's gonna be hell to pay," he said as the elevator doors opened.

When he arrived at the bank, he saw a long line of un-chipped customers waiting for a teller. He decided to use an ATM machine instead. Darius scanned his smartcard and stared at the camera built into the machine.

If they don't give me my money, I am going to start a revolution.

"For verification purposes, please state your name," came a synthesized female voice.

"Darius Prince."

"Welcome to JP Morgan Chase and Company, Mr. Prince. How may I help you?"

"Checking account balance."

"One moment please."

Darius nervously tapped his hand on the ATM as he waited.

"Mr. Prince, your current available balance is three dollars."

"Are you *sure?*" he asked.

"I do not understand. Please restate your request."

"Damn you!" he said, shaking his fist in front of the camera. "This is your last warning. Put my money back or else."

"I do not understand. Please restate your request."

If I'm going to start a revolution, I have to be sure.

He took a deep breath, and once again asked for his balance.

A long moment passed. "Mr. Prince, there has been a transfer of funds into your account. Your current available balance is nine thousand and three dollars."

He let go a heavy sigh. For now, he had proved his point but still, he had to be careful. They would stop at nothing to find out exactly what he knew.

▼ ▲ ▼

Darius walked into his apartment and was surprised to see his mother sitting on the sofa with Paris. He noticed his mother had developed a few extra wrinkles since he'd last seen her and her shoulder-length blondish hair was graying. She was also uncharacteristically dressed down in blue jeans with a white t-shirt and tennis sneakers.

"Mom, what are you doing here?" he said, looking at Paris who, by contrast, was dressed in a dark-blue business suit. Her legs were crossed and she had her hands clasped about her knee. "If you're looking to get back together, it's not gonna happen."

Paris frowned at him. "Darius, you need help."

"Yeah, right."

"Stop it," his mother said. "Please, both of you."

"Mom, I need to show you something."

He ran upstairs to his bedroom. When he returned, he handed her the article headlined *British Apollo Lands in Hollywood.* "Did you know they called dad a living god?"

His mother smiled sweetly at him. "That's just Hollywood talk."

"How come he never told me they called him British Apollo?"

"Your father was a very humble man. He never bragged about his achievements. You knew he was famous back in the thirties. But you never forgave him for abandoning us and, you never got to know him."

His parents had been protecting him. Obviously, this had something to do with his destiny.

He took off his jacket and flung it onto an empty chair, followed by his tie and shirt. He positioned himself in front of his mother and ex-girlfriend and flexed his muscles. As he admired his body, he wondered what else he needed to know in order to fulfill his destiny.

Paris sighed. "Mrs. Prince, he needs to stop doing drugs and see a psychiatrist."

"I stopped doing drugs right after dad died," he said, dropping his arms to his sides. Do you think that I would look this good if I were on drugs?" They both studied him as he raised his arms again in flex. He took a few steps back to better showcase his muscles and physique.

His mother stood up from the couch. "You look just like your father," she said, bringing her hand to her breast.

"Except bigger and stronger. Look at me." He relaxed and flexed his right bicep. "If he had thrown me the ball just once, I'd be playing inside linebacker for the New York Giants right now."

He saw his mom look at Paris with a knitted brow. He laughed and picked up two sixty-pound dumbbells and started curling them. He'd have to show them.

"He does have a point." His mother looked from him back to Paris. "If he was on drugs he wouldn't be in such good shape."

"That's what I keep telling her, mom."

"*Whatever*," Paris said. "There's something seriously wrong with you."

"You're just pissed off I broke up with you."

Paris paused. "Darius, they left me another text message."

Darius dropped the weights with a loud, heavy thud. He heard his mother let out a gasp as he turned to Paris. "They did?"

"They . . . told me . . . they told me that it is time you met."

"The Rebels, right?"

Paris nodded.

"How can I be sure that you're telling the truth?"

"Do you trust your mother?"

"She's the only one I trust."

"Tell him, Mrs. Prince."

His mother took a deep breath and exhaled. "Darius, she's telling the truth."

He saw tears forming in his mother's eyes. She'd always been honest with him. He slowly looked back to Paris. "Where do they want to meet?"

"They told me to text'em and they'd send an ambulance for you. They said you'd understand why."

Darius paused, deep in thought. *Brilliant!* By sending an ambulance, the Evil Ones would never suspect he was going to the hospital to meet with the Rebels. It was the ultimate in deception.

He looked at his mother who was nodding her head with tears of joy in silent approval and then shifted his gaze back to Paris. "Okay, I'm in."

"Good. Now, they also said you can *never* be too careful. Once you're admitted to the hospital, they might wait a couple days before contacting you."

"I understand perfectly." He nodded and paused. "Paris, did you take my Kennedy half dollar out of the fountain?"

"Of course not! But I did find your passport." She pulled it out of her bag and walked over to him.

"I've been looking for that. Where was it?"

"At *my* apartment. You know . . . the one I keep downtown . . . just in case we break up." She shot him a look of distaste and practically shoved the passport into his hand. "Anyhoo, it might come in handy if your so-called Rebel base is in Egypt," she said with a laugh.

Is that where it was? He stared at her, pondering the thought, and stuffed the passport into his pocket. "Are you sure you didn't take my Kennedy half dollar out of the fountain?"

Paris's eyes widened. Her lips thinned. "For the last time, I did not take your stupid coin out of the fountain."

The goddesses, then, that he'd freed from the painting were responsible for this. But why were they jinxing him? Were they punishing him for holding them captive all those years? He prayed that once he got to the hospital, everything wouldn't go drastically wrong.

"Hurry up and text'em," he said. "The fate of the entire world depends on it!"

CHAPTER 30

D ARIUS FROZE AS three orderlies dressed in blue scrubs wheeled a man strapped to a metal gurney past him. The man was in a straitjacket and struggling against four-point restraints.

"I don't care what you do to me," the man screamed. "I'll never tell you what I know."

This was his wake-up call, he thought, as he watched the orderlies load the man into a freight elevator. Darius knew if he didn't stay focused, he'd be next. Listening to the man's screams slowly fade away, he wondered if he'd ever get out of this hellhole alive.

He took a deep breath and continued down the dull grey hall. The finely polished floor made his shoes squeak and the unpleasant, sanitized odor of the facility irritated his nostrils and made him sneeze. "God bless you," he heard a young nurse say as she hurried past him. This was a sign, he thought, wiping the sweat from his brow. She was indirectly telling him to be careful even though God was on his side. Paris had said he wouldn't be contacted until the Rebels were absolutely sure that the Evil Ones believed he *was* crazy and there to get help. The ward was probably crawling with informants on both sides watching his every move. The patients were now as suspect as the hospital staff.

As he approached the nurses' station he saw three young nurses standing behind the counter. Dressed in purple scrubs, he realized they looked strangely familiar. He stared at the blonde, brunette and redhead and wondered why they looked so familiar. Then it struck him—his eyes widened. They were the three goddesses he had freed from the painting in his bedroom. Their hair was styled differently but he knew it was them.

The blonde nurse smiled and waved him over. Darius froze. What were they up to? He thought about the triple-jinx. Cautiously, he moved toward them.

"Hello, Mr. Prince." The blonde handed him a pen and placed a list of the hospital's rules and regulations in front of him. "Please empty your pockets."

Darius hesitated for a moment. Watching the other two nurses behind the blonde sort the patient's medications, he realized he had better hold on to a couple of things. He smiled at the nurse and reached into his pants pockets with both hands. Maneuvering around his cell phone, wallet, and passport, he carefully pulled out his keys, a bank receipt, and some loose change, and placed them on the counter.

"Is that everything?"

"Yes," he said with a hint of annoyance.

"Good." She placed the items in a bag and pointed to the bottom of the page. "Read it over and sign here."

He paused. Now that he was dealing with a divine intelligence, he had to be resolute. Who knew the true extent of their powers? Or, for that matter, their intentions?

Darius scribbled down his signature and looked into her deep blue eyes. "May I have a copy," he said. "I'd like to study it tonight."

She laughed. "Sure, but study hard. I'm going to test you in the morning."

Test? He wondered if they'd been the Devil's spies all along. If they were, he should've never set them free.

He placed his hands on the counter and leaned forward. "Rules are meant to be broken like lines are meant to be crossed." He folded up the paper and stuck it in his back pocket.

"Are you a Rebel, Mr. Prince?"

"Rebel?" he said, watching the other two nurses join her at the counter. They both acknowledged him with a friendly smile and continued working. Darius grinned and looked deep into the blonde nurse's eyes. "You're gonna have to figure that one out all by yourself."

She laughed. "If you're looking for something to do before dinner, the movie *Top Gun* is about to start playing in the lounge. I just adore Tom Cruise," she said.

"He's my favorite actor," Darius said, "but I think I'm gonna pass. I've seen the movie so many times." He noticed a young doctor emerge from an office behind the nurse's station. He was fiddling with a tablet computer as he slowly made his way toward them. Darius shifted his gaze back to the nurse, yawned and stretched his arms behind his head.

The brunette glanced at the doctor and then leaned toward Darius. "Did you know TC is in New York City shooting another Mission Impossible?" she whispered.

Darius held in a laugh. *Tom Cruise wasn't there to film the movie, he was there to meet with him.* TC might have fooled the three goddesses, but *he* wasn't fooled. On second thought, maybe he should see the movie. There could be a message hidden within the film that TC wanted him to see. If there was, then this just might be the first in a series of tests he would have to pass. Even though he had seen the movie a thousand times, he knew that if it was a test, and he didn't figure it out, his first test might be his last.

Darius thought back to his conversation with the goddess. Why, this time, did she refer to Tom Cruise by his initials? And why did she whisper? When the nurses turned to talk with the young doctor, Darius remained at the counter deep in thought. What had the nurse been trying to tell him?

Beads of sweat formed on his forehead and he felt his thoughts spiraling out of control. He didn't want to end up like the guy strapped to the gurney. He took a few deep breaths to calm himself. Then it dawned on him. This time, he thought, the goddesses were helping him. The brunette was indirectly telling him that TC was the leader of the Rebel forces he was there to rendezvous with.

Waves of euphoria rippled through his body even though he was confronted by an unwelcome truth—if it wasn't for the goddess, he might have jeopardized the entire mission. His smile faded. He should have known the moment the goddess reverted to using the initials TC that something was wrong. Obviously the young doctor was an evil spy. If he'd emerged from his office a second sooner, the doctor might've realized that TC was the Rebel leader Darius was there to meet with. Both of their covers would've been blown and their meeting would have to have been aborted.

That was close. Too close, he thought. He had to remember to say as little as possible and make like he was crazy until the heat was off. Still, he felt good knowing that the goddesses were on his side.

Darius winked at the brunette, and said, "G-L-O."

The nurses all looked at one another with confused faces. "G-L-O?" the redhead said.

He smiled. "Figure it out," he said and hurried down the hall toward the lounge. When he turned the corner he noticed a short dark-haired man wearing a black Fila sweat suit and a tall red-headed Irishman dressed in blue jeans and a white wife-beater t-shirt, both hassling a young black man. Darius stopped and stared at the number twelve on the back of the youth's New York Yankees white pinstripe baseball jersey. He wondered at the significance of the number and noticed the two thugs eyeballing him.

"Yo, you gotta problem?" the short heavyset guy said in a strong Brooklyn accent.

Darius slowed his pace but decided to keep quiet. This wasn't the time or place to start acting out. The audience just wasn't big enough. That would come later, he thought, at dinner, when he could play to a packed house. Then he'd give the performance of a lifetime, leaving no doubt in anyone's mind that he was certifiably insane. For now, he'd have to forego the movie. It was just too risky. He had to get back to his room and find a good place to stash his stuff. If things didn't work out as planned, he'd have to be ready to go at a moments notice.

CHAPTER 31

"WHAT DO YOU mean I can't see him," Laura said. "Visiting hours started at six."

The black adonis, who looked more like a bouncer than a security guard, looked up from behind the reception desk in front of the elevators at the end of the long lobby hall. "I'm sorry, but Mr. Prince is not receiving visitors."

"Is he alright?"

The guard stood up and flashed a pearly white smile. "I'm not at liberty to say."

"I'd like to talk to Mr. Prince's doctor."

"Do you have an appointment?"

Laura rolled her eyes. "No."

You need an appointment," he said and handed her one of the hospital's business cards. "Try calling in the morning."

Laura stared at the elevator doors behind him. Something wasn't right. Why wasn't she allowed to see Darius? When she focused her eyes back on the guard, Laura played it cool and decided not to argue the point any further. It just wasn't worth it. She did an abrupt about-face and headed back down the hallway. When she saw the woman she despised most in the world heading toward her, Laura stopped. Her heart raced. Wearing a floral patterned white dress with matching shoes and handbag, Paris Templar looked straight at her. She didn't seem to recognize her though and kept walking. Laura moved in front of her, blocking her path.

With her back foot sideways, she faced Templar head on. She jammed her hands on her hips and pointed her right foot toward her. Leaning forward, Laura said, "Look what the cat dragged in."

Paris removed her dark sunglasses and looked at her. "Laura," she said, "it's been a while."

"Three years to be exact."

"Not long enough in my book."

"Didn't I tell you to stay away from Darius?"

Laura pushed up the sleeves of her red sweat suit and took a menacing step forward. She shoved Templar with both hands. "Drop dead, bitch." Paris staggered back and then regained her balance. She dropped her bag and raised her hands in defense. Slowly, she walked around Laura, like a shark circling its prey. Laura moved with her—waiting for her to strike. When Paris abruptly stopped and lowered her hands, she could tell by the nervous look on Paris's face that she no longer wanted to fight and was backing down. Laura moved toward her with her hands on her hips and got in her face again.

"Still all talk and no action."

"Laura, I'm curious." She reached out and touched Laura's arm. "Did you buy this dreadful looking sweat suit at Walmart?"

She smacked her hand away. "I seem to recall your father saying in an interview that before he made his fortune, he used to buy your clothes at second-hand stores."

"Daddy's such the kidder." A bittersweet laugh escaped her. She picked up her bag and pulled out her checkbook. She scribbled in it, tore out a check, and handed it to Laura. "Now, stay out of our lives."

When Laura saw that the check was for one hundred thousand dollars, she stared at her in disbelief. "You manipulative little bitch. You think you can buy me?"

"Name your price and let's be done with this."

Laura tore the check in half and tossed the pieces into the air. "You're going to find this hard to understand, but I'm not for sale." She paused and leveled a condemning stare. "Let's put an end to this right here and now." She felt like scratching Paris's eyes out but when she raised her hands to do so, she had a sudden change of heart and lowered them.

"I'd love to but I'm late for an appointment," Paris said, and tried to walk around her.

Laura stepped to the side and blocked her path again. "You don't love Darius. All you love is money."

Paris reached into her bag and pulled out her Solofōn. "Get out of my way or I'm calling the police."

It wasn't in Laura Rigel's nature to back down, but a confrontation in the hospital could be dangerous or cause problems for Darius. She felt like knocking the bitch out but, instead, reluctantly moved aside.

"That's a good girl."

Laura stared into Paris's shallow green eyes. Did she even have a soul? Paris put on her sunglasses and gave her a fake smile. "Toodles," she said and strolled past her.

"Good luck trying to get past the security guard," Laura said.

Paris chuckled softly. "This is your last warning, Rigel. Stay away from Darius."

Laura watched Paris hurry down the hall. When she reached the reception desk, Laura's eyes widened. To her surprise, Paris waltzed right past the guard who never even looked up from his magazine. Laura stomped over to the desk as Paris "toodled" her again with the wave of her hand from inside the elevator. Laura glowered at the guard who was reading a magazine and slammed her hands down hard on the desk.

"I thought you said that Mr. Prince wasn't allowed any visitors." When he didn't respond, she reached over and ripped the magazine out of his hands. "How come you let her through?"

The guard stood up and flexed his muscles. "She's not meeting with Mr. Prince," he said and snatched the magazine back. "She has an appointment with his doctor."

"You were expecting me, weren't you?"

"You need some serious help lady. If you don't leave right now I'll see to it that you get the room right next to him."

"Is that a promise?" she said and stormed back down the hall.

What the hell was Paris up to?

CHAPTER 32

D ARIUS SAT DOWN at an empty table in the cafeteria and
gazed out of the ninth-story window. A rusty-orange glow
loomed over the horizon as the sun slowly set behind a backdrop of buildings
far off to the west. He realized he was only going to get one shot to convince
the Evil Ones that he was crazy. If he failed, the Rebels would never contact
him. An orderly placed a chicken dinner down in front of him which snapped
him out of his thoughts. When the orderly moved to the next table, Darius felt
a light smack on the back of his head. He glanced over his shoulder and saw
the two thugs standing over him.

"Winner, winner, chicken dinner," the Italian thug said and nudged his
partner.

Darius laughed. He glanced at the black dome camera on the ceiling in the
middle of the room and then looked at the orderlies, who were busy handing
out meals. With nowhere else to turn, he focused his attention back on the
thugs.

The Italian placed his hand on Darius's shoulder and squeezed it tight.
"You think you're better than us?"

Darius shrugged the guys hand off his shoulder.

The Irish thug slammed his hands down hard on the table and leaned
toward him. "*Yer* goin' to find it hard to laugh when *yer* jaw is wired shut," he
said.

What had he done? He needed to say something to defuse the situation—
and fast. Darius took a deep breath. "I don't think I'm better than you."

They walked around the table and faced him. "Bullshit," the Italian said.

Darius paused, averting their eyes for a moment. "I don't want any trouble," he said. "I'm here to get help."

"You don't fool us," the Italian said. "We know why you're here."

Darius grinned when he saw one of the orderlies rush over to his table. The orderly grabbed the thugs by the back of their necks and lifted them up. "That's enough," he said and walked them to an adjacent table. They sat down facing him. When the orderly walked away, the Irishman looked at Darius and started clucking like a chicken.

Darius lost his appetite. If he didn't do something quick this just might be his last supper. Looking around, he noticed that there were eleven other tables that were all occupied. As he tried to figure out what to do, he realized he'd made a serious mistake by not watching the film.

What was TC trying to tell him?

"I got invited to Camelot!" he heard a male voice shout.

Darius looked to his right. A young black man jumped up from a table and started running around the room waving a piece of paper. Without hesitation, the two orderlies rushed over and grabbed him. He resisted but they wrestled him to the floor and held him down while a nurse gave him a shot. Then they carried his lifeless body out of the room.

Invitation? That's it! He, too, would soon receive an invitation—but unlike the youth he was going to be invited to the Top Gun Academy. Tom Cruise wanted him to be his wingman in the apocalyptic battle of Armageddon. He paused. But why would TC choose him? He didn't know the first thing about flying jets. Then he realized that Tom Cruise would, of course, have the world's top fighter pilots teach him how to fly.

The Italian drew his finger across his throat.

Darius tensed. He had to work fast. It was crucial he show TC his leadership abilities before dinner ended. If he didn't, TC wouldn't invite him to the academy. And he couldn't let that happen, he thought, wiping the sweat from his brow. His only chance was to do the impossible and gain the respect of the thugs. If he could, he was going to the Top Gun Academy at the Rebel's secret base. If he couldn't . . . well, he didn't want to think about that.

When the orderlies returned and walked past his table, he overheard one of them say that Camelot was the hardest rehab on the east coast to get into.

Darius held back a laugh. Did they honestly think that he would be stupid enough to believe that Camelot was a rehab?

That's why the youth had the number twelve on his shirt. Just like he had to prove himself before he was invited to the Top Gun Academy, the youth had already proved his worthiness and was headed to Camelot to become the twelfth knight of Queen Elizabeth's roundtable.

Darius thought about his recent dream—the one where he was on a white horse leading millions into battle. Maybe it wasn't a dream after all, but a vision. *Of course.* After he proved himself at Top Gun, the queen would knight him, too, and send him on a quest for the Holy Grail.

First, he had to figure out a way to gain the respect of the two thugs. He looked at his full tray of food. What a waste. He stood up and cleared his throat. "Does anybody want my chicken?" Blank stares filled the room. Then, he noticed a pale heavyset man slowly rise to his feet.

"What do you want in return," the man asked. Instantly, Darius had everybody's attention. This was the opportunity he was looking for. He would now show off his leadership abilities and simultaneously make the Evil Ones think he was a lunatic. He picked up his tray and walked over to the man. "Gimme your three cookies."

When the man smiled and handed him his cookies, Darius placed the chicken on his tray.

"Thank you," the man said.

Darius grinned. He was making friends quick. "Anyone want a cookie?" Three hands flew into the air. He walked over to a middle-aged woman who had put her hand up first. "Do you have anything to trade?"

"I'll trade you my fruit cup for a cookie."

"Done."

A moment later everybody started to trade items they didn't want; everything from ketchup and sugar to salt and pepper were changing hands. He glanced at the orderlies who were both eyeballing him. He had better get back to his table, he thought. When he turned, he bumped into the two thugs. The fruit cup fell to the floor.

If he didn't think of something quick, he was going to end up in a dog fight.

Staring at the thugs who pushed out their chests and cracked their knuckles, he had a feeling that the orderlies weren't going to help him. After all, he started this mess. Now, they were too busy trying to calm down all of the patients who were running around the cafeteria screaming and trading their food. The only person he could rely on was himself.

"You're gonna pay for your disrespect," the Italian said.

Darius smiled half-heartedly and held out a cookie for each of them.

The Irishman smacked the cookies out of his hands. "*Yer* goin' to have to do better than that," he sneered.

The Italian pushed his man aside and moved in front of Darius. "Hey, we run the show around here."

There was only one way out of this. For now, he'd have to join forces with the Evil Ones. It was his only chance. As he readied for the highly difficult maneuver, he just hoped to God that Tom Cruise would realize what he was up to. It was a gutsy move but if he pulled it off, his leadership abilities would no longer be in question. If he didn't, he would be taken away in a straitjacket and tortured until he told them everything he knew.

Darius stood tall and reached into his pocket. "How much?"

"How much you got?" the Italian said.

Darius pulled out two five dollar bills. "Ten bucks." He handed each of them a crisp five dollar bill.

They grabbed the bills and started to argue about who owed the other what. Darius smiled knowing that he was now in control. He jumped between them and pushed them apart. "Listen guys, there's plenty more to go around."

They both grabbed him. "You holding out on us?" the Italian said.

"C'mon, guys, look around you," he said, motioning to the other patients. "There's power in numbers. If we work together we can shake down the entire ward in no time. Who knows what treasures we'll find."

They released him and resumed their arguing. Darius looked up and winked at the black dome camera he knew Tom Cruise was watching him from. His plan seemed to be working.

Finally they stopped bickering and turned toward him. "We could use a smart guy like you."

He grinned. The idea of running the ward and everybody on it made him feel powerful, superior. Darius felt a strong hand grab him by the shoulder. He turned and stared at the orderly.

"Okay, wise guy," the orderly said. "You're going to your room."

Darius stood at attention between the thugs and saluted the orderly. "Sir, I will not leave my wingman."

"We'll see about that," the orderly said and waved his hand in the air.

Darius looked at his new partners who were standing at attention, saluting the orderly, and then focused his gaze back in front of him. "Sir, never, ever leave your wingman," he said proudly. He felt a sharp stinging sensation on the back of his shoulder as if he'd been stung by a bee. His vision blurred and his knees buckled.

The room went black.

CHAPTER 33

"FINDING THE TWIN Leos is proving to be difficult," Raj said and locked the door behind him.

President Ramsey looked up from behind his cluttered desk. "Nobody said it would be easy," he said, and motioned for Raj to sit on the sofa. "I'll be with you shortly."

The computer broke in. "President Ramsey, you have an encrypted video call from the Supreme Leader, Mohammed."

Ramsey sat up and adjusted his white linen suit coat and tie. He took a deep breath and shifted his gaze to the middle of the room. "Put the call through." A life-sized hologram of Mohammed appeared. He was dressed in a white robe and head cover.

Mohammed's gaze was sharp and he acknowledged Ramsey with a friendly nod. "President Ramsey," he said, "the only person that fits your description is a man by the name of Darius Prince."

Ramsey shook his head, frowning with perplexity. "Impossible, he's not a pure Aryan or a Zoroastrian." He heard a laugh in the background. "Is somebody with you?"

"My brother, Zadam, and my wife, Roxanne," Mohammed said and glanced over his shoulder.

Ramsey stared at Mohammed in disbelief. This was disastrous, he thought. They were the last people he wanted involved. The supreme leader moved his gaze back to him.

"What makes you think it's him?"

"According to the Zoroastrian elders, the word *'pure'* in the document refers to Prince's bloodline on his father's side. It has nothing to do with his current religious beliefs since his father was a Zoroastrian and he can still become one. I was told to seek out a man with a royal last name."

"Of course," Ramsey said. "When the Zoroastrians fled Iran, fourteen hundred years ago, they became gypsies and changed their last names to their professions so they would remember who they were. Mr. Prince's family migrated to India and changed their name to Prince."

"Precisely," Mohammed said. "It's very likely he is a direct descendant of the Aryan king, Cyrus the Great, who founded the Persian Empire."

"That remains to be seen," Zadam said, pacing back and forth behind Mohammed. "But, if so, he's not the only one."

"What my brother is trying to say is that we, too, are direct descendants of Cyrus the Great. Legend has it that Cyrus's genealogy is linked to the mythological Aryan king, Jamshed, who ruled the city of Orion when the Evil One first came to this planet," Mohammed said. "In a desperate attempt to save our people, he ordered his mighty general to lead his subjects out of the holy land. They headed south toward the sun and settled in Iran."

"Do you think Mr. Prince knows about his heritage?"

"It's possible. And if he is of royal blood, Mr. Prince and his younger brother would be the rightful heirs to our ancestral throne before I or Zadam. Since we are no longer a monarchy, this is no longer of any consequence."

Ramsey thought for a moment. "If the genealogy on his mother's side is at all linked to British Royalty, he could claim to be—"

"*King of the World*," Mohammed said hesitantly.

"Not so fast," the president heard Zadam say. His accent was heavy. He stepped in front of Mohammed and flashed Ramsey the many medals pinned to his camouflaged jacket. They did little to impress the eccentric president.

"That interpretation is debatable," Zadam said. "When Queen Elizabeth finds out about this document and learns that you believe a crazy man is the Chosen One, you, too, will be committed to Gracie Square Mental Hospital."

Mental hospital? So that's where he was. He glanced at Raj who had looked back at him with a dumbfounded look on his face and then shifted his gaze back to Zadam. The Amazons were bluffing after all. Hopefully, he could reach him in time. Ramsey glared at this barbarian of a man in charge of the world's largest military. He had to act fast before word of Darius and the prophecy spread any further. He looked into Zadam's eyes as he listened to Mohammed's wife, Roxanne, laugh in the background.

"That's right," Zadam shouted, his hand pensively stroking his goatee. "Darius Prince is crazy and so are you. When the queen finds out, she'll have me remove you from power." He laughed. "And I'll personally see to it that you get the bed right next to him."

Roxanne moved next to her brother-in-law. Covered from head to toe in a green galabia, she clenched her strong jaw and looked at him with a snide grin. "I'm appalled that you'd even consider a man belonging to such a male chauvinistic religion to be the Chosen One."

"Silence!" Mohammed flashed her a condemning stare. "Mr. Prince is not a Zoroastrian. He is a Christian," he said and waved them back. He shifted his gaze back to the president. "Please excuse my disrespectful brother and overzealous wife. Now, I must warn you. If Mr. Prince is not the Chosen One this historical document speaks of, I will deny any involvement whatsoever and Zadam *will* remove you from power."

"I understand," Ramsey said. When the hologram disappeared, the president motioned Raj over. "I was afraid of this. Too many people know about Mr. Prince. We need to get him out of the hospital tonight."

"We have an agent in Washington, D.C. right now," Raj said. "I can have him in New York City within a few hours."

"Send him a schematic of the hospital and a recent photo of Darius Prince. The rendition should be carried out around midnight. That way nobody will know Mr. Prince is missing until he is safely in Egypt."

"And if he resists?"

"Under no circumstances is he to be harmed."

"Should the agent notify us once he has him?"

"No. I want a communication blackout until they are safely on the ground here."

"When Zadam learns of the escape he'll tell the queen you were responsible. How do you plan on convincing her that the prophecy is true?"

Ramsey stood up and walked over to the southern window. He gazed out at the Giza Plateau as darkness fell over the pyramids. "I pray that once I get him to the pyramids, something will happen so I won't have to."

CHAPTER 34

"**B**REAKFAST."

Darius lifted his head slightly and watched the orderly wheel a metal cart into the room. The sanitized smell of the room was replaced with the rich buttery aroma of bacon and eggs. Darius sighed and dropped his head back down on his pillow. When the orderly rolled the cart next to his bed, Darius sat up and swung his feet to the floor. "I'm not hungry," he said and pushed the cart to the side.

"So don't eat. It's a free country."

"You think we live in a free country?"

"Don't matter what I think," he said. "At nine o'clock you're scheduled to meet with Doctor Haus. And you *will* be there."

This was great news! The Rebels were ready to meet with him. He jumped up and started pacing back and forth.

"Man, oh man," the orderly said, shaking his head and chuckling. "After that stunt you pulled at dinner, I don't think they'll ever let you outta here."

"What time is it?"

"Quarter to nine." He placed a set of orange sweats and black slippers at the foot of Darius's bed. "Change into these. I'll be back in a few minutes."

"Why am I so tired?"

"The sedative they gave you at dinner," he said and headed for the door. "You're lucky you didn't wind up in the rubber room."

Darius held back a smile. When the orderly was out of the room, he let go of his smile and raised his arms in triumph. His plan had worked but he still had to be careful.

He sat down and removed the lid from the tray. The sight of the soft runny yolks and undercooked bacon made his stomach turn. It's probably drugged, he thought, and knocked the food onto the floor. When he saw the yellow egg yolk take the shape of the sun and the bacon curl up in the shape of a crescent moon, he wondered if the Rebels had purposely sedated him because he was bringing too much attention to himself.

That had to be it. He stood up and changed into the sweats. He had to remember to draw as little attention to himself as possible so the Evil Ones wouldn't suspect him of conspiring with the Rebels.

Darius put on the slippers and walked into the bathroom. He laughed at his reflection in the mirror. *I look like a convict.*

The sound of keys jingling in the door interrupted his thoughts and brought him back to the situation at hand. The moment he heard the door click open, he looked back in the mirror and said, "Showtime."

"Mr. Prince, time for your meeting."

Darius took a deep breath and exhaled. He'd have to keep up the act until he was behind closed doors with Dr. Haus. But even then, he wasn't so sure. He'd feel him out anyway—make sure the Evil Ones hadn't gotten to him as well. He walked out of the bathroom and saw the orderly standing behind a wheelchair.

"Did you have to make a mess with your food?"

"To you it's a mess. To me, it's art. I call it food art. Da Vinci would've been proud."

The orderly sighed. "It's a mess because I gotta clean it up. You wanna be sedated again?"

Darius glanced at the wheelchair and then winked at him. *These guys thought of everything.* Taking him to the meeting in a wheelchair would make him look helpless and weak. They would never suspect him now.

When the orderly wheeled him into the hall Darius was greeted with a round of cheers from some of the patients.

"You've become quite a celebrity," the orderly said. "For your own safety, I suggest you don't acknowledge them."

He's right. Now that the Evil Ones believed he was in need of therapy, he didn't want to give them any reason to second guess him. He had to do something to take the focus off himself. Darius jumped to his feet and started clapping and cheering for the orderly like a wild man.

"Mr. Prince, sit down!"

Darius remained standing and continued cheering him. When the patients finally settled down, he returned to his wheelchair and sat down.

"Another outburst like that and you're gettin' the needle," the orderly said and continued pushing him down the hallway. Once they reached the doctor's office, the orderly knocked on the partially open door and wheeled him inside.

Darius looked around the room. "Where's the doctor?"

"Have a seat. He'll be with you shortly."

Darius got out of the wheelchair and sat down on a wooden chair in front of the doctor's desk. Once he heard the door shut, he stared at the barren walls and then shifted his gaze to the cardboard moving boxes scattered around the room. Why was the doctor packing up all his stuff?

Something wasn't right.

▲ ▼ ▲

Where the hell was Dr. Haus?

Darius had waited for close to half an hour but the chair he was sitting in made it seem like hours. It was hard and uncomfortable; similar to what the police would use to interrogate a criminal.

He prayed the Evil Ones hadn't gotten to Dr. Haus like they had Mike and Norman.

Darius stood up and stretched his arms behind his back. He yawned and picked up a miniature foam brain off of the edge of the doctor's desk. He squeezed the spongy stress reliever and noticed it had BP-14 written on its side. Was this another code or message? A cardboard box on the floor beside the desk caught his eye. He glanced over his shoulder at the door and then hurried over to it. Full of framed photographs, he picked up the one on top.

He stared at the autographed photo. His heart raced as he read the inscription aloud.

Best Wishes, Tom Cruise.

He glanced at the foam brain and made the connection. They were testing his intelligence. BP-14 was a code Tom Cruise wanted him to crack. That's why the doctor was late. He was giving him time to figure it out before they met. If he could crack the code before the meeting was over, Dr. Haus would tell him the location of the Rebel base. If he couldn't, the doctor would recommend Tom Cruise find a smarter wingman.

The sound of keys jingling in the door startled him. He dropped the framed photo into the box and hurried back to the chair. He placed the brain back on the desk and sat down just as he heard the door click open. Darius turned his head and peered over his shoulder. A tall lanky man in his mid forty's strolled into the room. He held a coffee cup in one hand and a black leather briefcase in the other. Dressed in black slacks and a blue dress shirt with the sleeves rolled up, he placed the cup on the desk and his briefcase down in front of him. He sat down in his leather chair and opened the case.

"I'm Dr. Haus. Sorry I'm late."

Darius didn't say a word. He just sat there, staring at the case.

"Excuse the mess. I'm in the process of moving down the hall," he said and pulled a notepad out of the case.

So that's what he wanted him to believe. Darius grinned and looked at the doctor. "What else is in the case, Doc? Jewels? Money? Someone's soul?"

Dr. Haus chuckled softly and pulled a pair of wire-rimmed reading glasses out of his shirt pocket; he put them on and removed a file from the case. He placed the case on the floor to the side of his desk and flipped through the file. "So, you think you have a higher purpose," he said, looking up. "What makes you think that?"

Darius paused. He would play it cool and say as little as possible until he was sure the doctor could be trusted. "I don't know. I was hoping you would tell me."

The doctor took off his reading glasses and rubbed his eyes. "Please answer the question, Mr. Prince."

Darius nodded absently and looked around the room. "So how's TC?"

"TC?"

Obviously the doctor knew who he was talking about but was playing it off until he figured out the code. When Dr. Haus picked up the foam brain and started squeezing it, Darius realized the doctor was indirectly telling him that time was running out and he needed an answer. He had to figure it out before the doctor decided to abort the meeting.

Dr. Haus placed the foam brain back on the edge of the desk and put his reading glasses back on. He flipped through the file again and then removed his glasses once again and looked up. "Would you like to tell me what happened at dinner last night?"

"All I did was give away my chicken dinner, cookies, and money. I was just trying to show off my leadership abilities."

"The orderlies tell a different story. They say you incited a riot."

"They're lying."

"Why would they lie?"

Darius got up and started pacing in front of his desk. "Isn't it obvious," he shouted, "they're against me."

"Mr. Prince, please sit down."

Darius stopped pacing and reluctantly sat back down.

"Why would they lie?" the doctor said again.

"Because I won't tell them what I know."

"What is it you know?"

"Everything!"

"Okay . . . it's a start," he said and jotted down some notes. "What prompted you to give away your money?"

"I used it to control them and that's what scares me. I know it sounds strange, but it feels like there are other people inside of me. The person that emerged yesterday thinks he's a god."

The doctor jotted down some more notes. "Who do you think these people are?"

Darius grabbed the foam brain and started squeezing it again. "I have no idea," he said loudly. "All I know is that I'm having a tough time controlling them."

"Relax, Mr. Prince, I'm here to help."

"How do I know I can trust you?"

"It's called doctor-patient confidentiality."

Darius jumped up from his seat as if he had just hit the jackpot. "I figured it out," he shouted. "Sorry I took so long." He knew by the way Dr. Haus quickly sat up in his chair that he had gotten the doctor's attention.

"What exactly did you figure out?"

"I got to hand it to you, Doc. It was the toughest code I've ever had to crack."

"Code?"

Darius smiled and tossed him the brain. "The BP-14 on the brain. BP stands for British Police and if you subtract 1 from 4, you get 3. That means the British Police want me to go to the three Pyramids of Giza."

"Now we're getting somewhere." The doctor put down the brain and jotted down some more notes.

Darius tried to control his excitement and practically had to force himself to sit back down. He had successfully figured out the code and would soon learn the location of the Rebel base.

"According to your girlfriend, Paris, you took a three hundred thousand dollar loss at work. Tell me about that."

Darius took a deep breath and exhaled. "Doc, let's get one thing straight. She's no longer my girlfriend," he said, "I broke up with her."

"Do you regret breaking up with her?"

"No," he said. "My friends will say I'm crazy, but it's not safe for her to be around me."

"Mr. Prince, it doesn't matter what your friends think. Now, why don't you think it's safe for Paris to be—"

"What else did Paris tell you?"

The doctor paused briefly and glanced at his notes. "That you've been having dreams of the pyramids, Stonehenge, and the Devil ever since the comet Goliath exploded. Is that correct?"

"They're not dreams. They're visions. When the comet exploded, it told me everything. I have it all figured out."

"What have you figured out?"

Darius leaned forward. "If I don't get to the pyramids in time, there will be a huge war that the forces of evil will win."

"Excellent," Dr. Haus said. "We're really making progress. Now, we're going to play a word association game. I'm going to say a word and I want you to tell me the first thing that comes to your mind."

Darius took a deep breath and exhaled. "Okay, but make it quick," he said and leaned back.

Dr. Haus glanced at his notepad, and said, "Let's start with the word 'good.'"

Darius grinned and chuckled softly. "An old man with a long grey beard."

"How about 'evil?'"

"That's easy—a dragon."

Dr. Haus paused and picked up his coffee mug. He raised it to his lips and took a sip. "Tell me about the dreams you had about the pyramids."

'Somehow . . . I feel connected to them. The more I think about it the more I believe I have the power to—" He caught himself before he had said too much.

Dr. Haus leaned forward. "Please, continue the thought."

The doctor was definitely hiding something.

"Not so fast. I have a question for you."

Dr. Haus flashed him a phony smile. "Let's talk more about your connection to the pyramids. What power do you think you have?"

"I'm sorry, that's classified. There's only one man on this earth I will tell."

"Who's that?" Dr. Haus said with raised eyebrows.

"TC," he shouted. "Now, tell me the location of the Rebel base."

"TC?" the doctor said.

Darius saw a droplet of sweat trickle down the side of the doctor's face and realized that he had already said too much. His body went numb. Dr. Haus had masterfully lulled him into a false sense of security. He had skillfully extracted the information bit by bit with the precision of a surgeon. Even though the doctor had betrayed him, and a part of him felt like knocking him out, he knew there was only one thing to do. He had to try and help him.

Dr. Haus glanced at the box of pictures and looked up. "I get it. You saw the picture of Tom Cruise and think that we're friends."

"Doc, you can drop the charade. I know they've gotten to you."

Dr. Haus smiled and leaned forward. "Mr. Prince, I need you to listen to me. I don't know Tom Cruise. My sister gave me the autographed photo as a joke. 'TC' isn't particularly fond of psychiatrists."

"Doc, if you listen to me I can help you get your soul back."

"Mr. Prince, you are experiencing delusions of grandeur caused by the monetary loss you suffered and the shock you experienced when the comet exploded. You have bipolar schizophrenia coupled with financial insecurity disorder," he said, adjusting his glasses on his nose. He leaned back in his leather chair and pushed himself back from the desk a couple inches. He placed his elbows on the arm chair rests and steepled his fingers. "Right now you're experiencing the manic phase of the illness and, as a result, tend to believe that everything is aimed at you," he said. "It's very common for bipolar people to think that celebrities are trying to contact them."

"It's not an illness, it's a divine gift. I just happen to be more in tune with the universe than most people. Doc, I'm telling you . . . I have the power to help you."

"No, Mr. Prince, we're here to help *you*. I'm going to start you on a new drug called BP-14. It'll help balance you out."

"I'm not taking the drug; I'm not sick." He looked at the doctor's briefcase. "How do you sleep at night knowing that you sold your soul to the Devil? You tell Lucifer and his gang of Fallen Angels that my soul's not for sale."

"Mr. Prince, you're making this all up in your head."

Darius jumped to his feet. "That's what you Fallen Angels want me to think," he shouted.

"Mr. Prince, please sit down. Our session isn't over."

Darius placed his hands shoulder-width apart on the desk and leaned forward. "You know what the problem with you quacks is? Whenever you can't figure out what's wrong with someone, you label them as bipolar."

"This is your last warning, Mr. Prince. Please, sit down."

Darius leaned his weight into his arms and pushed his hands down on the desk top. He jumped up on it and looked down at the doctor who was visibly shaken. "Join with me before it's too late," he said and swung an imaginary sword through the air. When the doctor backed his seat up against the wall, Darius jumped backward off the desk and looked into his eyes.

"Remember one thing," he said. "Last time Christ came like a lamb to the slaughter. This time, when he returns, he will roar like a lion." He turned and headed for the door.

"Mr. Prince, do you think that you're Christ?"

Darius stopped. *Could he be the Messiah?*

"Mr. Prince, the door is locked. If you don't calm down and return to your seat, I will be forced to call the orderlies."

Darius turned and in a pseudo Scottish accent said, "If you don't give me the keys I'm goin' to cut your head off, Highlander."

Dr. Haus moved his seat forward and pressed the intercom button on his desk. "All stations, code green, Dr. Haus's office."

"You shouldn't have done that," Darius said. He picked up the uncomfortable wooden chair he'd been sitting in and raised it high above his head.

The doctor's hands trembled. He pressed the intercom button again. "All stations, code—"

"There can only be one," Darius said and swung down the chair. The doctor dove to the floor just as the chair smashed the intercom and broke into pieces.

"Okay, okay, okay," the doctor shouted. "I'll tell you where the Rebel base is!"

"Too late," Darius said and grabbed a chair leg off the desk. "The location has been compromised."

Dr. Haus scrambled to his feet and backed himself up against the wall. His body trembled. "Mr. Prince, you need to calm down."

Darius laughed and swung the chair leg through the air as if it were a sword. He moved around the desk and placed the splintered tip against the doctor's throat.

"You're lucky I'm learning to control the souls inside of me. They both want your head, but I told them you're not worth it." He withdrew the chair leg from the doctor's throat and tossed it to the floor. "You tell your associates," he said, jabbing the doctor's chest after each word with his index finger, "I will never, ever, tell them what I know."

"Tell them yourself." He pointed dismissively to the door behind Darius.

"Mr. Prince, stay where you are," came a deep voice from behind him.

Darius turned. Three orderlies the size of linebackers circled him. "It's gonna take an army of millions to take me down." He lunged forward and struck the orderly in the middle with a crushing blow to the temple. The orderly fell to the floor, unconscious. He felt another orderly grab him from behind while he watched the third pull out a syringe. Darius elbowed the man holding him hard in the gut and flipped him on his back.

"Two down . . . one to go," Darius said, brushing his hands together. He stared at the last orderly who cracked his knuckles and took a step forward. It was then he noticed that the orderly no longer had the syringe. When he turned to look for Dr. Haus, he felt the same sharp stinging sensation in his shoulder as he did the night before. His knees buckled and he fell to the floor.

As he lay there on his back, fighting to keep his eyes from closing, he noticed that the doctor seemed to be looking down at him with a supremely satisfied smile plastered across his face.

"*There can only be one,* Mr. Prince. There can only be one," he heard him say before everything went black.

CHAPTER 35

"**M**IND THE STUDIO for a couple of hours," Laura said and pulled her long blonde hair into a ponytail. "I have a hair appointment."

"Just make sure you're back by three," her student said. "I don't want to be late for my audition."

Laura jogged down the six flights of stairs and out onto the crowded city sidewalk. As she headed up Broadway, she tried to figure out what Paris was up to. Still fuming from the confrontation earlier at the hospital, she navigated her way through the tourists scurrying about the theater district. Who was Paris trying to kid anyway? She didn't care about Darius. Laura had been dead-on when she said all she cared about was money. Paris Templar was up to something and she was going to find out what.

After reaching the corner of 57th and Broadway, she saw a Harley motorcade heading south toward her. She turned right and walked toward Seventh Avenue. Midway up the block the motorcade roared past her. Her eyes opened wide. The limousine had Israeli flags on it.

Why didn't Sy tell her the prime minister was coming to town?

When the motorcade hung a right on Seventh, she had a hunch where it was headed. The prime minister often ate at Carnegie Deli, which was only two blocks up. She took a deep breath and hurried off after them.

From half a block away she saw a crowd forming outside of the deli. Her heartbeat quickened. She picked up the pace but when she neared the deli, she froze. To her surprise, the prime minister emerged from the limo with Sy

Kurtz. They were escorted into the deli by three agents dressed in black suits and sunglasses who quickly exited and stood guard outside.

Not only had Sy failed to mention he would be in town, but he had failed to make good on a promise long overdue. It had been three years since her father had died and she still hadn't been able to talk to the prime minister about it. There were a few unanswered questions about her father's death she needed to know and only he could answer. She was beginning to think she would never get to meet with him. Just this week Sy had sworn up and down that the next time the prime minister was scheduled to be in New York City, he would tell her and set up a meeting. Why had he failed to do so?

He better have a good explanation for this, she thought, as she jogged over to the three agents who were guarding the entrance. At wit's end, and in desperate need of closure, she smiled and tried to move past them.

One of the agents stepped in front of her. "Sorry Miss, the deli is closed," he said in an Israeli accent. "Please move along."

"Can you please tell the prime minister and Sy Kurtz that Laura Rigel is outside? They know me well."

"I have been given strict orders not to disturb them."

"It's okay," she said, "Sy Kurtz is a personal friend of mine. Just tell him Laura Rigel is outside?"

"Like I said, I have strict orders not to disturb them. Please move along."

When Laura responded by placing her hands on her hips, and glaring at them, two of the agents grabbed her by each arm. "Get your hands off of me," she shouted. She struggled to free herself as they escorted her to an awaiting suburban, but her efforts proved futile. "I really do know them," she said. "My father was killed while protecting the prime minister."

The agents didn't seem to care. They threw her up against the truck and patted her down. When they were done, she turned and faced them. "How dare you," she said annoyed.

"This is your last warning," one of the agents said. "Leave now or we're going to have you arrested."

Laura glanced at the entrance. It wasn't worth it, she thought. Sy was up to something but she couldn't hang around to find out what. If she did, she knew the agents would make good on their promise. She'd call Sy later and give him an earful.

CHAPTER 36

T HE DARKNESS THAT surrounded him was mysterious and
cold like two strangers passing in the night. Darius pulled the
pillow, wet with drool, away from his face and sat up. He swung his legs off
the bed and stood up. The shock of his bare feet hitting the cold hard floor
made him shiver. He ran his hand along the wall and switched on the lights.
He froze. On the back of the door he saw a white straitjacket hanging over his
dress shirt and suit pants.

They were getting ready to take him away.

He felt like jumping back into bed and hiding beneath the covers but when
he remembered the list of rules and regulations the goddess had given him, the
feeling faded. He pulled the paper out of his pocket and read down the list. He
didn't have to read too far. The guards did a bed check at midnight. He glanced
at the clock above the door; it was eleven-thirty. He still had time. Looking out
of the barred window over his bed, he knew he had to move fast. He would
escape tonight. When they came to check on him he would be ready.

Darius pulled his wallet, passport, and Solofōn out from under the mattress
and changed into his dress clothes. He placed the extra pillows he had found
in the closet lengthwise on his bed and laid a blanket over them. He turned off
the lights and walked into the bathroom. He ripped the shaving mirror off the
wall, unscrewed all the light bulbs, and hid behind the dark green shower
curtain. Every second felt like an eternity.

Just before midnight, he heard a noise at the window. *What the hell was
that?* He slowly tilted the mirror up and down and caught the image of what
appeared to be a woman standing over his bed. With the dramatic flair of a

magician, she whipped the blanket off the bed. Upon discovering only pillows, she pulled out a gun and aimed it around the room. Cautiously, she made her way toward the bathroom. Darius felt his heartbeat quicken.

As he waited to make his move, he heard the sound of footsteps in the hallway. Was help on the way? The faint sound of his assailants breathing in the darkness snapped him out of his thoughts. When he heard the light switch in the bathroom click on and off, he cocked his arm back and readied himself. Suddenly, the door to his room swung open and slammed hard against the wall. Light from the hallway flooded the room. He ripped open the shower curtain and saw a security guard tackle the woman into the bathroom and wrestle her to the floor.

Darius froze. The forces of good and evil were battling it out right before his eyes! But who was who? He wasn't gonna stick around to find out. He bolted out of the bathroom and tried to open the bedroom door but couldn't. It was locked. He turned and headed for the window. When he reached it, he was surprised to see that the bars had been melted. It appeared as though acid had eaten right through them. Mindful not to touch them, he climbed through the window and rushed down the fire escape.

It had been two nights since the new moon and there was barely any light to guide him. He released the fire escape ladder and climbed down. The moment his feet touched the ground, a tall heavyset woman holding a double-bladed axe stepped out of the shadows; she raised the axe high above her head and moved toward him. Slowly, he moved backward until his back was up against the building. He looked around the alley. There wasn't a person or security camera in sight and only one way out.

"Who are you people?" he asked.

She tossed him a pair of handcuffs. "Put those on."

Darius caught them and glanced up at his ninth-story window. The woman who had broken into his room was bludgeoning the security guard on the fire escape and attempting to throw him off.

Darius focused his gaze back to his assailant in the alley. "Put them on me yourself," he said and tossed the cuffs on the ground by the fire escape. When the woman moved over and scooped them up with the axe, Darius grinned and pointed up. Before she even had a chance to look up, the man's body landed on her, slamming her into the ground. He felt a sudden rush of adrenaline rip through his body as he watched the blood ooze from her head. The sound of the other woman racing down the fire escape snapped him out of his thoughts and back to the situation at hand. He rifled through the security guard's pockets and found a twenty-dollar bill and a business card for the Riddle of the Sphinx Café in Egypt. His heart raced as he stared at the picture of the Sphinx guarding the three Pyramids of Giza. Everything suddenly became clear.

Paris was right! The Rebel base *was* in Egypt. He darted out of the alley and jumped into one of the many taxis lining the street. "Gothic Hotel," he said and ducked his head down low. He took a few deep breaths to calm him himself but when he raised his head and peeked out of the back window, he felt a sudden surge of adrenaline rush through his body. His assailant was running toward his taxi.

He could see her clearly now. It was the woman he met in the Camelot Bar, Bella. How had she known which taxi he was in?

He pulled the twenty out of his pocket and held it up against the plexiglass divider. "Jackson's yours if you step on it," he said and glanced over his shoulder. He watched Bella leap toward the taxi with outstretched arms but just before she could reach it the taxi jerked forward and sped off downtown. The woman tumbled hard to the ground and disappeared in the traffic behind them.

Darius pulled out his Solofōn and punched in Laura's number. She answered after the third ring.

"Listen closely. I just escaped from the hospital," he said. "Some women tried to kidnap me."

"You okay?"

"Can you meet me at the Gothic Hotel?"

"I'll be there in fifteen minutes."

Darius heard a burst of static on the phone. So that's how they were tracking him, he thought. "I gotta go," he said and tossed the phone out of the window.

CHAPTER 37

D ARIUS JOGGED UP the sweeping cast iron staircase. When he
reached the landing, he stopped and stared out of a sixteen-foot
window overlooking the hotel entrance on West Broadway.

The deception ran much deeper than he originally thought. For all he
knew, they'd been watching him his entire life. He hurried through the busy
lobby that bled into the spacious bar and lounge and scanned the crowded
Soho hotspot.

The chic late-night crowd of celebrities, models, and artists, who were
either on display or displaying their newest artistic creations, sipped their
pricey martinis as the DJ set the mood with atmosphere-rich tunes. He finally
spotted Laura's purple sparkle salsa shoes at the bar. Without hesitation, he
pushed his way through a group of guys who were staring at her black halter
top and tight blue jeans from behind.

Darius grabbed her around the waist. "I almost didn't recognize you with
the new hair-do," he whispered. She spun around as if performing in a dance
competition. Her short, jet black hair had a stylish punk rocker look to it. She
reached up and hugged him. The familiar floral fragrance of her perfume
captivated him. The feel of her soft hair against his face made him tremble.
Darius gently pushed her away and took her by the hand.

"Come with me," he said.

"Are you hurt?"

Darius didn't reply. He led her away from the bar past a bevy of beautiful
models dressed in colorful designer galabias. When he noticed one of the

younger models staring at him, he smiled half-heartedly and looked back at Laura. "Coming here was a mistake."

He spotted a couple getting up from a table in the back and quickly pulled her over to it. He sat down on the crushed velvet sofa facing the entrance and stared through the crowd. Laura placed her purse on the copper-topped table and sat down next to him. He loosened the collar of his dress shirt and played with the silver chain around his neck.

Laura placed her hand on top of his. "Who tried to kidnap you?"

Darius pulled his hand away and pushed the hair back off his face. "A Russian woman named Bella that I met on my birthday. She just killed a guy who I think was trying to protect me. I thought I had given her the slip but she tracked me down."

Laura paused. "She tracked you down?"

"Had'ta be the GPS on my phone," he said. "Out of a dozen or so taxis, she knew exactly which one I was in."

"You sure she was trying to *kidnap* you?"

"Positive. But she won't find me here," he said, glancing at the entrance. "I got rid of my phone after I spoke to you."

Laura's Solofōn chimed with a text message. She reached into her purse and pulled it out. As she quietly read through the message, he glanced at the entrance again and then looked back at her. She had a stunned look on her face.

"What's wrong?"

Laura's face tensed. "Sy Kurtz—he's dead."

"What?"

A loud whoosh of air escaped her. "Earlier this evening he killed several people in a Mosque in Harlem and then turned the gun on himself." She paused. "I know he took it hard when the prime minister didn't sign the peace treaty and join the Eurasian Union but—"

"Sy didn't have a mean bone in his body. I betcha they drugged him."

"You might be right. I just saw him today with the prime minister at the Carnegie Deli."

Darius glanced at the entrance and turned back to Laura. "Our daughter appeared to me in a dream."

Laura fell silent.

"She was beautiful," he said, smiling, "like an angel. She pointed to the pyramids and told me to fulfill my destiny." Looking back at the entrance, his eyes opened wide.

"Darius, stop it! We don't have a daughter. We never did."

"Shh," he said, nudging her with his elbow, "the Russian, Bella, just walked in with her two friends."

▲ ▲ ▲

The three women were dressed in black leather biker jackets, short black leather skirts and black leather boots laced up to their knees. Laura never saw so much leather. She turned and looked at Darius, who was now holding a drink menu up in front of his face. "Which one is Bella?" she whispered.

"The woman in the middle who keeps looking down at her phone."

Had Sy lied to her? Laura ripped the chain from off of Darius's neck.

"Why'd you do that?" He paused, trying to fathom what was going on. After a long moment, he turned toward her. "So that's how they're tracking me," he said with an astonished look on his face. "I can't believe you sold me out."

"Darius, I know what it looks like but you have to believe me, I had no idea the chain was a tracking device," Laura said and reached into her purse. She pulled out some cash and stuffed it into his shirt pocket. "There's ninety dollars there," she said and stood up. "Get out of here now. I'll take care of them."

"I don't want your money," he said and grabbed her by the arm. "I want answers."

"Darius, there's no time." With her free hand she motioned to the women who were pushing their way across the dance floor. "You need to go," she said and pulled her arm free. She turned and casually made her way over toward the bathroom. Skillfully using the crowd to shield her, she glanced over her shoulder and saw Bella and her crew heading in her direction.

Thank God, she thought, and quickened her pace. The chain Sy had asked her to give to Darius *was* a tracking device. Just as she reached the bathroom, she looked back and saw Darius standing at the entrance to the bar. His arms were folded across his chest and he was staring at her. He shook his head from side to side as if to say he could never forgive her, and then turned and hurried out of the bar. Laura pushed her way into the crowded bathroom and barged into the handicapped stall. Three models were powdering their noses with what appeared to be endorphinate powder.

"Got an extra blast?" Laura said, smiling.

They dropped the vial on the floor and rushed out of the stall. Why would Sy want Darius tracked? She flushed the necklace down the toilet. More importantly, were they working for Sy? The sound of the bathroom door slamming against the wall snapped her out of her thoughts. Her heart raced. She placed a noticeable amount of endorphinate powder around her nostrils and then slipped the vial into her pocket. When she turned and opened the door, Bella was standing there with a confused look on her scarred face.

"It's all yours," Laura said. She wiped the white powder off of her nose as she listened to Bella's accomplices kick in the other stalls. Laura tried to move past her but Bella refused to move. She just stood there, staring at Laura as though she was trying to put a name to her face.

Laura pulled out the vial and offered it to her. "Wanna blast?" she slurred, swaying back and forth as if she was about to fall over.

"Out of my way, junkie," Bella said in a deep Russian accent. She pushed her to the side and checked the stall.

Laura moved over to the sink but kept a watchful eye on Bella and her associates in the mirror. She noticed a tattoo on the small of Bella's back—a red pentagram rested on the back of a yellow butterfly cocooned in a ring of purple.

It hit Laura that the women probably belonged to the same group that had infected Darius's computer with the pentagram virus. Laura splashed her face with water as she listened to Bella bark out what sounded like commands in Russian. Her associates responded with hand and head signals and then charged out of the bathroom. By the look of things, Laura had to admit that she was dealing with highly trained professionals.

She wiped her face with a towel and watched Bella slowly walk toward the bathroom door. When she reached it, she opened it halfway and looked over her shoulder. She shot Laura a longing glance that seemed to last an eternity before rushing out of the room.

Laura remained in the bathroom for a few moments and then cautiously made her way toward the hotel lobby. Why were they after Darius? A gut-wrenching feeling swirled in the pit of her stomach as she thought about her father. Why had he always tried to protect her, even when she was wrong? Her long suppressed suspicions about her father were aroused. But in this case, his overprotectiveness had placed her life at risk. Perhaps it was part of the package that came with being adopted. But, no matter how much it pained her, she could no longer deny the facts. He and Sy had purposely withheld vital information about Darius from her.

Should she fear for their lives? She thought back to the psychology class she had met Darius in during their freshman year in college. She smiled at the memory. Darius never missed a class and had told her that if it wasn't for the huge crush he had on her, he would never have gone. Her smile faded when she remembered the double life he had lived full of drugs and fast women, all held together by a web of lies he cunningly spun around her.

She sighed. If it wasn't for her father, she might have had the baby and stayed in the abusive relationship. After all, he swore up and down until the day he died that Darius was evil and was never to be trusted.

Maybe he was wrong. But now that Sy Kurtz was gone, she might never find out the truth.

From the top of the grand staircase, Laura moved the velvet curtains aside and watched the three women pile into an SUV. Who were these women? And why would Sy want Darius tracked? It just didn't make sense. Even though Sy was the one who had given her the necklace, she still had a hard time understanding why he would do such a thing. She cringed at the thought of being betrayed, but at the same time chuckled knowing that if the women were still following the signal, they would ultimately end up staring into the East River.

Were they *Ghostriders?*

If so, what did they want with Darius? At least one thing was certain; Bella definitely wasn't an IDF agent. The prime minister would never have allowed one of his agents to have a tattoo, let alone a tattoo of a pentagram. Something else was certain as well. There was more to Darius than her father and Sy had originally told her. Why did her father insist that he was evil? Granted, he did some terrible things when they were together—but evil? She wasn't so sure. He had even tried to make amends with her long after their relationship had ended.

The more she thought about Sy's involvement, the more she realized that Chaim Soloman was probably at the bottom of this. He was the one who wanted Darius tracked. Not Sy. He just used Sy to do his bidding.

As she made her way past some tough-talking British executives dressed to the nines, the idea that Bella might have recognized her made her uneasy. If her hunch was correct, and Bella was a Ghostrider, then she and Darius were in grave danger.

If the Ghostriders had intercepted the codes for the tracking device, which she strongly believed to be the case, then they were probably behind Sy Kurtz's death as well. There was no way Sy Kurtz, a staunch supporter of peace, willingly walked into a Mosque and opened fire. It was totally uncharacteristic of him.

She would have to split town until she had a better understanding of what she was up against. It wouldn't be long until Bella figured out who she was and came looking for her, too.

CHAPTER 38

A S THE TAXI arrived at John F. Kennedy Airport, Darius noticed soldiers patrolling the terminal. Armed with laser machine guns and bomb-sniffing dogs, he felt as if he had arrived at a futuristic concentration camp where escape seemed impossible. When the taxi stopped next to three soldiers dressed in fatigues, he raised the tinted window three-quarters of the way and sunk down into his seat.

He could hear one of the soldier's radios announce that President Walker's flight was going to be delayed. He wondered if the president was coming there to meet with him, but the thought faded as he listened to a news broadcast over the car radio—the president was scheduled to make an important announcement at the United Nations later that day. A moment later, he sat up stunned.

This was all Sy Kurtz's fault, he thought. Now that peace between the Jews and the Muslims had suffered another major setback, President Walker was abandoning the peace process for the chip. He had to be coming to town to announce that he was now in favor of a chip-based cashless society.

Traitor.

His zone ministers must have threatened to turn their voters against him if he didn't endorse it. Norman was right. Walker was going to sell out the country to ensure his re-election. Nero Technology's chip would most likely become the focus of his campaign. Darius knew this would be the final step before the seemingly elusive one-world government became a reality.

He had to stop him. But how? As he thought about his triumphant walk to work the day before, everything became clear. If he could mobilize the masses, then all he had to do was rally the people against the chip. Then, Walker would have no other choice but to abandon it. He didn't have a moment to waste. He had to locate the Rebel base and organize a revolution to stop the president.

"Cash, credit or chip?" the driver said and held up a barcode scanner.

Darius scanned his smart card and handed the driver the twenty dollar bill he had promised him. He let down his wavy brown hair, took a deep breath, and exited the taxi. As he hurried into the Delta Airlines terminal, feelings of guilt and betrayal seemed to sneak up behind him.

Why had Laura deceived him? Besides his mother, she was the last person in the world he thought would sell him out. Darius shook his head from side to side. He should have seen it coming. He had treated Laura poorly during their relationship and obviously she had never gotten over it. She had stayed friends with him all of these years for one reason—revenge. She wanted him to pay for putting her through those three years of hell.

But why had she come to his rescue in the eleventh hour? It was probably all part of her premeditated plan to destroy him. With every breath he took, the thought consumed him more and more. He vowed to get even.

When he reached the Delta Airlines check-in counter, he noticed a young man wearing a blue uniform with a matching cap standing in front of a large triangular logo. Instantly, he knew that he was in the right place.

The agent smiled. "Checking in?"

"I need a ticket on the next flight to Cairo." He noticed an armed guard out of the corner of his eye.

"Do you have a chip implant?"

"No," he said, shaking his head.

"The reason I ask is that if you'd had one, you wouldn't need a passport. I'd just scan your hand and you would have your ticket within seconds. You'd breeze right through security and immigration—speeding up the process of your entire journey. It saves time and money and makes your trip hassle-free," he said. "Think about it, no more long lines."

"Spare me the sales pitch," Darius said and handed him his smart card and passport.

The agent frowned. "Mr. Prince," he said, looking up at Darius, "will Egypt be your final destination?"

"That's none of your business." He noticed a twenty dollar bill lying on the floor. He stepped on it and slowly looked around. He knelt down on one knee and made like he was tying his shoe. When he felt comfortable that nobody was watching him, he lifted his foot and in one fluid motion scooped up the bill, stood up and nonchalantly slipped it into his pocket.

"It is my business," the agent said. "Egypt is the only country in the Eurasian Union that's not on-line with the chip. So, a temporary implant isn't mandatory unless you plan on traveling somewhere else within Eurasia. Would you like a temporary chip implanted into your right-hand so you can travel outside of Egypt?"

Darius took a step back. "Absolutely not. That's the number of the Beast."

The agent laughed and typed his information into the computer. "The next available flight is at 9:00 a.m."

Darius paused. By then the authorities would be looking for him in connection with the death of the security guard at the hospital. He kept his cool and looked up at the flight screen above the agent's head. "What about the 3:30 a.m. flight?"

"The supersonic jet is sold out. The last ticket was just purchased a few minutes ago."

Darius sighed. His brilliant idea to join forces with the Fallen Angels in the hospital had backfired and he had been replaced. Once again, his ego had gotten in the way of his humility. "Who purchased the ticket?"

"I'm not at liberty to say."

Darius glanced over his shoulder and noticed a gray haired lady in a rose print tank dress standing behind him shaking her head from side to side. He turned his attention back to the agent. "You don't understand. I have to be on that flight. It could mean the difference between life and death for all of mankind."

The agent rolled his eyes and sucked in a deep breath as he checked the passenger list. "There's one seat in first class that hasn't been confirmed."

"So, I still have a chance."

"I'm afraid not," the old lady from behind him said as she pushed her way past him. "That's my seat."

Darius stepped to the side. He stared at the frail old lady. She gave him such a nasty look in passing that he was sure there was divine intervention at work.

But who was she? Overwhelmed by the thought, his mind began to race.

The old lady was really the great mother goddess in disguise. She had purposely purchased the last ticket so he couldn't make the flight.

What did he have to do to gain her trust?

Darius felt like giving her a piece of his mind but played it cool and tapped her lightly on the shoulder. "Excuse me, Miss," he calmly drawled. When she turned, he smiled and said, "I will gladly pay you nine thousand dollars for your ticket."

"Sorry, my ticket's not for sale," she said. "I'm going to see my daughter who's about to give birth."

This time Darius flashed her one of his handsome smiles that usually allowed him to get his way with women. "First time being a grandmother?"

She scoffed. "Like you really care." She crossed her arms. "I saw what you did before and I do not approve of it."

"Sir," the agent interrupted, "flight 969 has been delayed until after Air Force One arrives. It was rerouted due to an electrical storm over the Atlantic. That gives you another half-hour for somebody to change their mind and give up their seat."

"Okay, put me on standby."

The agent handed him back his smart card and passport. "Good luck."

Darius put them away and looked at the goddess who stormed off toward the departure gate. Of course, he thought. She must've seen him pocket the twenty dollar bill. Obviously she had been disgusted by his actions.

No matter how he looked at it, he had just suffered a major setback. Handing over the money now would just validate his guilt. As he walked toward the departure gate, he realized he had to do something miraculous to prove he was worthy of being on that flight.

▼ ▲ ▼

Darius looked around the heavily guarded terminal for a sign. When all he saw were exit signs, he wondered if the goddess was trying to tell him that she no longer trusted him and that he was on his way out.

Overwhelmed by the possibility of being left behind, he realized he had only one option left. He would somehow have to tap into the spirit world and get God to overrule the great mother goddess's decision. His heartbeat quickened. If he failed, the flight would take off without him.

Darius closed his eyes and prayed for God to intervene. When he opened them, he saw the old lady shaking her fist at him. His heart dropped. His prayer had not been answered. Slowly, he started turning around and around in a circle. He had to figure out a way to break into the spirit world. If he couldn't, he would end up right back where he started—in the mental hospital or possibly even jail. He could feel the terminal walls closing in around him.

Spiraling out of control, he banged into a tall man covered from head to toe in a hooded burlap robe and fell backwards. "For Christ's sake," the man said and lunged toward him with outstretched arms. He grabbed Darius by the wrists, steadied him, and pulled him close. Darius could still hear the man's words echoing in his head but, try as he might, he couldn't get a good look at his face that was hidden beneath his gray-beard and hood. He shifted his gaze down and looked at the large wooden cross hanging from a leather cord around his neck.

Was the priest indirectly telling him that he was Jesus? After all, his mother's name was Mary. And, since Jesus and God were one and the same, if he was Jesus then he was God and ultimately controlled his own fate. The thought faded when he realized this was exactly what the Fallen Angels wanted him to think. Maybe he was still suffering from the effects of the song from a couple mornings ago that had made him feel immortal. He had to remember to keep up his guard. They'd stop at nothing to find out everything he knew.

He noticed the name "Mo" on the priest's name tag and everything became clear. Darius stared at him almost hypnotically, and then pulled his hands free. He reached up and touched his bearded face. "Moses?"

"Yes, my son?" His voice was deep, yet comforting.

Darius didn't respond, but, instead, just stood there staring. After a rather long awkward moment, Moses lifted his hands and slowly removed his hood.

"My son . . . help me . . . help you."

The words were like music to his ears. He had pulled it off. He had tapped into the spirit world and had connected with, of all people, the prophet Moses who was cleverly disguised as a priest. Relishing the moment, Darius gazed upon his long gray hair and unkempt beard protruding wildly from his elongated face. The wrinkles around his eyes and the lines gouged deep into his face were proof of the suffering he had endured while trying to make the world a better place. If there was anyone who had a direct line to God, it was Moses. If he could help him, then the prophet would ask God to intervene on his behalf. He had a feeling this was going to be his toughest challenge yet.

Darius smiled humbly. "Moses, how do I prove that I am worthy?"

"The good Lord says that if you give then you shall receive," he said with a southern drawl and handed Darius an envelope. "You can start by making a contribution to my mission."

Darius stared at the bold red letters that spelled out *MISSION POSSIBLE* and looked up stunned. Moses was indirectly telling him that his mission to get on the flight was possible. Darius reached into his pocket and handed him the twenty dollar bill he had found.

"Bless you, my child," he said, making the sign of the cross.

Darius looked at the goddess who was talking on the phone. She was watching him—and did not seem impressed. He turned his attention back to the prophet who smiled half-heartedly and walked away. Did he really think a twenty dollar donation was enough to get Moses to drop what he was doing so he could ask God to intervene? He had to figure out a way to prove his worthiness or he risked being left behind. Overwhelmed with the thought, he looked up at the departure screen. Time was running out.

He took off after the prophet, who was talking with an elderly couple.

"Moses," Darius said, interrupting their conversation, "I can help you."

"You already have."

"You don't understand . . . I'm a stockbroker . . . if there's one thing I know how to do, it's raise money."

Moses held up a hand to pause. "One moment," he said. "These beautiful children of God may be interested in helping us with our cause."

Darius glanced at his watch. He had exactly twenty-one minutes before Air Force One landed and flight 969 disembarked. When the couple excused themselves and walked off, the prophet turned and looked at him.

"My son, if I don't get any more donations before my flight departs, many orphaned children will starve."

"How much do we need to raise?"

"One hundred and ninety dollars," he said and handed him the six remaining envelopes. "But you must hurry. My flight to Tanzania boards shortly."

Darius stood at attention and gave him a snappy salute. "Your Holiness!" he said. "You can count on me to get the job done."

Moses smiled at him. "If you pull this off, God will shed his grace on thee."

"Let's hope you're right!" He turned and looked around the terminal. This isn't going to be easy, he thought. People in New York hated to give strangers money; everyone was always getting scammed. Darius spotted a middle-aged man reading the newspaper and headed over to him.

"Excuse me, sir, would you like to make a donation to help the mission of Jesus Christ Almighty?"

He looked up from behind his paper and scowled. "Not a chance, buddy. I'm not supporting your drug habit."

"Sir, I can assure you that all of the proceeds will be used to feed starving children in Africa."

The man scoffed. "I could give a rat's ass about the kids in Africa or your mission. Now beat it before I call the cops," he said and continued reading his paper.

Darius decided it was best not to argue with him and hurried off. He approached a woman who was talking on a pay phone and holding a young boy's hand. "Excuse me, Miss, would you like to make a donation to help the mission of Jesus Christ," he said and handed her an envelope.

She took the envelope and turned away from him. Darius ran his fingers through his hair and looked around the terminal as he waited for her to finish her conversation. He felt a light tug on his pant leg and looked down at the young boy.

"Mister, are you Jesus Christ?"

Darius paused. Why did people keep referring to him as Jesus? Did they know something he didn't? If they did, and he was Christ reincarnated, would they accept him as their savior and be willing to die for him? Or, would they curse his name and try to crucify him again? Did the children of the beast truly comprehend what a godless world would be like?

Darius smiled humbly at the boy. "No, I'm not Jesus."

The boy's mother hung up the phone and handed him back the empty envelope. She gave him a dirty look and pulled the boy away. Knowing that he now had two strikes against him, he searched the terminal for a friendly face. When he couldn't find one, he glanced up at the flight screen. His heart dropped. His flight was now boarding. He took a deep breath and thought about what the prophet had told him.

If you give, then you shall receive.

Darius ran over to the ATM machine next to the departure gate and scanned his card. When the machine told him that it was out of money, he realized that the Fallen Angels didn't want him on the flight either. They had purposely drained the machine of all its cash. He started to panic. The thought of failure tore through his mind with frightening complexity. He pulled the money Laura had given him out of his shirt pocket and ran over to Moses, who was soliciting the great mother goddess as she talked on the phone.

"All I have is ninety dollars," Darius said, panting and out of breath, "were you able to raise any more money?"

Moses sighed. "I'm afraid not. Unless a miracle happens in the next thirty seconds, our mission will fail."

Darius lowered his head. He had failed to have God intervene on his behalf and overrule the goddess's decision. He looked up and grabbed Moses's hand and placed the money in it.

"This is the best I could do," he said and turned on his heels to leave.

"It's a miracle," he heard Moses shout.

Darius stopped. He turned and stared at the back of a one hundred dollar bill the prophet was proudly holding in the air. Looking at Independence Hall, he noticed the phrase *In God We Trust.* He glanced at the goddess and then shifted his gaze back to Moses. "Did the goddess give that to you?"

"No," he said, "you did. Mission accomplished."

Darius wondered if Laura had made a mistake and given him more money or if, again, divine intervention was at work. Either way he looked at it, he had still failed.

The prophet waved goodbye and walked through the gate. A moment later, he felt a tap on his shoulder. He turned.

As if the sun had broken through a cloudy sky, a smile appeared on the goddess's face. "That was a very noble thing you just did," she said.

He took a deep breath and exhaled. "Even though I won't make the flight," he said, "I helped the children in Mo's orphanage and that's what counts." He smiled. "You better hurry up or you're going to miss your flight."

She smiled back. "My daughter just told me that the stork won't be coming for at least another week. So, I would very much like to make a donation to you," she said and handed him her ticket. "You have proved your worthiness."

Darius smiled from ear to ear. He hugged the woman and gave her a big kiss on the cheek. "How can I repay you for your kindness?"

"You just did," she said, fanning herself with her hand. "Now hurry up, you have a plane to catch."

CHAPTER 39

M OHAMMED STORMED INTO his palace office only to find his brother, Zadam, lounging in his leather chair. "Get your feet off of my desk and your butt out of my chair now," he said and moved toward him. "I have a conference call with President Walker shortly." When Zadam responded by leaning back and placing his hands behind his head, Mohammed leveled a condemning stare.

"My patience is running thin with you. Out of my chair. Now!"

Zadam cracked a thin smile. "Be careful, my brother," he said and slowly removed his boots off of the desk.

"Is that a threat?"

Zadam rose from the chair and shook his head from side to side. He chuckled softly. "I was referring to your call with the president. You know he is going to try to brainwash you into believing that Chaim Soloman had nothing to do with the recent act of war against the Muslim people." He slammed both hands down hard on the desk. "Israel must pay for their insolence. We must strike now!"

Mohammed moved around him. He quietly sat down at his desk and placed the file he had brought with him down in front of him. He opened it and looked at Zadam. "Patience, my brother. Israel will get what it deserves," he said with a smile. "The president is beginning to explore his Islamic heritage and will soon prove to be a formidable ally of the Muslim people."

"I do not trust him," Zadam said.

"Don't you have other matters that you need to attend to?"

Zadam grunted.

"Leave me."

Mohammed watched Zadam turn sharply on his heels and march toward the door. "Don't you dare do anything foolish, my brother. Revenge will be ours soon enough." Zadam turned. He looked evenly at Mohammed and then hurried out of the room, slamming the door behind him.

"Your holiness," came the computer intercom, "President Walker is waiting."

"Put him through."

A holographic image of the president in a navy-blue suit and red tie appeared in the middle of the room. The president was sitting behind his desk on Air Force One with his hands folded neatly in front of him. "On behalf of the American Union and its State of Israel," he said in a deep yet comforting voice, "I would like to extend our deepest sympathies to the families of the Muslim people who died a most tragic and senseless death today. Chaim Soloman would like to personally express his condolences. May I add him to the call?"

"Mr. President, that won't be necessary," Mohammed said sternly.

The president rose from his desk. "Your Holiness, I can assure you that this was not a premeditated act by the Israelis. After an autopsy was performed on the body of Sy Kurtz, a high dose of endorphinate powder was found in his body."

Mohammed raised the classified file in the air. "Mr. President," he said, "I know everything before you do." He stood up and dropped the file on his desk and slowly made his way toward the hologram. When he reached it, he stopped and looked up at the president. "The drugs prove only one thing."

"Open your eyes," the president said. "This was an act of sabotage by the Ghostriders."

Mohammed slowly shook his head from side to side. "You just don't get it, do you," he said. "The saboteur is Chaim Soloman."

CHAPTER 40

D ARIUS STRETCHED HIS arms high above his head. He yawned and looked at the young boy in the window seat next to him. The shade was drawn and he was watching a movie. He looked to be Egyptian. When he felt the plane encounter some turbulence, he finished the glass of water on his dessert tray and buckled his seat belt. He glanced at his Rolex. It was seven o'clock in the morning New York time so he mindfully moved his watch seven hours ahead.

"Excuse me, Mr. Prince."

He looked up and stared at a beautiful dark-skinned flight attendant that he hadn't seen before.

"We will be landing shortly," she said. She smiled pleasantly and picked up his tray. "Do you want your apple?"

"Apple?"

She picked up the shiny red apple and held it out to him. He stared at it and then looked up into her emerald green eyes. She was an African goddess cleverly disguised as a flight attendant. She was sent to test him. If he was going to succeed, he would have to stay calm and work things through. If he failed, she would never grant him access to the motherland. Darius felt entranced by her beauty; he reached out and took the apple. He raised it to his mouth but when he noticed her nametag, he stopped before taking a bite.

Evelyn? The past was repeating itself. She wasn't a goddess at all; she was *Eve*, the mother of all humanity. *Lucifer* had sent her to tempt him.

Darius grinned. He was getting good at differentiating illusion from reality. He realized that he was reliving the scene between Adam and Eve, only he wasn't going to make the same mistake Adam did. He was going to right the wrong that they had made in the beginning.

"Nice try, Eve," he said and tossed her the apple. He chuckled softly. "I'm not starting this shit all over again."

"Excuse me," she said in a tone that was supposed to make him believe she had no idea what he was talking about.

"You can drop the act, honey, your cover is blown." He smiled with a sense of satisfaction and put on his head phones. She turned and walked away. He had passed this test but was sure there were more to come.

Darius closed his eyes and listened to the song, *Light Up The Sky*, by Van Halen, as the plane prepared to land. He wondered if Eddie V truly believed that he could light up the sky with his electrifying guitar-playing. God had clearly given Eddie the divine gift of music, but he was still unsure as to what his gift to humanity was going to be.

CHAPTER 41

HE AIR WAS dry and the heat unbearable. Darius gazed out through the open taxi window at the afternoon sun. A hawk circled high above the stretch of highway that sliced through the arid desert landscape.

What if he failed to answer the riddle of the sphinx? Would he be devoured by the guardian spirit and end up in hell, strapped to a gurney, with swarms of demons disguised as doctors telling him that he was insane? And what if he did solve the riddle, but couldn't find the handprints at the base of the pyramid he had dreamt about? Would the illusion become reality or was he, in reality, delusional? But, then again, what was reality?

God, it was hot.

He wiped the sweat from his brow and shot a look at the car's rearview mirror. The driver was watching him. For an instant, their eyes connected. Did the young woman really think that he wouldn't know she was an Egyptian goddess in disguise? He had better keep an eye on her, he thought, watching her dark brown hair flap around in the hot breeze. She hadn't said a word to him since she had picked him up. There could only be one reason for that—the goddesses still didn't trust him. Not only did they not trust him, but they were probably pissed off that he had questioned their authority and had gotten God to overrule them. He had to keep up his guard. It was obvious that he was going to have to pass yet another one of their stupid tests; he felt like telling her to go to hell. It wasn't worth it, he thought. He noticed her dark eyes following him in the mirror again. What feeble-minded test was she going to try and insult his intelligence with now?

Darius leaned forward. "Let me guess," he said. "Your name is Isis."

"Not quite, but you're on the right path. It's Ma'at."

"The goddess of balance," he said, clapping his hands together, "I should've known."

"First time visiting the pyramids?"

"Nope."

Her smile stretched across the mirror. "Which of the three pyramids is your favorite?"

"King Khufu's." He leaned back, dripping with sweat.

"The Great Pyramid is overrated. Menkaure, the smallest of the three, is my favorite."

"Tell me about Khufu's pyramid," he said excitedly, "what's it like?"

She frowned. "I thought you said you've been to the pyramids before."

"I have," he said, "but not in this life."

"You're a philosopher then?"

"What'd you think I was, a liar?" Darius pulled his hair back off his face. "Listen, I'm sick of you goddesses constantly testing me. If you're not careful I just might upset the balance."

She paused. "The heat is getting to you. Close your window. I'm turning on the AC."

"Now you're giving me orders. Who do you think you are, my girlfriend?"

"Trust me," she said.

"Yeah, right," he said annoyed. "I'm at the point where I can't trust anyone."

"Then you will fail in whatever you do. A word of advice," she said, "it always takes two. You can't do it all by yourself."

Reluctantly, Darius rolled up the tinted window. As he began to cool down, he realized what was happening. The sun god, Ra, had purposely turned up the heat to drive him mad so he would pick a fight with the goddess and fail to win her over. If he didn't stay focused, he was going to end up right back in the hospital.

Feel better?" she asked.

"Yes. Thank you."

He scanned the horizon for the pyramids and spotted the capstone of the Great Pyramid in the distance. His heart raced as he gazed upon the ancient wonder—the one that called out to him in his dreams.

CHAPTER 42

"**I** STILL THINK WE should wake Lucy."

Artemis turned. Roxanne walked out of the steam-filled bathroom in a fluffy white robe. When she reached the foot of the bed, she turned and moved in front of a large mirror hanging on the wall in front of her. Artemis tied a towel around her torso and with the prowess of a hunter, slowly walked toward her. She moved behind Roxanne and began caressing her shoulders and neck, but stopped when she heard the familiar knock at the door. She glanced over her shoulder and watched her hardened general, Bellatrix, march into the room. Donned in a white leather suit, Bellatrix remained expressionless as she moved toward them. Artemis shot her a wry look. "You're late." When her general responded by averting her eyes and lowering her head, Artemis moved next to Roxanne who was brushing her long black hair. She nudged her to the side and began brushing the knots out of her own hair as she spoke to her in the mirror.

"There will be no need to disturb Lucy from her regressive sleep." She glanced at Bellatrix who was pacing back and forth around the room and then focused her gaze back to Roxanne. By the look on her face, it appeared as though she didn't agree.

"Your Highness, I beg to differ," Roxanne said. "Your condition has worsened. Now you act as though there are three goddesses inside you. One minute you're loving . . . and the next . . . warlike. It is as if you have the souls of Venus and Athena within you as well. We must wake Lucy."

"Silence," Artemis commanded. She had better stop this insurrection immediately, she thought, and turned to look at her lover. "It is you I am worried about. You have failed me for the last time." She turned back to the mirror and started brushing her hair again.

"Either I didn't satisfy you sexually, my Queen, or you think that I'm sleeping with Zadam."

"I am referring to Darius Prince and Miss Laura Rigel. But since you brought it up, are you sleeping with Zadam?" Roxanne had piqued her curiosity. Artemis glanced at Bellatrix who had stopped pacing and was standing motionless behind them.

"No," she replied, nastily. "And I didn't fail you. Bellatrix did."

Bellatrix cracked her knuckles and moved behind Roxanne.

"You don't scare me," Roxanne said and turned around to face her.

"Enough!" Artemis dropped the brush and moved between them. She looked at Bellatrix. "Tell me. How does a ditsy little dance instructor like Laura Rigel, who has no military training whatsoever, help Darius elude my elite team of Amazons?"

"She looks different from photo," Bellatrix said, her eyes radiating a disturbing madness.

"I'll tell you why," Artemis said, turning back to Roxanne, "she wasn't thoroughly checked out."

"Of course she was," Roxanne said. "They dated during college but for the most part she has stayed out of Prince's life up until recently. Our intelligence reports indicate she is not IDF and had no idea the chain was a tracking device."

"Did it ever occur to you that our reports might be wrong? Find her and bring her to me," she said and then turned back to Bellatrix. "I want to meet the woman who outsmarted my general."

"Yes, Your Highness."

"Roxanne, there's one more thing. Even though Paris Templar isn't a true blooded Amazon like us, she's the only one who has executed her orders flawlessly."

"That's because *I* trained her."

"You might have trained her, but Paris takes her orders from *me*," Artemis said adamantly. "She knows too much and now poses a threat to our operation. Take her to the underground lair and have her reconditioned. She will fight alongside our army of Amazons once the battle of Armageddon commences."

Roxanne stared at her in disbelief. "If that's the case, are Bellatrix and I next on Your Highness's hit list?"

"Don't be silly. But, if you lied about sleeping with Zadam you will be at the top of the list along with Princess Zara," she said with a devious chuckle.

It was a good shot, but it wasn't going to force Roxanne into entering a guilty plea. It wasn't designed to. It was more of a warning, if anything.

"What about the other person in *your* life?" she said sarcastically.

"Artemis shot her a wry look. "Roxanne . . . we've been through this a thousand times," she said sternly. "I don't see the need to go through it again."

"I beg your pardon, my Queen, but every time I see you two together it makes my stomach turn."

"I assure you that our relationship is purely strategic and totally platonic."

"It better be—or Your Highness will be next on *my* hit list," she said with a devious chuckle of her own. "That is, along with Princess Zara of course."

"Touché, my love." Artemis focused her attention back to Bellatrix, who still seemed frazzled at being outsmarted by Laura Rigel. She could tell with every breath Bellatrix took that her incompetence consumed her more and more. She had to redirect her general's focus. "Bellatrix, I need you to make sure Miss Templar agrees to accompany Roxanne to the underground lair immediately."

"And, if she refuses?" Bellatrix asked.

"Kill her." Artemis moved in front of Bellatrix and looked her up and down. "This time do not fail me."

"Da," she said and bowed.

Artemis shifted her gaze from Bellatrix to Roxanne, who was visibly shaken. "So . . . where do you think our little Zoroastrian will go?"

Roxanne shot her a condemning stare. "What do you care what I think?"

"I do care—that's my problem."

She paused for a few seconds. "The Pyramids of Giza?"

Artemis smiled and moved toward her. She placed her arm around Roxanne's shoulder and kissed her on the cheek. "You're so smart," she said. "I love you." Roxanne pushed her away and continued brushing her hair in the mirror. Artemis turned and looked at Bellatrix. "Contact our Amazon associates in Africa immediately and have them station their best warriors at the Pyramids. I want him protected at all costs."

Roxanne dropped the brush and turned toward her. "Your Highness," she hissed, "based on the intelligence gathered from the mental institution, I thought we agreed to kill him. Now you want to protect him?"

Artemis laughed. "You'll understand soon enough."

CHAPTER 43

D ARIUS STARED AT the Riddle of the Sphinx Café. It was as tall as a six-story building and similar in size to the real Sphinx, which guarded the pyramids thirty yards in the distance. He thought about the challenge that lay ahead.

What riddle would the sphinx try to outsmart him with? If the answer to the old riddle was *man,* maybe the answer to the new riddle was *woman.* He smiled. That would be too easy. His smile faded when he realized that if he failed to answer correctly, he would never learn the location of the Rebel base. He would have to keep up his guard, he thought, as he made his way between the six-foot stucco paws of the replica sphinx and into the café. Who knew what gods or goddesses might try to stand in his way?

Darius heard the oversized doors close behind him. He was immediately invigorated by the cold air that circulated throughout the café. The establishment was alive with tourists eager to spend their money on a cool drink. He hurried past the booths that lined the limestone walls and took a seat at the triangular black granite bar in the middle of the room. He glanced at his watch.

It was three-thirty.

Looking around, he saw that the ancient Pharaohs were watching him from their portraits mounted on the wall of each booth. Their eyes seemed to follow his every move. He ignored them and focused on a banner hanging high above the bar. The hairs on the back of his neck stiffened.

Answer the Riddle of the Sphinx or be devoured.

"I am Auset, your server," a female voice said from behind the bar.

Casting his gaze downwards, Darius stared into the almond-shaped eyes of the olive skinned bartender. Heavily lined in earthy tones of greenish black, her emerald green eyes shone like the thin eyes of a serpent. A golden headdress sat atop her long dark hair which fell in tapering ringlets over her neck. Her tight linen tunic, with alternating bands of dark colored scales, mesmerized him as it shimmered in the light. She placed a triangular coaster in front of him and handed him a menu with a picture of the sphinx on it. He looked back at the zoomorphic figure before him and tried to figure out which goddess Auset was.

"What can I get you to drink?"

Darius leaned forward and rested his elbows on the bar. "I'm here to solve the riddle."

She laughed. "That's what everybody says. What makes you so different?"

"I'm an Aquarius. We pride ourselves on being different."

She nodded in approval. "I like that. What's your name?"

"D-MAC."

"What kind of name is that?"

"It's not a name, it's a code."

She leaned toward him. "Tell me, what does it mean?"

"It's personal—between me and God." The smell of her sandalwood perfume entranced him.

"Please," she said, stretching out the word, "I promise not to tell a soul."

Darius shook his head as if to clear it. "Nice try."

"Can you give me a hint?"

"Only if you give me one," he said with a laugh. Her face tensed. She seemed edgy, nervous. "What's wrong?"

She looked around the bar and then leaned toward him again. "You're our only hope," she whispered softly. "You must solve the riddle and release us from this terrible curse."

Curse?

His lips tightened and he sat up straight. He hadn't expected this. He was now dealing with a supernatural intelligence. He closed his eyes and prayed to God for guidance. When he opened them, he saw the café for what it really was.

It was all an illusion. He should have known the moment he walked through the doors that his soul had been transported to the spirit world. If he failed to solve the riddle, the demons, cleverly disguised as patrons, would tear his body limb from limb and serve his soul to the sphinx.

"Are you ready?"

He nodded. She opened a sealed envelope and removed a card. She looked at it for a few moments and raised her eyebrows. "I've never seen a three-part riddle before," she said and handed him a pen and paper. "There are twelve different types of beer on our menu." She moved the menu back in front of him. "First, you must choose the correct beer and say why you chose it. Second, you must identify what the twelve beers represent and, finally, you must supply a name that is associated with them."

The sphinx had upped the stakes by increasing the riddle's difficulty. "Is that all?"

"No. You have six minutes to solve it starting now. Good luck."

Darius looked at his watch and read down the list of exotic beers. He saw that each beer represented a different country. There was Spanish, Omani, Norwegian, Danish, Japanese, French, Malaysian, American, Mexican, Jamaican, Jordanian and Australian beer. It occurred to him that if he chose one beer over another it would appear as though he was biased and favored one country over the rest. What was he missing? He turned and saw a young dark-haired girl dressed in blue jeans and a black t-shirt with a small u and large K emblazoned in white on her shirt.

"That's it," he shouted. There wasn't one correct beer. They were all correct. He had to unite the countries by mixing all of the beers equally into one glass. One down two to go, he thought, and scribbled down the answer. Now all he had to do was figure out what the beers represented and the name associated with them.

Without a second to spare, he wrote down the first letter of each country ... S-O-N-D-J-F-M-A-M-J-J-A. Repositioning the letters, he came up with the twelve months of the year. Could the answer be so obvious? This time he wasn't so sure and decided to search for a name to help him. He repositioned the letters and came up with the name Jason.

Of course. The beers represented the twelve labours of Hercules who was the greatest of Jason's Argonauts. A euphoric feeling overcame him. He glanced at his watch and noticed he still had three minutes left. He grinned at the thought of outsmarting the highly intelligent sphinx. It made him feel godlike, as if he could move mountains. He wrote down the answer and signaled for Auset.

"You still have a lot of time left," she said. "Are you sure of your answers?"

"Positive."

She reached for the paper but Darius snatched it off the bar. She smiled. "I'll be right back."

He felt a bead of sweat trickle down his face as he thought long and hard about his answer.

CHAPTER 44

DARIUS LOOKED AT the bartender. Still unsure of his answers, he suddenly realized which goddess she was. Auset was the Egyptian name of the goddess, Isis. He thought about the duality of the names and realized that two of his answers were wrong.

"Times up," she said.

Darius quickly changed his answers and handed her the paper.

"Are you a Zoroastrian?"

He paused. "What makes you think that?" His heart was pounding.

"You have a high forehead. It's characteristic of the ancient Aryan race."

"I'm not, but my father was."

She turned and typed his answers into the electronic cash register. He couldn't help but wonder if he should have stuck with his original answer. Suddenly, the window shields spiraled shut and the lights blacked out. An air raid siren blared through the darkness. Darius jerked backward and fell off of his barstool. On his back, in excruciating pain, he listened to the demon's high-pitched screams.

Staring into darkness, he heard footsteps rushing toward him. What was he to do? He hadn't come this far to have it end like this. He slowly drew himself up onto his knees and prayed for God to save him.

His hopes faded when he felt a hand with long, sharp fingernails touch his back. He knew once the demons were finished tearing his body to shreds the guardian sphinx would suck out his eyeballs, eat his brain, and then devour his soul.

"Get off me," he shouted. He tried to push the demons away, but there were too many of them grabbing and pulling at him. Finally, they overpowered him and pulled him to his feet. A loud roar thundered through the darkness. He felt the demons let go and saw the silhouette of the sphinx dance toward him. With nowhere else to turn, he decided to try and reason with the mighty beast. It was his only chance. Just then, the lights came on.

The sphinx was a *woman*.

Shocked, he stepped back into a crowd of people. They weren't demons who were going to dismember him but patrons congratulating him. When he noticed the woman was only wearing a costume, he breathed a huge sigh of relief and looked around the bar for Auset.

CHAPTER 45

"DARIUS IS AT the Riddle of the Sphinx Café."

Ramsey jumped up from his chair and looked at Raj who seemed equally surprised. "Get some agents over there now."

Raj returned to his phone. "Keep him there until reinforcements arrive. And remember to exercise caution. He's wanted by the American Union for murder." He hung up and made another quick call. When he finished, he turned and looked at Ramsey. "We're looking for him and he comes right to us. How lucky."

Ramsey was not amused. "Luck played no part in this. The will of Allah has brought him to us." He turned and opened the safe hidden behind the portrait of his wife. He carefully removed the lion sword from its case along with a well-worn leather belt. He looped the belt through the back of the silver sheath and wrapped it tight around his waist.

"Get my helicopter ready," Ramsey said. "And just in case Mr. Prince gets past our men, deploy some plain-clothes agents to the pyramids as well. Especially, the Great Pyramid. I have a feeling that's where he's headed."

Ramsey moved around his desk and hurried over to the southern window. Gazing out at the Great Pyramid baking in the sweltering heat of the late afternoon sun, he gripped the smooth handle of the lion sword and prayed he wouldn't have to use it.

CHAPTER 46

NOTHING COULD STOP him now, Darius told himself as he watched Auset emerge from the kitchen. Why had she left the moment the lights went out? Something wasn't right.

He noticed a set of keys in her hand as she danced her way toward him. His suspicions faded when he realized what they were for. She handed him the keys and fawned over him as if he were a celebrity. Darius responded by feasting on the attention.

"Are these the keys to the Rebel base?"

She laughed. "Not only are you handsome, but you're funny too. They're the keys to your new Lamborghini Diablo."

The crowd of people around him gasped with excitement. Everything suddenly became clear. This was how they planned on getting him to the Rebel base. The moment he started the ignition, the secret location would be displayed on the dashboard computer. And, being that they supplied him with a race car, he had a feeling a high-speed chase was about to begin. When Auset moved back behind the bar, the crowd slowly dispersed.

Darius leaned forward. "So . . . where's the car?"

"Relax, Mr. Prince. It'll be here in half an hour." She handed him a black knapsack with the sphinx on it. "Here are some other gifts," she said, smiling. "Can I get you something to eat?"

Darius paused. How did she know his name? He stood up and stepped back from the bar. His heartbeat quickened. Auset was a *spy* for the forces of evil. That's why she had asked him if he was a Zoroastrian and then snuck off to the kitchen. They had planted her there just in case he showed up. It was all a setup. After he was done inspecting the Great Pyramid they would follow him to the Rebel base and destroy it. He had to get out of there—and fast.

"Is there something wrong?" Auset asked.

"Yes," he said, stepping toward her, "I'm starving. Can you get me a cheeseburger?"

"I can do better than that." She placed an ice cold beer in front of him. "I'll have the chef whip up an authentic Egyptian meal with lots of mezzas. I'll be right back," she said and disappeared back into the kitchen.

Darius placed the keys into the knapsack and slung it over his shoulder. He grabbed a pack of matches off the bar and rushed out of the café.

The intense dry heat hit him like a brick wall. Every breath made him feel like he was cooking from the inside out. He heard thunder rumbling in the distance. A storm was approaching.

They would soon be looking for him, he thought, shielding his eyes from the light with his hand. He needed to disguise himself. He ran over to a Bedouin vendor standing with his camel and tent near the real sphinx, and traded his watch for a pair of tan shorts and velcro sandals, a straw hat, cheap sunglasses, and a souvenir shirt with the three pyramids on it. He quickly changed in the tent, secured the pack to his back, and took off.

Nobody would recognize him now, he thought, as he blended in with the thousands of tourists scurrying around the Giza Plateau. He glanced over his shoulder and headed north toward the Great Pyramid. Shortly thereafter, he saw armed soldiers looking around so he made a quick left toward the Pyramid of Khafre. Once again, he glanced over his shoulder. This time, he noticed three black women following him. He picked up his pace and headed toward the Pyramid of Menkaure.

Dark clouds rolled across the sky. Lightning flashed and a gusty wind began to swirl. Upon reaching Menkaure, he looked up and saw a brilliant flash of light. As if it were hurled by the mighty god, Jupiter, himself, the lightning bolt struck the pyramid's capstone. The earth shook and a thunderous boom echoed across the plateau. Darius backed himself up against the pyramid as rubble rained down around him. Watching tourists scramble for cover, he heard a voice in the distance shout, "Halt." Three men dressed in tan suits ran toward him. He had to move fast. The much smaller Queen's Pyramids were to the left of Menkaure and he took off in that direction. Running against the flow of stampeding tourists heading towards him, he felt the hot desert wind sweep across the plateau. It created a blinding sandstorm that made it difficult to breathe.

Coughing and spitting, he covered his face with his hat and braved his way through the storm. He felt the rain begin to fall. Hopefully the storm had bought him a little more time. He circled back around to the south side of Menkaure. Seemingly out of nowhere, the three men he had managed to elude suddenly reappeared. Armed with laser hand guns they surrounded him.

"Mr. Prince, turn around and put your hands up against the pyramid," one of the agents said.

He paused for a moment but when he realized there was no escape, he turned and followed their orders. He stared at the huge weathered limestone block and remembered that the little girl in his dream was pointing to the Pyramid of Menkaure.

After a long moment, Darius heard one of the agents order him to turn and face them. As he did, he saw the same three women sneak up behind the agents and shoot them with lasers. The agents fell to the ground, either unconscious or dead. He turned and stared at the women dressed in short yellow tunics.

They must be Bella's associates, he thought.

Darius removed his hat and sunglasses and tossed them to the ground. He clenched his fists and took a menacing step forward. When one of the women said that they were there to protect him, he couldn't believe what he was hearing. She had a strong African accent and spoke with the authority of a tribal leader. He noticed a tattoo on her arm of a red pentagram resting on the back of a yellow butterfly encapsulated in a ring of purple. He froze. *They* were responsible for the pentagram virus!

Why were they now supposedly there to protect him? He stared at the men lying face down in the wet sand.

"The men are alive," she said. "Guns were set to stun."

Darius looked up and she tossed him her weapon. He snatched it out of the air and looked at the settings. When the men slowly started to move, he dropped the gun in the sand. Whatever the case, he had to find the handprints from his dream. As the women watched over him, Darius inspected each of the pyramid's stones from top to bottom. The moment he found the stone from his dream, he knew it immediately. He picked up a jagged rock and frantically chipped away at a crusted layer of sand that had formed on the stone. The sand was hard and looked as if it had been caked on over many centuries. The rain stopped and he glanced up to see the setting sun break through the clouds. Little rays of sunshine struck the stone. He could feel the adrenaline course through his veins like a mighty river as he stared at the two weathered handprints he had come so far to find.

He took a deep breath and placed his hands onto the handprints embedded in the stone. He was not at all surprised when the stone began to move.

CHAPTER 47

C OMFORTABLY KNEELING ON her bed behind him, Roxanne pressed her large naked breasts against Zadam's muscular back. She caressed his broad shoulders and tended to his troubled mind.

"View this new turn of events as an opportunity," she hissed.

"You call being fourth in line an opportunity?"

"At least you are in line." She laughed. "Patience, my little lamb. Your day in the sun shall come."

"Talk is cheap." He turned and faced her. "How do I know that everything will work out as you say?"

She flipped him on his back and pinned his arms to the bed sheets. "The stars never lie. Trust me, when everything is said and done, you will become King of the World and I shall be your queen. All the others will become nothing but faded memories."

CHAPTER 48

T HE LIMESTONE BLOCK that lay dormant for thousands of
years slowly disappeared into the sand. It was as if all the
water from the downpour had been diverted under the one stone and turned
the sand beneath it into quicksand.

Darius raised his arms in triumph. His heart pounded hard against his
chest as he stared into the secret passageway. He smiled knowing he was
about to find out what his higher purpose was. He glanced over his
shoulder. Where were the three women—his protectors? The men still lay
face down in the wet sand, but the women were nowhere in sight. He
turned back to the passageway and stared at the stone steps that led down
into a dark cave-like tunnel.

"Mr. Prince," came a loud voice from behind him, "put your hands in the
air and step away from the pyramid." Startled, he turned to find himself
looking into the barrels of three laser assault rifles held by soldiers in
camouflaged fatigues. Once again, the Fallen Angels were trying to stop him.

"Mr. Prince," came the voice again, "put your hands in the air and step
away from the pyramid."

Darius didn't raise his hands but, instead, stepped backward into the
pyramid. Just then, three laser beams raced toward him. Instinctively, he
dropped into a split to avoid being hit and was shocked to see an opaque
magnetic force field appear over the entrance and absorb the shots. He jumped
to his feet and watched a soldier attempt to enter the passageway. His efforts
proved futile as he was zapped like a bug and sent flying back through the air.

Darius grabbed a torch off of the wall and struck a match; with the lit
torch he slowly headed down the dark stone staircase. He could smell the

past. A mixture of stone, sand, and dust lingered in the cool stagnant air. He counted the steps as he descended and when he reached the thirty-third one, he stopped and then stepped onto the sandy floor.

The torch he'd been carrying went out and a soft golden light illuminated the room. He dropped the torch and gazed around the chamber. In the middle of the room, a hand-sized triangular-shaped diamond radiated the soothing light. It sat atop a solid gold altar that was perfectly aligned with a thirty-foot ceiling that came to a point. It seemed as though he was in a smaller pyramid beneath Menkaure. As he walked toward the altar, he felt almost godlike; his super-ego burned like a star inside him. To his surprise the light grew dimmer and dimmer.

Suddenly, a loud clicking sound echoed around him. Sand began to pour through holes in the walls and ceiling, quickly filling the room. His heart pounded hard against his chest.

The chamber went dark.

CHAPTER 49

D ARIUS TILTED HIS head back to gain a few precious seconds before the sand would completely cover him. The pressure of the sand squeezing the air out of his lungs was nothing compared to the thought of being buried alive.

Was the power radiating from the diamond connected to his thoughts? It had to be. The light had started to dim the moment he felt immortal. He had to demonstrate that he didn't suffer from hubris. He thought back to that fateful day at the beach twelve years prior when he had braved the strong ocean currents to save a young woman from drowning, and had almost drowned himself.

The memory of her panicked screams replaced the sound of the falling sand. Battling against the riptides and strong surf that pounded his body and mind, he had finally reached her. After struggling to save her, he too had been on the verge of drowning but the thought of letting her go to save himself never entered his mind. Reliving the joy he felt when he walked her up onto the beach, he was forced to take his final breath.

Was this how his life was going to end?

While struggling to hold his breath, he felt a strong vibration beneath his feet. He could feel the sand slowly moving away from his body. He had to hold on. Just a few more seconds, he told himself . . . just a few more seconds. After a long moment that seemed more like an eternity, his head broke through the sand. He let out a loud groan as he gasped for air. Still surrounded by darkness, he felt the sand rush away from his chest. He tried for a deep breath, but a violent cough erupted from deep within his lungs. Suddenly, the diamond flooded the chamber with fluorescent black light. Coughing and spitting, he wiped the granules from his dry thirsty mouth. Now, knee-deep in sand, he breathed easier, knowing that he had passed the final test. As the sand disappeared through thousands of small holes on the chamber floor, he brushed himself off and gazed at the wall in front of him.

He marveled at the ancient drawings the black light revealed as he made his way around the altar toward the wall. When he came face to face with the Star of David, he stopped. He noticed a star on each of its six points, as well as a few star clusters positioned on or around the star's planes and main axis. Slowly, he traced the grand trines with his finger. He remembered that the two interlaced triangles mapped the position of the major stars of the heavens with the major axis along the Milky Way, from Sirius to Altair. The three belt stars of Orion were perfectly aligned with three pyramids positioned below. His discovery was confirmed. He was standing in a smaller pyramid beneath Menkaure.

The pyramids on the wall were the original pyramids that had been built in alignment with the belt stars of Orion twelve thousand five hundred years ago. Why had the ancient Pharaohs hidden them beneath the pyramids? As he connected the pieces of the ancient puzzle, he recalled that scientists had dismissed the Orion Theory when carbon dating suggested that the pyramids were only forty-six hundred years old.

He glanced over his shoulder at the altar. Could it be some sort of ancient control panel? He looked back to the wall in front of him. There were symbols of the earth, air, fire, water, moon, stars, and sun to the right of the Star of David. He read the inscription above them, "Airyanam Vaejo." A chill shot down his spine. Airyanam Vaejo was the homeland of the Aryans. If the Aryans had built the original pyramids, why did the Egyptians build over them?

He had a feeling he was about to find out. Still pondering the thought of a cover up, Darius removed his knapsack and moved back behind the altar. He brushed away the sand from around the diamond and noticed two handprints in the form of a triangle surrounding it. When he placed his hands on them and his thumbs and index fingers touched, his hands locked in place. Struggling to free them, he felt the diamond release the power embedded deep within his soul.

CHAPTER 50

T HE SILENCE THAT fell over the military battalion was as unsettling as the decision he would soon have to make. As the ancient mystery surrounding the pyramids unfolded right before their eyes, Ramsey watched the continuous beam of energy race skyward out of the capstone of Menkaure. He knew exactly where it was headed. He glanced at Raj who was now standing next to him and then tilted his head back and stared into outer space. "Can you bind the chains of the stars of the Pleiades or loosen the bands of Orion?"

"What did you say?"

"Keep an eye on Orion's belt."

Ramsey shifted his gaze toward the constellation. When the energy beam struck Mintaka, the dimmest of the three belt stars, the pyramid fell still. A brilliant flash of light lit up the western sky, turning night into day and quickly back to night again.

Was the universe going to explode? He watched Mintaka relay the energy to the other six stars of the Orion constellation. A glowing ghostlike image of the mighty hunter wielding his sword high above his head shone through the darkness of space.

"The power of Orion is preparing to return to this dimension," Raj said, excitedly.

Ramsey rubbed the smooth black handle of the lion sword. Now that it was clear that Darius Prince was the Chosen One, he would soon have to play God. Still deep in thought, he watched the six stars simultaneously send their energy back to Mintaka. The star shined, for a moment, with a magnitude that appeared to be brighter than the sun.

Ramsey shielded his eyes from the light with his hand. Was Darius Prince responsible for putting three of his agents into intensive care? And what of the death of his agent in New York? When the starlight dimmed, he watched the energy beam split into two and head in opposite directions. The beam heading southeast raced through the belt stars Alnilam and Alnatik on its way toward the star Sirius; the other beam headed northwest and struck the constellation Taurus's main star, Aldebaran.

Ramsey stood in awe as the brilliant red eye of Taurus the bull, Aldebaran, relayed the energy to the V-shaped cluster of stars, the Hyades. Branded in white, a bright image of the bull's head and menacing horns appeared as if preparing to charge Orion. Marveling at the divine display of power, he watched the other beam strike the Dog Star—Sirius.

Raj gasped. "Sirius just redirected the energy beam."

As the beam raced northeast out of view, Ramsey realized that Raj was right. He wasn't meant to find the Zoroastrian—the Zoroastrian was meant to find him. He turned to Raj. "Come on. We can track the beam's trajectory on the helicopter computer."

They hurried over to the president's helicopter, which was protected by a perimeter of soldiers, and climbed into the rear cabin.

"Computer, give me a visual of the Milky Way," Ramsey said.

A holographic image of the light beam soaring through the stars appeared inside the cabin.

Through the cabin window, Ramsey kept a watchful eye on the stars of the Hyades. They remained illumined as they distributed the energy amongst the seven brightest stars in the shoulder of the bull—the Pleiades. A spectacular image of the bull's head and shoulder branded the sky in white. He marveled at its majestic beauty and shifted his gaze back to the hologram.

Ramsey repeatedly stabbed his right index finger at a cluster of stars toward the upper left. "The beam appears to be headed toward the Bootes constellation."

"The beam," Raj said, "is forming one of the two grand trines in the Star of David that Aje spoke of. If I'm correct it will strike Bootes's main star, Arcturus, next."

King Arthur's Star, Ramsey thought. Were the stars foreshadowing the coming of a king?

Ramsey looked at Raj. "Do you think Darius Prince's fingerprints are on the gun?"

Raj shrugged. "You're not still thinking about killing him. Are you?"

Ramsey fell silent. Raj's words dug deep into his soul—so deep that he wasn't sure if he could ever truly know enough about the Zoroastrian to make that decision. He had wrestled with the thought day and night for the past fifteen years, but the reality was that he would soon find himself at the crossroads of history. When that time came, he prayed he would make the right decision. He shifted his gaze back to the hologram just as the beam impacted Arcturus. There was a sudden burst of light and the beam changed directions.

"Computer, where is the beam headed?" Ramsey glanced out of the window and noticed the stars of the Pleiades dim as they relayed their energy back to the stars of the Hyades.

"The light beam will impact the star, Algenib, in the Pegasus constellation, in nine seconds."

Ramsey tried to remember which horse Pegasus had been compared to in the Book of Revelations. He looked back to the hologram just in time to see Algenib relay the energy to its sister stars in the constellation. An image of the mythological winged horse, branded in electric white, shone like an angel in the sky.

Pegasus, he remembered, had been compared to the white horse that the conqueror rides during the Apocalypse. Was *Darius* the prophesized king who would come forth to deceive the nations of the world? He took a deep breath and exhaled.

Loosening the bands of Orion just made his decision that much harder. If he killed Darius, he might become the most hated man on the planet. That, he could live with. But, if he allowed Darius to live and he turned out to be evil, he would have failed to do his job. And that, he couldn't stand to bear.

"Unfortunately, I have a job to do, Raj."

"And so do I. What if Darius is really good and the sword is to be used on the female Chosen One Aje identified? Think about it. Maybe she is the one who is evil."

In synchronicity, the stars of Pegasus and the Hyades relayed their energy back to Algenib and Aldebaran which in turn unleashed their energy back into the grand trine matrix and at the constellation Cetus. Simultaneously, the two energy beams struck its main star, Menkar.

"The grand trine is complete," Ramsey said.

Raj took a deep breath and turned toward him. "I can't tell you what to do," he said, "but I must remind you that you are not a god. Only God has the right to take a life."

"I wish it were that easy Raj. Allah has entrusted me with the lion sword and I will not let him down." He looked up into the sky. "When the time comes for the decision to be made, Allah will be there to guide me."

Ramsey and Raj watched Menkar relay the energy to its sister stars. An overpowering image of the many-armed serpent-like beast, the Kracken, appeared in the center of the hologram.

Did this image herald the coming of the *Beast?*

Ramsey's heart raced as the stars of Cetus relayed their energy back to Menkar. The star briefly shined like the sun before sending two beams of energy back to earth. One struck the northern Sahara desert and the other returned to the Pyramid of Menkaure.

CHAPTER 51

STRUGGLING TO FREE his hands from the altar, Darius saw a beam of energy strike the diamond. He felt the energy surge through his hands and into his veins. His body shook violently. It was as if two worlds were colliding deep within his soul. A moment later, his hands were jettisoned from the altar.

Darius flexed his hands in front of his face. Once again, he felt godlike. Immortal. But the feeling faded when he heard the thunderous roar of jet aircraft over the pyramid and his name being called out over a loud speaker. He grabbed the diamond and the three scrolls he saw lying in the sand, placed them into his knapsack and hurried up the stone staircase.

His heart was pounding.

When he reached the top step, he gazed through the protective force field. With the prowess of a skilled hunter, he eyed the perimeter. Hundreds of armed soldiers, some on foot and some in armor-plated vehicles were waiting for him.

What the *hell* had he done?

Mobs of civilians were being held back by soldiers in riot gear. People, young and old alike, dropped to their knees in prayer. He could sense hysteria in the air.

Were they worshipping *him*? He wasn't so sure. Still, he had to be careful. The Fallen Angels would do anything to sway him to their side. Anything. And that included worshipping him as a—"

A helicopter spotlight shone down from above. He took a deep breath and stepped through the magnetic force field.

The hot desert air surrounded him as did a platoon of soldiers thirty feet in the distance. Armed with laser machine guns, they readied their sights and took aim.

Darius's senses felt sharper. When a black fat-tailed scorpion silently emerged from the sand by his heel, he squashed it without even looking down.

"Darius!" came a loud voice from a helicopter above, "this is President Amon Ramsey. We come in peace. Drop the pack and put your hands in the air."

Peace? Darius scoffed.

There was nothing at all peaceful about a battalion of soldiers aiming their weapons at him. This wasn't what he had expected, but then again, everything that had happened that day had been unexpected.

He sensed fear in the hearts and eyes of the soldiers and felt like he could lay waste to entire armies. He looked to the shining stars of Orion for guidance. It was right then that everything became clear. He had received the power of Orion, the Hunter. But, if he was now the hunter, who or what was he hunting? One thing was certain, he thought, as he took a step forward, no one was going to stand in his way.

CHAPTER 52

FROM THE CO–PILOT'S seat in the hovering helicopter, Ramsey watched a fighter jet fly across the waxing crescent moon. "Hold your fire," he shouted and glanced at Raj who was seated behind him. When the pilot angled the helicopter down, Ramsey looked back at Darius Prince who was illumined by spotlights. He gasped as three laser beams struck Darius in the chest causing him to fall backward onto the ground.

"Get me down there now," Ramsey shouted. He checked the multisensor display in front of him. A moment later, he looked up stunned. "The guns were set to kill."

"Are you sure?" Raj said, leaning forward.

"Positive. No human being could withstand a blast like that." This was disastrous, he thought. If the Chosen One died before he was able to find out the truth, his hopes and dreams would be lost forever.

"Find out who fired those shots."

He prayed to Allah that Mr. Prince had somehow survived. As they neared the ground, the helicopter blades stirred up a blinding dust cloud of sand. When he felt the helicopter touch down, he swung open the door and hopped out. He shielded his eyes from the sand and rushed over to Mr. Prince who was lying on his back, surrounded by soldiers.

"Stand back," Ramsey commanded. He threw off his suit coat, rolled up his sleeves, and knelt down next to Mr. Prince. He felt for a pulse. Other than a large burn-hole on the front of his shirt, he couldn't believe the Zoroastrian didn't have a scratch on him.

Darius's fingers started to move. Without a second to waste, Ramsey stood up and ordered a soldier to fasten a titanium band around his neck. If Darius could survive a blast like that, there was no telling what he could do. After the band was in place, he motioned for his men to help Mr. Prince to his feet. Two soldiers reached down and grabbed Darius under the arms while a third lifted him up from behind.

"Mr. President," Raj said as he reached the scene, "I have some bad news."

Ramsey turned. "What is it, Raj?"

"Our three agents were pronounced dead on arrival."

Ramsey cringed. "I was afraid of this. Did we get the forensics on the gun yet?"

"No. We should have the report within the hour."

Ramsey turned away from him. The Zoroastrian was now standing on his own, brushing the sand off of himself. His face was sunburned, and his lips were dry and cracked. The hole on the front of his shirt continued to smolder.

"You tried to kill me," Darius said, coughing and spitting.

For the moment, Ramsey's excitement was offset by the decision plaguing him. "If we wanted you dead, you already would be," he said. "The guns were set to stun."

Darius ripped off his shirt and threw it to the ground. "What's this thing around my neck?" he snarled.

Ramsey took a step back. Who or what was he dealing with? He pulled out an electronic device and held it in front of Darius's face. "If you try to escape or harm anyone, I will press this button and you will cease to exist."

Darius laughed. "If you kill me, my soul will return in an instant and be housed in another body. If that happens, you'll never find me."

This was not how he envisioned his first meeting with the Zoroastrian. Ramsey moved forward. "Do you think you're a god?"

Darius chuckled softly. "Press the button and find out."

Darius had issued a challenge he could not back down from. Ramsey looked into the Zoroastrian's eyes and offered him the device. "You do it."

Darius reached for the device, but then dropped his hand to his side. "You're dealing with a power you don't understand."

It was evident by his reaction that Darius still believed he could be killed by normal means and was unaware of the lion sword—the *only* weapon that could now kill him. He would use this to his advantage.

The president scoffed. "I know what I'm dealing with," he said. "It's *who* that worries me."

He slipped the device back into his pocket. "Take him away."

CHAPTER 53

"**F**OR THE LAST time I didn't kill anyone."

Dressed in desert-colored fatigues and strapped to a metal chair by his wrists and ankles, Darius struggled to free himself. He watched the Egyptian president remove his sword belt and place it down on his desk. The sight of the protective sheath concealing the sword's twelve inch blade sent a chill up and down his spine.

Darius cursed under his breath. "Torture me and I'll never tell you what I know."

With his hands shoulder-width apart on the desk, his captor leaned forward and leveled a condemning stare. "You expect me to believe that three unidentified black women killed my agents and then just vanished into thin air."

"At first I thought the women were after me, but when your agents showed up I realized that the women were really there to protect me. They killed your agents. Not me."

"Mr. Prince," the president said, "I want to believe you but there are half a dozen eyewitnesses who say that you killed them."

"They're lying."

"Your doctor at the hospital claims that you assaulted him and earlier had tossed a man off of a fire escape. Is he lying as well?"

"Okay . . . I assaulted him," Darius said. "But I never tossed anyone off the fire escape. Bella did that."

"Bella?"

"She's the one who broke into my room and tried to kidnap me."

The president shook his head, frowning in perplexity. "Two orderlies also filed assault charges. Are they lying too?"

Darius paused. "No, but Dr. Haus is. He's on their side."

"Whose side?"

"Evil's!" he shouted. "For all I know, you're on their side as well."

"How do I know *you're* not the one who's evil?"

"Don't turn this around on me," Darius said. "If you're not evil then why'd you send your agents after me?"

"You're wanted by the American Union for murder."

"I told you . . . it was Bella who killed the security guard. Not me!"

The president picked up a business card lying on the desk. "Then how did you get this," he said and held it up in front of his face.

Darius paused. He stared at the crinkled card with *Riddle of the Sphinx Café* printed on it, and said, "After Bella tossed the man off the fire escape, I went through his pockets to see who he was. If it wasn't for *that* card, I wouldn't be here."

His captor raised an eyebrow. "You came here because of the card?"

"My destiny brought me here."

The president stood motionless in front of him.

"I'm telling you," Darius said after a long pause, "somebody's setting me up."

There was a firm knock at the door. Darius turned. A short man wearing a white robe with matching head cover rushed into the room. He looked at Darius for a moment as if he were a circus attraction, turned to the president, and whispered something into his ear. By the look on the president's face, he could tell it wasn't good. When the man left the room, the president wrapped the sword belt around his waist and pulled the belt tight. He positioned the sheath over his left hip and walked over to the southern window.

"You have become quite a celebrity," the president said, peering out the window. "The entire city of Cairo is standing outside, waiting to see the man with the power to light up the sky." He took a deep breath and slowly exhaled. "That makes my decision that much harder."

"What decision?" Darius watched the president turn and walk toward him.

"What to do with you," he said, pulling the curved sword in one fluid motion from its sheath.

The sight of the razor sharp blade slashing through the air made his heart race. "I'm telling the truth," Darius insisted, "I never killed anyone."

"Your prints were the only ones found on the gun."

"I didn't kill anyone," Darius said again as President Ramsey moved behind him. Was he gonna cut off his head? Overwhelmed by the thought, he struggled harder against his restraints. He could hear his captor's deep breaths, but he said nothing. The ringing of the telephone on the president's desk suddenly broke the silence. When the president emerged from behind him and answered the call, Darius shouted, "Help!"

His captor frowned. He held the phone tightly against his ear. After a long moment, he said, "Good work, Raj. Tell Mohammed and Queen Elizabeth that I will get back to them shortly. And find Aje and bring him to my office immediately."

Darius wondered if this was all part of some twisted psychological game his captor was playing to try and scare him into confessing. He watched the Egyptian president hang up the phone and move in front of him. With the sword still drawn, the president leaned against the front of his desk and spoke to him.

"The star Menkar sent two energy beams back to earth," he said. "One landed in the desert and the other went back into the pyramid and seems to have affected you. Tell me . . . do you feel any different?"

"My thoughts aren't scattered like they were before. When I stepped out of the pyramid, I was completely aware of everything around me and felt," he paused and looked around the room, "practically immortal. But I no longer feel like that." Even though the feeling still seemed to come and go, he thought it best to keep that fact to himself.

"How about physical changes?"

Darius flexed his arms, but try as he might, he couldn't break the straps that bound him. "My eyesight's improved but I don't have any super human strength if that's what you're asking."

"Did the women have any markings on them? Birthmarks? Tatoos?"

His tone sounded friendlier to Darius. What was the president up to? He stared at the razor-sharp sword that his captor still had drawn.

"Yes," Darius said coolly, "one of the women had a tattoo of a red pentagram resting on the back of a yellow butterfly."

For the first time, a smile appeared on the president's face.

"Praise be to Allah." Ramsey placed the sword into the sheath and knelt down before him. "I am pleased to report that three unidentified black women were in fact sighted firing lasers at you," he said, loosening one of the straps around his ankles. "They are part of a secret organization of women known as the Ghostriders or Amazons. They've been watching both of us for a very long time."

Could Paris and Laura be Amazons? Consumed by the thought of betrayal, he felt his heart drop. It was all starting to make sense. Paris was the one who introduced him to the hedge fund manager he took the hit with, and Laura had given him the tracking device.

If the pentagram was associated with the Amazons, and they were responsible for infecting his computer, then the hit he incurred was all part of a plan to ruin him financially so they could control him. They used Paris's millions and the pension account to lull him into a false sense of security. Even the woman who put him on hold at his firm's trading desk was probably in on it.

He took a deep breath and exhaled. How could he have been so naïve? What bothered him most was the way Paris had so skillfully manipulated him into admitting himself to the mental hospital where he met Dr. Haus. It all seemed so obvious now.

"Do you know who any of these women are?" Darius said.

"I recently learned that my wife was one of them," the president replied, letting out a long whoosh of air. He stood up. "I was hoping you might know."

"You can start by questioning my ex-girlfriend, Paris Templar."

"She's gone missing. What about Laura Rigel?"

Darius paused. Still unsure of her role in the grand scheme of things, he decided it was best to keep her out of it for now. She had, after all, ripped the chain off his neck and helped him escape. "Laura has nothing to do with this," he said, confidently.

"Laura's a Virgo, right?"

"Yeah," Darius said. "Why?"

"Strange as it may seem, astrology has a lot to do with your destiny. I'll fill you in later. Now, is there anybody else you can think of?"

"The Russian woman, Bella, and her associates. That's it."

"Okay," President Ramsey said as he moved behind him. He removed the titanium band from around his neck. "The Amazons will stop at nothing to sway you to their side. Soon, the entire world will be brainwashed into believing that you are evil," he said and untied the straps around his wrists.

Darius rose from the chair and grabbed the president by his shirt collar. He pulled him close. "If you hadn't received that phone call, you would've killed me."

"I know how you're feeling," Ramsey said, his body shaking, "but I swear I wasn't going to kill you."

After a long moment, Darius released him. "You don't know how I feel or the pain I've suffered." He watched the president regain his composure and straighten his shirt.

"You think you're the only one who's suffered?" Ramsey's eyes were ablaze. "When my grandfather and father couldn't find you, the pain of failure was so great, they committed suicide and placed the burden of finding you upon my shoulders." The president began pacing back and forth in front of him. Darius could see that he was edgy, nervous. "Then when I thought I had found you, I insisted my wife and son come with me to meet the man I had spent the last fifteen years searching for." Ramsey stopped pacing. His face was passive and his eyes filled with regret. "That day there was an attempt on my life. I escaped only to watch my wife and son burn to death."

Darius recoiled.

"I was abandoned by my father and then I lost my wife and son—all in search of the Chosen One. But I never gave up and I'm thankful I didn't."

Darius had been staring across the room and out the window as he massaged the circulation back into his wrists. He held his left wrist still and looked straight at the president. "My father abandoned me, too."

Ramsey nodded sympathetically as if to say he understood. "Did you know our fathers were friends?"

"They were?"

"My father was convinced your father was the Chosen One."

"You keep referring to me as the Chosen One. Why?"

The president moved back behind his desk. He pulled a framed document out of a drawer and placed it down in front of him. He motioned for Darius to join him.

Darius looked at the grandfather clock across the room. "Your clock has stopped."

The president laughed. "I'll tell you about it one day. I don't suppose you can read Egyptian hieroglyphics?"

"Nope." He leaned over and stared at the Star of David emblazoned on the top of the yellow papyrus. "But I can tell you that the same two interlaced grand trines were on the wall of the pyramid," he said and stood up straight.

"Grand what?"

"Grand trines. They're astrological symbols. King David had two in his birth chart—I have three."

"Ahh," Ramsey said as if his life's work had just yielded a major discovery. "Your three grand trines are the keys that activate the pyramids. Did the hexagram show star positions?"

"Six stars on each of the points and a few star clusters. But what stood out most were the three belt stars of Orion on one of the star's planes."

"What else did it show?" The president seemed eager.

Darius paused. Had he said too much? Even if he had, did it really matter? Regardless, he was getting to the point where he knew he had to start trusting someone. The taxi driver, Ma'at, had made that point very clear. The president could have killed him, and didn't, but hadn't he already proved that he wasn't the enemy by releasing him? And hadn't their fathers been friends? Darius smiled pleasantly at the president. "Three pyramids were aligned with the belt stars of Orion," he whispered, as if in confidence.

"Impossible. Carbon dating negates the Orion Theory."

"That's because the Aryans built the original pyramids. Not the Egyptians. Your Egyptian ancestors merely built over them."

"You saw proof of this?"

"The writing was on the wall." Darius looked back at the document.

"Now that I have seen what the pyramid can do, it makes sense that my ancestors would hide such power from their enemies. In 1910, my grandfather found this prophecy under the sphinx. It foretold of a Chosen One and the future of the things to come," Ramsey said, tapping the prophecy.

"I *can* read it," Darius said excitedly. "*Somehow* I can read it." When the president looked at him somewhat skeptically, he cleared his throat and read the prophecy aloud.

> "In a time when Islam rules the world a fireball from space will align over the monoliths and pour its knowledge upon the land. A pure Aryan-Zoroastrian who has the power of the pyramids embedded in his soul will connect to the divine energy released by the heavenly bodies above. He will have the power to retrieve the Sword of Orion and crown a young prince, king. The Chosen One will hold the fate of good and evil in the palms of his hands."

Darius looked up at the president. "Did you ever think the word *pure* might have been referring to my soul?"

"No, but my wife did." The president reached into the drawer again and pulled out the three scrolls Darius had found in the pyramid. He shut the drawer and placed two of them down on the desk.

Darius grinned. "Where do I find this sword?"

"That's what we need to find out." Ramsey unraveled the yellow papyrus from within the scroll's cylindrical ivory case.

"What if I'm also the prince the prophecy speaks of?"

Ramsey frowned. "Prince William is," he said sternly. He carefully placed the parchment on top of the glass frame and smoothed it out with his hand. "I've never seen this language before."

Darius chuckled softly. "Who would have ever thought that an Aryan and an African would team up to fight the forces of evil? When Ramsey responded with a reassuring nod, Darius nudged him aside and studied the document.

A few moments later, he looked up stunned. "Evil is much more powerful than you think."

CHAPTER 54

PERCHED HIGH UPON her throne in Buckingham Palace, as if she was looking down from Mount Olympus, Queen Elizabeth stared at the holographic image of the small, yet most powerful man on the planet.

"Rubbish," the queen said. She glanced at the priceless pear-shaped diamond at the top of her royal scepter. "By divine right, Prince William is the Chosen One."

"Not according to President Ramsey's document," the supreme leader said.

"Why was I not told of this prophecy sooner?" She watched him adjust the green belt around his white robe.

"It is not a prophecy," Mohammed argued. "Rather, a document of historical significance."

"Call it what you will," she said with a hint of annoyance. "Now, why was I never told of it?"

"Ramsey's family kept it a secret."

"That defiant man is nothing but a nuisance. He is always trying to undermine my authority. This time he will pay dearly for withholding information."

"President Ramsey is a devout Muslim but under the new circumstances, I tend to agree with his decision."

"That's not the point," she said sternly.

"For now, Ramsey poses no threat to us. This is his last chance to prove to us, to himself, and to the world, that his family did not die in vain and that he is not a failure."

"He's a spoiled brat. A prime example of nepotism," she said as she gazed around her grand throne room. The massive chandelier hanging above her head illuminated the diamond in her scepter, creating a kaleidoscope of colors that shone throughout the room.

Maybe I can use Darius to my advantage.

She focused her gaze back to the holographic image of the supreme leader. "What other secrets do you think the defiant president has hidden up those sleeves of his?" she said, staring at the diamond in her scepter. When Mohammed didn't respond, she lowered her scepter and focused her sharp gaze back to him. "You're positive that Darius Prince comes from royal blood on his father's side."

"Yes. Zadam and I are related to the same line of kings on our mother's side, but since the bloodline comes from his father's side, if we were to ever reinstate our monarchy, he would be first in line to the throne, his brother would be second, I'd be third and Zadam—"

"Must be furious," she said with a laugh and rose from her throne. Her white satin gown flowed behind her as she gracefully walked down the plush red carpeted steps toward him.

She stopped and stood face to face with the Napoleonic ruler of the Muslim world.

"I must point out," he said, "that since the Zoroastrian's mother is of English, Irish, and Scottish descent, if the bloodline on his mother's side is linked to British Royalty, Darius could claim to be—"

"*King of the World,*" she said, finishing his sentence. She moved the scepter back into the light.

"The media is already heralding him as Apollyon the Destroyer, the third king or Antichrist mentioned in chapter nine verse eleven of the Book of Revelations, as well as the Messiah Supreme since his mother's name is Mary and his father was known as British Apollo."

"How does that make you feel?"

"It's not my plan, it's God's plan. My mission is to spread the word of God. That's all."

The queen shook her head. "As of late, the media has placed the blame of the current economic depression on my head. For the first time since Diana's death, I am fearful for our lives—especially for Princes William and Harry and Princess Zara."

"You'll get no sympathy from me," he said. "We're all under the microscope."

"You mentioned that the prophecy references the ancient Sword of Power, Excalibur."

Mohammed frowned. "The *document* references the ancient Sword of Orion, which your ancestors renamed Excalibur."

"Rubbish. I'll wager anything that Excalibur is hidden in another dimension and Stonehenge is a gateway that leads there."

"What are you up to, Your Highness?"

"Strategy. Ramsey may prove useful after all. For now, tell Zadam to back off until we find out what else he knows. Commend the president on a job well done and have him deliver the Zoroastrian to me at once."

"You're going to use the Zoroastrian to get you the sword?"

"Precisely."

"If the Zoroastrian is successful in his quest, what makes you think that he will give it to you?"

She turned and headed back up the dais to her throne. "I am going to make Mr. Prince an offer he can't refuse."

CHAPTER 55

"**Y**OU'RE SAYING THAT God abandoned us?"

Darius turned. President Ramsey shook his head and dropped down in his chair in complete and utter silence. "It looks like he had no other choice," Darius said, listening to the air whoosh out of the leather cushions. "It was either that or be overthrown." When Ramsey didn't respond, he turned back around and read through the rest of the scroll.

"Listen to this," he said excitedly. "When God unveiled his crown jewel, the earth, to the Evil One, the temptation to destroy the material world proved to be far too great. The Evil One postponed its attack on heaven and came to earth on a comet that impacted the planet with such force that it plunged the world into a frigid darkness."

Ramsey stood up from his chair and moved next to him. "So God underestimated the power of the Evil One and trapped him here?"

"The moment evil landed," Darius said, "God destroyed the spiritual bridge that linked heaven and earth."

"Does it say when this happened?"

Darius nodded. "About 26,000 years ago."

"I find it hard to believe Allah would use our souls as bait."

"It was the only way. Evil will always attack the material world first. Only when it's completely destroyed, will evil resume its attack on heaven." Darius paused and looked away, deep in thought. After a long moment, he focused his gaze back to the president. "Let's say Jesus Christ underestimated evil. Would Allah intervene on the battlefield and help him fight?"

"Yes, the Muslim people would march behind him into battle."

"Good. Then we're both in agreement."

"Not so fast; Christ was not a god, he was a prophet."

Darius chuckled softly. "If we're both working toward a common goal of getting into the kingdom of heaven, where all people can coexist under one god who has no name, then we must put our religious differences aside."

"I agree," Ramsey said. "The battle should be good versus evil. Not one religion versus another."

"By the way, whatever happened to the other energy beam that landed in the desert?"

The president turned sharply on his heel and hurried toward the southern window. When he reached it, Darius carefully unraveled the next scroll as he listened to Ramsey bark out commands.

"Computer, give me a visual of Alpha Team at the Crater."

"Negative," the computer replied, "satellites are down."

▲ ▼ ▲

President Ramsey gazed up at the three belt stars shining through the vast coldness of space. He took a deep breath.

"I rarely speak of this anymore, but I believe that a specialized gene programmed with the knowledge of the ancient ones lives in the Sirius star system."

"Interesting," Darius said.

Ramsey turned and walked back to his desk. "I find it fascinating."

"Not your theory—this scroll—it talks about me and my soulmate."

There was a knock at the door. He watched Aje follow Raj into his office. "Can you believe that Alnatik is once again the brightest of the three belt stars?" he heard Raj say to Aje as they walked toward him. Ramsey realized Aje had shaved off his beard. He looked much better, he thought. When they reached the front of his desk, Ramsey noticed Aje's hands tremble at the sight of the Zoroastrian.

Ramsey rubbed the smooth handle of the lion sword with his right-hand and with his free hand motioned for Darius to continue.

"Not until you put away the sword," he said.

The president shot Darius a longing glance. After a rather long but awkward moment, he unbuckled his sword belt and removed the sheath. He placed the sword back in the mahogany case and secured it in the safe behind him.

When Ramsey turned back around, he realized by the smile on the Zoroastrian's face that he had gained much more than he could ever have imagined. "I have honored your request," Ramsey said. "Now tell me. What does the rest of the scroll say?"

"It says that once I find something called the *Star of Life,* my soulmate and I will have the power to defeat good or evil."

Could one of the twin Leos be his soulmate?

Ramsey looked at Raj and Aje who were now seated in front of his desk. He shot Aje an approving smile and focused on Raj. "Please tell me that you have found some information about the twins."

"Not yet," his aide said. "I should have some names for you soon."

"What's the Star of Life?" the Zoroastrian interrupted.

"It's the Persian equivalent of the Holy Grail," the astrologer said and crossed his legs. All eyes were focused on Aje. "It's believed to be buried beneath the lost city of Orion in an impenetrable time capsule."

Darius laughed. "A kind of modern day Noah's Ark."

"Precisely," Aje said. "All holy texts as well as all of life's creations are believed to be hidden there and protected by the Knights of the Zodiac." He paused. "Around the fifteenth century BC, God spoke to the Persian prophet, Zarathustra, and reintroduced religion to the Aryans. Zoroastrianism is considered by most scholars to be the world's first monotheistic religion."

"That's debatable," Ramsey said, tapping his desk. "Some believe it was dualistic in nature with a god of good and a god of evil, while others believe it is the mother of all major religions."

"You really believe there are ancient guardians living beneath some lost city called Orion?" Darius asked.

"The Knights of the Zodiac may not even be knights at all," Aje replied. "They could be a numerical representation for the precession of the twelve equinoxes."

Ramsey turned to Raj. "What's he trying to say?"

"About every two thousand one hundred and sixty years the ages change," he said. "There are twelve ages, so, if we multiply twenty-one sixty by twelve we find out that we are just about at the end of this 26,000-year life cycle."

"Which is also the end of the Mayan calendar," Ramsey said thoughtfully.

"Precisely," Aje said. "In the beginning of this cycle, Alnatik was the brightest of Orion's belt stars and perfectly aligned with the Great Pyramid, but it dimmed as the star cooled."

Ramsey watched Darius study the final scroll. "Does it say anything else about you and your soulmate?" Ramsey felt his heartbeat quicken. A moment later the Zoroastrian looked up.

"It says something about aquatic—"

"Triplicity?" Aje said.

"Yes."

Ramsey noticed the astrologer's hands start to tremble. "What's wrong?" he asked.

The astrologer didn't answer. He just stared at Darius as though he were the Devil himself.

"Aje, what is aquatic triplicity?"

"It is a grand trine," he lisped, "but this one is very powerful. It is in the water signs of Cancer, Pisces, and Scorpio."

Ramsey's eyes widened. He glanced at Darius and then looked at the astrologer. "Darius has three grand trines."

Silence filled the room. They were all looking at the Zoroastrian.

"According to Nostradamus, the third Antichrist is said to be born with a grand trine in aquatic triplicity," Aje said slowly, almost in a whisper.

Ramsey reached for the handle of the lion sword. When he realized that he had put it away, he nonchalantly slipped his hand in his jacket pocket. "Computer, display Darius Prince's birth chart." Would it show the Zoroastrian with the grand water trine?

A colorful hologram of Darius's three interlaced grand trines in yellow, red, and blue appeared rotating over his desk. "The Islamic nine-pointed star," Ramsey said, and looked at Aje.

Slowly, Aje stood up. "Computer, display the grand trine of the Antichrist." A green triangle, pointing upward, appeared rotating next to Darius's three interlaced grand trines.

Ramsey could feel a nervous tension fill the room as he watched Aje study the grand trines like a detective analyzing a crime scene. His mind flooded with thoughts. What if Darius did possess the aquatic triplicity grand trine? Did that make him evil? Was he going to have to kill him after all?

"Does he have the aquatic triplicity grand trine or not," Ramsey said impatiently as Aje continued to analyze his birth chart. Ramsey glanced at Darius and noticed a bead of sweat roll down his temple.

"Am I, or am I not, the Antichrist?"

The silence that ensued was unnerving to Ramsey. He could feel his heart rate quicken again.

Finally, the astrologer broke the silence. "The Zoroastrian has the aquatic triplicity grand trine."

Ramsey could hear the lisp return to the astrologer's voice.

"There has to be a mistake," Darius said, nervously.

"Aje, are you sure?" Ramsey said.

"Positive."

Ramsey froze. He looked at Darius who he saw was visibly shaken. If he didn't kill the Zoroastrian and he turned out to be evil, the thought of knowing that he could have stopped him and didn't paralyzed him. He couldn't seem to find his voice.

"President Ramsey," the computer said softly, "while Darius Prince does have some water in his chart, he does not possess the water grand trine the astrologer speaks of. He possesses an earth grand trine, an air grand trine and a fire grand trine. The astrologer must have associated the blue grand trine in Mr. Prince's chart with water."

Ramsey breathed a huge sigh of relief as he watched Aje frantically recheck his calculations.

▲ ▲ ▲

"Does that mean I'm just as powerful as the Antichrist?"

"Yes," Aje said. "You have the missing element the Antichrist needs to defeat good, just as the Antichrist has the missing elements you need to defeat evil and achieve balance."

Darius took a deep breath and exhaled. Would he be able to reason with his soulmate once he found her? When that day came he would be ready, he thought. He watched Ramsey look at Aje questioningly.

"Could Darius have two soulmates?" Ramsey asked.

"Anything's possible when you're dealing with the supernatural," Aje replied. "But it's highly unlikely. The Bible only tells of one Antichrist."

Two Antichrists? Darius felt his heartbeat quicken.

"The Bible was rewritten," Ramsey said. "But since we are dealing with a supernatural intelligence, we must try to think like it. To me, it makes perfect sense that evil would have a backup."

"If you're right," Darius said, "then my job just got a whole lot harder."

Raj jumped out of his chair. "If Christians find out that they have been lied to and there are two Antichrists, instead of one, the effects would be—"

"Devastating," Ramsey said. "Not only would it send fear into the hearts and minds of billions it could trigger the collapse of all organized religions."

"Precisely what evil wants," Aje said. "But I must warn you, the Devil's plan is dynamic. Once you think you've figured it out—think again, because the plan changes."

As Darius listened to them go back and forth, the reality of what he was up against started to sink in. His godlike feeling faded and he no longer felt immortal. For the first time since he received the power of Orion, he felt unsure of himself. How could he possibly reason with two Antichrists? And what about the beast he had to hunt? A chill shot down his spine. What if he was the one being hunted? But, then again, if he had the power to light up the sky, then he had the power to do anything. He smiled. Orion had returned to him.

"What gender did the Frenchman say the Antichrist would be?" Ramsey asked.

"A male!"

Ramsey paused. "Nostradamus was wrong. He predicted the Antichrist would be a man when in fact it's a woman."

"Not necessarily," Raj said. "If Darius is evil then he, too, would be considered an Antichrist."

"Right you are," Aje replied.

Darius scoffed. He looked at Raj, who cracked a thin superficial smile and then focused on Aje.

"Mr. Prince, do not take this personally," Aje said.

Darius's face tightened and his eyes narrowed. He held the astrologer's accusatory stare for several seconds.

"If I turn out to be evil, I'm coming for you and Raj first." Darius shifted his gaze from Aje who was visibly more shaken than Raj to Ramsey. He could tell by the cross look on Ramsey's face that he was not at all amused.

▼ ▲ ▼

"You need to control the power inside you and stay strong. Help us get you where you need to go," Ramsey said.

Ramsey was right, he thought. The power seemed to come and go and he was learning how to control it, but if he couldn't take the pressure from Ramsey's aide and a frail old astrologer, what would happen when the media got hold of him? After a long moment, he took a few deep breaths to calm himself and continued interpreting the scroll.

"When Jupiter is retrograde and Venus is in Sagittarius, a portal will open at twenty-nine degrees Aquarius. A grand cross will appear in the heavens and align with the pit of darkness at which time the aquatic triplicity will reverse. If the soulmates do not act when the portal is open, the Phoenix will take flight and darkness will fall upon the land."

Darius looked at Ramsey who had walked out from behind his desk and was pacing in front of the southern window.

"The birth and death of Venus," Aje said. "According to Mayan cosmologists, Venus was birthed back in 3114 BC. This marked the beginning of the great Mayan cycle. And," he said, pausing, "Venus will die in Sagittarius at the end of this cycle in December of 2012."

Darius looked at Ramsey. "Love will cease to exist?"

"That's up to you and your soulmate." Ramsey said. He slowed his pace and seemed to go into deep thought.

"Starting in June," Aje said, "Venus will start making a retrograde loop across the top of Orion, which is a very rare event. The last time this occurred was in 9792 BC and it will occur again on December 21st, 2012."

Ramsey stopped pacing. "Venus's first retrograde loop marked the last flight of the Phoenix."

Darius chuckled softly. "You're not worried about some mythical bird. Are you?"

Ramsey nodded his head up and down slowly. "The Phoenix is symbolic of a cataclysmic magnetic pole shift that'll send us right back to the Stone Age. It's possible the shift could occur again during Venus's retrograde loop. And that's what worries me."

"Only God knows that," Aje said. "But, according to Darius's chart he was born when Jupiter was retrograde. And—when it's retrograde—it appears to spin in reverse and usually has a negative effect on people. But, since Mr. Prince was born with a Jupiter retrograde, it has a positive effect on him. So, in essence, he's strongest when it's retrograde and Venus is making this loop across the top of Orion."

"Is that when we'll be able to defeat evil?"

"Yes, but only for a short time. Once the sun aligns with the galactic equator, the portal will open for exactly twenty-nine minutes. It's imperative you and your soulmate activate both of the grand trines in the Star of David during this time. If you succeed, your soulmate's negative grand trine will be added to your three and balance will be achieved."

"And—if I fail?"

"Your three grand trines will turn negative and the balance will shift. One second too soon or too late will be—"

"Doomsday," Ramsey said. He paused as if deep in thought. "What if Darius dies before he finds his soulmate?"

"If Darius has only one soulmate, his grand trines would be gifted to her and she would have the power to defeat good or evil all by herself. If, by chance, his soulmate dies, her grand water trine would be gifted to him."

"And if he has twin soulmates?"

"Darius's grand trines would be split in half and divided equally among them," Aje said. "Together, they would have the power to defeat good or evil. But, if Darius is alive and one of his soulmates die, then the surviving twin would receive the other half of their soulmate's grand trine—not Darius. Only if both soulmates die would Darius receive their negative grand trine. He would then have—"

"The power to defeat good or evil all by himself," Ramsey remarked.

"Precisely," Aje said.

Silence filled the room. Darius noticed that Ramsey and Raj were both staring at each other the way two people do when they seem to know something others don't. He shifted his gaze back to the astrologer who shot him an accusatory stare and continued speaking.

"In order to activate the entire Star of David you will need your soulmate's cooperation and the Star of Life. The last time the portal was open, Jesus Christ was said to have been born."

Darius felt like he had been kicked in the head by a horse. "The odds of my pulling this off are astronomical," he said.

"And astrological," Aje replied jokingly.

The computer interrupted. "President Ramsey, the satellite feeds are being recalibrated. They will be up and running in thirty seconds."

"It's about time. Give me a visual of the crater and patch me in to Alpha leader. Aje, what do you make of the other beam that landed in the desert?"

"Since the two beams originated from the star Menkar, and Mr. Prince received the power of Orion, the Hunter, then that means the beast—"

"Computer, abort the mission," Ramsey shouted.

When the hologram appeared, they watched in horror as the three helicopters lost control over the crater. "Allah, forgive me," he heard Ramsey say over and over again.

Caught in a whirlwind, the helicopters formed an equilateral triangle and spun violently out of control. Simultaneously they crashed down into the black onyx crater and burst into a ball of flames.

The transmission ended. Darius watched as Ramsey rushed over to the southern window. This was a wake up call, he thought.

"Computer, scan the area for survivors," Ramsey said.

"No surviving life forms detected," the computer replied.

When Ramsey turned, Darius saw pain etched into his face. Raj rushed to the president's side.

Ramsey sighed. "Those soldiers were like my sons. Raj, notify their families and give them all Medals of Honor."

"Yes, sir," he said and moved across the room.

"And find me the twin Leos."

The phone rang. Darius noticed how tightly the president pressed the receiver to his ear. The president listened with an intent expression and then hung up; he hadn't uttered one word. He tossed Darius the knapsack with the diamond in it. "The Queen of the EU wants you to go to Stonehenge and attempt to retrieve the Sword of Power. You leave for London tomorrow."

He froze. "What's going on at Stonehenge?"

"You will know shortly."

"What if you're wrong and I'm also the prince the prophecy speaks of?"

Ramsey leveled a condemning stare. "Your job is to retrieve the sword and give it to Prince William so he can become king. Under no circumstances are you to keep it."

"And if I refuse?"

"Knowing the queen, she's going to make you a deal you can't refuse."

CHAPTER 56

"OFF WITH THEIR heads," chanted the Romanesque mob outside of Buckingham Palace. Darius moved away from the helicopter and stared through the heavy wrought iron gates at the sea of black and yellow raincoats being beaten back by EU soldiers in riot gear. It was late in the afternoon and the sight of the smoky-colored teargas coupled with the agonizing screams of the bloodthirsty crowd tore through him like a roadside bomb. He felt disoriented. Everything seemed to move in slow motion. As the guards ushered him toward the Ambassadors' entrance on the southern side of the palace, he felt like breaking away and leading the people in revolt. The thought faded when he heard the palace doors thunder shut behind him.

The guards led him down a passage and through a door leading back outside to an inner quadrangle resembling a town square. He remembered Ramsey's words. Stay focused. Stick to the plan. Darius took a deep breath and arched his shoulders back. He followed the guards through the grand entrance and down a marble hall lined with priceless statues and paintings. He marveled at the life-size statue of Mars and Venus locked in an everlasting embrace and then ascended the sweeping grand staircase past portraits of Queen Victoria's immediate family. Their eyes seemed to follow his every move. When he reached the landing, he was led into a small decorative room where he was searched in front of two life-sized white marble statues of Queen Victoria and Prince Albert in Roman costume.

If he were to make it to the next level, and stay there, he had to be able to tell the difference between illusion and reality. The Fallen Angels would do everything in their power to confuse him and turn him to their side.

"Follow me," the guard said in a staunch British accent. He ushered Darius into an adjoining room. "This is the Green Drawing Room. Have a seat. The queen will be with you shortly."

When the guard left, Darius gazed around the two-story high stateroom. It was elegantly decorated with gilt seat furniture, Sevres porcelain, and vibrantly colored green silk walls lined with immense portraits. A massive twinkling chandelier hung like a crystal stalactite from the elaborately coved and domed ceiling enshrining the treasures beneath it.

As he listened to the rain rhythmically pelt the huge rectangular windows, he noticed a large wooden crest hanging on the far wall. He strolled across the lavish red carpet bordered in gold and stopped when he came face to face with Prince Charles' coat of arms. An eerie feeling overcame him as he admired the intricate details of the symbolic crest.

The beast Aje spoke of was staring him right in the face. It had the head and mouth of a lion, the body of a leopard, and the feet of a bear. On the lion's head was a crown of gold and its right paw pointed to the harp of David.

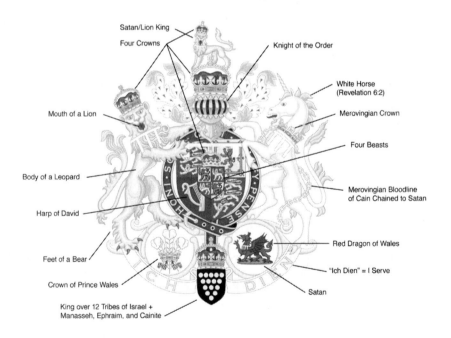

Darius thought back to his conversation with the bartender at the Camelot Bar. Was the harp in the crest proof that the Messianic bloodline from the House of David of the Tribe of Judah was indeed passed on to the kings of Ireland, Scotland, and England?

▲ ▼ ▲

"Mr. Prince, Her Majesty is ready to meet with you."

The guard led him to another set of doors in the middle of the northern wall. The guard stopped abruptly and stood at attention. "Remember," he said, without looking at Darius, "to bow and whatever you do, don't turn your back to Her Majesty." He waved the back of his hand in front of a scanner built into the wall, pushed the doors open, and ushered Darius into the queen's opulent baroque-style Throne Room.

What type of deal was the queen going to offer him in return for embarking on a quest for the Sword of Power? He gazed at her highness who was sitting upon her throne in all her glory. When he reached the two thrones standing side by side on the middle of the dais, he bowed and looked up at the queen who was seated on the throne to his left. He wondered why Prince William was not by her side.

The queen adjusted the priceless crown resting comfortably on her head. Her short silver hair glistened under the shimmering light of the immense crystal chandelier along with the rest of her crown jewels.

"I shall get right to the point," she said in a demeaning British tone, asserting her superiority. "You need me far more than I need you."

His mother had once told him Queen Elizabeth was a Taurus who had Capricorn rising and a moon in Leo. He could use this to his advantage. Being a Taurus, she would most likely remain fixed on her ideas and determined to get exactly what she wanted. She would come off serious and dignified due to her Capricorn rising, and her moon in Leo would make her proud, domineering and the center of attention. Now that he had the power of Orion, he had to establish *his* superiority and make it perfectly clear that she needed him more than he needed her. If he did, he had a feeling she would bow to his demands. She was the most powerful woman on the planet—and a stubborn one at that. This wasn't going to be easy.

"Quite the contrary," Darius said, coolly. "Have you taken a look outside lately?"

"Don't flatter yourself, Zoroastrian. They want your head just as much as they want mine. That's why I am going to make you a deal."

He heard a door open from somewhere behind him. Darius started to turn but caught himself before he had turned too far and, instead, looked over his shoulder. The five-foot-ten-inch princess strolled into the room dressed in a white-satin galabia that swept across the famed red carpet as she walked. She appeared calm and deliberate; she neither moved too quickly nor, he was sure, would she ever act in haste. Her blue eyes eluded his as he watched her long blonde hair glisten in the light. She paid him no attention as she walked past him and up the dais. She sat down on her grandfather's throne to the queen's left and leaned back comfortably. Darius nonchalantly stole a glance at her three-inch heels, and then focused his gaze back to the queen who stood up and moved in front of her. For a moment, he couldn't help but think of the moon's eclipse of the sun. He cracked a thin smile and listened to the queen regain control.

"Mr. Prince," she said in a friendlier but still condescending tone, "if you can get me the Sword of Power, my son and I will abdicate the throne in favor of Prince William becoming king. You will become his knight and my granddaughter's knight in shining armor."

The princess stood up and moved next to the queen. "Have you gone mad? I'm already married."

"Bollocks," she said in a demeaning tone. "You don't even have sex with the man." She turned and looked at Darius. "This is my granddaughter, Princess Zara."

"Pleasure to meet you," he said and bowed graciously. When he straightened, he heard the queen say, "The princess is my thirteenth heir apparent."

Zara stared at her grandmother. "My Queen, I will not abandon my husband for a man I do not love."

The queen scoffed. "Since when has our family ever married for love?"

"But he is a freak of nature."

"That's not a nice way to speak about your future husband," Darius said.

"Silence!" shouted the queen. "Get me the sword and you shall have my granddaughter's hand in marriage. You will become a distinguished member of our Royal Family and William will become king of both England and the Eurasian Union."

Darius could feel his polar opposite sign of Leo stir from within. He paused. If Ramsey was wrong, and *he* was the prophesized prince destined to become king, he needed to be within striking distance of the throne. He would also need help navigating his way through the kingdom of the Antichrist in search of his soulmate. He needed to level the playing field and cut a deal that could provide him with both. He shot a longing glance at Zara and focused his attention back to the queen. "That's not enough."

"What else could you possibly want?"

"Change the line of succession."

"Impossible!"

"Then I will keep the sword and your family will die."

"And you will be a king without a kingdom," the queen laughed. "You need alliances. If you agree to my terms," she said, "you'll be aligned with the most powerful kingdom on the planet."

"My kingdom is the Kingdom of God," he said.

"So is my grandson's," she said sternly. "William is a direct descendant of Israel's Royal Houses of Judah and David—just as Jesus Christ was. Not to mention his Merovingian bloodline that makes him a direct descendant of Christ. It is his destiny to become king."

"I'll be the judge of that," he said and winked at Zara. "Personally, I don't believe Christ had kids, but it is possible he's related to Christ, David, and Judah through the Legend of the Scarlet Hand. Now, if I do decide to give Prince William the sword, I will be next in line for the throne just in case something should happen to him." He looked at the queen, who seemed to be at a rare loss for words, and then shifted his gaze to Zara. "Call it our golden parachute." When Zara's smile stretched across her beautiful face, he focused his gaze back to the queen. "Do we have a deal?"

"Yes," Zara interrupted. "I like the way he thinks."

"Silence!" the queen shouted again. "On behalf of Princes Charles and Harry, I reluctantly accept. But, I'd like to make it known that I am only accepting your terms because it is in the best interests of the family that they both step aside."

"I can't speak for Charles, but Harry won't mind," Zara laughed. "He never thought he'd become king anyway." She looked at Darius. "What guides you?"

"My faith in God . . . and the stars," he said. "I'm an Aquarian and have a good mix of earth, air and fire in my chart, so my intuitiveness and deep imagination tend to guide me. And you?"

"I happen to be a Tauren like my grandmother. Contrary to you, I base my life on what is practical and real—not what is imagined. I consider astrology a science and know a thing or two about it. We are both very passionate and strong willed people. So . . . if we can work out our differences . . . and you make me the center of your universe," she said with a laugh, "we can make a very formidable couple."

"That remains to be seen."

"I'm serious," she said. "The only way we wouldn't be compatible is if you were a water sign."

Darius raised an eyebrow. "Water sign? Why do you say that?"

"I am an earth sign. So . . . if you were a water sign . . . together . . . we would make . . ."

"Mud," he said, finishing her joke and chuckling softly. Darius thought for a moment. Zara wasn't a Leo but she might be able to use her influence to help him find his twin soulmates. He grinned. He had just cut himself a sweetheart deal, but when everything was said and done, could he trust them? Most of all, could he trust himself?

"If you live up to your end of the bargain Zoroastrian, you will become next in line for the throne as well as William's knight and champion. The Arthurian Legend will be reborn in my grandson and the British Royal Family will be restored to their original greatness."

"How do I get the sword?"

"My scientists have concluded that Stonehenge is some sort of gateway. So far, nothing can penetrate it except inanimate matter; food, weapons etc. But we think you can."

"Let's say you're right and I go through some type of wormhole in space. How do I get back?"

"We will implant you with a chip that will act as a homing device."

"No way."

"You must."

"Then the deal is off."

"Do as you wish, but don't blame me if you don't come back."

He winked at the princess and coolly said, "Don't worry, I'll come back."

"Then it is settled. You leave in the morning."

"When do I meet Prince William?"

"The Duke and Duchess of Cambridge are on holiday until tomorrow. I don't want them, or anyone else, to know about our little deal until you have successfully returned with the sword."

"This is a fairy tale in the making," the princess said.

Enamored with the thought of becoming a member of the Royal Family, Darius watched Princess Zara walk down the red carpeted steps toward him. When she reached him, she moved her head forward and whispered softly into his ear. Intoxicated by the sweet scent of her perfume, he grinned and softly kissed her hand.

CHAPTER 57

T HE DAWN'S EARLY light shone into the room through a blue
and yellow stained glass window etched with the moon and stars.
Darius yawned and stretched his arms behind his head. The cascading light
moved diagonally across the bed and divided him in half with the moon above
his head and three stars beneath his feet. He reached over to caress the
princess. When he felt nothing but the silk sheets, he sat up and looked around
the room

Princess Zara was gone.

Her side of the bed didn't even look like it had been slept in. Had their
tryst been only a dream? There was a loud knock at the door. A rather
distinguished gray-haired man in his late sixties, wearing a white jacket with
polished gold buttons and gold fringed epaulettes, walked into the room. He
was holding a silver platter.

"I'm not hungry," Darius said, hardly giving him a glance. He threw back
the covers and climbed out of bed. He put on the camouflage fatigues that had
been laid out for him and looked up. He saw three intertwined triangles on the
platter's shiny exterior and realized that he wasn't being served breakfast. The
man was holding a shield with his three grand trines on it.

"Mr. Prince, the only serving I do is to my queen and my country. I am an
admiral in the Royal Navy," he said. "That means you salute me."

Darius tucked in his green camouflage shirt and lazily saluted him.

"Princess Zara has instructed me to give this to you." He handed him the
shield. "She says it was forged by the god, Hades, himself. Personally, I think
she's crazy and you are a fool if you think you can get through the
magnetic force field surrounding Stonehenge."

"The hero and the fool are one and the same," Darius said. He held the lightweight shield up in front of his face and stared at his slightly distorted reflection. With everything he'd been through he looked pretty good, he thought. He looked at the admiral who handed him a sealed envelope.

"A message from the princess."

Darius placed the shield on the bed and read the note quietly to himself. He smiled at her words of encouragement, but his smile faded as he thought about the daunting task that lay ahead.

If he failed to retrieve the sword, would the people who came to believe in him suddenly turn around and abandon him just like his father did? The thought disturbed him but it also gave him the added incentive he needed to succeed. Darius took a few deep breaths to calm himself as he listened to the admiral finish his briefing.

"Any questions?"

Darius, at a loss, didn't say anything.

"I'll take that as a no. Get ready. We leave for Stonehenge within the hour."

CHAPTER 58

O UT OF THE helicopter window, Darius gazed upon Stonehenge for the first time. His heartbeat quickened. Flashes of green and white light pulsated throughout the stones from top to bottom like a screen of an old television that had lost its signal and turned to static. Battalions of armed soldiers scurried around the Salisbury Plain like ants guarding their queen. Jet aircraft thundered through the overcast sky.

As they neared the ground, he felt his hands start to pulsate just as they had the morning after the comet exploded. He flexed them in front of his face and realized he was connected to the power radiating through the megalithic ruin. It reminded him of the inborn sacred bond between mother and child. A static electric shock distracted him from his thoughts. He looked at the admiral who was strapped into the copilot's seat.

"Did you feel that?" Darius said.

"Feel what?"

Darius didn't respond but, instead, stared hypnotically at the megalithic ruin. Drawn to the constant humming sound emitted by the magnetic field, he felt as if it was calling him. When the helicopter touched down on the lush green plain thirty yards from Stonehenge they were immediately surrounded by soldiers.

The admiral jumped out of the helicopter and saluted his men. When a few soldiers looked curiously into the cabin, Darius grabbed the knapsack and the shield and stepped out onto the Salisbury Plain. The ground was spongy and moist. He could feel the energy flow beneath his feet.

Darius slung the pack over his shoulder and followed the admiral toward the stone circle. Like a salmon's genetic programming that guides it upstream to spawn, he felt instinctively, almost hypnotically, drawn to the magnetic field. With every step, his hands pulsated even stronger. When they reached the stone circle he was ordered to stop. Static electricity crackled in the air around him. He felt the raw power resonating from the magnetic field upon his face. It was warm and inviting. The pack was secured to his back and he was handed a laser handgun and holster.

He tightened the belt around his waist and looked at the admiral. This was his moment of truth, he thought.

The admiral saluted Darius. "May God be with you."

With the shield in his left hand and the gun secured to his side, he took a deep breath and stepped through the magnetic field.

There was a blinding flash of light followed by a deafening crash of thunder. He found himself immersed in a river of soft purple foam that carried him faster and faster down a long winding tunnel. With every twist and turn it seemed as if his speed was accelerating exponentially. It was then that he realized that he was traveling through the magnetic fabric of space—aether. He saw a glimmer of light at the end of the tunnel and then everything went black.

▲ ▲ ▲

When his vision returned, Darius found himself standing within a complete ring of stones. He blinked his eyes and gazed around at what appeared to be the Salisbury Plain. The air was cool and damp. Shafts of sunlight shone down through the partially cloudy sky. The magnetic force field was gone and the soldiers had vanished. A bluish mist blanketed the grassy plain, and an overpowering silence loomed all around him.

There was no ambient noise: no trains, no planes, no automobiles. The world he had traveled to seemed void of any modern-day technology. A flock of geese flew overhead.

"Look at what you've done," Darius heard a male voice say with a British accent.

Darius drew his gun and aimed it at the mist. "Who's there?" he said, waving the gun around in different directions. "Show yourself!" He tightened his finger on the trigger and slowly turned around in a circle. The silence was unbearable. "This is your last chance," he shouted. "Show yourself."

After a long moment, a tall man with flowing silver hair and beard emerged. Dressed in a black cloak, he walked toward him with a long wooden staff in his right-hand. When the old man reached him, he stopped and waved his staff high into the air as if he were going to cast a spell on him. Darius aimed the gun directly between his beady, blood-red eyes.

"Your weapons are useless in this world," the old man said. He peered into a small crystal ball on top of his staff.

"Who are you?"

"My name is Arcturus. I am the wizard who guards the gateway," he said, shaking his head. "You have deactivated the portal."

"Can it be reactivated?"

"That is entirely up to you. You have come for the sword?"

"Yes." The sun burst through the clouds and burned off the last of the early morning mist. "But how do I reactivate the portal?"

"You must retrieve the Sword of Power. If you are successful the portal will open."

"Where is the sword?"

"Patience," he said, "leave your shield here and come with me."

"Can you at least tell me where I am?"

"You are in a parallel dimension where time and space act differently than in your universe."

Darius stared at him in disbelief. How was that possible? Pondering the thought, he leaned the shield up against one of the outer stones and followed the wizard out onto the plain.

"Tell me," Arcturus said loudly. "Why do you wish to possess the sword?"

"To heal and rid the world of evil."

Arcturus stopped walking. He turned and looked directly into Darius's eyes. After a long moment, he grinned and chuckled softly. "I can lead you to the sword but its guardian will decide whether or not you are worthy to possess it."

"Guardian?"

"The goddess of the lake protects the sword."

The thought of having to pass another one of their tests made his blood boil. Hadn't he already proven enough?

"I must warn you," Arcturus said, snapping Darius out of his thoughts. "You are the twelfth and final Knight of the Zodiac to come for the sword. All the others have failed and died here."

"I'm not like the others," Darius said. He followed Arcturus across the plain, his breath coming from his mouth in small white clouds as they walked. Darius remained silent in thought as they traveled for what seemed like miles.

Finally, they came upon two stallions tied to a tree. When Arcturus stopped, Darius moved next to him and gazed out over the plain. Clouds rolled across the sky like armies charging into battle.

"Where is this lake?"

"Patience. Have you ever ridden a horse?"

"Couple of times."

The wizard sighed and waved his staff high into the air. Out of nowhere, a glassy lake appeared in front of them.

"Unbelievable," Darius said, stretching out the word.

"No, magical," the wizard said, and lowered his staff. "Magic is the missing element that binds the universe together. In this dimension there are no limitations to what one can do."

Darius smiled. "The illusion has become reality."

"The lake was always there—you just couldn't see it."

Were magic and aether one and the same?

The wizard moved toward the shoreline. He raised his staff high into the air again. This time, the wind picked up and the lake began to stir. He could hear the wizard's chants swirl in the howling wind. When the sky roared with thunder, the wizard plunged his staff into the lakebed and let go. A lightning bolt struck the orb on his staff and electrified the lake.

"Come quickly," he shouted.

Darius moved next to him. The wizard motioned for him to step into the lake.

"I'm not going in there."

"You must. It is the only way."

Darius stepped hesitantly into the water. He quivered and fell to his knees as a strong electric shock surged through his body. The pain was unbearable—he felt as if he was going to die. At just that moment he stood up and relaxed and, unbelievably, slipped into a state of bliss. The lake fell silent.

Below the calm water's surface the goddess appeared floating on her back. She was dressed in a luminescent gown that shimmered like silver moonlight on the water. Her long, blonde wavy hair floated weightlessly in the shallows. When their eyes connected, he felt as if the goddess had looked deep inside his soul. She extended her arms and thrust a silver sword into the air. He stared at his reflection in the shiny steel as water trickled down its razor-sharp blade.

"Take the sword," Arcturus said.

Darius glanced at the wizard, who had mounted the black stallion, and then focused his gaze back on the goddess. Her watery brown eyes seemed to fill the lake with salty tears. He pulled the sword from her hand and raised it high above his head.

Darius froze. He felt the power from the sword course through his veins. *He* had succeeded where all others had failed. He lowered the sword and jogged up onto the shore.

"I am the *one*," he said, swinging the sword through the air.

Arcturus opened his mouth as if to speak, then he closed his mouth tight and tossed him a belt with a long sheath attached. "Put this on," he said barely moving his lips.

Darius wrapped the belt around him, and slid the sword into the sheath. He took up the reins and mounted the white stallion. When he put his feet into the stirrups, he looked at the wizard and nodded.

"Ride, Darius. Ride!"

The air was electric and their pace was brisk.

Darius held on for dear life as he and the wizard galloped hard across the plain toward Stonehenge. As they rode side by side, the wizard spoke to him.

"Do you feel the power of the sword?"

"Yes! Nature, the sword, my soul—they're all connected." Darius stared at Stonehenge in the distance. His stomach fell and his chest heaved. He looked at the wizard. "Why isn't the portal working?"

"Stay focused and ride," Arcturus said. "Ride!"

As Darius accelerated past him, Stonehenge flickered with a sudden burst of light. His heart raced. The portal had a pulse. "Come on," he said, knowing that he was the heart that powered it. The closer he got, the more frequent came the bursts. Static electricity crackled in the air around him. Suddenly, green and white light pulsated throughout the megalithic ruin. Darius grinned with a sense of satisfaction as he listened to the familiar humming sound surge across the plain. He was going home.

Once again, Darius felt godlike, immortal. He was the prince the prophecy foretold of—not Prince William. He was going to keep the sword.

Suddenly, the force field disappeared. He looked at the wizard. "Did you do that?"

"No, you did," Arcturus said and dismounted his horse. "You are *not* the one."

Darius paused. How could he have been so foolish? He should have known his thoughts were connected to Stonehenge—just as they were to the diamond in the pyramid. But if he had the power to escape from the pyramid, then maybe he had the power to activate the portal again, he thought, as the wizard moved toward him.

"Give me the sword."

"Not yet," Darius said, "I think I know how to reactivate it. He closed his eyes and thought long and hard about bringing the world into a state of peace from one that had been manipulated into a constant state of famine, war, and corruption. When he opened his eyes, Stonehenge still lay dormant. He felt himself spiraling out of control. What was he to do? He couldn't just die here. Everything was going as planned and now he was going to be stuck in this godforsaken place for the rest of his life. He wasn't going to let that happen.

He closed his eyes. This time, he thought about all the good deeds he had done in his life. As the images played over and over in his head, he hoped that this would work. But when he opened his eyes, once again, he was confronted by the same unwelcome truth. He exhaled deeply and bowed his head in defeat. "I have failed."

The wizard moved in front of him. "On the contrary, you have succeeded."

Darius looked up and stared into the wizard's eyes. "Have you gone mad?"

"Darius, in your dimension good has already defeated evil."

Darius scratched his head. "How is that possible?"

"That's something you are not yet meant to understand."

Was he really going to die here?

"There's gotta be a way to reactivate the portal," Darius said and moved toward the stone circle.

"I'm sorry, but there is not."

"There are no limitations to what one can achieve," he said. He slid the sword into the sheath and began inspecting the stones.

"You must accept your fate."

Darius ignored him and scaled the ruin.

"Get down here now and give me the sword. I must return it to the goddess at once."

"Darius continued to ignore him and searched the top ring of stones for anything—anything that could reactivate the portal and get him home. After several minutes, he saw a triangular-shaped indentation on one of the stones. His eyes widened and his heartbeat quickened.

He knew exactly what to do. Darius pulled off his pack and carefully removed the diamond. He placed it into the triangular shaped indentation and jumped to the ground. Suddenly, a beam of white light shot out of the diamond and into the sky. As he watched the beam race into outer space toward the Orion constellation, he wondered why the portal hadn't reactivated.

At just that moment, the beam struck the middle star of Orion's belt, Alnilam. A brilliant flash of light distracted him from his thoughts as it lit up the entire constellation. An image of the mighty warrior appeared in the sky. The image slowly faded as the stars relayed their energy back to Alnilam, which swelled to gargantuan proportions. The star collapsed back to its original size and released its godlike power in opposite directions within the grand trine matrix.

As the two energy beams raced through the belt stars to complete the grand trine, Darius dropped to his knees and prayed for a miracle. When he finished, he glanced at the wizard and then watched both beams converge on the star Arcturus. "The second grand trine is complete," Darius said, and stood up. The star glowed with the energy of the sun and then beamed its energy back toward them.

Time seemed to stop—everything moved in slow motion. He watched the beam strike the diamond and explode into a burst of light that momentarily blinded him. When his vision returned he saw that the portal was reactivated.

In one swift motion, Darius pulled the sword out of the sheath and raised it high into the air. He smiled and moved next to Arcturus. "I *am* the one," he said, sliding the sword back into the sheath.

The wizard dropped his staff and faced him. His face tensed and his lips thinned. He placed his boney hands on Darius's shoulders and pulled him close. Darius looked into the wizard's blood-red eyes.

"Darius, listen to me. You can stay here and become king, leaving things as they are, or you can risk everything and go back to try and save your world again. But, I must warn you that if you do decide to go back, you will be giving evil a second chance."

"If good already defeated evil, doesn't that mean I was successful?"

"Yes, but—"

"So, if I go back again, the outcome should be the same."

"The outcome can change," he said, shaking his head. "Evil will learn from its mistakes. As we speak, evil is trying to turn back time so it can return to that fateful day when it lost. I know it's hard to imagine not returning to your world, but sometimes in order to see the future we must turn our back on the past."

Something's not right, Darius thought. Why was the wizard trying to keep him there?

Darius paused, deep in thought. "How do I know you're telling the truth?"

"Trust me," Arcturus said sternly, "evil will not make the same mistake twice. As it is, I can see Lucifer already has a strong hold on you."

Darius picked up the shield and stared at the portal, contemplating his fate. He slid the sword back into the sheath and looked at Arcturus. There was that brief moment of silence one experiences while making a pivotal decision at the crossroads of history. Darius took a deep breath and exhaled.

"That's a chance I'm gonna have to take," he said and jumped back through the portal.

EPILOGUE

D ARIUS HEARD A loud crash of thunder; surrounded by blackness, he shivered in the pouring rain. The foul stench of acrid smoke filled his lungs and soured his stomach. His vision was blurred. All he could see were dark shadowy images of people wandering around him. His heartbeat quickened. He was back! He pulled the sword out of the sheath and raised it high into the air. When his vision came back into focus, he dropped the shield. The sword fell to his side.

What had he done? Thick plumes of black smoke rose high into the air from funeral pyres scattered around him. Ash fell like fallout from the blackened sky. The apocalyptic landscape made it seem as if the earth had been plunged into a nuclear winter.

Darius stared at the hundreds of dead servicemen strewn across the plain. He should have listened to Arcturus. Why had he come back? Why? As he walked past the soldiers heaving corpses onto the raging fires, he wondered how all of this could have happened in the few short hours he was gone.

"You are responsible for this, Zoroastrian."

Darius turned. The pessimistic admiral, who doubted him from the beginning, moved in front of him. He was wearing a dark green poncho over his uniform. His face was flushed and his thin gray hair was soaking wet.

"Take a good look around Zoroastrian," he said. "Everything has changed. Everything!"

Darius thrust the sword high into the air. "Behold, the Sword of Power!"

The admiral seemed exasperated. He didn't seem the least bit interested in him or the sword. He looked Darius straight in the eye, and in a chillingly cold tone said, "Now you can help us burn the bodies of those who were raptured."

"Raptured?" Darius said. The word chilled him to the bone. He felt a turbulent mixture of abandonment, rage, and guilt tear through his soul. He pushed his wet hair back off his face and lowered the sword. He thought about his family and friends. Had they been raptured, too? He sighed deeply. He never even had a chance to say goodbye. Everything happened so fast. Or had it? He remembered what Arcturus had said before he left. Evil will not make the same mistake twice—the outcome can change.

Darius's face tensed; his eyes narrowed. He grabbed the admiral and pulled him close. "Queen Elizabeth . . . the princess . . . Prince William . . . are they alive?"

"Yes."

"Tell me. How long have I been gone? How long?"

The rain fell harder. "You've been gone a long time, Zoroastrian. A little over nine months."

"Nine months?" Darius felt his heart drop. He felt his mind go numb. He released the admiral and staggered backwards. Nostrils flaring, face flushed, he tilted his head back and stared into the unforgiving sky. "Why God? Why?" he shouted.

"I'll tell you why," the admiral said. "God has abandoned us."

God abandon us? The admiral's spirit seemed vacant as did the soldiers who fell in behind him. He could sense a deep raw anger, as if it were seeping from their pores. He had to bring God back to them. He raised his sword high into the air and stared at the men.

"God hasn't abandoned us. You've abandoned yourselves. God is in everything," he said, waving his hand in the air. "Limit God's existence and you will be limited in your own." He looked at the admiral's blank stare and suddenly felt alone. He had achieved the impossible, but now everything seemed to be going so terribly wrong. "Just this morning, everything was fine and now—"

Lightning flashed and the sky thundered. "This morning?" the admiral said, frustrated. "Zoroastrian, I told you, you've been gone for nine months! For Christ's sake, Princess Zara is about to give birth to your child. We all thought you were dead."

END OF BOOK ONE